WAILING TEMPEST

CORRUPTED REALMS – BOOK ONE

T. B. PHILLIPS

Wailing Tempest
Corrupted Realms, Book One

Published by Andalon Press
Copyright © 2022 by T.B. Phillips

Cover design by Lynnette Bonner of Indie Cover Design, images ©
  stock.adobe.com, File: # 299836923
Map artwork by Cary Beshel
Book interior design by Stewart Design, https://StewartDesign.studio

ISBN 979-8-9872191-0-2

Books by T.B. Phillips

Chilling Tales
Ferryman (October 2022)
Don't Pay the Ferryman (Expected June 2023)

Corrupted Realms
Wailing Tempest (May 2021)
Howling Shadow (September 2021)

Andalon Saga

Andalon Origins
Andalon Project (April 2022)
Andalon Paradox (Epected Winter 2022)

Dreamers of Andalon
Andalon Awakens (June 2019)
Andalon Arises (July 2020)
Andalon Attacks (December 2020)

Children of Andalon
Andalon Legacy (September 2022)

Helpful Tidbits

The Relics
The Bláth de Saol – Blossom of Life
Healing – Rose/Ruby
Resurrection – White Lily/Pearl
Corruption – Black Iris/Onyx
Sight – Hydrangea/Emerald
Fire – Begonia/Garnet
Water – Hyacinth/Aquamarine
Air – Aster/Lapis

Bláth de Eolas – Blossom of Knowledge
Powers and Description Unknown to our Characters

The Bláth de Cumhacht – Blossom of Power
Powers and Description Unknown to our Characters

The Places
Fainnotherr – Fairy Realm
Enatherr – Human Realm
Luchorpár – Gnome Realm

N
W
E
S
NORGAARD
MIDLANDIS
BAY of WINDS
DUNE SEA
CROSSTON
PORT of ENAT
RIVANIA
ENATHERR

N
W
E
S
Deamhan Palace
Fainnotheria
FAINNOTHERR

Part One
Through the Fainnen Ring

Chapter One

I was young when he arrived in Fainnotheria, infantile of mind and naïve in my own form. I lacked the confidence only experience brings and yearned not for wisdom but instead for ignorant rebellion. My reflections upon his arrival are filled with wonder – trepidation for the fate of my people – but wonderment for the knowledge I gained by his meeting. Oh, that he had never crossed through the Fainnen Ring.
– Lamentations of Nastauria

The forest darkened, marked by the incoming horde filtering the sun. Alistaria lifted her eyes, too terrified to look away from the shadow of death. Fear descended upon her, and the scores of wings buzzed against her ears. Their vibration matched the rapid pulse of her heart, throwing her into panic and sending her running toward the city walls. With a leap she was airborne. Her own wings outstretched and beat with a flurry. She gained speed, careful not to fly too high or reveal her fleeing form to the invaders above.

The Skygate closed slowly as she made her approach, and stalwart guards braced against the pending attack. They waved wildly, urging the girl toward safety. Looking behind she saw others of her kind following. She was not alone when tending the roots, and frightened faces shared her urgency. This was not the first time the invaders had caught them unaware, and each Fainne knew what would happen if caught. She landed beside the soldiers and turned to aid those who lagged behind.

A young Fainne, her cousin Restarian, had flown too high and his delicate frame was caught by muscular arms. They pulled as he struggled, bringing him toward needle-sharp teeth craving flesh. Strong jaws bit at his neck as he writhed, thrashing and kicking while wrenching his body from their death grip. He broke away and plummeted toward the canopy below. He flapped his wings to escape to safety, but the effort proved hopeless as two more pairs of arms plucked him from the air. They lifted him high toward a waiting mass of hungry vermin.

Alistaria took three steps and tried to surge to her cousin's aid. She lunged into the air but returned to her bare feet when strong hands grabbed her wings. She turned to meet the eyes of the sentry – cool blue and intently focused with warning. He pointed to the East and the girl relaxed. The king's army, the Kern, had released from their perch and streamed upward with silvery spears aimed forward. She watched as the elite warriors, clad in shimmering golden armor, collided with the Banshee invaders and their primitive weapons of bone and iron.

The sentry, wearing the silver armor of the city guard, urged her inside. "Hurry," he begged. "Go inside! Let the Kern do their work while we secure the Skygate."

"I will," she promised, but her feet lingered and her eyes remained fixed on the battle above.

The golden armor of the Kern glistened as they weaved in and out of their attackers – clashing wildly with the charcoal grey skin of the Banshees. The delicate features and small bones of the Fainne made them appear far nimbler than the heavier Deamhan – whose jagged jawlines and pronounced cheekbones appeared more demonic than fae. The Kern darted in and out – their agility a weapon against their larger foe.

"Hurry," the sentry begged. "We must shut the gate!"

"Shut it," she said without diverting her brown eyes from the melee. "Restarian needs my help."

Two Kern had pulled the attention off her friend, and his attackers danced in the air with their spinning weapons. The boy struggled, and the larger of the Banshees turned his body just in time to counter a thrust of a silver spear. The tip caught the meat of Restarian's wing, causing him to cry out and tear it further. He tumbled from the arms of the laughing Deamhan, and plummeted to the forest floor – crashing against clawing branches that ripped his skin while cushioning impact.

Alistaria dove downward through the canopy, ignoring the shouts of the blue-eyed guard. She reached Restarian and landed softly upon bare feet beside him – barely disturbing the moss as she settled. All around the boy the green lichen had been painted red with his blood. His eyes were closed, and his breathing labored as she knelt beside him with concern. She gently checked his neck for injury and found his back had broken from the impact. It was a killing blow, and he should have been left for Síth Morkur.

A hiss from the ferns roared the arrival of a Banshee. His massive chest heaved as he lumbered toward her, breathing deep before bellowing an alarm to his counterparts above. She would be overrun by his kind before long, and she must deal with him quickly if she were to save her friend. She raised her hand to summon any lingering power she could draw from the forest.

A silver blur streaked past as a newcomer rushed the attacker. Flying at full speed his shield met the Deamhan's chest, knocking his wind and interrupting his hellish scream for aid. Both Fainne and Banshee sprawled onto the ground, tumbling and rolling – coming to rest in the undergrowth of the forest floor. The larger of the two was the first to recover and rushed the newcomer. Shocked, Alistaria watched as her savior – the guard from the Skygate above – regained his footing and parried a heavy blow.

"Hurry," he commanded through gritted teeth. "Heal him so we can get back to the city!"

She nodded and bit her lip slightly while focusing on Restarian's injuries. She knew she shouldn't heal him. He was dying, and his soul belonged to the Síth and his flesh to the Ganshees the creature commanded. But besides the heir to the throne, Restarian was her friend, and she must try. It was good they lay on the forest floor; the healing powers residing in the roots of the great trees would channel easier as she worked.

Iron and Fainne silver crashed as fighting raged, but she ignored their clatter. Her concentration only broke when the flittering of tiny wings buzzed all around. *Cursed Ganshees,* Alistaria thought, waving her hands and shooing them off her friend. The horrible little creatures dispersed, but several remained, biting at Restarian's skin with sharp teeth laid out in rows.

The vile critters lacked noses, but they could sense his dying flesh from miles away. If left to work, they would devour and clean an entire carcass in less than an hour. She mustn't allow them to do the same to her friend. Fed up with their harassment, she summoned a bit of power from the mighty roots thrumming below her knees. Channeling it through her hand she zapped each one with a fairy bolt, sending them scurrying off to watch the battle above and bite at fresh wounds.

The lifeforce remained in Restarian's limbs, but was severed cleanly within his spine. Should he actually survive, he may neither walk nor fly unless she acted quickly. She closed her eyes and allowed the vibration of the forest to pass through her thoughts. The resonance hummed a tune of life for Fainne healers, allowing them to mend and heal but not to resurrect those who ceased to live. That art belonged to another – stolen long ago from her kind. She was a novice in this craft and focused on the severity of the boy's wounds. It was possible she was not skilled enough to mend him completely, but she must try.

A second Banshee had landed beside the first and the pair converged on the sentry, driving him closer to Alistaria. "Do it," the soldier called with urgency, "and let's be gone from this place!"

"I need a moment longer," she pleaded. The resonance had tuned with Restarian's pulse, vibrating invisibly beneath her hands held an inch above his neck. Soon the bones within responded, crackling as they popped into place and restoring the pressure around his nerves. The boy gasped and she shushed him reassuringly. "Rest easy," she cautioned, "I'm not finished."

He grunted and closed his eyes against the pain as she urged blood to again flow into the damaged areas. His wings fanned and air fed new growth that seemed to accelerate around the gash from the spear. The healing succeeded, and the boy would fly.

"Now!" the soldier cried, pointing toward the sky. Three more Banshees swooped down to aid the others. He parried a thrust from one of his attackers and countered with a slash across an exposed hamstring. The beast fell to the ground and roared. He spun and blocked a blow from above, falling to one knee and bashing his shield into the knee of his foe. Bones shattered and the Deamhan screamed displeasure into the sky – causing others of his kind to turn toward them.

Alistaria jumped to her feet and reached for Restarian's hand, half-dragging him behind as she abruptly flew skyward. He beat his wings with purpose as he followed, ignoring both pain and the terrifying screech of trailing Banshees. Alistaria glimpsed beneath them and smiled with satisfaction as the sentry followed. He surged upward and past – clearing their way to the Skygate. Before long they had reached the portal and tumbled inside as a panting heap. The waiting guardsmen slammed the heavy door shut behind them, locking it into place.

As she untangled her limbs from the others, she noticed piercing eyes casting judgement upon her actions. They were deeply set in a hallowed face, anciently carved and more distinguished than the younger Fainne. She blanched under the king's stare, suddenly hotly aware of the recklessness of her actions.

"Foolish child," he sneered with displeasure. "Your brashness could have caused them to breech the city." He gestured to the shimmering dome set atop the ramparts. "This shield has lasted centuries, older, even, than I. The Banshees have never succeeded in their raids, yet you nearly invited them inside Fainnotheria."

Alistaria felt her knees weaken and her wings began to tremor, urging her to take flight and flee the royal chastisement from her grandfather. Yet she planted her feet and drew tall in his presence. The girl stood under his full gaze and raised her chin. With indifference to his rank she exclaimed, "My *brashness* saved your grandson's life, King Betarian. You should be thanking me instead of criticizing."

"Thanking?" He blinked in surprise at her boldness. "Gaw!" He spat. "I believe you are as dangerous to our court as your mother. She was your age when she betrayed us."

A woman's voice interrupted the king. "Would you have rather driven me from court, Betarian? If I recall it was your fondness for me that allowed me to remain. I dearly called you father at one time in case you've forgotten. Or is it simply," she asked with an eyebrow raised, "you've reserved more punishment for the daughter I was, than the criminal I became, and you so grievously blame?"

He spun in anger to meet the eyes Nastauria. The woman was a force to be reckoned with when docile, but her words flowed torrential when riled. "I punished you enough," he proclaimed. He waved to his grandson who jumped to his feet and hurried to the king's side. "Come," Betarian ordered. "Explain your role in this foolishness." The monarch then turned on his heel, striding off to find a better vantage point to view the battle raging above.

Restarian glanced at Alistaria only once as if to offer a grimace of both sorrow and thanks.

Nastauria waited until the king and her nephew had departed. Then she turned to the blue-eyed sentry standing near the Skygate. "You rescued my daughter," she offered without even glancing at her daughter. "What is your name?"

"Torian," the guard crisply replied.

"Thank you for coming to her aid, Torian," she said with both an air of regality and the smile of a grateful mother. That bearing would never be lost, despite that her titles and inheritance were stripped forever.

"It was *my* honor, my lady."

"Did you know she was my daughter when you followed her to the forest floor?"

"Honestly, no," he admitted. "I saw only a Fainne in trouble and her lending aid."

"Then why didn't you leave them to the Banshees and Ganshees? If Restarian was dying, his soul belonged to Síth Morkur."

His eyes flicked toward Alistaria and returned to meet her mother's. The woman's stare was as intense as the king's. With candor he answered, "I admired her loyalty to her friend and..." He paused.

Nastauria, impatient and not willing to draw out the conversation, demanded, "and what?"

"I also admired her boldness, my lady."

The woman nodded and motioned for Alistaria to follow. Once she was alone with her daughter she said, "You acted bravely, and of that I'm proud. But your grandfather and I each sensed your healing of Restarian. Be careful with that," she cautioned, "a healing of that strength could draw nearer those who would do you harm. Especially," she added with concern, "if you steal what belongs to the Síth."

"I'm sorry, Mother. I will be more cautious in the future."

"In the future?" Nastauria chuckled. "In the future I'd advise you not to risk your life so recklessly."

The girl could only nod her head. There were no words with which a worthy argument could be made.

Chapter Two

He was not the first human to cross the portal, and indeed he wasn't the last. He wasn't even the first to bring harm to the Fainne. No, I never saw the threat he posed. To me he epitomized beauty. I yearned for his touch, the sweet temptation that offered so much more then my own kind could provide. I longed for his mortal passion. Alas, he brought only beautiful pain and suffering while shattering my youthful spirit.
– Lamentations of Nastauria

Brown eyes shot open and Alistaria jumped from her hammock. Violence had erupted throughout the city, with Fainne silver colliding against iron and the clash of it waking the sleeping court. With the softest of breeze and lightest of movement she swung her legs over the side and bolted to the hall. The leaf structure swayed in her wake, forgetting her presence as it slowly settled to a stop. Soon it would cool as well, as evidence of her slumber fully erased from the night.

The hideous screech of the Banshees met her sensitive ears. She covered them with her hands as she flew into the courtyard and toward the Tree of Life. The Fainne were unaccustomed to loud noises within the shield – their home a sanctuary from all but the most delicate sounds of the forest. She despised these vile beasts!

At the base of the tree's long roots stood a line of silver armor where city guardsmen held the invaders at bay – pushing against a squad of enemy. Amongst the lower branches blurs of golden-clad Kern zipped around, bravely defending the citizens hidden within the ancient wood. Alistaria landed nimbly beside Restarian, taking note of the dagger in his outstretched hand.

"What will you do with that?" She asked coolly of her friend, walking toward him on bare feet and taking a perch beside him.

"Stick it in a Banshee, I hope," was his reply. By the shaking of his hand she doubted he could ever strike dead a living thing.

She took note of the unsteady worry in his voice and spoke this time with only a hint of sarcasm. "Well, I'm sure you'll nick one or two before they gut you."

"Thanks," he said with a smirk. Friends since birth, the cousins had often shared jokes at each other's expense. She knew he'd welcomed the jab, even though he longed to join the Kern just as their grandfather had done but his father could not. It galled Restarian to be a root tender instead of a fighter, and she sympathized he never would.

"How'd they get in?" She asked. With worry she looked to the night sky. The reassuring shimmer of the shield let her know it held.

Restarian pointed toward the Skygate. Another line of guardsmen held the heavy door with their bodies, pressing against a mass of Banshees pushing through. Torian was there – the blue-eyed sentry who had risked his life for hers. He currently led the effort to secure the portal. She realized he wasn't suited in his armor, and must have been off duty when the breech occurred. *Such dedication,* she thought, *that his first action was to return to his post.* With a final heave the Fainne pushed back the invasion and dropped the bolts into place. Fainnotheria had held.

Beneath her feet Alistaria watched as the Kern descended upon the enemy below – wetting the roots of the sacred tree with Banshee blood. Soon the battle ended and she and Restarian joined the other healers tending to the wounded. Tears filled her eyes at the carnage. Though easily healed, the scars of evil would remain both on their skin and within the hearts and minds of the brave soldiers.

While she worked her eyes fell upon a slain Deamhan nearby. The hideous beast offended her eyes – its presence a disgrace to her kind. *They should all be destroyed,* she considered, *slaughtered and scattered instead of driven away to their palace each time.*

"Alistaria!" The shout came from the heart of the roots. She turned and found her mother and King Betarian standing together. Nastauria beckoned her daughter.

"Yes, Mother?" She asked while landing softly upon the sacred soil, careful not to disturb the roots of the Tree of Life. She touched one gently to feel the pulsing pleasure of the spirits within. As long as the tree lived, so would her people.

"Your grandfather demands your audience," her mother declared. "Attend to him and heed his order as your king." As she spoke, she turned her eyes away from her daughter but added over her shoulder, "After you are dismissed you shall give to me an audience as well."

"Certainly, Mother," a confused and now worried Alistaria promised. She watched as Nastauria strode away – head held high with the bearing of the queen she would never become.

"Come, child," The king's harsh voice commanded. "You don't keep the elders waiting."

She turned and he lead her beneath the roots into the sacred Chamber of Life. She drew breath. Only the elders of the court were allowed to meet in the most holy of places, except when a child ceremoniously watered the Blossom with their blood. Letting out her gasp she followed.

The roots here felt warmer, pulsing with the rhythm of the forest despite its seclusion within the walls of Fainnotheria. The entire city was built around the great tree – the oldest and the first planted by the Great Spirit. The spirit had planted three in total. The first she gave to the children of the forest to tend, and bid them to heal the roots of every tree in the wood. They kept them free of parasites and flowing always with the lifeforce of nature.

Alistaria knew little about the other two she gifted the races, but one she knew belonged to man – a gift the guiled race spurned. She had given to them the Tree of Knowledge. Driven by selfishness they had cut it down to build walls for their shelters. Their abhorrent discard of her gift had driven the Great Spirit to mercilessly disregard their kind. She turned her back and left them to their fateful whims and open to invasion from the Shadow Realm. She left them to rule themselves with the ignorance they had demanded.

The third belonged to a mysterious race of beings. They shared the realm with mankind, but burrowed deep underground in caves hewn from rock. The Great Spirit had taken pity on the gnomes and their wretched poverty, granting them a tree of their own. The story of this third race had always been Alistaria's favorite, and she had always been disappointed the elders could not provide more detail of their lives or their legends. None even claimed knowledge of the purpose of their tree. She only knew of these mystical persons by their collective name – Luchorpán.

The king led his granddaughter to a place deep beneath the roots. The room was dark and lit only barely by the arrangement of glow stones. They had been carefully placed in a circle between the elders and the relic. She shied under the gaze of the ancient Fainne – each far older in appearance than even Betarian – bowing her head in respect while stealing glances at their withered faces. They sat around a barren patch of earth that appeared tended as if ready for planting.

Where a giant bush had once rested, only a withered vine remained, illuminated by the glow of the stones. The pathetic branch offered shrunken leaves and a tiny red rose frozen in perpetual bloom. Alistaria gasped when she stepped upon holy ground that once held the Blossom of the Fainne, tears of reverence falling from eyes that befell the sorry remnant of its former glory. Her utterance caused the elders to nod their approval.

"At least the daughter shows more respect than the mother for the blessed site," one of the elders proclaimed. The woman was the oldest – celebrating her two thousandth year of life. Erania was her name. Her piercing green eyes were the classic emerald of the Fainne and shone brightly with her wisdom from behind wrinkled skin. Meeting her gaze Alistaria thought she even detected kindness.

"You bled for the Blossom already, have you not, child?"

"I have," Alistaria agreed, feeling the tip of her finger where the thorn had pierced delicate skin of youth. Her ceremony had occurred two years before, granting the power to draw energy from the relic. She had immediately felt the presence of the healing rose, and faintly sensed the ghostly remains of the missing blooms. Upon those the magic of her people had once relied, but no longer.

"Do you understand the importance of the shrub that was stolen from our midst?"

The daughter of Nastauria nodded, not realizing the elders awaited a recitation of their history.

"Then tell us, child," her grandfather commanded with impatience lining his voice. "Tell us the story of the Blossom and how it came to be stolen."

Alistaria nodded vigorously and choked back her nerves. She had listened intently to this story many times as a child, despite the shame it brought to her mother. The girl swallowed and recanted the best she could.

"The Bláth de Fainne," she said, "is the Blossom upon which balance depends."

"Balance for whom, child," Erania demanded.

"Balance," Alistaria replied, "for both our fae realm and also that of the humans against the shadow. The bush stood for more than two hundred thousand years as the tether to our realm. In our possession it kept the Deamhan under our control. Even the Ganshees obeyed our command whilst she grew beneath the roots."

"Describe her blossoms, child," Erania said with a wave of her hand to continue.

Alistaria continued, "She flowered with the blooms of the elements and also power, healing, life, and death."

"How did they manifest?" Erania asked.

"Power was a morning glory – representing the dawn of our hope – vibrant like the strength it represented. While it blossomed, our kind could do more than zap harmlessly," she snapped her fingers as she spoke, causing a tiny spark to appear in the darkness. "We could summon lightning from the heavens and explode boulders. With her begonia, hyacinth, and aster, we could wield fire, ice, and air as well as the Great Spirit herself – as long as the blossom remained on the vine."

"What of the others, child?"

"The white lily represented resurrection, our mastery over death, while the bold Iris represented corruption. As black as death, the bearded petals dripped with the evil that resides in the heart of the Deamhan. As long as they bloomed, the Banshees feared our power and our people roamed the forest unmolested while tending the roots."

"And if they were plucked?" The elder asked.

"They could be planted to grow in a different place," she said, "but they will not grow as flowers. They would reemerge as precious gems without the roots of the Tree of Life nearby."

"How long does it take to grow if replanted?" Erania questioned.

"Once planted, the blossoms require the full six days of Tempest before returning."

King Betarian interrupted, obviously impatient with the ritual of the elders. "And what happens to the Deamhan during Tempest, child?"

"They sleep." Alistaria spoke with confidence. She well knew her history. "Girtrán the Great commanded them to slumber every thirty days, saving our people from their cunning and hatred for our being – even if only for the duration of the storm. He did this when he revealed to us their wickedness that lay within. They once looked like us, but instead were of a different realm. They cloaked themselves with enchantment to fool our ancestors and live among us, but Girtrán revealed their true forms as the Banshees we saw today."

"So you fully understand why the storm does not rage over Fainnotheria?"

"It is a sign of their corruption and limited to the east where the vile nest. As their evil swirls within their hearts, the storm rages above their heads while they slumber."

"And when they are awake?" The king seemed eager to move the discussion along.

"Much as in today's attack, they raid Fainnotheria with desire to steal what remains of the Blossom of the Fainne."

"What of it remains, child?" Erania showed more patience than the king, but her voice suggested Alistaria should finish her story.

"Only the Blossom of Health remains, ancient one. Our ability to heal each other and tend the great trees was not lost when the shrubbery was wrenched from its bedding – when it was uprooted and stolen away to Enatherr."

"Who purloined the symbol of our power, child?" One of the other elders had asked the question, a man whose name Alistaria could not recall.

"Radviken," she replied. "Radviken the Vile... Radviken the Vain, the Purloiner, the Fashioner of Lies. No matter which title you bestow upon him, he is the schemer and betrayer, the reason for our misery, and the bringer of our downfall."

King Betarian asked with whispered guile, "How did he earn these titles, grandchild?"

Shocked that he had acknowledged their familial connection, she inclined her head at the oddity. In all her one-hundred years he had never called her anything so intimate. "He earned them," she said, "with my conception. He lured Nastauria into his bed and learned of our secrets. After leaving his progeny within her womb he wrenched the holiest of artifacts by its roots and made off to the portal from which he entered – leaving us to fight off a horde of Deamhan until this very day."

"And where is your father now, child?" Erania's eyes let enough pity slip through that Alistaria raised her head with regal bearing as she had learned from her mother.

With confidence resembling an elder fueling her voice the girl said, "He resides now in Enatherr, the human realm where we cannot travel except during Tempest."

"We cannot remain there beyond Tempest like we once could. That was before he stole our power and sealed his realm from ours," Erania agreed, "but a half-blooded child of man can easily walk among the humans after the storm has passed." She waved a wrinkled hand and a root raised as a chair. She motioned for the child and said, "Join us and listen to how you will serve the Fainne, Alistaria – daughter of Nastauria's sin. Learn of the redemption you may bring to your mother and help her regain the title of Princess of the Fainne."

Alistaria sat.

CHAPTER THREE

I confess that I have sinned grievously against others in my rise to power, but know that my ascension was purely intended. I would lament had I the ability of contrition, but that virtue requires penitence. Rulers cannot afford sorrow or regret, not over casualties sacrificed for their own kingdom.
– Confession of Radviken

The buckboard bounced along the road, landing harder than usual due to the heavy sacks of grain. The load was piled high – the fruits of a plentiful harvest, but none belonging to the carters earning a wage and hopefully warm beds during Tempest. Piotr let out a grunt as the force of the impact shook his seat. As usual, Boyd laughed at his pain and earned a spiteful look.

"Oh, relax," the stout passenger told the driver. "You always take things too seriously, and it shows by the pain in your arse."

"I can't help it," Piotr – the taller of the two – replied. "I'm cursed with an arse for a best friend."

"Better an arse than an uptight coin pincher."

"Just be happy I found us this job. We've two days until Tempest and I'd like to stay in an inn, this time."

"You have something against barns?" Boyd asked with a sly smile.

"Aye," Piotr answered, "and so do you. I know you like to flirt with tavern wenches instead of the livestock."

"What a friend you are," Boyd insisted, "if it weren't for picking on me, you'd have no one to talk to. I can't help it if the women love me."

It was true. The ladies were always so charmed by Boyd they acted strange around him – often causing trouble wherever they went. Piotr had never understood their interest. He wasn't much to look at, being shorter and slightly overweight. It must have been the stout little man's charms.

"Besides," Boyd continued, "If it weren't for getting on my nerves, you'd have nothing to do all day. You already leave me doin' all the work!"

Piotr held up the reins and shook him for Boyd to see – he'd been driving every load and doing most of the loading while his friend loafed in the sun. The young men shared a laugh at Boyd's joke, but Piotr stole a worried glance at the sky. He always felt uneasy around Tempest, and never trusted it wouldn't arrive early despite the king's steadfast hold over the elements. "What *do* you have against *honest* work?" He asked his friend to get his mind off the storm.

"Well," Boyd said, "for one it doesn't pay as well, and for another it often makes my muscles sore."

"Your kind of work will make our necks sore if we're caught," Piotr protested. He felt their purse, weighing it and their expected earnings against the prospect of six days in a barn. Boyd was right. If they wanted to stay in an inn, they'd have to find *unsavory* work as well as the carter job they were on. Perhaps a small heist wouldn't hurt. "What do you have in mind?" He finally asked, though he immediately regretted asking. Boyd's schemes were notoriously flawed and unlucky.

"I'm so glad you asked, my distinguished friend! Old man Potter rolled out two kegs of brandy to age in the storm, and I've got a buyer lined up."

"I don't know, Boyd. That sounds risky... and heavy."

"We've got this cart through tomorrow, don't we? We only need to move it a few blocks to a tavern by the docks."

Mention of the harbor district sent Piotr into an immediate attack of anxiety. "Count me out," he said with a dismissive wave, "I'm not going near the docks."

"Why not?" Boyd asked.

"Because the Thieves' Guild nearly pinched us last time! No sir, I'll decline. Never mind the fact they told us never to be seen doing jobs around their turf! They know our faces and will kill us on sight, so find something else!"

"C'mon, Piotr, that's the easiest one I could find. You want to stay in an inn, don't you?" Boyd watched his friend expectantly, hoping he'd find wisdom in his hairbrained schemes. Finally he added, "A warm inn with cozy fireplaces, three square meals a day, and pretty wenches?"

"Jails have three square meals a day, too, Boyd. No thanks, I'll settle for the barn."

"You've got no sense of adventure."

The buckboard bounced again, and Piotr gritted his teeth. He would sleep well that night for sure. His body ached and his mind was exhausted. Maybe Boyd was right. Maybe they needed one big score to finally relax and stop taking these odd jobs before Tempest. Then a thought struck him.

"Maybe Miss Tamee will take us in again," The taller man said.

"Are you kidding me?" Boyd asked. "She said never come back!"

"I know she said that, but it was two years ago when we hit adulthood. She wanted us to see the world since we were officially grown... and we have."

"The world? We've shoveled horse stalls in Rivania, fish guts in Enat, and spent two months in jail in Crosston. That ain't seein' the world, Piotr."

"No, but the sheriff's wife was as big as the world, wasn't she, Boyd?"

"Don't bring that up. I didn't know she was married when I met her in that tavern."

"You're just lucky she denied everything to her husband to get him to you set free." He paused as if considering then asked slyly, "Or was it she forgot you altogether?"

"She won't never forget me," Boyd said with a grin. "She took me 'round the world, that gal!"

"Just think about it. We could go back to Tamee's and ask her for a job bouncing customers and keeping the girls safe. You know, the job Markey did when we were growing up in the house."

"I miss Markey. Having him around was like having a father or big brother – always teaching us things and showing a better way to do it. He had a thief's mind, a warrior's strength, and a lover's heart, that man! Seems a waste for him to join the Storm Riders." Boyd said.

"I'm sure he's doing fine," Piotr said fondly of the man. He had indeed been like a father to them both. "But you know the Warden gave him no choice but to take the job. Not after what he did to protect Madeline." The carts ahead turned off the main road to the silo. Farmhands were already lined up to move the sacks, so Piotr pulled alongside. "You ever wonder about the Tempest?" He asked his friend.

"What about it?" The shorter, stockier man asked.

"Why does the king allow it to happen? If he's *all-powerful* why doesn't he stop the storm from coming every thirty days instead of letting it rage for six?" Piotr pointed to the barn. Cattlemen were already driving the herd, bringing them indoors for the purge. "This all seems like a big waste of time for a wizard. Don't you think he could stop the entire thing from happening?"

"I don't know," Boyd said truthfully. "But imagine if the crops didn't wither during Tempest, and you had to plow them under every time you planted. Now *that's* a lot of work!"

They watched as robed priests bore out three shrouded bodies, placing them high on the funeral stands for the storm to claim.

"Who do you think those are?" Boyd asked.

"I know one is old-man Perkins. He passed two weeks ago, and they had him stored in the barn. I saw him when we picked up the wagon. He scared the mutton out of me, lying there on the hay!"

"How do you think they disappear, the bodies? And why do they only disappear during the storm?"

"You know how," Piotr said. "Tamee told us all the stories."

"Yeah, but do you think pixies are real?"

Both men fell quiet, thinking of the *other* creatures who roamed Tempest. Finally Piotr spoke. "I know Banshees are."

"Yeah, me too," Boyd agreed.

"At least those can't hurt you. They just kind of roam around screaming all night. Markey once said he stood face to face with one and could see right through it. They can't actually cross over, he said, only their ghostly spirits do."

"There're worse things than Banshees," Boyd added. "I'd hate to run into a Cat Síth, or a three-headed hound, or a Skinwalker."

Piotr laughed. "There certainly aren't three-headed dogs and Pucas roaming around. And Cat Síths are silly. I've seen plenty of black cats in my day, and none of them were out to steal my soul."

"Ever see one with a white spot on its chest?"

"Well, no," Piotr said honestly.

"Then there you go. When you see one, don't say I didn't warn you."

One of the farm hands pounded on the side of the cart, indicating they were finished unloading. Piotr flicked the reigns and turned the cart toward the foreman's quarters. He'd have a table set out to pay the carters their daily wage. While they rode, he stole another glance at the perfectly cloudless sky. *One day we'll be caught without a place to stay,* he thought, *then what'll we do?*

Chapter Four

I saw no harm in speaking openly about the Bláth de Fainne, considering the permanence it held in our world. I never believed it would be stolen, especially by him. He was my lover and friend. He confided in me the secrets of his world as well. It seemed to a young girl a harmless thing to show him the source of our power – and to tell him of its history...
– Lamentations of Nastauria

Alistaria emerged from beneath the roots of the Tree of Life. She chose to walk instead of fly to her mother's chamber – emotion coursing her veins and muddling her thoughts as she mulled the elders plan. *Can I do this thing they demand? Surely, I'm not capable,* she worried.

The entire scheme was ridiculous. The notion that she – a mere child by Fainne years – could succeed in the venture was foolhardy. *Certainly the elders have more sense than this. Surely, they can put together a plan using only the Kern, instead of depending on me to aid their attack.* Bewildered she approached her mother's door.

She pushed it open to find Nastauria was not alone. Sitting across from the princess was the young blue-eyed sentry from the Skygate.

"Ah... Alistaria," her mother said. "You remember Torian?"

"Yes," the girl blushed slightly.

She found him much more handsome now that she had a solid look at his features. There was never a moment to really study him before. His ruggedness stood out from the other Fainne. His muscles were more deeply defined – stronger and standing slightly taller. His jaw was broader than the others and his facial hair thicker. And his eyes… As blue as water they contrasted the emerald or yellow of most. Occasionally light turquoise would appear in a newborn, but Torian's shone much more brilliantly. Whether green, golden, or blue, any color was better than her own dusty brown – surely a mark of her father's vile seed.

"Mother," she said, tearing her eyes away from the visitor. "You must send him away so we may speak privately."

"Yes," Nastauria said, "we *should* discuss your journey."

Alistaria was taken aback. "How did you know?"

"I didn't, but I presumed. A mother has a way of knowing things regarding their children. And you…" she trailed off, choosing her next words. "Let's just say that you offer the elders a single option in their war against the Deamhan. My role in our people's fate set you up for this dangerous undertaking." Her bearing slipped for only a moment when she added, "The least I can do is offer survivability."

The girl looked again at Torian. He met her gaze and nodded along with her mother's words. *So he's agreed to come along.* "I do not need a nursemaid, Mother. I promised the elders I'd travel alone and involve no one else. By bringing him I'd have broken both my promises before even venturing to begin the quest." For no reason except to inflict pain she added, "Besides, Mother, I'm not you. I don't make a habit of betraying my people or breaking my word."

Without flinching Nastauria replied harshly, betraying the hurt in her voice, "I deserve that, but you are mistaken in believing you can succeed alone."

Alistaria at once regretted making the slight. It had not been easy growing up, especially when the entire court knew her the daughter of Nastauria's sin. Despite that hardship, she had never treated her mother with such indignity.

"I'm sorry," she said, "please forgive me. It's just that I promised the elders and King Betarian I would do this alone and without aid."

"My father oversteps," Nastauria snapped. "He may be king of the Fainne, but he holds no authority to send my daughter into danger without consulting my guidance on the best course." More calmly and worthy of the queen she should be, the mother added, "I will deal with my father and you will travel with Torian."

"I cannot!" Alistaria protested.

"You must. There is a chance you have too much human blood and may not transport without his aid. Furthermore, once you cross the portal, the journey will be treacherous. The Deamhan will be deep in slumber and will cross over in their dreams, but the Ganshees will be very real. They will harangue your path the entire way."

"Will I have Fainne magic?" Alistaria asked.

"I don't know," her mother admitted, "but I doubt it. Though your father's blood courses through your veins – and you may feel it since his blood first watered the replanting in his realm – I cannot say for sure." The older woman suddenly frowned, worried by an unspoken thought. "But even if it did, the magic may feel different for you." With a dismissive wave of her hand she added, "In truth, I hope you may fully draw upon the Blossoms in that realm, though you may have to bleed on each in order to do so. Like the bleeding that fed the healing rose, his lifeforce feeds the other seven blooms. If you can somehow connect to it, you will have more strength than you know. Remember," Nastauria stressed, "you *must* bleed on the Blossom as soon as you can!"

"How will I find it, much less feed it, Mother?"

"That's beyond my knowledge. But know you have a full six days of difficulties until respite, and by then Torian will have returned to our realm." She turned to the young man with sadness in her expression. "He will find himself deep in Deamhan territory – maybe even their palace – and will face a terrible journey while returning to Fainnotheria."

"I'm not meant to stay beyond the storm." Alistaria admitted, reaching into her pocket and holding up a tiny satchel of spores. She stared at it intently and her mother's eyes focused as well.

"What is that?" Nastauria asked curiously and just a little worried.

"Spores with which to plant a Fainnen Ring within the walls of Radviken's fortress," Alistaria said excitedly.

Her mother's face softened. "So you're not to retrieve it, you are to plant the means by which the Kern are to gain access?"

Alistaria nodded. "The elders cautioned I only have six days to find and enter the place he keeps the Blossom. The best of the Kern will stage in that spot of our realm and search for the portal I leave behind. It will be up to them to retrieve the Blossom and escort it and I to Fainnotheria."

Nastauria's eyes grew wide with concern. "So this is an assault on both Betarian's enemies," she mused aloud. "Radviken's palace stands in their realm where Clíodhna's is in ours."

Alistaria nodded. "Betarian will lead the Kern to the Palace of the Deamhan and attack Clíodhna's sleeping Banshees. By placing the ring in the Human Realm, I will give grandfather access to transport through."

Nastauria nodded. The arrangement was fair and the plan more sensible than she had assumed. "It has merit," she admitted. "But Betarian is a fool to think Clíodhna won't detect his attack. She's smarter than he gives credit." She paused to allow some sorrowful memory pass, then added, "Nonetheless, you will take Torian along. Let him guide you to the Port of Enat and north to Radviken's home of Norgaard. You will find him there for he loves it dearly. He spoke fondly of that farmland nestled south of the Windswept Mountains, and he would have built his palace there."

"How will I remember all of this, Mother?"

Nastauria handed her daughter a small book with flax binding. "This contains my most intimate thoughts and memories of his treachery, but will also provide you with the secrets he told an innocent girl during seduction. This is the weapon you will need along the way, Daughter. This," she rested her gaze on the blue-eyed sentry and added, "and the sword of *this* warrior."

"What will I do, Mother," Alistaria asked, "once he is gone and I find myself alone in Enatherr? I will not know my way or who to trust."

"Trust no one," her mother snapped. "There is no trusting humankind. They are selfishly arrogant, and their bodies bear evil souls that will consume your own. Trust them not while anticipating their betrayal."

"So I should avoid them?"

"Of course you should. Stay in the shadows while you search for the Bláth de Fainne."

"You aren't coming," Alistaria declared with finality. "I don't need you and I won't have you."

"Your mother insisted," Torian said.

The calmness in his voice nearly made her beg him to come along. She yearned to remain as even tempered as he, a feat while the world around her fell apart. Confidence had never been one of her virtues. Instead she quivered inside like a coward begging to return to the safety of her room. She looked up from packing her satchel and stared into his eyes – his beautiful blue eyes.

"I won't deter you?" She asked.

He shook his head. "No, you won't," he said. "You're stuck with me for six days," he replied.

She pointed to the sword at this side. "Will you get me one of those?"

He shook his head again. "No. Fainne silver will draw too much attention to a girl seeking the shadows. I've been told the humans covet the fineness of its forging. My advice is you play your strengths."

"My strengths?" She cringed at his implication. "Because I'm a woman? Just what do you suggest *are* my strengths?" She fumed. "Just because I'm female doesn't mean I'm weaker than you." Realizing another possible meaning she added, "And I won't use my body in any fashion to complete this quest!"

He blushed. "Of course you wouldn't... I meant..."

She raised a sharp eyebrow and waited.

"That's not what I meant at all," he said. "He turned his eyes to the floor and shyly said, "When I first met you, I was impressed by your courage. Remember I witnessed you turn away from the Skygate to save the prince? I admire your bravery. You would have fought that Banshee even if I hadn't arrived."

"Well," she said, taken aback by the unexpected compliment. "Thank you." She blushed a little herself and added sternly with a waving finger, "I would have done that for anybody!"

"So you two aren't..." he drifted off, searching for a delicate way to ask if she and Restarian were mated.

"Most certainly not!" She exclaimed. "He's my cousin! There's no way we'd..." She felt a little vomit tickle the back of her throat and added, "Eww!"

Torian notably relaxed, almost pleased – and that caused her a new worry.

"Don't get any ideas of your own," she said. "I won't be stuck on a journey with someone who only wants to paw at me!"

"So you *are* taking me along?" He asked with a smile.

"Yes," she said, "it seems that I am."

"Taking him along where?" Restarian asked from the doorway.

"Nowhere," they both answered in unison.

The prince pointed at the satchel she had packed. "Then why've you packed for a journey? Obviously, you're taking one." He pointed to the similar satchel on Torian's shoulder. The sentry's armor was gone – replaced by a simple tunic and breeches. On his feet he wore moccasins. "And it seems he's dressed for you to *take along.*"

Alistaria pulled her friend inside, shutting the door behind him. "I'm sworn to secrecy, Restarian. I'd love to tell you, but I can't."

"Sworn to secrecy by whom?" He asked.

"Your father, *the king.* Also by the elders."

"Is that all?" He chuckled and asked, "Which elders?"

"All of them," she replied.

"Well then," he sighed. "You *mustn't* tell me. Because I talk to *each* and *every* one of them daily," he said sarcastically, "including my father. In fact," he added, "I may even go tell him now that you *invited* me along to Enatherr." He turned to leave.

Torian grabbed the prince by his shirt, pulling him close and pressing his face in his. "You wouldn't do that, because it's a lie."

"Relax," Alistaria said as she squeezed between the two, saving her friend from certain embarrassment. "That's how we tease. It's called sarcasm."

Restarian shrugged without taking his eyes from the sentry's – daring him to press forward. "Just because I'm a healer and you're a warrior, doesn't mean I can't dispatch you, guardsman." Both Torian and Alistaria looked down at his hand. In it he held a silvery dagger. It was inches from the soldier's sternum.

"Put it away, Restarian," she commanded. "He's a friend, and my mother ordered him to go with me."

"Worry not, Cousin," he said with a sudden grin and laughing eyes. "I merely wanted to offer you this knife for your journey. Besides, your bodyguard already confirmed your destination with his reaction." He tossed the blade on her hammock and left.

Torian's eyes followed him as he left. "Will he be trouble?"

"Not at all," she replied. "He's only sore he's not coming with." She noticed the tension in the sentry's posture and added, "Lighten up. He doesn't even know how to use that thing." She picked it up and turned it over in her hands, admiring the craftmanship. Sliding it into the empty sheath on her belt she said, "Thank the Spirit that I do."

"Do you really?" He asked with a raised eyebrow.

"No," she replied, "not one thing except which end to point."

Chapter Five

The Fainne girl was a wonder. She was the most beautiful woman I'd ever met, and she fell deeply in love with me. Stealing her secrets was never my intent, but I saved my own world by doing so. Never in my wildest dreams did I imagine the power I'd brought back.
– Confession of Radviken

Port Enat always had a northern chill about it at night, even when the Tempest wasn't bearing down. The old-timers said it had something to do with the breeze from the mountains to the northeast, but the superstitious claimed the icy wind came from the dune sea in the northwest. The land was enchanted, they believed, and the source from which the Tempest carried the Banshees and Ganshees from their forest hidden within the Dune Sea.

Many an explorer had perished crossing those dunes, but the survivors told tales of strange mirages shimmering on the horizon. But instead of water, as one would expect in a sea of sand, each telling boldly claimed ghostly trees as tall as the mountains beyond. Most travelers, however, never made it past the cliff-lined ridge overlooking the dunes. That was plenty far enough to know nothing good could cross that desert alive. The dead, of course, would cross it no matter what.

On this night Piotr shivered atop the cart, cursing Boyd for dragging him into another half-baked job that could land them both in jail. His eyes scanned the shadows, searching for the constable or squad of city guards. Worse, every time a cat meowed, he jumped out of his skin – worried it was the Síth come to claim his soul. When the rear of the wagon lurched, he nearly screamed aloud.

Spinning around he found Boyd had loaded the first cask of brandy. "Good gods, man! You gotta let me know you're sneaking up on me!"

"Be right back," Boyd said with a wink, turning to trot off toward old man Potter's distillery. A few moments later he was wheeling the second cast at a fast run, with two large dogs chasing behind.

"For Radviken's sake," Piotr muttered, swinging down to catch the runaway barrel before it careened down the street and into a crushing mess. It nearly rolled over him, but he caught it just in time. He and Boyd quickly heaved it to the rear and jumped aboard as the dogs reached the wagon. One of them leaped and nearly tore a hole in his leg.

Boyd sat grinning in the straw. "You gonna drive us out of here, or play with the doggies?"

With a roll of his eyes, Piotr jumped into the driver's seat and gave the reins a snap. Soon they were racing down the street with the dogs barking their chase.

Boyd leaned forward, "When I planned the job, I figured we'd do it a little more stealthy-like." He pointed behind them. Five more dogs had joined the chase and were barking merrily from behind. "This isn't at all what I had in mind."

"Me neither," Piotr muttered. He pulled the cart into a left turn that nearly turned the entire thing over, but it crashed onto all four wheels once he again straightened it out.

"Oh, blast," said Boyd.

"What now?"

"Three strays and a blind beggar's dog just joined in the chase. You really do have us in a pickle, mate!"

"Me?" Piotr gawked. "You brought the blasted dogs, not me!"

"I only brought two. You somehow have the entire canine population of Enat chasing us." He made a *tsk* sound in his mouth. "You've really fouled this job up, Piotr."

"I?" Piotr flashed his friend a glare. "How did *I* foul it up?"

Boyd pointed. "Watch the road, please?"

Piotr turned to find they had burst into the market square. It was late, but several merchants were still hawking their wares. A fish monger leaped out of the way just as they crashed through his table.

Salmon and trout flew into the air and Boyd caught a sturgeon in both hands. "Lucky day!" He proclaimed.

Piotr turned. Some of the dogs had given up the chase, choosing instead to attack the fish littered about the square. Only four had ignored the catch of the day. A thought sprang into his mind and he turned the wagon toward a meat seller. "Grab that ham," Piotr shouted to Boyd, "and that rack of ribs and those sausages!"

His friend nodded, realizing his strategy. He stood and nearly fell from the buckboard as he retrieved the items. People shouted in the square behind them as the dogs sprinted between their legs. Then a whistle echoed down a side street and the men exchanged a look. A constable was in pursuit.

Piotr held the reins steady as they continued toward the water-front. "Get ready to throw sausages," he said as he turned toward Boyd. The man had frozen between bites, his mouth stuffed full of the meat and chewing noisily. "What are you doing?" He yelled. "Those were for the dogs!"

His friend shrugged and tossed the ham over his shoulder. Both men followed its trajectory with their eyes, flinching when it caught the constable in the chest, knocking him from his horse. Four more dogs stopped to fight over the discarded meat and both men exchanged another look. They rounded another bend and emerged in the waterfront.

"Which tavern is it," Piotr asked.

Boyd pointed. "That one," he said, "the Crabby Mistress."

Piotr turned the wagon and made for the front door. Pulling to a stop both men quickly jumped down to find only one dog was still in pursuit. It was a mangy brown mess with only one eye and half a tail. How it kept up was a mystery to the men.

"That's the beggar's dog," Boyd offered with a shrug. He reached down and handed it a sausage. It ate greedily, nearly taking a finger in its first gulp.

The two men pulled both casks from the buckboard and rapped on the door. The keeper poked his head outside and looked around – ensuring the men weren't followed – then held out a sack of gold. The sound of constable whistles caused him to change his mind and shut the door without handing over a cent. Leaving the casks, they both jumped onto the wagon. The mangy dog followed. With a shake of the reins they were off again, with the dog once again in pursuit. Behind them the door again opened and strong arms pulled the brandy inside.

They didn't get far before two large men stepped into the road. Piotr hauled in the reins and they lurched to a halt. One of the brutes held the horses while the other circled the wagon with a crossbow, aiming it at Piotr.

"Friends of yours?" Boyd asked.

"I was about to ask you the same thing," Piotr replied.

"Thieves' Guild," the man with the crossbow said. "And you two ain't supposed to be around here."

"Tell you what," Piotr said as he got down from the wagon, motioning for Boyd to do the same. "You can have our wagon and everything in it," he said, hoping they wouldn't notice it was currently empty, "but we've," he looked the way they'd come and spotted four city guardsmen running their direction, "got to run."

In a flash he was off with Boyd and the one-eyed dog trailing behind. He only looked back once. Both guildsmen were taken into custody by the guards – obviously mistaken for the two men joyriding through the market square. Once they were safely out of the waterfront district, the stopped to catch their breath.

Boyd tapped Piotr on the shoulder and pointed the way they'd come. "How much was the deposit on that wagon," he asked.

"Pretty much the price of an inn for six nights," Piotr replied.

"So we're sleeping in the barn again?"

The taller man nodded. "We're sleeping in the barn again."

"Beats jail," Boyd said with a smile, tossing the dog another bit of sausage.

Chapter Six

He came to our realm unaware, having drifted into slumber within a Fainnen Ring. A circle of mushrooms, he'd thought, and nothing menacing. An innocent piece of nature and the perfect place for a rest. When he had awakened the forest around him had changed. The trees were larger and the canopy higher than those around his home. He had wandered several days before I'd found him staggering with confusion and full of terror of the many things he had seen. The Cat Síth was one of them, and Clíodhna was another.
— Lamentations of Nastauria

Many years had passed since Alistaria last journeyed deep into the forest. Other than the tended roots around the city, much of the forest had fallen to neglect since the Deamhan stepped up their attacks over the past hundred years. The vigorous raids had taken a toll not only on the Fainne, but also on the forest itself. Death and decay had already worked into most of the larger trees. The situation was more dire the further east she and Torian journeyed.

She could smell the musk of rotted wood as they passed a broad trunk. She paused, holding up a hand for her escort to do the same. He took up a defensive position, something he had learned to do during the first day of their journey, realizing finally there was no arguing with the girl once she set her mind to a task. She leaned in close to the bark, feeling the pulse of lifeforce within.

"Beetles," she said. "They burrow deep and lay their eggs. The larvae are what devour the tree, damaging and killing it over time."

"Is there anything you can do?" He asked.

"Yes, but not without drawing attention to our whereabouts. As soon as I connect to the roots the vibrations will draw the Banshees - even this far out."

The soldier shivered despite the warmth of the forest. "There are other things just as dangerous in this wood," he warned. "Much of it's darkened over time and won't be long before Fainnotheria is all that remains of our realm. Eventually, even the city will disappear."

"That's the fear of the elders," she agreed, "and why they asked me to make the journey. Unless we restore the Blossom, even the Tree of Life will wither too. The fate of our people is uncertain."

"What lies beyond the forest?" He asked. "How badly has the world deteriorated?"

"I don't know, but mother has told me the stain of the Deamhan has spread far and wide. She believes they've corrupted more than the trees, spreading their darkness to the soil as well. I've heard the ground in their lands has crumbled into vast caverns, spewing molten rock the further one journeys eastward and north." She pulled her hands from the bark, patting it gently as if to tell the tree there were nothing she could do, even if she did empathize for its plight. They were kindred – both the forest and the Fainne – destined for extermination via slow decay.

She began moving again toward their goal. They would find the Fainnen Ring after a full day's walk at their current pace, but neither was in a hurry. Remaining quiet and avoiding attention was their main concern. Both knew what they were looking for, since knowledge of the rings were common among their kind. Every child knew to avoid them in the forest – these portals from another world brought monsters more dangerous than the Banshees to prey upon the Fainne.

"What do you think the humans will be like?" Torian asked. "I'm actually excited to see one."

"Mother says they appear very much the same as us. Their ears are shorter and rounded – something I never understood. I asked her once if that affected their hearing and she said that it did, but not much. Their men grow full beards that are thicker even than yours." Alistaria suddenly laughed despite her efforts to remain quiet.

"What's so funny that you'd laugh so loudly and risk our detection," Torian asked, shushing her scornfully. But her outburst had made him smile as well. He was enjoying himself despite a quick look around them to ensure they hadn't alerted any threats.

"Mother said that many of the humans are quite plump."

"Plump? What does that mean?"

"Fat. You know, with rounded bellies and extra chins. Some of the men grow their beards to cover their many chins," she said. "They get that way by putting sugar on their food and drinking fruits and grains they've fermented."

He gasped and turned to her with rounded eyes. Aghast he asked, "Fermented on purpose? Whyever would they do such a stupid thing?"

"Apparently they like it better that way. It affects them, making them to act strangely and have blurred vision."

"How is that a pleasurable experience?" He wondered.

"I don't know. Mother said she tried some my father had made for her – something he called wine. It didn't appeal, and had a different effect."

"What happened to her?"

"She fell deeply asleep and awoke with a tremendous headache that even midsummer daisy couldn't help to ease." They both fell quiet after mention of Nastauria.

After a while Torian asked the question burning inside. "So she really did tell him the secrets of the Blossom? That part of the story isn't a myth?"

"She did, and he took advantage of her innocent trust." She paused, searching for the right words to say. He was so eager to know more about her mother, but she couldn't tell him all she knew. "Humans are evil, Torian. That's the sum of it. They would sooner destroy our world as they've destroyed their own."

Her escort fell silent as he considered, but she could tell something still troubled him deeply. After a while he asked, "So you really are half fae and half human? I'm not surprised you hate them with such passion."

"I am," she admitted. "But my heart is full Fainne. I've no desire to ever meet a human, much less show sympathy for one. The only thing I despise more than them are the Deamhan."

Sounds of a struggle and shouts for help suddenly rose through the forest, reaching them from the path they had travelled. Someone was in trouble and his cries begged mercy.

"That's a Fainne," Torian exclaimed, drawing his sword and lifting into the canopy. He paused and motioned for Alistaria to follow. "Come along," he said, "I won't leave you alone."

She looked eastward down their intended path and hesitated. "It could be a trap," she said, "and we're so close to our goal!"

"Someone's in trouble," he insisted, "and my duty is to protect." He waited only a few more seconds before flying off to investigate, leaving her behind.

Alistaria abruptly felt cold and alone, aware of her vulnerability in the forest. *What if this is a trap?* She wondered. She looked once more toward their destination then lurched into the air, following quickly behind Torian as he raced toward sounds of trouble.

They soon emerged in a clearing – one through which they had already passed. There they found a Fainne backed against a tree and swinging a silver sword wildly. It was clear he had no experience with the weapon, and the three circling Banshees laughed at his ineptness.

As they neared, Torian and Alistaria paused in the air, suddenly recognizing the trapped fae.

"It's Restarian," she whispered, lurching forward to lend aid.

But the sentry caught her by the wing and heaved her backward, pointing toward a bush behind the Deamhan. It shook and was shoved aside as a large beast emerged. Alistaria froze in place, hovering and watching as the black forest cat leapt into the air – revealing a white spot on its chest as it lunged. It dug sharp claws into the nearest Banshee.

"Cat Síth," she exclaimed with a gasp.

The Deamhan howled and screamed for only a moment before the mighty cat found its larynx, ripping it out and rendering it silent. The other two Banshees fled in terror, leaving their companion behind to be devoured in both body and soul. They rose into the air and swiftly flew, abandoning Restarian to the same fate as their comrade.

The boy backed further against the bark of the tree, holding his sword outstretched as if it were a relic to fend off demonic presence. The beast circled, measuring his threat with the blade. It finally must have decided he offered none and leapt, meeting Torian's shield in midair.

The sentry had dived downward in a blur with such speed that Alistaria hadn't even noticed him begin to move. With shield outstretched, he deflected the pounce and sent the beast tumbling to the side. But he miscalculated the blow and was pushed aside himself, rolling into and under the legs of Restarian. The prince dropped his sword and so did Torian.

Alistaria watched as the beast regained its feet, limping slightly and baring teeth at the duo. As they scrambled for their swords the mighty cat transformed, twisting and turning on the ground as its muscles stretched and spine expanded. Soon it rose, looming over the others, and now wearing the form of a man.

His black skin was as dark as in cat form, velvety and soft and still covered by fur. His teeth were orange and as sharp as a feline's. His eyes glowed yellow with anger and focused with a glare on Torian. He placed his foot upon Restarian's blade, locking it tightly to the ground and forcing the boy to back away once more. The sentry scanned the foliage for his dropped shield.

"Do you know who I am, Fainne?" The Cat Síth asked.

"I do," Torian admitted. "You are Síth Morkur, King of the Beasts."

"Then you know what I am here to claim?"

"You can't have him!" Alistaria screamed into to the forest as she swooped down from the air. Her silvery blade flashed as the beast-like man turned. With a casual wave he pushed her strike aside and sent her off course, coming to rest beside the others. A crimson line formed on her hand as the knife cut deep with her impact. She watched helplessly as large droplets of blood fell to the forest floor.

Restarian knelt beside his friend and took her hand in his, going to work at once to heal the wound. Síth Morkur laughed.

"You Fainne are so quick to heal one another that you forget to leave what is rightfully mine. Whatever falls in the forest belongs to me," he reminded them of the lore. "Two days ago this one fell," he pointed to the prince. "His soul is owed to me."

"He wasn't dead," Alistaria protested. "I merely healed his wing and mended his neck."

The foliage beneath Síth Morkur's feet trembled then moved aside as hundreds of Ganshees raised into the air. They orbited their master as he loomed above the Fainne. They chittered and laughed at the death they would soon consume.

"My children tried to claim him," he explained as several sprites whispered in his ear and pointed at Alistaria, "and you sent them away empty handed. I shall claim what is mine." The Síth took a step forward but froze when a voice announced the arrival of another.

"Then take my soul in exchange for his," Nastauria challenged as she emerged into the clearing. "I've no duty left in this world. I'm shunned by my own kind and my title is stripped, but I *am* the Princess of the Fainne, no matter what my father has proclaimed. Take me in the child's stead – a princess for a prince – and let them continue on their quest."

Alistaria flexed her mended hand as she watched the exchange, barely comprehending the sacrifice. Abruptly she understood and rushed to her mother's side, hugging her close. "No," she begged, "I caused this, not you. Please don't leave me, Mother!"

Nastauria nodded to Torian and he stepped forward, pulling the girl free. "I'm sorry," he whispered, "but I vowed to her that I would allow her to aid you in this way if it came to this."

Alistaria cried as he hauled her off. Through tear-filled eyes she watched her mother casually take her place beside the king of the beasts. Nastauria raised her hand and made a sign in the air – a motion to slumber – as she had done so many times before to help her child sleep. The girl's eyes grew heavy then, as she found she could no longer fight off its affects. She fell limp in Torian's arms and drifted silently into the realm of peaceful dreams.

Nastauria watched as the duo carried off her sleeping daughter. Once they were out of earshot Síth Morkur broke the silence.

"You're running out of souls to offer me, Princess of the Fainne."

Without even a glance for the Síth she answered, "I've kept all my bargains with you. Thank you for scaring away the Banshees."

"I shouldn't have interfered," the Síth replied. "The price of my interference raises each time I give you aid."

"Then why did you?"

"It's becoming a bad habit," he said solemnly, as if he indeed regretted his part. With a sigh he added, "But I understand you must see this ugly business through that you began years ago." He shook his head with distaste and spat on the ground. "Dark business for a Fainne to undertake."

"It reminds you of another?" She asked.

"The *other* requests darker things of me than you would dare to imagine. Your motives are not the same although you share a common goal."

"Does she yet suspect my transgression?"

"She does, but only the narrative you placed," the Síth said with reassurance in his voice.

"And Radviken?" Nastauria turned to face Síth Morkur, boldly staring the spirit in the eye as they spoke. "What does he suspect?"

"His vanity blinds him still, but he knows about the girl. It won't be long before he realizes the truth about all the children and your part in the deception."

"Then I must trust she will act as I hope, and plays the role I've led her toward. I must hope that she succeeds in her goals on her own from this point forward."

"You should have been a Síth, Nastauria. You would have made a stronger one than I."

"Let's see if I can live up to that when the time comes, shall we?"

"Now," he asked with a sly smile – words hissing from his mouth as he spoke. "When can I cash in on this latest soul you've promised me?"

"When it expires naturally, and not a moment sooner." "I've heard that before, so many times," he sighed then added, "but it is truly mine?"

"Given freely, the flavor is sweetened, or so the legend goes?" She asked.

He licked his lips with anticipation. "Given freely the flavor is *sweetest*," the spirit agreed.

Chapter Seven

*As soon as I met him, I'd known in my heart my life had
changed. I merely had no understanding of how at the time.
My life is ended now, though my body lives on. I gave to
him my soul the night I showed to him the Blossom, so
I have no more to offer – not even to a Sith, though that's
a sacrifice I'm ready to make. Remember me not as the
princess who betrayed her people, the girl who performed
that vile act was a mere husk animated by misguided love.*
    – Lamentations of Nastauria

Alistaria awoke in a clearing, blinking sore eyes against a black
sky dotted with the stars of night. Such a beautiful sight, the stars.
Each winking and teasing a story as they comforted the inhabitants
of the world beneath. But which world? She sat up with a start,
anxious panic suddenly coursing her body. All at once she remembered her mother's sacrifice and wailed.

Both Torian and Restarian rushed to her side – offering comfort
and urging her silence. But they held no power over her emotions,
nothing could curtail the mourning that screeched from her lungs
like a Banshee's howl. Thus she keened until she no longer had the
energy to hold her body upright. She lay upon the soft earth and
wept until sleep returned.

When she awoke the second time, she felt warmth upon her face
though her heart felt icy and void. Opening her eyes she blinked

them against the piercing rays of the sun. Oh, how she loved the sun. Often, she would fly above the canopy to bask in its warmth and feel upon her skin the regenerative power of its beam. Now she surrendered to its power, soaking in the heat and hoping it could restore the emptiness that filled her heart.

Why, Mother? She wondered in her mind. *Why would you sacrifice your soul for Restarian?* She rolled to her side and saw that he and Torian practiced blades by a stream. *Pathetic and useless he is in a fight,* she thought. *What worth would he have to our people that is greater than your own? Especially* you, *the princess Nastauria?*

They stopped abruptly when they realized she stared, and sheathed their blades. Torian held back this time, and allowed Restarian to comfort her alone. When he tried to hug her, she shied away from his touch and pulled herself upright to glare at the sentry still by the stream.

"She arranged that with you before?" she asked.

He nodded. "She worried by saving him you had drawn the wrath of Síth Morkur."

"The real reason she sent you along?"

"Yes," he admitted, "I was to escort you to the portal and see you inside. I won't accompany you further if that is your desire."

"My desire?" She boiled with rage inside. "My desire is never to look upon you again. I *desire* that you leave me now to my fate and never interfere in my life. My *wish* is that you die at my enemy's blade and tooth!"

"Fair enough," he said, turning his body and pointing to the place where the meadow met the forest's edge. "I've kept my promise and escorted you to the Fainnen Ring. Your fate is no longer up to me."

She blinked at the circle of shrooms – boldly standing against the green grass – and fearsome doubt returned. *I'm here,* she realized. *All I have to do is enter the portal and cross into the other realm.*

Restarian spoke. "I can come with you," he offered. "The Tempest will be raging so I can only remain at your side for six days. But I would offer any help I can."

"No," she quickly snapped. "You're the reason she's dead! That same selfishness drove you to come along, even though you were hunted by the Síth! Because of *you* my mother is gone, and I cannot let her sacrifice be in vain!"

"I'm sorry," he begged. "You will be lonely, and I've been learning the sword," he urged.

"Trained on it for one day?" She laughed mockingly at his pathetic offer of chivalry. "No," she said with more determination than before. "You'd be a distraction. Besides, you'll be stranded in Deamhan territory at the end of six days – prey to their merciless savagery and doomed to cross days of barren rock."

Something in the distance caught her eye and she pointed past the meadow. Restarian turned his head to gaze upon the hellish landscape beyond. Blackened rock was all that remained of a wind-swept tempest of fire. In the distance, she could see it raging and heading their way.

"So that's why they push into the forest," Torian realized. He pointed to a massive horde of Banshees taking flight ahead of the fiery cloud.

She nodded. "And why they enter the Human Realm during the Tempest. It's destroying their dominion while also purging the other."

"Then you must hurry," he said. "Get a head start so you may find shelter."

She nodded, climbing to her feet and picking up her satchel. Without looking back she hurried forward, entering the ring expecting instant transportation. She waited but nothing happened. She turned around in circles, looking up and down and side to side – suddenly worried this was not a portal after all.

"Go," Restarian urged.

Panic set in. "I can't! I don't know how it works!" She turned her eyes to the sky and watched the horde approach.

Suddenly Restarian seemed to understand. He retrieved Torian's satchel from the ground and thrust it into his arms. "Sorry," he said to the sentry, "but she must have too much human blood to travel, and needs a Fainne to bridge her across – you're much more the protector than me." With a shove he sent the sentry toppling backward into the ring. In a blinding flash the pair were gone.

Restarian watched them disappear into thin air, then turned to face the advancing horde. With a shaky hand he raised his father's silver sword, holding it the way Torian had shown him earlier that morning. The numbers against him were insurmountable – with thousands descending in advance of the fiery tempest. One walked in front of the rest, standing out like a rose among weeds.

His sword arm wavered, and he slowly lowered the tip as she approached. Her beauty was unmatched, more dashing than any Fainne he had laid eyes upon – yet she was clearly a Banshee. Her blue eyes met his green with a loving smile as the horde held back. Only the woman approached. She placed a tender hand against his cheek and stroked his skin, gazing into his eyes with a lover's yearning.

"Why did my son travel to the Human Realm?" she asked. "Why is he traveling with the Princess of the Fainne?"

The prince fought to keep his mouth shut, urging silence against the magical draw of her caress. She smiled tenderly and kissed him gently against the lips, leaving an intoxicating air behind. All at once he could taste her beauty and was driven to yield to her questions. Her scent drew him forward and she gently turned him to face the Fainnen Ring.

"I ask you again, young Restarian. Why did my son – stolen from my birthing bed – travel with the daughter of Nastauria? What scheme does my nemesis hold for my only progeny?"

He tried to resist at first, but her spell was strong. In the end he told her everything. He felt his mouth moving on its own, speaking and detailing their mission as they had explained to him. After he had finished, she snapped her fingers and reality rushed in.

"Do you know who I am, child?" She asked with a tender smile.

He nodded.

"Say it, Restarian, son of King Betarian. Say my name so that your ears know it as well."

"Clíodhna," he replied with a trembling voice.

"Good." She placed her hand against his chest, feeling his heartbeat as it pulsed out both fear and desire. "And who am I?"

"Queen of the Deamhan," he said with tears trailing his cheeks.

"Go then," she commanded, placing a crystal in his palm and wrapping his hand tightly around it. "Follow them to Enatherr. Go where I cannot. Learn what you can, and return to me in six days." She kissed him once more and whispered a command in his ear – one that he would be compelled to carry out – and then shoved him with her palm.

Restarian flew backward into the Fainnen Ring, blinded by intense light as he transported. As he tumbled to the other realm he stared longingly at her beauty and silently swore he would obey his new queen.

CHAPTER EIGHT

Merging the Tempest was my only mistake, but even it turned out beneficial. It purged death and corruption from Enatherr and disposed of it in Clíodhna's realm, adding to her people's misery. It made no matter to me, and the Fainne blamed her for the diminished forest instead of me. But I had conquered death – both my own and that of the kingdom.
– Confession of Radviken

The sky had darkened, heralding the imminent arrival of the Tempest. Though the winds did not yet rage, the dense fogbank loomed on the northern horizon – creeping ever closer with its harbinger of death. In the distance howling winds could be heard, and upon them rode the wails of the Banshees. The wise were shut indoors for the duration of the storm, and would remain in their place of safety for six entire days.

Boyd and Piotr were not so lucky. They had been turned away from several places. Without enough money for the steep price of the inn, they tried the temple. Those doors were already bolted in place and knocking proved futile. The greedy priests ignored all pleas. Frustrated, they returned to the farm they had worked as carters.

The foreman fumed when he recognized them, demanding the price of the lost cart. Thankfully no one had identified them as the culprits of their midnight brandy heist, so they merely forfeited the deposit as well as their final wages. In return he allowed them to spend the week in the livestock barn.

Piotr held up the purse containing their final coins. "We're going to be hungry," he said to the man, "we'll need provisions for six days."

With a heavy sigh the man shoved two full water jugs into Boyd's waiting arms. "This will hold you," he said, "but you'll have to forage for food. Anything left outside will be withered and gone by the end of the storm so you can have what you find."

"Please sir," Piotr begged, "there isn't much to be found this close to Tempest."

The man pointed to the garden and slammed the door, sending them on their way with the heavy slide of bolts.

The garden had been mostly picked over, but they found a pair of gourds and a handful of onions. Those, and the leftover sausages from the night before, made for paltry rations at any time, much less during Tempest.

"I could run to the inn for some beggar scraps," Boyd offered.

Piotr eyed the storm. "There isn't time. It'll be upon us within hours."

"The waterfront's closer," Boyd offered with a smile.

"No. Absolutely not," Piotr said, "I won't even consider that option." But a simple peek inside the barn – and a whiff of fresh manure piles – set his feet toward both the waterfront the Crabby Mistress. "Come along, dog," He said to the beggar's pup. It eagerly followed.

"He needs a name," Boyd suggested of the animal.

"No, he most certainly does not."

The Crabby Mistress had already been shuttered against the storm, but a woman opened the door to empty last minute bedpans on the stoop.

"Thank you kindly, miss," Boyd said as he tipped his hat in a gentlemanly fashion.

"We're closed for Tempest," she muttered back, but moved too slowly to bar access to the two men.

"Have any brandy, miss?" Piotr asked as they pushed their way inside.

"Strange you should ask," she said, "we just acquired two casks last night." She hurriedly shook the last pan and then gathered the others to follow. "But we're not serving during Tempest, sirs! You'll have to leave."

The tavernkeeper was a large man – a mountain, actually. He had his back to the entrance as he busied himself with Tempest preparations. When the pair approached, he was drying mugs with a dirty towel.

"Two fingers of brandy each, good man," Boyd plopped his stout frame onto a stool and added, "and a biscuit for our dog!"

"No dogs allowed," the man growled, turning to recognize the newcomers. "Besides that, we're closed for Tempest!"

The woman hurried to the bar, wiping her hands on her apron. "I tried to tell them, Harveigh, but they barged through anyways!"

The brutish keep reached under the bar and drew out a club, hoisting it and slapping it against a meaty palm. "I'll be asking you nicely at first and then not so nicely, but either way you'll be stepping outside of my tavern." "Well, Boyd," Piotr remarked, "It seems we've discovered why they call this place the *Crabby Mistress*." To Harveigh he said, "No worries, good sir, we'll simply turn our selves over to the magistrate and let him know where to find Old Potter's brandy."

"You wouldn't..."

"Aye, but I've known this man since I was a mere toddler," Boyd offered with a smile, "and I can assure you he's a conscience as wide as Enatherr. He always aims to keep his promises. Besides, this close to Tempest a jail would feel quite cozy."

"What's keeping me from killing you now and setting you outside for the Tempest? There'll be nothing left of you to find after the pixies and Banshees devour your bones." Harveigh stepped forward with the club, still tapping it against his palm.

"Well," Piotr said, "only the possibility that the Thieves' Guild won't take kindly to you killing their own."

"I didn't know you were guilded when I first hired you," the large man said doubtfully. He paused and stopped tapping the club as he considered his options.

Ah, thought Piotr. *There's your weakness! You fear the guild as well as speak of fae. Could you be superstitious as well?* He decided to play his hand and pressed.

"Aye, that we are." He said. "We took this job, interestingly enough, as a lure to see who would hire non-guilded thieves. There'll be a penalty for that, by the way." Piotr was improvising, but that was one of his gifts. He could talk his way out of any situation – not as well as Boyd, who could be convincing even when he was speaking nonsense. "You're welcome to check our credentials with the guild master, but Tempest is about to hit." A roar of thunder announced its arrival just as he if he had timed it. "Ah, but it's too late and you'll have to wait six more days to do so." He leaned in. "I'll tell you what... Since we're here, we'll waive the penalty in exchange for a six night stay in your guest room. We will be taking payment for the brandy up front, however."

Harveigh still appeared doubtful, but the Thieves' Guild was not a group anyone wanted to trifle with. He finally nodded and tossed a full purse onto the bar. "That's for the casks," he said. "You can stay in the guest room, but you best be leaving my girls and my food stores alone. You'll eat only when we do." He pointed at the animal and added, "The mangy dog stays in your room. He doesn't get a share of food, and eats only off your scraps."

The woman eyed the dog closely. "I've seen this dog before," she said, "but I can't remember where. What's his name?"

"Bastard," Boyd said. "Lucky," said Piotr at the same.

The two men exchanged a look – Boyd's was amusement and Piotr's was irritation. Finally, the taller man said, "His name's Lucky Bastard, because he's the luckiest sort of dog."

"How lucky," Harveigh asked. "He don't look very lucky. He actually looks a bit unfortunate, missing an eye and a bit of tail."

Boyd dug into the purse and drew out a gold coin. Turning to the woman he tossed it to her, saying, "Miss, would you mind so much scrubbing him down? It's bad luck not to bathe a dog during the start of Tempest. The smell draws the Banshees into your home."

"I've never heard that," she protested. "Sounds made up to me!"

"Oh, no," agreed Piotr. "It's a habit every dog owner should have if he wants to reap the fortune off a good-luck dog. Besides, we can't take chances with the Banshees, now can we?" Turning to the tavern keeper he said, "Isn't that right, Harveigh?"

Despite his confusion, the large man wouldn't admit his ignorance – especially when it came to his superstitions. He nodded and shooed the woman away. "Get on with it, Martha! Clean him up good so they don't come in!"

"Thank you kindly, miss," Piotr said with a grin. "Now, which way is the guestroom?"

Chapter Nine

*Clíodhna wasn't always filled with evil, nor was she
an enemy of the Fainne. She simply fell under the same
spell as I... and suffered the same terrible fate. Sometimes
that's enough to change a woman's heart and inclination.*
– Lamentations of Nastauria

Torian awoke with a start – muscles cramped, and his limbs
pulled close to his body. His knotted fingers and toes radiated pain
as they struggled to uncurl. He finally found his footing and stood,
stretching and finding new muscles willing to spasm and render
him once more to the ground. His head spun with the pain and
he stumbled.

The world around him had changed drastically and he found he
lacked sense of direction. None of the usual landmarks remained.
The trees were gone, with only petrified stumps occasionally sprout-
ing from thick yellow sand. Gone also was the Fainnen Ring, the
circle of mushrooms replaced by a windswept pattern in the sand.
The grains seemed to flow from the center of the drawn power,
twisting and bending them to an invisible force.

He looked around for Alistaria, suddenly aware of her absence.
In her place he found Restarian asleep beside him – curled in the
same contorted position in which he himself had awakened. Stranger
still was the prince's back. His wings were gone and only two slits
in his tunic revealed they had once adorned his shoulder blades.
Panicked, Torian felt for his own and found nothing. Even their ears
had shrunken, small and rounded with tiny lobes.

He kicked the prince into alertness. "Get up," he commanded.

Torian then turned around to find his bearings. In the far distance he spied a large mountain range where he had hoped. *North,* he realized, *just as in our home.* Between him and the peaks Fainnotheria should have stood amidst the Great Forest and the tended trees. Instead he found only a barren waste. The wind howled unabated across this sea of dunes, sweeping up grains of dust and swirling it into his eyes and mouth. He gagged against the intrusion and helped Restarian to his feet.

"Where are we," the prince asked, wincing from pain of his own.

"Through the portal thanks to you, although I don't understand why Alistaria isn't with us."

"Maybe she wandered off," Restarian said. "I'll go look." He arched his back as if to launch into the air. His face abruptly fell, clouded with confusion.

"You can't fly. We no longer have wings in this realm." The sentry pointed to the dunes all around. "*Everything* is different here."

"What is that on the horizon? It looks like the storm we saw on the other side, but it's changed."

Torian looked the direction the prince pointed. Storm clouds raged in the distance – full of lightning and black with heavy rain. They swirled against the sky but were not filled with the fire they'd seen before. "I'm guessing that's how the Tempest appears to the humans." he said. "Come," he beckoned, "that's where she'd be headed. We must journey into the storm until we find Alistaria. Nastauria mentioned a place called Norgaard and said we'd find it in the furthest point north in this realm. If we discover that place, we'll also find her, I'm certain."

Restarian walked in silence behind the soldier. So many thoughts swirled in his mind – conflicting and troublesome ideas threatening his conscience and his duty to the Fainne. *I've betrayed Alistaria,* he remembered. *I told her of the plans to invade the realm.* Realization slammed him right in the gut. *I warned her of my grandfather's attack!* But the woman had been so beautiful. His mind muddled for a moment, wondering briefly why warning her had been wrong. He suddenly yearned to think only of her and not Alistaria or the fate of his kind.

The taste of Clíodhna lingered upon his lips. Her scent danced within his nostrils. He could feel her breath as she drew nearer. He must serve. He must...

"Are you even listening to me?" The soldier had stopped walking and they nearly collided. He pointed to a patch of sand. "It's deeper here than in other places. I nearly sank into it. You really need to pay attention."

"I'm sorry," Restarian said as he broke from the trance – suddenly embarrassed by his desire to betray everything he held dear, just for a chance to lay beside the woman. "My thoughts wandered off, I guess.... I was thinking of... of her."

"Yeah, I've been thinking of Alistaria as well, but don't worry. We'll find her." They walked a little further, careful to avoid the deeper sand. It was becoming easier to recognize the difference in dunes. "I think the wind is picking up as the storm grows nearer."

Restarian looked closely at the clouds. Once or twice he thought he saw silvery shapes weaving in and out, but couldn't make out the forms. He shivered out of fear. "Then we need to get out of these dunes before it hits us fully."

Torian pointed to a steep incline leading to a plateau. "More importantly," he said, "we need to get over that before it arrives, or we'll never make it over."

"It's like the land just fell away," the prince remarked.

"Aye, or was ripped away," the soldier agreed. "Everything here is different – unworldly, as if an unseen hand bent it to its will."

The journey took several hours – slowed by the shifting sand and the howling wind, but the duo never rested. Eventually they reached the bottom of the outcropping which served a decent windbreak.

There they were able to study the ridge in search of an easier climb. They settled for a steeper section that offered better hand holds.

Restarian had a tougher time than Torian during the ascent. He watched as the stronger fae pulled himself easily up the ridge – finding the outcroppings with strong fingers that hoisted his muscular frame. When he tried, he found he was clumsier, lacking the upper body strength to continue once he made it halfway. He dangled there, staring at the soft sand below and yearning to give up.

"What's wrong?" Torian called down from above.

"I'm tired," the prince admitted. He pulled his body onto the lower ledge and sat on his knees – catching his breath and flexing his hands. "I need to rest here a while."

"That's not wise, your muscles will grow sore unless you keep moving. You'll wind up stuck there. Best to keep moving!"

Restarian stared up at the stronger Fainne, suddenly understanding why he disliked him so much. His entire life he had been wasted while yearning to be a warrior like his father, Justarian and his grandfather Betarian before him – but his talent was for healing like his mother. Though he was born the second prince under the king, he had never been free to participate in sports or dueling. His entire schooling had been tending roots and honing his *weaker* craft.

He watched this soldier now with what he finally understood was jealously. Pure and simple, he yearned to be a protector and a fighter instead of cowering like when the Banshees came. The Banshees. His thoughts drifted to the horde and how he had frozen before their queen. The only brave act he had ever committed was sending Torian with Alistaria – but even that proved futile because here he was with the soldier instead of her. *She must be in peril,* he thought. *If she made it to this realm at all.*

The woman… She had been so beautiful and her voice held such allure. *She had called Torian her son,* he remembered. His eyes drifted to the soldier once more – taking in his stronger frame and blue eyes. *He isn't like us because he isn't one of us,* he considered. *Is he a Banshee like her, disguised as a Fainne and hellbent on finding*

Alistaria? He knew the notion was ludicrous. *If he is her son, then why would he lived so long among us?*

"Hurry," Torian urged from above.

Unless, Restarian considered, *he aims to kill her before she completes her quest.* He languished to remember the rest of Clíodhna's command, but the words had slowly faded along with her kiss – her sweet kiss and soft caress. *So beautiful and perfect, she was.*

He shook free of the spell, suddenly determined to protect Alistaria. He had to keep her memory at bay, even if it meant ignoring his own betrayal. Every time he thought of her, he yearned to serve her beauty. *Her beauty is unmatched.*

With renewed strength he stood on unsteady feet and found another handhold. He pulled himself up and onto the next ledge followed by another until he reached the top. Torian reached down a strong hand to help him over but Restarian ignored the offer, choosing instead to do it alone. He swung his leg up and over and lay there – panting and exhausted but victorious in his effort.

When he finally stood upon his weakened legs, he looked eastward toward the storm. It was nearly upon them and truly a tempest without comparison. The swirling shapes in the clouds were more clearly recognizable, despite their translucent form. All around the sky, silvery Banshees dove in and out of the clouds – half in their realm and half in this – but seemingly unable to fully cross over.

"Hurry," Torian commanded.

Your air of superiority will end soon, traitor, Restarian thought toward him. *I'll reveal your plot against my cousin and stop you.* He considered once more the final words of Clíodhna, *Go where I cannot. Learn what you can, and return to me in six days.* Who then, was the traitor but he? He fought once more to shove the sight aside. *But I will not return to her.* He placed a hand to the mouth she had so eagerly kissed. *My role is at Alistaria's side.*

Chapter Ten

I blame the Síth for the issue, he had cursed me with lies and promises of a progeny to further my kingdom. A foothold in each realm, he promised, but deceit set two women against me. My dynasty will not be complete until I can do more than bring balance to the realms
— Confession of Radviken

Radviken, King of Enatherr and Lord of the Realm gazed into the crystalline structure. The Blossom of the Fainne appeared different in his realm, something that had surprised him all those years before when he brought it over. The vine had transformed instantly when he awoke inside the circle, the brown sinew replaced by the glass-like stalks. The flowers had changed as well – each bloom consisting of a different precious stone. They were all here, these many years after – each serving his whim except for the gift left behind for the Fainne.

That gift had been the rose of healing. They would suffer much following the loss of their relic, and he left behind a symbol of his benevolence for her, if not for her people. To this day he wasn't certain he hadn't erred. By his grace the Fainne would retain their one craft – dominance over dying and the ability to heal – while he gained mastery over death and life itself. The magnificent power to wield magic he kept as well, reigning in power over each of the elements. The greatest gift to himself, he knew, had been the dominance over corruption.

He ignored all stones but the one giving him power over sight. He focused on the heart of a blossoming emerald, searching its secrets and making them known in his mind. The storm within reflected against his eyes as he searched his kingdom for the girl. She shouldn't be here. Not in his realm nor her own, but he had dreamed of her arrival. The Blossom shook when it sensed his thoughts, eagerly welcoming his daughter. *But to which woman did she belong?* A Deamhan had entered his realm, but he did not know if it was the girl or another working alongside her.

He had taken precautions against visitors from her realm long ago, having changed the portals themselves. He locked them from travelers such as she, in case their rulers led an organized attack. She must have had help, but that did not matter. Fainne and Deamhan alike would have been scattered across the realm – separated from their own kind. If she survived the journey, she would have randomly landed in one of the other rings far away from her party.

It took many decades for him to fully understand both the rings and the coexistence of the realms – how proper balance kept Enatherr free from the Shadow Realm's taint and the Fainnen greed. The Fainne had not understood their world was merely an echo of Enatherr, and they had selfishly kept the Blossom for themselves while draining the life from his. Only the Human Realm mattered, he knew, for it kept the most dangerous evils from theirs.

Footsteps and a clearing throat announced the arrival of his Storm Warden. Nodrick's black armor seemed to absorb the light rather than reflect it, and his only adornment was the brightly stitched cloak upon his back. It depicted luminescent bolts of lightning, the mark of his station as General and Lead Searcher. On his hip he wore a broadsword with four stones set into the hilt and pommel: A diamond, a lapis, an aquamarine, and a garnet. Each represented the gifts of dominance over the elements – and the power to reach them farther. These had been rewards for loyal service to his master. He could only receive one more without rivaling the king's might – an emerald reflecting sight over the realm. The other two gems Radviken never shared.

"You summoned me, my lord?"

"A Deamhan has crossed through a portal," the king explained, "I was awakened by the Blossom's excitement."

"It has been many years since they've tried. Do you think this is the business of the queen?"

"No," the king said with a heavy sigh, "Clíodhna dares not try a second time, not without help. I believe this to be Nastauria's offspring, finally of age, and difficult to find without also sending out my Searchers. They are stronger at dowsing, and we'll need their help to find the Deamhan."

"A Deamhan could not have traveled alone," the Warden agreed. "If a Fainne has also travelled, what do I do with them, my lord?"

"They will be easier to dispatch since their powers are useless in our realm. But find and bring them to me. We shall train those chosen to elevate by giving them sport before the fae are expelled upon conclusion of Tempest."

Nodrick bowed deeply. "I'll send Storm Riders to fetch them. In addition to the sport, may I suggest a strong message for the King of the Fainne? One that will prevent his further interference with our realm?"

"Perhaps a warning *is* due for my adversary. I've never properly repaid him for the hospitality denied me when I roamed the halls of his Fainnotheria. Seek the intruders between Midlandis and Crosston. One portal activated in the forest north of the Port of Enat, and another near the Dune Sea. They will exit the desert from the west, and cross the mountains there. Send a Searcher with each pair of Riders. Patrol every road to Norgaard, but do not neglect the forests and bandit trails. No doubt they will avoid the roads. Bring each found to me personally."

"Your will is spoken, my lord."

"Nodrick," the king added, "We will again be visited by Síth Morkur during this Tempest." The name weighed heavy on the king's tongue. He despised the Master of Beasts, but owed him gratitude for the favors granted many years before. "Prepare him rooms and give to him our fullest hospitality. Let me know of any special requests he may have."

The mage bowed and left the king alone to his musings. The Síth were a strange race of being – ageless and as old as the world. They walked freely between all realms, and were ambivalent to the concerns of each. Their impartiality bothered him, and their true purpose not fully understood.

Alas, it was Síth Morkur who first lured a young Radviken through the Fainnen Ring, setting the course for a future king and damning the Fainne to a diminished fate. He feared the Síth, but he could not challenge or remove their existence – not without breaking the delicate balance he had fought so long to establish.

The Tempest was one such accomplishment. When he had first travelled to the Fainnen Realm, his own faced relentless famine during agonizingly long growing seasons. The evils of the Shadow Realm roamed free in Enatherr, and the former king did nothing but bow and scrape to their interference.

Now that Radviken controlled the Blossom, the realm held balance. His farmers enjoyed thirty set days of growth followed by six days of purge. Following the Tempest the farmers would once again plant their crops and the livestock would calf and lay eggs. The cycle continued monthly without fail. Their prosperity endless, hunger had been eliminated.

Radviken also kept the evils of the Shadow Realm at bay, much in the same fashion the Blossom had crushed the Deamhan under King Girtrán's heel. The shadows surrendered to his power, doing his bidding and forced to obey without question. The king was all that stood between their unquenched desire to sow chaos and the harmony of prosperity. If the Fainne should fade away it mattered not to him.

Turning to the Blossom, he gazed at his reflection in the Emerald of Sight. He could see he had grown noticeably older than he ever had, and the effects of the bloom seemed to wear off much quicker than when he first mastered the magic. If he did not replenish several times a day, he would appear feeble before his subjects – better they view him a god.

He pricked his finger along a thorn and dripped crimson atop a glistening pearl. *Resurrection also brings rejuvenation,* he mused. At once the lines of his face smoothed and his back felt straighter, but not the full restoration he would obtain by the conclusion of Tempest. By then he would once again achieve full strength and youthful vigor.

"You stare at the Blossom like you still search out its secrets," a hissing voice declared from behind. "Have you not uncovered them all in the time I've given you?"

"Síth Morkur speaks lies to the king, tempting deception with a forked tongue. You gave nothing to me, except to lead me toward my destiny."

"Bought and paid for!" The Master of Beasts growled. The air in the room changed with his voice, and darkness pushed the light aside. It strobed and the king's vision blurred as if watching a mirage. When he blinked his eyes, he found the Síth had moved quickly, pressing the velvety black skin of his face against Radviken's cheek. The stench of his orange teeth bore death and decay as he hissed at the wizard. "You will do well to remember the source of your power is a gift, one that was once bestowed upon the Deamhan and taken by the Fainne before it was stolen back several times by each. The grace by which it lays with you is tenuous at best. What you have been given can be taken by another – just as your own realm's Blossom was stolen from your ancestors."

"You, Síth Morkur?" The king faltered, cringing against the heat of the spirit. "Will you take it from me and wield it yourself?"

"You know I cannot, but there are others who can. Others who can bring true balance to the four realms." "I *have* brought balance," Radviken bellowed, drawing upon his bearing and stretching again to full height. "I healed my world and enjoy dominance over the Shadow Realm!"

"If you say so," the Síth shrugged off his words. "As we speak, powers conspire against you."

"Will you aid me as before?"

Síth Morkur answered truthfully. "I've not decided if I shall interfere any more than I already have. Forces are in motion that even *I* may not have the power or willingness to stop. Your vanity has injured many in the other realms when actions were taken long ago. I pity your position, Radviken. I truly do."

"The ruler is always hated for his benevolence, by those at his feet who will never understand his sacrifice."

The Síth laughed at the king's words – a rumbling sound from deep in his chest that chilled Radviken's skin, raising bumps along his arms and tickling his spine. The spirit's cackle raised his haunches like a dog sensing danger. His laughter subsided, the creature asked, "What have you ever sacrificed, Radviken?"

"Love, for one."

"You are capable of loving only yourself. What have you truly sacrificed for your realm?"

"My children," the king said with a solemn candor. "I sacrificed my children. They are doomed to lives without their father, kept from my embrace and tender wisdom."

"So you believe. In truth they were saved from your injury," the Síth explained. "Saved from the pain you so graciously inflicted upon their mothers. Even now your blood coursing within theirs can unravel your hold over that Blossom, so hurry, lord of man, learn true balance before your realm finally topples under the weight of the swinging pendulum." The room completely darkened with the words of the spirit.

When light returned, Síth Morkur had left Radviken alone but not in peace. The king swayed from a drain upon his power, momentarily feeling mortal. He staggered to the open window of the tower – raised high above his realm – and gazed upon the Tempest. The first day of the purge was at hand, and he had six days to find the girl and any others of his children who travelled in the storm.

Part Two
The Tempest

CHAPTER ELEVEN

We had both journeyed to the forest for our births as tradition demanded. My child came first, the heir to his evil. Her harbinger fell second. Or so the world must believe.
– Lamentations of Nastauria

Alistaria awakened alone. Every muscle screamed agony within her body, and she whimpered with fright. Curled like a hatching chick, she tried desperately to realign her back – an effort that rewarded each struggle with newfound pain. Every movement added to her misery, and her twisted legs further knotted with cramps that reached her toes. The torment lasted several minutes before she could finally straighten – all the while drenched by chilling rain and battered by icy pellets. The cold further distressed her joints as pain radiated through her tiny bones. She shivered and begged to return to her realm.

After she could finally move, she called out for the others, screaming the names of her friends. "Torian," she cried. "Restarian! I'm here and ready to journey!" She waited each time for an answer, but none came.

The only echo had been the distant shriek of Banshees wailing their vile language. If they descended – and her mother was wrong about their form being ghostly – she would be in no shape to fight them off. Suddenly embarrassed by her lack of caution – and worried she would draw their attention – she moved away from the Fainnen Ring and safely under the canopy of nearby trees. Deafening thunder drummed in her chest and she flinched with every flash of lightning.

Every strike quickened her pulse and sent panic coursing through. Beyond that, though, she felt something else – a dark vibration like that of a drum. It called to her, pulling her to step into the open and accept the electricity surging in the clouds above. Coming to her senses she wrapped her arms about her and shivered. She knew she must find comfort during this storm.

Seeking warmth she huddled against the trunk of a pine and felt for the comforting thrum of its roots. Alistaria had tended trees since she was barely able to walk – trained to detect their lifeforce without effort. The absence of pulse coursed panic through the girl and she frantically dug downward. Perhaps, if she could place her hands closer to the tap, its sentience could be found. But that, too, proved futile. Understanding replaced confusion as she realized her powers had fled altogether.

The Blossom of the Fainne awaited and she wasted valuable time. Thinking of the mission forced upon her by the elders, she rose once more to her bare feet and put one in front of the other – choosing a direction and walking. Eventually she would surely find shelter and warmth. Six days she would have to endure this storm, suffering both its pain and its dangers. She had no time to huddle in fear.

Despite her mother's warnings she must find a population of humans. Surely respite would come in the form of dry clothing and a fire. She would find it faster if she flew, even in the storm. She tried to fan her wings and once more found futility. Those – like her powers – were gone. She had only just reached the realm of humans and already had been beaten. Tears mixed with the icy rain as she decided to press onward.

She willed herself forward. Every step took immense effort as she traveled in the storm – bare feet sinking in mud when they weren't pricked by thorns or burrs. Mostly she slipped in the wet puddles, falling several times for lack of traction. The ground here vastly differed from the soft moss of the forest in Fainnotheria, and she would travel no further unless she found a way to protect her soles.

Stumbling, Alistaria leaned against another trunk. Drawing the silver dagger from her satchel she apologized to the tree.

"Please forgive me," she begged. "I wouldn't do this, but I must. It's the only way."

With heavy remorse she created a deep wound, carving off a section of bark. Kneeling on the ground she sawed this in half then shaped it to match the size of each foot. Satisfied the smooth side would fit nicely against her skin, she cut strips of leather from the hem of her dress. These she wrapped and tied until she stood upon the bark, flexing and testing it would remain in place.

She placed another hand on the exposed section and spoke penitently. "Your skin will heal," she promised, "but mine may not. I beg you to understand this transgression was in the direst of need."

She abruptly stepped back with alarm as flittering movement descended from the clouds like a plague of locusts. Still backing she watched as thousands of tiny Ganshees ravaged the wounded tree with their razor-sharp teeth, devouring first the tender section she had carved and finally felling the entire pine to the forest floor. More joined the others in their feast – rendering the arbor to dust upon the wet ground. Alistaria wept for the loss, mournful over the destruction her greed had caused the living being.

Several of the vermin converged around the girl, sniffed around her feet and tasting her wounds on the air. After a moment they must have decided no matter how badly the girls feet ached, the injuries weren't grievous enough to consume her flesh over. In minutes the tiny creatures had moved on to find a discarded carcass left in the bushes by a predator. This too they consumed, ravenous with their need to consume the dead.

Alistaria fled deeper into the forest, her feet now protected by makeshift shoes. The second attempt was easier, and she moved more quickly – confident of her traction. Without the pain she was able to think more clearly.

Mother is surely dead, she worried. *Sacrificed so Restarian would live on.* She would never understand the choice – it made no sense to

Fainne laws or her station – but she couldn't continue to blame him. *If Síth Morkur had claimed Restarian*, she realized, *Mother would have stood to inherit the crown despite grandfather's wishes.* Even if Betarian refused to acknowledge their relation, the title would have eventually passed to Alistaria. The thought repulsed her. *Is that why I saved him despite his wounds? Was it out of compassion for my friend or my aversion to someday wearing a crown? Could mother's choice have been the same?*

A hideous screech sounded from her left and she whirled. The abrupt movement placed her off balance and she fell, striking her head against a branch. The blow merely stunned her wits as her vision swam – gazing upward at several swirling images of Banshees. Slowly her eyesight settled, and the visage of terror focused into a single staring face.

The Deamhan lurched forward, biting, and clawing at Alistaria. She flailed her arms and kicked wildly, missing each time but relentlessly fighting off the attack. After a moment the monster pulled back, hovering over her frightened form. The girl slowly realized her mother had been correct – the Banshee was no more than an apparition. Translucent but seemingly real, the ghostly specter sat atop the Fainnen princess – infuriated by the inability to touch her with its gruesome claws or teeth.

The Banshee howled - speaking with its shrill and shrieking language. But instead of piercing her ears, Alistaria found this time she could understand the guttural tones beneath the scream – as if the Human Realm had slowed them down enough to understand.

"You are lucky I found you while in this form, child of Nastauria," the beast chided. "Though my mistress wishes you dead, we'll have to meet again on the other side for me to finish the job."

The words formed in Alistaria's mind – twisting together and opening a new world of understanding. "Why can I suddenly understand you?" She asked, furious at her folly in believing it could cause her harm.

The beast cocked his head, as intrigued by her words as she with his. He hissed in her face, then bit at her mouth but passed right through. She jumped back with a squeal. The beast laughed at her reaction and said, "You speak blasphemy, daughter of Nastauria! I'll rip those lips from your face for uttering our sacred speech!"

"I don't understand what you mean," she insisted, but the Banshee suddenly leapt into the air and joined his brethren in the swirling clouds. Alistaria trembled with fright as she hurried deeper into the forest.

Restarian halted behind the taller Torian, once more nearly colliding with his heavier frame. The Fainne had been leading them on a dogged pace, rarely stopping except to occasionally sip from their waterskins. But something ahead in their path had caused the man to dig his feet in solidly, as if unsure of their possibilities. The prince strained his ears to listen and the rushing torrent of a raging water could be heard. He pushed beside the guardsmen to see around him, and his eyes grew wide at the obstacle ahead.

A swollen river stood between them and the far banks, carrying death and debris upon its dangerous current. Deer and elk floated or swam among the mighty trunks of fallen trees, swarmed by Ganshees determined to devour them in entirety. Nothing would survive a crossing – not without risking both concussion and drowning. The far bank was just as formidable, as the flowing water cut into steep mountains with loosed boulders tumbling down their faces.

"We can't cross here," Torian explained. "It's far too dangerous."

Restarian turned his eyes upward above the steep cliffs. Above a splashing waterfall he saw what appeared to be a gentle pass. "There," he said. "Perhaps if we can reach that point, we can safely cross the mountains."

"I don't like it," the sentry said. "Getting across is one thing, but up and over that bank is another. Even if we reached the top of the waterfall, there's no guarantee that pass doesn't lead into taller cliffs. With this storm I'd rather find a safer route." With that he abruptly turned south along the bank and moved carefully along the shoreline.

Restarian eyed the waterfall. *It appears passable,* he thought. *If we can just make it up that bank, I know we can make it.* Without glancing at his companion or giving warning he leapt into the river, swimming hard but swept into the fierce current just the same. It carried him swiftly past Torian as he tried desperately to reach the other side.

"You fool!" The guardsmen screamed over the thunder. With a splash he had also entered the water, swimming with the current and urging the prince to do the same. "Let it carry you, and aim for those trees!" He pointed to a grove down river and diagonal to where the pair swam.

Restarian understood. He would never reach the bank directly across from them – not with the strength of the stream – and the trees gave him a reasonable target. He kicked his legs hard but feared placing his face in the water lest he lose sight of the debris. Once he turned to check on Torian, and watched a large trunk rushing toward him.

"Look out!" he cried, thankful to see the other man duck beneath the surface. He swam along, watching and waiting for the soldier to resurface. After what seemed an eternity, he saw him break through the foam.

What did I do? He wondered. *I could have allowed it to strike him, ending any threat to Alistaria here and now.* But is that what he wanted? This man had saved them both before, and showed no evidence of treachery. *But if he is a Deamhan,* the prince considered as he swam, *then he deserves to die no matter who he is or what he's done. All Deamhan must die.*

Splashing and gasping for air, Torian reached for another log. Ganshees – angry at his disruption, bit and clawed at this fingers until he once more let go. He went under and came back up several times before he drifted close to the opposite shore.

Restarian fared little better – hitting his head upon a rock and momentarily losing sight of the grove. He willed his legs to kick and his arms to pull against the water until he found Torian's outstretched grasp. With a grunt both men reached the bank, digging into the soft mud with their fingernails and clamoring to safety.

The guardsmen wasted no time turning on the prince. "Are you crazy? You nearly got us both killed!" He leapt to his feet and felt around at his soaked gear, turning his satchel upside down and spilling the contents. "Our rations are fine, but my waterskin floated off!" Feeling his side he thankfully felt his sword remained.

Restarian hadn't thought about stowing their valuables. A trembling hand felt inside his pocket and wrapped around the firm formation of the crystal. Her crystal. The Banshee Queen had shoved it in his hand as he plummeted to this realm, and he couldn't afford to lose it – whatever it was for. *What am I doing?* He wondered. *She is a Deamhan – the Queen of them all. Even she deserves death.*

Unfortunately, his own satchel was completely gone. So were the weeks' worth of rations he'd packed. "I still have my waterskin," he was happy to find, offering the guardsmen a drink. "Besides." He pointed at the waterfall – further up the bank then he'd hoped, but they were certainly closer to their goal. "We are close and can make it from here. All we have to do is continue up this bank, and I think we can. We climbed worse in the desert."

Torian's eyes seethed with anger as he pushed past the prince, shoving the waterskin against the boy's chest. Without offering to help, he scrambled up the rubble and onto the first ledge. Restarian followed quietly, wondering at the purpose of the crystal in his pocket as he pulled himself beside Torian.

Can she communicate with me through it? He wondered. *Is it magical?* A more terrifying thought made him lose his grip and nearly fall. *Can she now follow us through the portal?* He pushed his worries out of his mind and focused on the task at hand. The rest of the climb proved easier than it had appeared from the other bank, and soon they had hiked the distance to the waterfall.

The guard said something atop the ledge while looking down the cascade, but his voice was drowned by the rushing roar. It mattered not what he had said, Restarian's mind was again fully returned to the crystal. *Is it a way for her to find me after I return to our realm? It could be a trap,* he thought. *No,* he reasoned, *she could have killed me then, beside the Fainnen Ring, if she wanted me dead.*

"What do you know about the Deamhan?" He asked Torian after they had set off up the pass.

The soldier shrugged. "Same thing as everyone else, I guess. They attack us because they want to steal what's left of the Bláth de Fainne. They want the final Blossom so that they can heal their bodies of the curse.

"That won't work," Restarian explained. "For that they'll need the black iris of corruption. Healing won't do much but tend their wounds."

"Then I don't know," the sentry shrugged. "Maybe they're after something else."

Or someone *else,* the prince considered. "The corruption," he asked, "do you think it's true, then? That they were like us before?"

"I don't know," Torian said. "You're grandfather's the king, what has he told you?"

Restarian wondered at how the guard deflected the conversation. Either he really had no opinion, or he hid some love for the vermin. "He said they were a long time ago, and they too lived in Fainnotheria at one time. But they were only hiding among us, and were eventually driven from the Tree of Life and forced to live in the barren waste where they built the palace." He paused, thinking of the story told of King Girtrán. "He also said his great grandfather had later cursed them for again stealing the Blossom. They had it in their possession for five hundred years, and our kind suffered a deep famine as a result. The king stole it back, marking their bodies so they could never again hide among our kind."

"They are hideous," the guard agreed. "But I've heard their queen is beautiful." Torian remarked. "They say she epitomizes beauty – or that's what I learned in the nursery."

"She is…" Restarian agreed. "Ravishingly so."

Torian turned. "You talk as if you've seen her. Have you?"

"Most certainly not!" The prince panicked as he denied the accusation. His hand felt the crystal in his pocket, though, and he swore he could once more feel her lips upon his. Clearing his throat he added, "That's what I've heard from the stories, as well." Changing the subject he asked, "You're from the nursery? Are you an orphan, then? Don't you have any family?"

"I am," Torian said with pride. "As for family, I was apprenticed to the city guard as soon as I reached my seventieth year. The barracks have been my family ever since. I wouldn't ask for anything else, and the other soldiers have been good to me. I worked my way up to Skygate detail by the time I turned ninety. Hopefully soon I'll be elevated to the Kern."

Restarian chuckled at his optimism. "My father never got past Skygate, and he was a prince before…" His mood changed. "Before he died at their hands."

"I heard the tale," Torian admitted. "They share the story with each new recruit as a lesson that no Fainne is safe. It's still a mystery how he died, but the Deamhan are cunning and often prey upon those cutoff from the rest."

"Did you know him, my father?" Restarian asked, eager to hear the stories.

"Not well," the guardsman said, "but I remember he was brave and took his duty seriously."

Maybe Torian isn't so bad. Maybe the queen was wrong and he isn't her son, the prince considered. Changing the subject again, he asked, "Who do you think your parents were?"

"I don't know," Torian said truthfully, "and I really don't care."

Doubts still lingered and Restarian realized the possibilities. *It is possible, then,* that *I'm questing with the son of Clíodhna!* His hand moved absently to the silvery blade at his side – it was his father's once. *It would be easy now to run him through from behind. No one would ever know the truth, and his body would never be found high upon this mountain.*

He slowly drew the blade, nearly clearing sheath when a voice in his head resounded. *Stay that blade or suffer my wrath,* it seemed to say, oddly sounding just like the Banshee Queen had issued the command.

He slammed it home as his eyes grew wide with fear. Looking up into the clouds he saw a swirling circle of Banshees within the storm. He also released his grip on the crystal and hurried to catch up to the sentry atop the summit. Though the mountain was not too high, the air was cold enough for the rain to have turned to snow. It thickly coated the path leading up and over.

"Look," Torian said as they looked out upon a green basin. Two cities spread in the distance. One to the north and one to the south. They had clearly cut off much of their journey by crossing the mountains. "The northern city must be Norgaard," the soldier suggested. "Let's hurry and find the Blossom!"

"I don't know," Torian said. "there could be much more to travel ahead, it may be several days further north."

Restarian nodded, following him downward and gripping the hilt of his sword the rest of the way. If this Fainne turned out a Deamhan, he would kill both the son and the mother. That was no longer a question in his mind.

Chapter Twelve

She brought first the human into our realm, and then forced his offspring upon us as well. The girl I tolerated out of hope she could someday prove useful. The boy I allowed in the nursery, only because it would rile his mother. But eventually I made a decision I never admitted to my daughter.
– Journal of King Betarian

The winds outside howled with rage as Piotr enjoyed the quiet warmth of the Tavern. It wasn't often that he found himself resting comfortably in a bed – even one he had to share with Boyd. This Tempest had turned out a lucky one. The sweet smell of stew and cornbread drifted down the hall from the kitchen, and he licked his lips at the savory thought of a full belly.

Next to him, Lucky began to snore – just a little at first, but as he revved up, he sounded like the storm blowing outside. That was fine with him, as well. He was used to sleeping beside blustery snorts, he'd been sleeping through Boyd's for years. But then he learned the animal – who knew not a command and clearly had no training – had one trick behind his devious single eye.

Pfft. The sound was simple – just a simple puff of air to the ears – but proved an offense upon Piotr's nose. It happened just as he was breathing in – the worst time if you were to ask anyone who owned a flatulent dog – and choked him with an eye-watering retch. He coughed and gagged as the scent overcame the lovely smell of stew. Instead of venison and onion, Piotr swore he tasted rotten egg mixed with the gravy found in the bottom of a privy – how he thought of that particular odor, one would never ask in mixed company – so leave that ponderance be.

He wanted so badly to vomit, and even tasted the bile as it rose to his throat. This, it turned out, proved to further season the smell and added another round of gagging. He coughed until he could no longer breathe properly, gasping and pressing against the closed window while searching for air – any air – that hadn't been filtered through a canine's bowels.

Indeed, a tiny stream of wind beneath the pane proved his savior. It blew in with a steady stream, and he sucked that air like it was sweetened with honey – savoring the refreshment and not caring at all how he would appear to any who walked in the room. Truth be told, when he opened his eyes, he found three children watching intently from the window across the way – to them he appeared to be licking the sill like a simpleton. This didn't bother him either – he let them laugh at his expense – until their mother came to see the source of their laughter. After one inaudible gasp she scurried them out of view of the obviously demented pervert.

With a groan he rolled over and faced Lucky, who had decided at that very moment he would lick the source of the smell with the same exuberance that one would attack sweet rolls at the fair. Piotr gagged once more and rushed from the room, slamming the door behind him and shutting in the dog. He knew that he may have to sleep in the common room and decided Boyd deserved that bed – and the dog – more than he. He hoped the shut door would trap enough of the smell to ruin the night for his friend, later.

Piotr rounded the corner of the kitchen and found the others seated around a small table. Boyd paused in the telling of a story in which even Harveigh seemed deeply attentive. Martha, the woman who had cleaned up Lucky, shot Piotr a watchful look of mistrust – she would take more convincing of their supposed guildship than the tavern keeper – but stood to pour him a bowl of stew. Two other women stared longingly at Boyd as he spun his yarn.

One of the women was named Harriet. She was a wide-eyed young woman whose job it was to keep the customers buying drinks. She was quite pretty – a tiny yet buxom little thing – and seemed utterly infatuated with Boyd. She batted her lashes as she listened to his tale of a beautiful Banshee Queen and thrall – gasping at how the fairies stole their magic for themselves.

Boyd, it seemed, wasn't the least bit interested in Harriet, his eyes fixated upon the other woman. Sophie was a plump lass with rosy-red cheeks and a rump that needed two chairs to hold her heavy frame at the table. The scullery maid listened intently, but seemed much more interested in dipping large pieces of cornbread into her bowl of stew. These she soaked until the drippings fell from her fingers then popped the entire lump into her nearly full mouth. Finding the spoon lacking efficiency for the broth– she picked up the bowl and dumped it down her gullet. As soon as it hit the table empty, Martha immediately spooned another helping for the girl. Boyd, of course, stared intently at the leftovers drooling down her chin. She was exactly his type: messy and round.

Uh oh, Piotr thought as he slid in next to his friend. He kicked him softly under the table and shook his head with a stern *no*. Luckily Harveigh hadn't noticed Boyd's preference, and was busy watching Harriet for any inappropriateness. Hopefully she would keep the man's full attention while Piotr kept Boyd away from Sophie.

"You're just in time, Piotr!" Boyd hadn't taken his eyes off the girl to address his friend. "We're telling Tempest stories."

"He was just telling us how the Banshees were tricked by a fairy king and their magic stolen," Harriet explained. "Isn't that's why they visit our world during Tempest. They're searching for a lost bush?"

"Is that so?" Piotr raised an eyebrow at Boyd who shrugged. "I thought it was a tree they sought."

"Not according to Tamee," Boyd insisted. "The Banshee Queen's bush was stolen and hidden in our world. Since King Radviken barred her entrance to Enatherr, she sends her minions every Tempest to find and steal it back."

"I'm pretty sure it was a tree the pixies stole," Piotr argued.

"Definitely a child," Harveigh muttered, breaking his silence. "That's how *I* heard it." Piotr was correct earlier in assuming the man held strong superstitions within his giant head.

Recollection of a story heard long ago entered Piotr's memory, and he realized Boyd was right. "I think it *was* a bush." All eyes turned to him and he shrugged. "I just remembered Miss Tamee telling this story when we were foundlings in her..." He paused, not wanting to admit they were raised in a brothel. "... in her boarding house. "The way we heard it told, the Queen and her Banshees can't step a physical foot on our world unless her blood feeds the bush that was stolen. That's why all we see are their ghostly spirits wandering around, they're searching for it and for a way to water it with her blood. Only that will break Radviken's spell and allow her children to roam Enatherr."

"Well then," Martha said with a huff. "Thank goodness they can't get through! Tell me the story you both heard."

"I don't remember it all," Piotr admitted.

"I do," Boyd said and all eyes turned to the stout thief and waited. He paused, drinking in the attention, then began the tale of King Octavian.

In the far west of Enatherr, where the Dune Sea now resides, once stood an enchanted forest, the home to the Fainne who tended the roots of the Great Trees. They and the humans had formed a balance despite sharing a realm. The humans agreed to farm only the eastern region and the fae would agree not to cross the Westron River. The agreement worked well for more than a thousand years.

The Fainne stood with one foot in two realms – sharing Enatherr with the humans and the Luchorpán, and Fainnotheria with their cousins who dominated that realm. They warred with the other fairies, vying for control of the mystical relics that held open the portals between the realms. In their lust for magic the Fainne had stolen the relic entrusted to the humans, keeping it for themselves while trying to also steal that of the Banshees. This opened an even darker portal – one threatening King Octavian's kingdom.

He ruled during this time of warfare between the fairies. The eighth king of Enatherr, he refused to choose sides in the conflict – choosing neutrality for his people and shielding them from the hardships war brings upon the land. Despite his efforts, war proved inevitable when cunning interlopers forced his hand. As a result, he committed fully to an endless war that continues to this day.

In the far north of Enatherr – in the high mountains looming over Norgaard – lived the quiet race of Luchorpán. They also kept to themselves, burrowed deep underground and mining the rich minerals hidden within the rocky depths below the range. Though they enjoyed peace with Octavian and his human kingdom, they had not sent an envoy to the realm since the days of the first kings. King Calug's arrival had proved a surprise of great importance.

His entourage had presented themselves in flowing robes of red silk gilded with golden trim, trailing behind their king who clad himself in a sharp suit of crimson armor adorned by a crown of rubies. Their race was quite a sight, being much shorter and stockier than the human onlookers. Though not all wore beards like the stereotypes whispered through the ages – many wore intricately braided and beaded whiskers of every color. The king himself wore a brilliantly orange beard adorned with diamonds trailing down in descending sizes.

Octavian greeted him warmly, inviting the king to a private audience but Calug refused – demanding the presence of their generals and advisors.

"We're called to war," the Luchorpán king had warned, "and we desire your aid."

"I'm sworn to neutrality in the war between the fae and will not interfere.

"I'm not speaking of choosing sides. This new darkness that has emerged is the product of their greed and hatred for each other. A great evil is sweeping the land as we speak. But to defeat the Shadow Realm, we need their magic. Come with me and retrieve your own while I lay claim theirs. That will end the wars and seal away the Shadow Realm."

Deeply concerned for the obvious fear that had driven this noble king south, Octavian welcomed Calug to court and met with him at once with their war leaders – hearing the plight that plagued his people and would eventually spread to destroy his own kingdom. What he learned shattered his notion that peace would survive the new threat.

"They have too much power," the Luchorpán king explained. "And while the fae hold both Blossoms, we have no way to protect ourselves from the shadow creeping in. Surely your people have told tales of evil tidings?"

"Aye," Octavian had said. "Skinwalkers and dark demons have made their way into our forests."

"Then we must seal the realm. Join me against the fae to claim their relics! They constantly war over their many Blossoms – neither side content with the portion they control. Each time they war the Deamhan or the Fainne gain a different power over their enemy, and they wield it despite the consequences to us. Our realm won't survive the onslaught of a full invasion of shadow!"

"So far," Octavian said unconvinced, "the fae hostility has been directed at each other. I've no proof of this evil that you described, except for whisperings. Tell me of this shadow that darkens our realm."

"Indeed, a shadow it is," insisted the stouter king, shaking his head in such a way the diamonds shook in his beard, "and it casts darkness over our valleys and your farmlands." He leaned in and lowered his voice to a whisper. "It has even discovered our caverns below the surface!"

With a trembling hand, Calug drew a parchment from his vest. Upon it someone had sketched a beast unlike any Octavian had seen.

His heart raced within his ribcage at the thought of such a monster walking freely upon the fields of Enatherr. "Why is there a horse drawn beside it?" The king had asked.

"That's for scale."

Octavian's heart fluttered and the room swam. The creature in the drawing was at least fifty times larger than the equine. "And that's loose in your caverns?"

"No." The Luchorpán's face lit up and beamed with victory. Pointing to a small man leaning over the maps he added, "Not anymore. General Cróga here slew it."

The human king stared at the simple man with disbelief. He would not have picked him as a soldier, much less a general.

"Retrieve the gift we brought King Octavian, Cróga! Bring it so that he shall share in our victory and feel urgency toward driving the Fainne from our borders."

The little man nodded and hurried off.

"What do you propose, Calug? What is your plan to seal the portal?"

"When the Great Spirit gifted us our trees, he also granted power to the fae he kept from us." Placing a hand on his beard he touched a gem. "They each were gifted a blossoming bush that contained all the powers of the Fairy Realm.

"Yes," Octavian agreed. He knew this as the source of their warfare. "In possession of the shrub they draw power over life and death and healing and pestilence."

"They also can harness power over the elements themselves." The Luchorpán stood and waved his arms as he spoke with animation. "Imagine harnessing power over wind, water, earth, and air! We could eradicate famine and suffering among our people, and live as long and prosperous as they!"

The human king stood frozen with alarm – suddenly aware of a different darkness that resided within the stalwart king of the Luchorpán. "I will not aid you in this war, Calug," he vowed quietly.

"What?" The stout fellow turned with rage simmering beneath his regal bearing. "Have you not heard a word I've told you? Have you not listened to the dangers breaking through to our shared realm?" In that moment Cróga returned with a retinue towing a small wagon. Inside was a bulging load covered by a simple tarp. "Here you will change your mind, lord of neutrality! Feast your eyes on the end of your people if you do not aid me!" With melodramatic showmanship Calug ripped off the covering.

King Octavian felt his body freeze with fear while his mind grew alert with panicked curiosity. A furred talon the size of a haystack lay in the wagon. The severed edge was tinged with dried blood, proving definitively the beast had been recently slain. "This..." he tried to speak but his words tripped over his awe. "Is this what emerged from your caverns?" "No," The Luchorpán king replied. "It's what emerged from the portal, a rift between realms caused by Fainnen warfare! Join with me," he urged, "and let's seal the Shadow Realm from ours." He leaned in with a sinister sneer and added, "In doing so, let's also drive the fae forever from Enatherr!"

Harveigh interrupted. "So what about the crystal and the bush?"

"The crystal *is* the bush, but that came later," Boyd said while eyeing Sophie. Thankfully the tavernkeeper was so enraptured with the story he didn't notice. "They fought a fierce battle against the fae, and drove them from the realm. Then the two kings even crossed over into the Fairy Realm, and took the war to both factions."

"What happened to their bush and the magic blossoms?" Martha asked.

"Calug double crossed Octavian and kept it for himself – protecting only his people from the Shadow Realm."

"I've heard about that," Harveigh said slowly. "They plagued our realm for thousands of years until Lord Radviken travelled to the fairy world and stole the remaining bush. Then he used it to lock out the Shadow Realm from ours and trapped the Luchorpán forever under their mountains."

"Why did he create the Tempest?" Sophie asked, confused.

"He didn't, not according to Tamee," Piotr said. "That was a product of corruption, one a Fainnen king marked them with. Radviken merely brought it through the portal and allowed it to purge our world, she said."

"Why would he do such a thing like that?" She asked.

"There was no longer balance between the realms," Piotr said softly. "With both bushes now in this realm, the growing cycles were out of control. Crops grew but never died, meaning they couldn't produce more than a single yield. Also, people and animals would die, but never decompose."

Boyd nodded. "So he brought over the Tempest and it comes every thirty days. The Banshees who come through can't harm us, but are seeking the bush with every storm, not a baby or a tree."

"So what keeps them from crossing fully over?" Harveigh asked.

"That was the deal made by King Calug. He brokered a deal with the Deamhan, allowing them to keep their own Blossom when he stole King Octavian's rightful magic from the Fainne. In order to come through, the war between the fae must end. They would have to work together with their enemy to come to our realm. He locked them in theirs, and they can only cross through portals with each other's assistance. That was something he knew would never happen."

"How did Radviken travel in the first place?" The tavernkeeper wondered aloud.

"Before he went to their world there was nothing at all to bar our way. Humans could pass over anytime they fell asleep in a fairy ring. But he locked it so we must be accompanied by either a fairy or a Síth," Piotr explained. "So now it's impossible."

"What happens if the Banshee Queen's blood touches the bush?" Martha asked.

Piotr shrugged. "I guess all of Radviken's spells are broken, since she's the rightful owner."

Harveigh interrupted. "That's what I heard the child's for. If the child of Radviken bleeds on the bush, it breaks his spells." Exhausted, he pushed away from the table and yawned, then motioned for the women to leave. Martha sent the others scurrying to their beds. Once they were out of earshot, he announced to Piotr and Boyd, "I'm going to bed. Best you two remember my deal. Leave my girls alone!"

Both men nodded and when the opposite direction of him.

"I'm sleeping on the couch," Piotr announced when they reached the common room. "You and the smelly dog can share the bed."

"He can't help it if he gets a bit gassy."

"No, but you can by laying off giving him those sausages he likes."

CHAPTER THIRTEEN

She brought the most recent war to Fainnotheria, but the blame for more than a century of bloodshed ultimately falls upon me. She knew what I did, even if she didn't understand how. Of all my lamentations this is the one to which I paid the most reparations. I finally set it right, even though it nearly destroyed the one I loved.
– Lamentations of Nastauria

Nastauria watched as King Betarian readied the Kern. It had been two full days since the Deamhan had ceased their raids, and usually this time was spent shoring up defenses and resting – the Banshees always renewed their attacks following the Tempest. Instead of resting, the king and the Fainnen elders had planned a different strategy. In more than a thousand years no Fainne had planned an outright attack on the Deamhan.

He hadn't donned the golden armor since Nastauria was a child, and seeing him wear it now brought sentiment of those times. Without her mother, she had lived a loveless life, and his apathy to fatherhood was evident even then. She always had believed her brother would have held the warrior's affection, but Justarian never achieved placement with the Kern. His death while holding the Skygate had been as much an embarrassment to Betarian as she had been.

"So this is it," she said to her father. "You truly sent my daughter on a mission of sacrifice. Was she simply a distraction to ensure Clíodhna watched her and not your army of invasion?"

"Of course not," he insisted. "She served another role than merely that. Hopefully she will be successful in the Human Realm – opening a portal for us to enter and retrieve the Blossom. This stands to pose a dual victory. We shall defeat the Deamhan while they sleep and strike Radviken in his palace."

"So you intend to guide her return through the portal only if she is successful?" She awaited his response with ice in her heart and hatred in her eyes.

"Just pray she *is* successful," he said curtly. "Let this serve as your final penance – just as I've lived without a daughter, so may you." He stormed off, retrieving his gear and joining the others.

"You'll lead them personally? Who'll rule after you're dead?" She chided his turned back, causing him to whirl around.

"You know very well the answer. My grandson will rule in my absence if I fall."

"You don't know?"

"Know what?" He demanded.

"Restarian travelled with Alistaria to Enatherr. He's there now with her. If she doesn't return, neither will he."

"You play me?" He said with seething anger. "You bait me with your words, but I am not foolish enough to fall. He's not half-human and will return following the Tempest. I'll be there to meet him when he does."

She smiled warmly, letting him know just how cunning his daughter could be. Despite her withheld title, she ensured he would never fully deny her as his child. His manipulation had surely passed to her. "The other child joined her quest as well, the one I stole so many years ago from Clíodhna."

The king grew red with anger. She had beaten him with her trickery. "Regardless," he said. "Then he'll remain at her side over there because of their human blood. Even if she *does* succeed, I've half a mind to leave them both there. That abomination should never have been conceived, much less born."

Nastauria ignored the slight upon her daughter, and said with a smile, "I wish you good fortune on your war, Father."

He turned and addressed the elders. "Hear this," he said, "if I fail to return, this woman has neither my title nor favor. Give my crown to another!"

Hushed whispers echoed the chamber as he and his gilded army raised into the air. The shield above flickered and then faded as they rose above the canopy. Nastauria watched them fly off into the night long after the shield had returned. *He at least has incentive not to abandon Alistaria, and must push deep inside the Deamhann palace. He will have to reach Clíodhna's throne room if he is to journey through any portal my daughter leaves in Radviken's.*

"Nastauria," the voice belonged to Erania the elder.

The princess turned and with pleading eyes said, "Clíodhna's child can unite us, Erania. There is a chance, one that our kind is not capable of bringing about."

The elder laughed. "If her child survives, you mean? There are so many obstacles ahead and so many forces working against success in the Human Realm." She shook her head, suddenly solemn. "I hope you're right, Nastauria, but forgive my pessimism. The age-old question of nature versus nurture is at play here. I'm afraid the child's blood and the greedy interference of our world will overcome any good intentions or potential for unity."

"Unity is the only way, Erania. If both Fainne and Deamhan can work together, we will recover both Blossoms as well as our true homeland. Then they can have this realm and we can return to our own."

"Your father thinks that by destroying the Deamhan we can turn our attention on achieving that same goals. He would rather use the Kern instead of leaving our fate in the hands of children."

"You heard him," Nastauria said. "His plan for balance is also in the hands of a child."

Erania frowned. "Thanks to your scheming treacheries, I now fear for the fates of three children. You are so much like your father, and your plans much the same." She sighed. "But at least you had the wherewithal to send them all into the Human Realm."

Nastauria paused, cringing against the old woman's revelation. "You knew?"

Erania nodded. "I suspected, but suspicion is often rooted by truth. I pray your plan – whatever it is – works in the favor of our kind... and theirs."

"Then I have your support and that of the Council of Elders?"

"No. We will never support you, Nastauria. That endorsement would be foolish and imply approval of your methods." The old woman placed a feeble hand on the princess. "But if her child succeeds along with your plans, we will support the outcome."

(HAPTER FOURTEEN

*My father believed he'd hidden the child forever, but the Síth
and had I made a pact of souls. He did my bidding when
he carried the child through the portal, and not my father's.
If one thing redeems my Fainnen kind, it will be this savior.*
— Lamentations of Nastauria

Restarian should have been able to sleep easily after hiking two
days over desert and mountains, but he found little rest. He and
Torian had decided to set up a camp, and chose a tiny cave nestled
into the mountainside. From there they overlooked the city they
believed was Norgaard. They spent much time scheming a plan for
their arrival, but they had finally settled in for the night.

The prince lay with his back to the guardsmen, staring at the
crystal in his hand. It was ordinary, except for a blue tint to the
center. The clear exterior was very hard – seamless without a single
crack or chip. It wasn't large, only about the size of the tip of his
index finger – perfectly round, seemingly formed with magic and
not by nature. He stared unblinkingly until his eyes began to water.
Finally, after what felt like eternity, he drifted into slumber with his
hand tightly wrapped around the object.

His dreams carried him far into Fainnotherr. He was aware
then of his ethereal form – pleased no harm would befall him by the
terrible Banshees sleeping all around. He tiptoed over their bodies,
careful not to disturb. But stealth was difficult – the ground not
padded with moss as in Fainnotheria, instead the blackened rock
crushed and crackled with every step, a harbinger of death and decay

that would also plague his own kind – if Clíodhna had her way. He yearned to return to his kind and to his grandfather's side.

But he was torn by a need to also protect Alistaria. Even as he tiptoed through his Deamhann dream, she was alone – most likely lost and afraid in a world unlike her own. He silently prayed to the Spirit she would succeed before the sixth day. In the meantime he had his own job. He must keep eyes on Torian.

A soft voice called from across the pile of sleeping Banshees. "Come, prince. Join me at my side."

His eyes made out Clíodhna sitting upon a throne and dressed in a flowing gown. Her beauty was perfectly recreated in his dream – every detail imagined from her gradual neckline to a single mole upon her chest. "How did you do this?" He asked. "How did you enter my mind so fully that you appear real even in my dreams?"

The queen laughed kindly and answered, "You are under my spell, Restarian. Though the power of my people is greatly diminished, I can summon enough trickle of the magic promised to my people long ago. Your people can do the same, and occasionally one among you can conjure or affect a mind just as I."

"Nastauria…" He wondered. He was thinking of the way she had entranced her daughter in the forest and placed her into slumber.

Clíodhna hissed at the name but recovered her bearing. "Yes," she admitted, "like that vile woman."

"You know her?" He asked.

"We were friends, long ago. Met in the forest as children, we formed a bond despite the warfare of our clans. My fondest memories were spent playing with her among the forest floor, until we eventually grew apart and adopted the hatred our people bear for one another," she explained.

Restarian's eyes grew wide with disbelief at the obvious lies. "The daughter of the Fainnen king and the Deamhann queen were friends? How can this be?"

"Hatred does not exist among the very young and is learned or passed down as children age. We did not care Fainne or Deamhan,

Fainneshee or Banshee at the time. But the reality is that our people were once intermingled," she said. "Our blood was and is the same and our histories shared." She pointed toward the sleeping Banshees on the ground. "Only when your ancestor stole the power from my people, were we trapped in those hideous forms by that vile King Girtrán."

"How are *you* so..." He paused, blushing at his childlike foolery.

"How am I so beautiful?" She asked.

"Yes," he agreed. "Is this another conjure, are you as vile as they? Have you beguiled my eyes to see you in this form?"

She approached and took his hand, suddenly making him corporeal in her presence. Sudden fear coursed his body and his pulse quickened – ready to force his body to flee. But she gently placed his fingertips against her face, rubbing them gently along her cheek and chin. She ran them along her soft lips and against her teeth – as perfectly formed as his and just as pearly shone. When she let go, he pulled his hand back slowly – her touch lingering on his lips where she had kissed him before.

"You are not beguiled, Restarian, son of Betarian. You see me in my natural form. That was the gift given to my people by your ancestor. He allowed our queen and her female offspring to always have beauty. He promised one day one of us would sire a son who is also perfect in form and free of his spell of corruption."

"Who then," he asked, "is the father? Who sired Torian?"

"So that's his name, then? Given to him by Nastauria after she stole him away, no doubt. His father was my only love, a visitor from the Human Realm brought on a quest by Síth Morkur. Together they schemed to disrupt our world and steal the Bláth de Fainne, as you call it, and take it away to his realm."

"Radviken," he said with a gasp. "He left a child inside of you like he did Nastauria?"

"Yes, young prince. He left us each with child and left both in despair following his departure."

"Why didn't you follow him?"

"I tried, after my child was stolen by Nastauria, to journey to him and tell him of her deceit. I eventually found a way, by capturing a Fainne and using them to travel. I made it through the portal but his Storm Riders found me and brought me before him, now a king. He was not happy to see me as I had foolishly hoped, and he punished me by locking the portals with his own blood. Now I'm bound until my own child sets me free, but he is off doing the bidding of Nastauria."

He considered Torian and Alistaria. "So he truly does not know…" He suddenly felt bad for earlier wishing Torian's death. "Despite his blood, I should not have judged him or treated him with contempt."

"You are very wise and intelligent, grandson of Betarian. Perhaps there is promise for peace between our people once again." She wheeled around and walked to a crystal structure and added, "After the king's days have ended, of course." She beckoned for him to follow. "Behold the remnants of the Blossom."

Restarian examined the structure – formed like stalks of a plant and resembling vines. Even the leaves were crystalline. It did resemble the vine from beneath the Tree of Life, but was most certainly not living. "I don't understand. This is not a plant," he said.

"No, I don't suppose it is," she agreed. "Once the blooms are plucked, this is the result of what's left behind – and how it's viewed in the Human Realm."

"Someone plucked the blooms from…" he was dumbfounded. With confusion he asked, "Who plucked these blooms?"

"If he were still alive, we would ask your great-great-great grandfather. Girtrán was the one who betrayed my people and condemned them to perpetual subservience to the Fainne." With obvious loathing she added, "When he stole their beauty and marred them instead to match the demons of the Shadow Realm – destined to sow fear in the world we once tended."

"Where?" Restarian asked. He felt the dream began to fade around him as something drew his slumbering mind back to his body. "Where did you once tend?"

"Why *this* realm, of course." she answered with a smile. "We were the tenders of the forests in Fainnotheria before the great war between races. That realm belongs to you, not to the humans! It was they who forced your kind through the portal."

No, he thought. *That isn't right!* This *realm belongs to us!* Mistrust began to build once more, and he eyed her closely. "What is it you want of me? Do you want me dead?"

"No," she replied. "I want you to help me retrieve the bush stolen by Radviken. Then you will give the healing rose over to me, and return through the portal with your people. You will leave mine in peace and I will assist you in winning yours back from the Luchorpán."

"I cannot do any of that! I *won't* do that!" He protested. The throne room suddenly spun around him, and he felt himself drifting away.

She felt him going and called out, "Place the crystal upon the person of my son. Find him and slip it into his satchel or his clothing, but do so quickly. I must answer his questions as well as yours!"

Abruptly he awoke.

Torian shook Restarian as he slept, bringing him to consciousness with a jolt. "Get up," he said. "Someone's coming up the mountain!"

"What? Who would dare be out during Tempest?" The prince asked lazily, wiping sleep from his eyes.

"They appear to be soldiers, from the look of them. They're climbing up the slope. I see three in total, each atop four-legged beasts."

Torian looked again. Two were unassuming, simply adorned with light armor with swords at their sides – but the third seemed unworldly. The storm seemed to swirl above his head with rain falling around instead of atop he and his fellow riders. Somehow, he knew it was that rider who diverted the wind and rain.

"Hurry," the guardsmen said, "grab your sword and be ready!"

Terror seemed to grip Restarian as he drew the silver blade. He wasn't ready and he knew it. Though Torian had taught him the basics, the prince would need many thousands of hours of practice before he would be ready to swing it in real battle. *Much less against a foe wielding magic,* the guardsmen thought.

"Just stand behind me and get against the wall. If they capture or kill me, drop the sword and surrender. You'll be back in our realm in a few days."

The prince nodded.

Good, the boy isn't stupid, Torian thought. He readied his feet for the first attacker. He'd rather wait for them to come to him, using the cave as a defensive shield rather than expose his flanks to both the men and the elements. At least here he could force them to fight one by one. He waited with anticipation, with seconds stretching into what felt like hours. The approaching soldiers were purposely taking their time.

Certainly they don't know we're here, the guardsman thought. *They couldn't have seen the glow from our fire, not from way down there. Surely, they just happened upon the cave!* But any belief in coincidence soon diminished when an amplified voice boomed into the chamber around them.

"Surrender, Fainne, and present yourself for testing." The words echoed around them.

"How does he know we're Fainne?" Restarian asked.

"Shh," Torian warned, "I don't know!"

"Give up," the voice continued, "and your punishment will be swift."

Moments later a soldier advanced on the cave, swinging a sword at Torian. The Fainne parried and moved to the side, flawlessly executing a counter attack that the attacker blocked with a parry of his own. Fighting was difficult without wings, Torian realized, and he focused his next thoughts on defending against a relentless flurry of strikes.

Finally, the attacker tired and Torian proved his superiority with a sword. The man's arm sagged just enough with fatigue that a silvery blade was thrust into the exploited opening. Torian pulled out as quickly as it went in, sending the man tumbling backward with a kick. The Fainne barely had time to rest when a second attacker swooped in with as much ferocity as the first.

But fatigue had also worked its way into his own defense, and he slowed as the attacker swept high and low with his blade. One misstep would cost him his life, and the Fainne relied upon a move he learned fighting in the close quarters around the Skygate.

As the man lunged with a fury, Torian stepped backward to allow him entrance. Finding the cave more cramped, the longer sword of the attacker dragged along the ceiling of the cavern – sending sparks flying as it slowed. The opening to the man's chest was large as Torian spun and kicked a second time, connecting solidly and sending the human toppling backward toward the cliff's edge. He stood there, waving his arms for a moment – and their eyes locked. The human was suitably shocked to have been bested, and it showed on his face just before he lost balance and fell to the rocky floor below. The Fainne watched him lying there only briefly, then waited for the third man.

Abruptly a flash of light filled the cavern and a blur rushed in. Torian spun but had been blinded by the sudden eruption of power. He swung his blade wildly but only made contact with air. He whirled and swung again, missing this time as well. He blinked against the spots as Restarian cried out with a desperate scream for his help.

The prince blinked against the flash of light – suddenly blinded and fearing Torian had been as well. Bravely he held the blade forward, but knew there was little he could do. A gush of wind announced the entry of the third attacker rushing by Torian and sprinting toward him. In a panic he sheathed his blade and grabbed the satchel beside him, thrusting Clíodhna's crystal inside. A moment later he felt a blade prick against his arm and a strong hand grab his wrist. He cried out for help as brute strength pulled him to his feet. Another flash of light erupted, and his vision swam once more.

The next thing he felt was coldness as the attacker pulled him from the cave and into the night. He tried to dig in his heels and slow his kidnapping, but the dagger across his arm had been poisoned. He felt his knees buckle and his limbs become numb. Just before he blacked out, he felt himself tossed across the back of a horse and tied tightly to the saddle.

Torian's eyesight returned not long after the attacker had fled. Blinking in the darkness of the cave he searched for Restarian. The prince was gone, he realized quickly. He felt around until he found his satchel and the prince's waterskin. Fatigue crept in as he scanned the cave for any of their discarded belongings.

Staggering as he moved, he hurried to the entrance and looked out into the storm, searching the slope for the bodies of his attackers. The body of the first man had already been consumed by the Ganshees – not even a bone remained inside the armor. He retrieved the black leather gear, figuring it better suited than the simple tunic he wore. *If I'm attacked again,* he thought, *this will afford better protection.* He walked to where he had kicked the corpse of the second – nothing remained at all, not even his armor. Either the man had recovered and fled, or he had been dragged off deeper into the forest. Torian had no time to find out.

The gear fit him well, providing both warmth and protection from the chilling rain. He was most thankful for the boots. The blackness of the leather would also provide camouflage when traveling during the nighttime, and the hooded cloak would hide his face from those he happened to meet – though he doubted he could fool other riders.

He hated to leave the warmth of the cavern, but more humans may come in search of him or for the armor of their fallen comrades. He looked toward the city in the north. It was several day's walk at best. He needed one of the beasts like the men had ridden upon. He yawned deeply and his eyes were growing heavy. He also needed rest. The southern town was closer, he realized, and would offer both. He set off right away, moving swiftly through the trees and careful not to leave tracks that could be followed.

Chapter Fifteen

It would be unfair to blame my father for the recession of our kind. Our dynasty had already ended before his reign.
   – Lamentations of Nastauria

Alistaria emerged in a large clearing. Ahead lay miles of groomed farmland and open fields for grazing. What had once been acres of forest, humans had slashed and burned – killing thousands of living trees and using the fertile ground to feed their greed. Turning a mournful look toward the way she'd come, she felt exposed and vulnerable. In all her life she had never stepped foot in such a lonely place. She yearned to feel the happy thrum of healthy roots once more.

Slowly she willed her body to move. Cramped, hungry, and exhausted she pushed forward across the open field. Surrounded by rows of plants of every kind, the girl marveled at the size of the vegetation. Corn grew taller than her in some places, and flowing stalks of unharvested wheat swayed in others. The humans enjoyed so much abundance that they hadn't even taken the time to claim the bounty of every field. In these, thousands of Ganshees had already descended – devouring pods of grain and eating the stalks to the root. Some lifted their hideous faces to watch the girl pass by, but thankfully most ignored her presence.

She had heard stories how the humans had ruined their world, but nothing had prepared her for the blatant irreverence. The geometric lines of planted trees, vegetables, and even their structures clashed so openly with those of her home. Living beings were to be nurtured and not dominated, she believed – but these creatures had bent and broken everything to their will. Suddenly she grew homesick for the flowing and natural shapes of Fainnotheria. She could never live among these heathens who so wantonly desecrated nature, and yearned instead to return to her realm.

As she passed through corn rows, Alistaria trembled at the closeness of the Ganshees. Accidentally brushing her arm against a stalk earned chittering protest and snaps of displeasure by razor sharp teeth. She did her best to avoid another encounter, and, as she moved deeper into the emerald maze, the Ganshees were fewer and the leaves more abundant. She squeezed under a stalk – broken in the wind – and her face came too near a pair of the pixies fighting over an ear of grain. One of them snapped in her direction and took a piece of flesh from her cheek – narrowly missing her eye.

In a panic she took off in a run, heedless of disturbing more of their feasting. She rounded a row just as lightning lit up a monster standing in her way. Alistaria had never seen a scarecrow, nor did she understand its purpose – or why humans would hang one to decorate their fields. She did, however, understand the evils of shadow and their presence in both her realm and the human's. The flash of light illuminated what appeared to be a hideous Draugar, tied with arms outstretched and head rolled to one side.

She tried to stop but slid in the mud, crashing into the beast with jarring impact – its arms wrapping around her as she scrambled free. Looking up she watched as the head rolled toward her, staring with unseeing pits that once were eyes. Two Ganshees emerged from the sockets and hissed, and she forced out a frightened cry. Her wail echoed in the storm, joining that of a host of Banshees swirling in the clouds above. With a moan and a whimper she took off running once more. Overhead, more Banshees answered her call – swooping down to investigate the source of the sound. Several luminescent beasts swirled around her, tittering at her fright and biting at her body. They chased her toward a rectangular structure.

She could clearly see that the building had large doors closed against the storm. She fled faster to reach their safety, unable to pull her eyes from the pursuing creatures. Her skin crawled under their hungry gaze, sensing their desire to pierce her flesh with rotting teeth. Not watching the path ahead, Alistaria tripped over several pieces of lashed timber.

Now tangled in a mass of tiered structures, she imagined the dangling ropes as snakes crawling across her skin. The more she struggled, the tighter the entanglement squeezed. She breathed deeply, trying to calm her mind and return it to reality. *What are these?* She wondered. At first, she believed them cages, but then realized they were temporary structures, built high to hold tightly wrapped bundles high above the ground. *Not bundles,* she realized, *but shrouds!* The humans had offered their dead to the Ganshees. The entire structure was crawling with the vermin – each crawling upward to devour their meal.

The Banshees flying above laughed as she fought to free herself from the funeral pyres, further binding herself with every struggle. The ropes now wrapped around her arms and legs, and some had found their way to her neck. She cried out again – causing the Deamhan to snicker at her peril as the entire structure fell. The tiny pixies now surrounded her, confusing her skin with the shrouded forms now toppled and laying atop Alistaria. She rolled to her hands and knees and felt new pain as tiny razors bit through her flesh.

One of the shrouds had pulled away. She looked up to find clouded eyes staring back – deeply set with death and belonging to an old woman. Next to her a man looked down upon her violation of his grave – his mouth open to the Ganshees feasting on his tongue within. To her horror there were corpses of all ages, each with half-eaten flesh falling from their bones. Once the Ganshees had flensed the flesh, they would devour those as well.

As she struggled, she found her bonds tightening – pulling her face closer to the rot-feasting pixies. She felt their bites on her arms at first. Slowly they spread to her legs and the tender flesh of her armpits. Tears flowed against their tearing teeth and her pleas grew into inaudible wails.

She weakly turned her head toward the watching Deamhan and begged, "Help me!"

"See?" A male Banshee said to the others. "She clearly understands our speech. Hear her plead with us? She begs redemption from the fate of all Fainne!"

"Her pleas are in vain," another commented. "Let's leave her now to face the sins her kind deserve. Had they not wrought so much suffering on us, she would receive our mercies."

"Come," the first encouraged. "Leave her and let's be gone." He leapt into the air and the second followed.

The third - a female, she thought but couldn't be sure – lingered. She leaned in with tender compassion behind scarlet eyes. "No one deserves this fate, not even a wicked Fainne. If I had hands in this world, I would lend you aid," she promised, then turned and flew upward to join the others.

Alistaria groaned against the restraints, then wriggled a hand free. Inching her fingers toward her belt, she felt for her silvery blade. Pulling it free she worked on the nearest lashing. Sawing as quickly as she could, she felt it tug then snap as she dropped a few inches. Now able to move her entire arm, she worked on the other bonds. Soon the girl felt her body fall and braced against a hard thud against the ground. The Ganshees continued to bite at her flesh as she struggled to her knees, crawling from the heap of death.

Finally free of entanglement but not the pixies, Alistaria rolled on the ground the best she could, crushing as many as she could beneath her bodyweight. Lightning surged overhead, filling her with a sudden rush of power unlike any she had ever felt. The rhythmic beating as if of drums pounded within her soul, and fairy sparks flew in every direction from her body – casting off many of the tiny creatures. With dagger in her hand she swatted away several more, stabbing one and pinning it to the wet mud. Pulling the weapon free she watched in horror as its companions dove on their dying comrade and ignored the Fainne. Turning away from the carnage she sprinted toward the building and its waiting doors.

She tried the latch, and it gave, freeing them open. With a heave she pulled, greeted by the stench of dozens of animals and several days of feces. She retched and turned, hoping to find another shelter, but found the Ganshees had gathered into a hovering ball. They turned in unison and flew toward Alistaria. She quickly ducked inside, pulling the doors firmly shut.

Ignoring the smell the best she could, she found a pile of hay and collapsed. Hopelessness consumed her thoughts and her mood darkened. Unable to tend her wounds they would surely fester. She had never felt so grim or hopeless all at once. She would never find the Blossom in time, and what she had was running out.

Chapter Sixteen

Dog farts are nostalgic. They remind me of growing up with Boyd
– Piotr

The common room couch was actually more comfortable than it looked. Even better, the musky leather smelled far better than Lucky and his expressions. In no time Piotr was fast asleep and dreaming. It was the same dream he often experienced when resting comfortably during Tempest – instead of cramped in the mucky corner of a crowded barn. He dreamed of the fae realm.

The trees in his dreams were always magnificent. They were tall and twisted with broad trunks and large roots that thrummed with a pulse of their own. He loved this place, and always wished upon waking he could return to tread the mossy floor below the towering forest. In this particular vision he floated above it with delicate wings that buzzed in the air. There were others beside him, laughing merrily as they took turns placing hands upon the roots and cleaning the great trees of insects or disease – tending roots, they called it. But then, as with every time he dreamed this fantasy, the Cat Síth came.

He was the reason for Piotr's own superstition, and why he loathed Tempest so badly. Every time he dreamed of this world during the storm, the Síth made an appearance. In this case – as most – he dragged Piotr away from the others and carried him to the edge of the forest. Ahead was a fairy ring, that simple circle of mushrooms that seem so benign. The cat had transformed into a man with delicate fur along his humanoid body – velvety and strange. His dark eyes gazed into Piotr's as he bore him into the ring, whispering as a flash of light lit up the night.

"Forget," he said softly, "but never fully."

A loud scream bellowed through the tavern and Piotr's blue eyes shot open with alarm. In an instant he had sprinted to the guest room, mortified to find Harriet had snuck in to visit Boyd while the others slept. The cry had come from Sophie, who had already been paying her respects for quite some time. The result was a cacophony of shrieks and hair pulling that woke the entire place.

Piotr shot an angry glare at his friend. "We've been over this sort of thing before, haven't we?"

Boyd merely shrugged, then agreed, "Aye, but I can't help it I'm so irresistible to women."

Piotr never understood the attraction to the short and awkward looking fellow, but he was right – women loved Boyd, and usually fought for his attention. "Get dressed," he commanded the culprit, "and grab our things. He'll kill us and throw our bodies to the storm for this!"

Boyd nodded and leapt from the bed, throwing on clothing he found on the floor, the chair, and even the headboard. While he hurried, he muttered, "I really can't help it," he insisted. "I even told her *no*, this time! But she insisted, and the girl had her way with me!"

"I'm sure she did," Piotr muttered with doubt.

By then Harveigh had stormed down the steps from upstairs, screaming for Martha to return to her rooms. With the devil in his eyes he raised the club and shouted, "I gave you one rule!" The club came down, narrowly missing Piotr as he added, "Stay away from my girls!" The piece of smooth lumber raised again, this time swinging sideways at the tall thief's head.

"Actually," remarked Boyd, "you also said to leave the food alone and share ours with the mutt... I'd say two outta three ain't bad!"

This only further enraged the tavern keeper, and he unleashed it wildly against Piotr, still the nearest. The tall thief ducked and bobbed out of the way, wishing for something he could use to fight back. The man was definitely stronger, so he used his quickness to avoid the blows. "It wasn't his fault," he protested. "He told her *no*!"

"That's right," Boyd agreed while pulling up his pants. "I told her *no*, but she insisted on having the time of her life!"

"You're not helping!" Piotr shouted as his friend, ducking another blow that splintered a support beam beside where his head had been. To the angry tavern keeper he pleaded, "We'll leave if you want us to, just please let us go peacefully."

"You'll leave out of here in pieces," the bigger man promised. He finally turned his attention toward Boyd, now fully dressed and sneaking past. He had their satchels on his back and the sleeping dog in his arms. The stout thief froze as a blow swung down at him.

Before it struck his friend, Piotr grabbed a mug from the bar and swung it at Harveigh – striking his temple. The club went wide and arced to the floor, followed by the big man himself. The girls in the guestroom momentarily stopped fighting when their boss crashed to the floor. You could have heard a pin drop in the new found silence.

A tiny *pfft* came from deep in the rancid bowels of the beggar's dog, followed by a shriek from upstairs. Martha had left her room despite Harveigh's order, and believed him dead by Piotr's hand.

"Murderers!" She screamed. "Bloody murder is what this is!"

This set the other two girls in a tirade of their own, and Boyd and Piotr sprinted to the door. Wrenching it open, the taller man shooed his friend outside and into the Tempest. The cold wind hit them nearly as hard as the icy rain, blowing the door from his hand. They left it swinging in the storm as they hurried down the street.

"What were you thinking?" Piotr shouted at Boyd over the howling.

"I wasn't," Boyd admitted. "I just couldn't help myself. She's the purdiest woman I've ever seen!"

"That's what you said about the last one," he reminded.

"Well, she was!" his friend reasoned, "Right up until the moment I met this one!"

Other than the two men hurrying through the rain – one clutching a now awake and irritated wet dog – the streets of Port Enat were deserted. Not even a constable would be fool enough to be caught out in the Tempest, so they never expected to see three riders coming down the street. They slowed their gait and stared as the duo hurried past.

"Peter?" Boyd asked.

"What?"

"Did you just see three riders?"

"Yes, and so did you. What about them?"

"Do you think those were Storm Riders?"

"I don't think so, but why do you ask?"

"Well," Boyd explained, "They just turned around to follow us."

An alleyway opened up between streets on the left. And Piotr quickly pulled his friend in that direction. It was opposite from their intended destination, but the duo had used it once before to duck the Thieves' Guild. Once they were around the corner they again broke into a sprint. The clap of horses' hooves echoed the rider's hurrying their pace as well. Thankfully, they'd have to dismount to further pursue.

The best part about being a thief in a city you know well is quickly finding your way out of sticky situations. The duo did just that – slipping behind a weathered sign and past a loose storm water grate.

Boyd handed Piotr the dog and jumped down beside him in the sewer. "I've never been inside one of these during Tempest."

"No one has, Boyd."

"I wonder why that is?" he asked as he retrieved Lucky.

"Because no one else is ever stupid enough to get kicked out of a warm tavern and sentenced to running through the streets during Tempest, Boyd."

"Like I said, 'twasn't my fault."

"I know," Piotr agreed with more than a hint of sarcasm, "you're just too irresistible."

"Exactly."

They were able to move quickly through the sewer, despite the rising water around their ankles. Had they entered later during the storm, they would probably have drowned. Each pondered this silently as they hurried to the spill over on the edge of town. Piotr, seeing something ahead, slowed and held up his hand.

"What is it?" Asked Boyd.

"I'm not sure," he said. "It looks like a dead cat. Or a dog. I can't tell from here."

Boyd made a show of covering Lucky's solitary eye. "Don't look, Bastard. I'd hate for you to see someone you recognize!"

They crept along until they could clearly make out a horrific sight. It was – or until then it had been – a dog who found its way into the sewers to die. The carcass had laid undisturbed until Tempest, and was covered with tiny insects with lacy wings. Piotr crept forward to get a closer look.

"Careful with that, Piotr," Boyd cautioned. "If those are what I think they are, you'll be in for a hurtin'!"

"I don't think they're pixies, Boyd."

"Yeah? Well… you said the same about them Storm Riders, yet you ran from those guys in the street. I figured you'll finally start listening to me soon."

"Not a chance." Piotr reached out a cautious foot and jabbed it into the animal. A flurry of wings rose into the air and dozens of sharp toothed pixies snapped at his face – hissing and buzzing as they chased the pair down the sewer. Out of breath and with pulses throbbing, Boyd and Piotr finally rested after the fae had for certain given up the chase.

Boyd grinned like a child who had just found candy in the cushions. "Oh boy!" he said. "You should have seen your face!" He thrust Lucky into Piotr's arms and waved his own around like he was swatting mosquitoes. "Aaaaahhh!" He said mockingly as he spun around in circles – bug-eyed and mouth open like a fool. After he'd stooped to laugh, he kept chuckling awkwardly – even after realizing Piotr hadn't joined in.

Finally, after some time of staring at but ignoring his friend, Piotr said, "I can't believe they're actually real!" What he didn't say aloud, he said in his mind. *And they look just like in my dreams!*

The storm clouds had lightened by the time they reached the farm, meaning that morning of the second day had come. They would weather the final five days of Tempest in the barn after all, despite their best efforts. The effect of the storm could already be seen, the thief noticed solemnly. It had already ravaged the farmlands, killing every crop in the fields and withering them to the root. Even the bodies left out for burial had been rendered by storm, knocking over their burial pyres in its fury to consume what was offered by the priests. All around them the green of the land had transformed into hues of brown – even the trees were without leaves. In five more days the cycle would begin anew, and fresh crops would be planted, and the forest would bloom. *What would Enatherr do without the storm?* He wondered.

Lucky trotted behind as they approached the barn, eager for the dry warmth within. Boyd pulled open the doors and the pathetic party of thieves entered while holding their noses against the stench. Both men froze when they realized they were not alone. There, upon a dry haystack slept a young woman. Her face and her arms had been battered, bruised, and clawed during the storm. Chunks of meat were missing from her exposed skin, although many of her wounds had scabbed over during the night. She required immediate attention.

Boyd started to wake the girl, but Piotr held him back. "Let her sleep," he said. "We'll attend to her after she's rested. Something tells me she's been through a worse night than we."

"Look at this, Piotr." Boyd felt the hay next to her and lifted a knife made of shining silver. The craftmanship was exquisite – intricately designed and folded with as much care as the hardest steel in Enatherr. "Tamee told us tales of these," he said with awe in his trembling voice.

"Put it down, Boyd, it doesn't belong to us."

"And look here," Boyd insisted. The girl's tunic had been carefully stitched with two long slits running down her back. "These are for wings, Piotr."

"That's enough," the taller man cautioned. "Let her sleep and return her dagger. We've no quarrel with this child."

"We could take her to Tamee," the stouter of the two insisted. "She'll take her in and treat her wounds."

"Tamee's in Crosston, that's a full day's ride from here," Piotr protested. "Three on foot."

Boyd pointed to the livestock all around. "I see many horses available, and we know where they keep their wagons. We could make it by nightfall if we hurry."

"No," he shook his head. "It's too much of a risk and we haven't slept all night."

"We'll take turns sleeping along the way. For Radviken's sake, Piotr, she's burning with fever."

Piotr looked closely at the dagger Boyd had found. *It does match the tales,* he thought. He considered also the pixies in the storm sewer. *So many things about this Tempest are strange, so I guess anything's possible.* He cleared his throat and asked quietly, "Do you really think she's a fae, Boyd?"

"Fae or not, she's real sick and we've five more days of Tempest. We've no medical supplies, and no one will open their doors to strangers during the storm."

Piotr considered his friends words. *He's right of course, only we can help this poor girl.* Off in the distance, sirens wailed – rising up from the waterfront. Constables had surely been notified of the incident in the tavern. "Fine," he said. "We'll risk it, but we'd better hurry."

"I'll get the wagon," Boyd said, hurrying to choose the best horses.

Piotr looked around the barn, taking in the smell of the muck and the feces. *Yes,* he thought, *that smell just about sums up this Tempest.* He bent down and picked up a fallen satchel, surely dropped by the girl when she collapsed. Inside he found rations akin to hard tack and pemmican – these he recognized. Several herbs and salves were also packed, along with a waterskin.

The flax binding of a book caught his eye, and he reached in to pull it out. Holding it in a shaky hand he opened to the first page. *Lamentations of Nastauria,* it read, and Piotr followed the words with excitement. It was a journal began by a young woman, it seemed, and each page offered insights to another world. Placing a trembling finger on the first line, he followed the thoughts of the mysterious woman.

I was young when he arrived in Fainnotheria, he read, *infantile of mind and naïve in my own form. I lacked the confidence only experience brings and yearned instead for the rebellion of ignorant youth. My reflections upon his arrival are filled with wonder – trepidation for the fate of my people – but wonderment for the knowledge I gained by his meeting. Oh, that he had never crossed through the Fainnen Ring. Oh, that I had never met Radviken.*

Piotr closed the book with eyes wide with excitement. He carefully stowed it in his satchel to read later. He *was* a thief, after all, but the guilt for taking it flooded instantly.

Chapter Seventeen

"My son was a beautiful sight, born upon the forest floor. He was bold and stubborn, forcing his mother to work throughout the night. But when he finally came, I found him magnificent. His eyes were the blue of his father's and just as entrancing. I only held him briefly, for when I awoke, he was gone from my life."
– Sorrow of Clíodhna

Torian reached the city just as a new day dawned. The sun rose slowly from behind the mountains to the west, changing the terrible blackness of Tempest into a more tolerable gray. There were no gates – they weren't needed in the Human Realm since warfare had been eliminated under Radviken. With the citizens sleeping soundly in their beds, no one noticed as he strolled into the town and slipped into a stable.

The structure was delightfully warm after crossing desert and hiking over mountains. The soft pile of hay provided a cozy place for him to settle, and he pulled his satchel close to his cheek – serving well as a pillow. Both heart and mind settled quickly, and he soon drifted steadily to sleep.

His dreams found the forest of Fainnotheria as he had left it. Thrumming roots called from every direction and the dense canopy invited him to perch on its highest branches. He tried his wings – thrilled to find they'd returned. He couldn't imagine life without the freedom of flight, and he zipped around to regain their feel. He laughed his joy into the air as he flew – unhindered as in the Human Realm.

Movement in a clearing caught his eye. A woman stood there, dressed in a flowing gown and most certainly with features of a Fainne. He hovered for a moment, searching for Banshees in case of ambush. Finding none he investigated.

"Why are you alone this far from the city?" He asked, still hovering above. "Would you like an escort to Fainnotheria?"

The woman laughed then smiled sweetly. "No," she said, "I'm afraid I'm not welcome there, and this is as close as I dare wander."

"If you're not from the city," he asked, "then where is your home? Surely it's not safe in the forest this near the Banshees."

"They will not harm me," she promised. Changing the subject she asked, "What is your name, stranger who cares so much about my safety?"

"I'm called Torian."

"Then I shall call you Torian the Chivalrous," she said with a smile. "Why are you so boldly flying around so far from the city, yourself?"

Suddenly aware he was in a dream, he paused awkwardly and floated down beside the woman – joining her on the forest floor. She hopped up on a fallen trunk and patted the space beside her. He eagerly joined her atop the stump. "I'm apparently dreaming," he said. "Which is strange because this feels so real."

"Sometimes you can exist in both dreams and the waking world at the same time," she explained. "Especially when you are dreaming across the realms."

Torian's eyes grew wide with understanding. "Like the Banshees? They fly during Tempest and walk the Human Realm, but aren't fully there. Are they dreaming in our realm? Is that why they do not attack Fainnotheria during the six days of the human Tempest?"

"That is exactly what's happening, only don't refer to it as the human Tempest. The storm wasn't of Radviken's making, and has plagued our realm for many centuries – even before he opened it to theirs. He's only learned to control it since stealing the Bláth de Deamhan."

"You mean the Bláth de Fainne?"

"No, Torian. I meant what I said. The Blossom did not always belong to your people. I'm sure you know the story how King Betarian's great-great grandfather stole it from the Deamhan and enslaved them."

"King Girtrán's tale?" He asked. "Every Fainne knows that history."

"Yes," she answered. "That is why they're so angry – they want it returned to its rightful resting place. Until that happens there will not be balance between the human and fae realms."

Torian said nothing. He considered her words thoughtfully, questioning why she would blaspheme so openly. Finally he asked, "You are not Fainne?"

"No, Torian. I'm not. I promise to tell you everything, but first I have questions for you. Do you know who your parents were?"

"I have no parents," he replied. "I was raised in the nursery."

"Have you ever wondered about them? Wondered at who they were and why you were given up?"

"Truly I did," he said. "Every day I wondered."

"And now? Would you like to know?"

He shifted his weight, suddenly uncomfortable and afraid. "That's one wish that would never be granted. No one knows the truth of my origin."

"Nastauria knows."

"I doubt that's true," he laughed. "She would have told me if she knew."

"Did you not wonder why she chose you to protect her daughter on this journey across realms?"

"She said it was because I protected her when the Banshees attacked. She believed me a capable protector."

"It wasn't only that, Torian." The woman's face grew sad as her eyes focused on a distant memory. "She knew that you were her only way home."

"I don't understand."

"Nastauria's daughter is half human, did you know?"

"Yes. She is the product of her tryst with Radviken the Vile. Everyone in Fainnotheria knows that."

"Did you know that he locked the realm? That a Deamhan could only travel through the portals if accompanied by a Fainne?"

"I did," he said. "That too, is common knowledge. What does that have to do with Alistaria."

"Just as a Deamhan cannot travel to the Human Realm without a Fainne, her human blood cannot return to our realm without the help of a fae."

"I don't understand."

"Torian," she said, "you are the son of Clíodhna, Queen of the Deamhan. Nastauria knows this and that is why she chose you to escort her daughter – even after the elders ordered her to travel alone."

"No," he said. "That's not possible."

"Think, Torian the Chivalrous. Why would they order her to travel alone if not to leave her stuck on the other side?" She smiled tenderly as he absorbed her words, placing a warm hand upon his shoulder while offering reassurance. "I'm sure they gave her a way to open a portal once she reached Radviken's palace?"

He nodded. "They did. A satchel of mushroom spores is what they sent."

"Then they planned to send the Kern to attack the sleeping Deamhan and capture one or two with which to travel. They would pass through to his palace while the Deamhan became trapped in the Human Realm. You didn't land in the same portal as she, did you?"

"No," he said. "I arrived with Restarian, and she went somewhere else. We haven't been able to find her. I'm sure we'll find her in Radviken's palace, and King Betarian will have already killed the Deamhan and will come to our aid."

Her eyes grew wide with sudden alarm. "He plans a full attack, and not a raid? That cannot be so!" She leapt from the trunk with alarm, suddenly staring up at Torian with fear behind her once confident eyes.

Realizing his blunder he hopped down to join her. He should not have told this woman their plans.

"We've all been deceived," she said, waving her hand.

Torian instantly awoke in the stable, gasping and panting with muscles sore as when he traveled the portal. Though he found himself once again in the Human Realm, he could smell the lingering scent of the woman he'd met. *Who was she?* He wondered. *Her beauty was truly unmatched.* The image of her blue eyes lingered, and his mind wandered once more. *She said she wasn't a Fainne,* he realized with alarm. *Surely, she wasn't Clíodhna!* He thought. Then a moment of terror seized him as he realized. *She* is *the queen!*

He threw open the door to the stable and looked out upon the storm. Though it was difficult to tell with the cloud cover, it was past midday. *I'm losing time,* he thought, *and must hurry.* Turning, he considered the animals in their stalls. Several were of the type ridden by the men who had attack them in the cave. They kicked and snorted their protest over the open door, and Torian considered his options.

The men did not ride upon them bareback, but upon leather seats strapped upon their backs. Looking around he found one hanging from the wall. *It looks simple enough,* he considered, *with places to insert my feet so I don't fall.* Heaving the saddle from the wall, he made his way to the nearest stall.

The beast within was as dark as those ridden by their attackers. It stared at Torian, watching him approach and shifting his weight uncomfortably. "Easy, boy," he said to the animal. "I've no idea how this works, so I'll need you to go easy on me." The animal snorted loudly and bobbed his head – a good sign, he assumed.

Standing beside the animal, he hoisted the saddle up and over the animals back, causing it to protest immediately. It tried to move away from him, turning its head away and sending the leather contraption sliding to the ground. It struck with a loud slap in the dirt, sending hay scattering and the other beasts into obvious panic. They paced their stalls and eyed Torian doubtfully.

Picking it up, he used his body to push the animal gently against the wall, intent on trying again. He placed it gentler, this time, kneeling to fasten the buckle underneath its chest. It protested, but did not budge. He gave the seat a tug and it held. Satisfied, he coaxed the horse forward into the open area of the barn. Placing one foot in the stirrup he grabbed the horn above and heaved his frame upward, swinging the other over the side. Comfortable but somewhat unsure what to do next, he placed his hands on the saddle and closed his eyes.

Bracing himself for whatever came next, he spoke aloud. "Go." Nothing happened. "Walk," he commanded, but the animal stood frozen in place. He gently nudged the animal's side with his heels and tried again, "Go!"

The beast shot forward, racing toward the door and freedom beyond. Torian had not expected the sudden burst of speed, and held on dearly for his life. Just as they reached the door, the weight in the loose saddle shifted, sliding to the right and toppling the Fainne with it. Luckily, his feet slipped free and was not trampled as he slammed against the ground. The animal continued running – through the open door and into the city beyond.

CHAPTER EIGHTEEN

Piotr had never driven a wagon during Tempest. From the anxiety he felt from the horses, he could tell they'd never been taken out in one. Leading them from the barn had been difficult, and hitching them to the wagon had almost proven disastrous. They resisted the snap of reigns but finally started forward with resignation. Other than a few startled bucks at the first lightning strikes, they finally settled, though. After that he held them steady enough, and soon they were ready to travel.

He had prepared a bed of straw in the wagon, and hastily threw together a makeshift shelter out of old canvas. It wasn't perfect, but would keep most of the rain off the girl. He looked up when Boyd brought her out of the barn. She was tinier than he had first noticed – just a waif of a thing.

"She's light as a feather, this one." Boyd said as he set her upon the straw. She hadn't even stirred when they tried to wake her, and slept a dangerous sleep. They would have to hurry to Crosston. "She's burning up badly," Boyd observed. "This fever will kill her if we don't get there soon."

"Aye," Piotr agreed, "I'll go as fast as I can, but don't wanna flip us over in the process." He flicked the reigns and the horses moved, leaving the farm behind and headed east out of Enat.

Boyd reached into the sack and felt around, pulling out an odd-looking bread. "This is strange, isn't it? Resembles hardtack, but not like any I've seen. He returned it to the satchel and shrugged. "She's packing light. Other than that dagger of hers, she seems to have little more than a beggar. Hell," he added, "look at these homemade shoes on her feet. Ain't nothing but tree bark and wrappings. How does a beggar girl like her get her hands on such a fine weapon?"

"Maybe she stole it," Piotr offered, but his mind was on the book he'd found. He was too embarrassed to even tell Boyd he had stolen it from her things.

Boyd held the blade in his hand, marveling at the craftsmanship. "I'm telling you; I've heard stories about these things. This is a fairy sword, I'm sure of it."

"Maybe it's from one of the wee people, and she won it after catching one and letting him go?"

"No," the stout man disagreed. "That ain't how it works. Didn't you ever listen to Tamee's stories? They don't flit around offering wishes, that ain't their style. They're miners and craftsmen, themselves. Haven't you ever heard stories of chores getting done during Tempest?"

"You mean like the one about the sick cobbler who was in bed during the entire storm?"

Boyd nodded eagerly. "That's the one. When he awoke and went into his shop on the seventh day, all his shoes were made for the next month. They even went as far as fixing his tools and improving his stretching racks."

"Yeah, I never understood that one," Piotr admitted. "What do the brownies get in return for their charity?"

"Not a thing," Boyd suggested. "And they're called gnomes. Tamee said they have so much wealth from digging under the ground that they feel the need to give back to good humans with deserving hearts. But they don't like to give up their gold, so they help them with favors, instead."

"Well, hopefully we find some along the way to help us, then. We're gonna need quite a bit of help when we get into Crosston. I just hope Tamee takes us in."

"She will," Boyd promised. "She always does."

The duo rode in silence for a while, and Piotr allowed himself to get lost in his thoughts. It *was* a good thing they were doing for the girl – getting her help and maybe saving her life. Besides, they needed out of Enat. There would be a manhunt the moment Tempest let up. And this time, they'd have more than the Thieves' Guild after them.

Lucky growled deeply then barked.

"Get off her!" Boyd suddenly shouted.

Piotr jumped where he sat, whirling in his seat to find Boyd fighting off a pair of pixies hovering around the girl. "Don't let them bite her," he shouted. He hadn't thought of them. They may have to deal with them trying to do to the girl what he saw them doing to the dead dog in the sewer.

Boyd picked up the silvery dagger and swung at one, making full contact and sending it crashing to the road. The others immediately raced toward their comrade – now lying still on the cobblestones – and commenced devouring their own.

"Nasty little creatures," Piotr remarked.

"Aye," agreed Boyd, "They're worse than in the stories."

Piotr felt a shudder run down his spine, thinking of all the tales Tamee had told them as children. "Let's hope they're the only things *remotely* like the stories." A wail in the distance caused both men to flinch. They paused, listening intently to the silence that followed. After several moments of only the howling storm, Piotr remarked, "only wind, thankfully."

The second scream was closer, and both men realized at once it came from the forest on their left. It was followed by another – much like the others but filled with more agitation. Soon the trees were filled with shrieks and shrills that made the forest seem alive with conversation.

Boyd leaned forward, "What do you think it is, Piotr." The girl beside him groaned and he looked down. Her eyes were closed but she was fighting to regain consciousness. "She's mumbling something I can't make out," he said. Leaning in closer he listened intently.

"She's calling them back," the girl muttered.

"Calling who back?" He asked. "And to where?"

"Clíodhna," she said weakly, "is calling her children."

Boyd sat up with eyes wide and fear pulsing through his heart. "Piotr," he asked, "who is Clíodhna?"

Piotr frowned, recalling a story from long ago – one Tamee would tell them on the nights that terrified her little foundlings and encouraged them to do their chores and to behave when told. He had also read the name in the journal he found on the girl. "She was the queen of something if I recall. Is that right?"

"Queen of the Banshees, maybe?" Boyd asked with a quivering voice.

"Yeah," Piotr replied, suddenly very afraid. "That was her. Is that the name the girl just muttered?"

All at once more than a hundred spirits shot out of the trees, gliding on the wind and racing over the road and through the wagon. They spun in the air wrapped around each other like newborn snakes in the water – spinning and wailing their misery into the storm. Several made a second pass in the air, streaming by the wagon – their mournful wails more distinct from the others.

Piotr shouted out with alarm. Boyd screamed. Lucky howled. The girl stirred and tried to stand, losing her balance and landing in the straw. The Banshees rose into the air as a writhing mass that disappeared into the clouds above.

As they left, a strange quiet entered the storm and all that could be heard was the soft howl of the wind, Piotr let out a laughing roar of triumph. "Did you see that?

Boyd had a different reaction. He collapsed in the wagon holding his chest. "I think they've killed me, Piotr! I've never been so frightened in my life!"

"Relax," the driver said. "You'll live to annoy me another day. But *wow*, that was a rush of excitement!"

"Excitement? That was the most terrifying thing I'd ever seen," Boyd complained. Lucky whimpered beside him as if to agree.

It took a while for both men to get over the moment, but soon their pulses slowed to normal. They each fell silent for quite some time, afraid of what they'd encounter next.

Chapter Nineteen

My father never chastised me for what I did to Clíodhna. Rather, he laughed when I told him about the child and dared her to recover him. I may have brought her war upon us, but he fanned the flames of her anger. Alas, his punishment of me was over the other child.
– Lamentations of Nastauria

The Palace of the Deamhan held none of its former glory. Once a bastion of life and strength, the structure had been marvelous – built with magic and shining in exquisite splendor. That was no longer the case. Betarian stared at the crumbling ruin lying ahead as he flew, marveling at how time and decay had robbed the Deamhan of both dignity and hope. Of course, his ancestors had been the catalyst of their destruction, but his people could not know the true history. A Fainnen king had once forced these vermin into submission, but this king would not settle for less than their annihilation.

A former bustling city, the streets had been erased by steaming fissures and spewing fumaroles. The only building that still stood – once shining with gilded towers, but now encased within a thick carapace of ash – teetered precariously as if it would crumble at any moment. He focused his eyes on a structure with six spires reaching upward into the heavens.

"There," he told his commander. "The palace and Clíodhna's sleeping brood will be found within."

The man nodded and signaled the Kern. Each held spear at the ready as they hovered. The king was pleased. Now was certainly the time to attack – with every Deamhan deep in hibernation and half between the Human Realm and their own. What he was about to do was akin to murder, Betarian knew – but he would rid the realm of the screaming Banshees once and for all.

"Attack," he commanded, and the golden blur zipped toward the waiting palace. The king followed. In his excitement he envisioned the peace that would follow. *No more raids upon Fainnotheria,* he thought. *No more worry the Bláth de Fainne will be stolen. We will finally enjoy true balance.*

He watched as his army split as previously agreed – one force to each spire. They descended upon the great hall below, forced to land by a lowered ceiling over the steps and to walk the rest of the way. Each soldier shared his excitement, and eagerly looked forward to the purge of the nested vermin.

King Betarian would right the wrongs committed by his ancestors. *Perhaps I will restore this palace,* he mused. *I will return the Blossom to its original resting place and bring balance to the realms.* He smiled at the thought of the forest taking over the hellish landscape passing beneath. *All things will be as they were,* he thought. *No, as they* should *have been.*

He reached the spire along with his main force and marveled at the structure – seamlessly constructed as if it had been carved from a massive stone. The platform was sloped and forced his entire squad to land. A wide staircase led downward, and he led the Kern into the structure below.

Darkness enveloped his senses, dulling his vision and heightening his hearing. His ears perked at the stark void, feeling for either movement or the sounds of slumber. Neither reached him. Suddenly the hairs on his neck stood to attention. *Something is wrong,* he sensed, *so very wrong.* He held up his hand and his column halted on the descending stairs. He pointed at two scouts and pointed down the hall. His hand flashed in the battle language of the Kern – *Investigate,* he commanded.

The pair had been gone only a moment when sounds of battle erupted ahead. He sprinted ahead with his squad on his heels. As he rounded the entrance to the hall, he found the other Kern had emerged from the spires – brutally ambushed by the Deamhan. He continued to hold his column – afraid to commit his entire force. The Kern had emerged from the spires and immediately been set upon by the waiting defenders. *They were awake,* he realized. *Awake and waiting for our attack.*

He watched as the tide turned for just a moment, his army pushing toward the center of the great hall. Then he had a sobering thought. *Their numbers are the same as every other raid upon Fainnotheria. Surely, they haven't been attacking with their entire force.* Understanding rushed in. They had moved to flank. Sounding the retreat, he ordered his squad the way they'd come – up the spire and to the landing above.

Orange teeth and glowing eyes met them atop the stairs, cutting down his Kern as they fled the gruesome trap – enemy now above and below and his force trapped on the stairs. One Banshee locked swords with the king, leaning in and biting at his neck as it shrieked its ghastly cry. Betarian stumbled, losing his footing and falling into the golden horde pressing at his heels. When he toppled over – pushed to the stone by his own men – he tried to stand. Each time he found his balance the screaming fervor of his men rushed by, sending him reeling once more. When he finally placed his legs securely beneath his heavy armor, a rush of Banshees fell upon him – pulling him once more into the spire and down the spiral stairs.

At the same time King Betarian had arrived at the palace, thousands of Banshees had arrived at the walls of Fainnotheria. At their lead stood Clíodhna in her splendid beauty – flawless and entrancing to all who watched their arrival. Nastauria even marveled, though her reasons differed from the other Fainne. A voice from behind made her turn.

"She's here because of you," Erania said accusingly.

"Perhaps," Nastauria agreed, "but our feud is shorter lived than the rift between our kind. Were they truly like us before we stole the Blossom?"

The old woman nodded. "We were very much like them before their appearance was marked. We share much with the Deamhan, but we are different in many more ways than looks. Or so I understand. Though we eventually won the Blossom, I believe we lost so much opportunity for peace and cooperation between both of our kinds."

"Have you considered what I said about unity?"

The elder laughed. "Child, I consider that same hope of yours every day. But there is no hope for the lasting unity you desire. Bigotry and prejudice will keep our kind apart."

"Bigotry and prejudice are rooted in upbringing and fed by fear," Nastauria said. "Despite our differences in appearance, we *are* the same species. Beneath their skin their emotions are ours."

"Fear," the elder said solemnly, letting it roll of her tongue. "Fear has a way of fueling division, and is truly the evil on which our time is wasted fighting. The Deamhan are not our enemies – that honor belongs to fear." She pointed at the roots of the Tree of Life. "It pains me to say, but this tree belonged to her people when ours resided in Enatherr and it remembers her."

"Radviken had told me the same, but it feels odd to hear it from the lips of an elder. So it's true? We were the intruders on her realm?"

Erania nodded. "Do you not feel how the roots pulse harder when Clíodhna is near? It's as if they know her kind tended them before we. The Blossom will do the same in her presence because it yearns for her blood."

"The tree and Blossom will accept her rule, but I doubt our kind will understand as easily," Nastauria said.

"They never do. The Fainne are blind and deaf to the world around them, paying attention only to their stomachs when they rumble. As Fainne, we place too much emphasis on kings, gifting away too much dominance over our lives."

"Hopefully that will change. My prayer to the Spirit is that their eyes open to the dangers of placing too much trust in men like my father. Absolute power has corrupted him, and they should be wary of his outstretched hand."

"His time is drawing near," Erania promised with a tinge of regret mixed among the hope. "Only hardship will awaken their sleeping minds."

"That is exactly why I cannot wait for him to either succeed or fail in his current attempt to destroy the Deamhan. Since she has arrived on our doorstep, I fear he has already failed."

"I fear the same, child," the elder replied.

Nastauria placed a hand upon the roots and turned toward the elder. "If I do not have your support, may I at least count upon your help?"

The old woman sighed, then nodded. Stepping beside the princess she placed both hands on the pulsing veins feeding the tree. "Yes," she said with wonder, "they truly thrum for their mistress. They call out to her so strongly I find myself compelled to aid you – even if it goes against the urgings of my heart."

The shield above shimmered as the power feeding it waned. A few heartbeats later, and it dissipated completely.

Clíodhna watched with puzzlement as the shield over Fainnotheria wavered then disappeared. *Surely this is a trick,* she thought. As she hovered above the city, she focused on two women standing over the roots of the Tree of Life. *Nastauria,* she realized. She did not know the woman beside her, but recognized her as an elder – ancient in years and feeble. *She has allies in her scheme, so this is* certainly *a trap.* But she signaled her brood and they descended slowly, landing beside the two women. Her Deamhan fanned out but did not attack, hovering as the people of the city ran screaming for shelter.

"I expected we would meet again," Clíodhna said to the princess. "I'd hoped for it, actually. What I did not expect was for you to welcome your conquerors inside. Could it be that you are finally ready to die by my hand?"

Ignoring her threat, Nastauria asked, "You laid a trap for Betarian?"

"I did."

"We figured you might." She pointed to the cavern beneath the roots. "What you seek lies within. I offer it freely with only one request in return for my aid."

The Banshee Queen laughed. "You are a poor negotiator, my former friend. You offer something I can claim with my presence alone. The Kern are defeated, and you only have a light force of guardsmen. Besides," she added, "we are already inside the shield."

"You will grant me this boon," Nastauria insisted, "because I alone have the answers you seek."

"How do you know what I seek?"

"You recalled your Banshee from the Human Realm for a single reason – you had learned of the children's plan. Know these things."

The queen raised an eyebrow and waited.

"The young soldier aiding Alistaria is not your son, and they will bring the Blossom directly to you and will finally reunite our people. Now you wonder what happened to your true progeny. The truth is that two conspired against you on our birthing night, but I am the only one who can offer those answers."

"You will offer those answers willingly?"

"I will, along with the rose blossom you will find in the cavern beneath the tree."

"Then tell me," Clíodhna demanded.

"I will, but not here. Take the bloom – it is what you most desire – and I will go with you. Then you will have the truth you demand."

"Spoils offered seem too good to be true, but who am I to pass on a chance to have my Blossom *and* a chance to exact revenge on the one who brought me most harm." The queen immediately spun on her heels, hurrying to the chamber. Heedless of any trap waiting within, she skidded to a halt before the ring of glow stones. Her eyes grew wide with pity at the sad state of the withered vine and the single red blossom. A throat cleared from the corner of the room and she turned to find the collected Council of Elders watching her with fear.

"So it is true?" One of them asked. "You will lay claim to what's left of the Blossom and strip us of our power to tend the remainder of the Great Trees? They will surely pass from this realm, and we will all be left with nothing!"

"Fools," she answered with flashing anger. "Radviken did us all a service by stealing it away to his realm." With a gesture to the pathetic vine she added, "You proved to be poor stewards, and do not deserve to hold the power."

She examined what was left of the bush, carefully choosing the correct place to make the cut. *Here,* she thought, *where the bud meets the stalk there is a slight pulse.* With nimble fingers she snipped the blossom from the vine. Abruptly the stalk shriveled and died. With satisfaction she watched the blossom in her hand change as well. What once had been a delicate rose transformed into a ruby red gemstone.

Finally holding power over healing she waved to the collection of Fainne elders. Their eyes reflected the glow stone – faces gaunt with fear and shame over the lies they had told generations under the guise of history. They were now lost and without direction, just as their people will be.

She smiled at their plight – well deserved for the curse their ancestors imposed upon her kind – and walked with confidence from the chamber, ignoring the wails within. Once she emerged, she motioned for Nastauria to follow. "Come with me," she commanded, then leapt into the air. Her Banshees followed and so did the princess. With a fierce buzzing of wings they left Fainnotheria and returned to the Palace of the Deamhan.

Chapter Twenty

Nastauria will pay for her deception, though I shall not be the one to swing the fatal blow. She was my friend long ago, and who am I to go against nostalgia.
– Sorrow of Clíodhna

Restarian awoke with several men staring at him like a specimen. He recognized none of them and wondered which had been the soldier who had removed him from the cave. The sulky fellow sitting by the fire couldn't have done it, he was too old and slow. He was more focused on stoking the fire than the young Fainne bound and displayed. The man standing next to him seemed too eager to please the older human – waiting for the slightest indication he had a need that deserved his attention. He must be a domestic sworn to attend his master. His eyes returned to the old man and wondered, *Is this the mighty Radviken the Liar? The scourge of the Fainne?* He didn't look very kingly if he was.

The other man in the room was clad in black leather armor from head to foot. He was a menacing type – despite that his face was fully covered. He never spoke or uttered a sound. He also never shifted his weight – an odd behavior for someone wearing heavy armor. *Him.* It must have been him who captured Restarian – or someone like him.

"Searcher Cainnech, tell me again why you and two Storm Riders failed to bring them both?" The older man asked without averting his eyes from the fireplace.

Black leather replied, "He was an expert swordsman and took out both riders in my escort. I only grabbed the weakest in my haste."

Weakest? Restarian thought. *That must be me.*

"He must have been an expert indeed, to drop two riders when a Searcher was with them. I ask again why you failed to bring both? Did I not order you to capture all Fainne who crossed through the portal?"

"Only this one held the resonance, my liege. I could not confirm the other wasn't human."

He called him, my liege, *as in king. He* must *be Radviken the Vile,* Restarian decided.

"Bumbling fool," Radviken muttered. "If a human is traveling with a Fainne, then they are also a threat. Worse, they could be Deamhan and deserved further testing! Order the others to neutralize *all* threats. I can no longer afford one of *them* reaching the Blossom."

"Right away, Lord Radviken. My mistake is inexcusable, my lord."

"Yes, it most certainly is," the king replied. "Searcher Cainnech, you are on report, and unless you redeem yourself, I will be forced to demote you to Rider and you will lose access to my power. I only choose to share with my most *efficient* Riders, and not only my most loyal sycophants. *Ensure* you find him at once."

The attendant noticed Restarian watching and said, "He's awake, Lord Radviken."

"Bring me the sword he carried." The steward bowed and walked to a table, bending over a silvery blade laid upon a silken cloth. The old man turned from the fire and pointed the red-hot poker at the prince. Restarian watched it with wide eyes, suddenly aware that it glowed red hot from the coals. "You are long way from home, child," the king observed.

"I am not a child," the boy replied.

"No," the old king mused, "I suppose not. Your kind age differently than we. When I met Nastauria she was ancient by our standards, but young by yours."

Restarian flinched from the heat as the poker hovered near his face. Radviken seemed not to care if he burned him or not, and carelessly waved it around. The prince tried to pull away, but his bonds were too restrictive.

"This sword, child. I've seen it before. It belonged to King Betarian's son, Justarian, when I visited your realm. By its appearance with you, I assume two things. Either he is dead, or you are a thief."

The red-hot tip of the iron grazed Restarian's face and he let out a yelp.

Radviken insisted, "Answer me, child!"

Defiance growled from the boy's throat as he said, "I am not a child. I am a prince and you will address me appropriately!"

The man seemed puzzled, scrunching up his face as if in deep thought. Finally he nodded. Oh yes, you favor Justarian and must be Betarian's grandson. Justarian *is* your father?" A smile spread across the old king's face and he asked, "Or are you the child of Nastauria?" Turning to Nodrick he added, "Now that would be an interesting turn of events, if you were."

"Justarian was my father. We lost him to the Deamhan, so I'm the crown prince and I order you to release me at once."

The old man stood, still carrying the poker. "You are in no position to order me around, child. Also, it is ill advised to inform your kidnappers of your status. Before, you were a mere trespasser, and I would have considered allowing you to disapparate at the end of Tempest." He shrugged. "For I'm a benevolent ruler, and would have returned you to your realm."

Restarian felt ill, suddenly aware of his mistake. "And now?" He asked.

"Now, I am thinking of ways to drive pain through your grandfather's heart. That callous prig deserves to feel retribution for once." Radviken held the iron so close the skin on the boy's cheek turned warm and red.

Flinching from the heat and worried over Alistaria, the prince asked, "And if I had been the child of Nastauria?"

Radviken replaced the poker to the fireplace and took the sword from Nodrick, turning it over in his hands. "Then I would have killed you immediately. But since you've asked that question, I must assume her child made it to Enatherr. Where is the child now?"

Restarian's eyes flashed to the tip of the poker laying in the fire. It was iron, and even if it had not lain in the fire, it would have brought him much distress. Fear rushed in as his face pulsed with anticipation of its touch. *I cannot give her up,* he thought. *Not even if they torture me with that!* He shook his head and clamped his mouth shut. "I won't give you any information," he said, "not even if you torture me with that iron!"

Radviken turned his eyes to the fire and smiled at the poker. "Oh," he said with amusement, "you think I would torture you with that primitive tool? Though its metal would indeed cause you discomfort, I have something else in mind for the crown prince of Fainnotheria." Leaning in closely he whispered. "I don't need that tool to extract information. With the Blossom, I have powers that inflict much more pain than hot iron ever could."

A searing heat returned to the spot the poker had nearly touched the prince's face. Slowly it intensified, burning flesh without leaving a mark and crawling toward his eyes. When he cried out with agony it abruptly stopped – replaced by a burning cold that crept down his neck toward his chest. He shivered against a new kind of pain.

"Yes," said Radviken, "I can sense you understand what I mean. These methods are cruel but have purpose, I assure you. Shall we begin with Nastauria? Did she bear me a child?"

"No!" Restarian screamed. The pain had a mind of its own, by now, and sensed his lie. His entire body burned with intense heat as if he'd been dipped in hot coals."

"Did I forget to tell you that my magic can not only inflict pain, but also detect deceit? The pain comes from your own mind when you speak falsely. Tell the truth and the torment will sooth – replaced with pleasure." The old man pulled up a chair and sat before the prince. "We'll start simpler, "Did Nastauria give birth to a child?"

"Yes." The simple word brought great comfort to the prince, replacing the sensation of flames with one of comfort. Abruptly he felt as safe and cozy as in his mother's arms.

"Good. Where is that child now?"

"I don't know." It wasn't a lie, so the feeling remained. He caught his breath and swallowed, preparing his body for another round of agony.

"Did she travel with you through the portal?"

"No." It wasn't a lie. She had traveled with Torian. He relaxed his muscles. He would beat the wizard at his game. Lies were easy to avoid when you could tell half-truths.

"Is she in Enatherr?" The king asked.

"I don't know."

Radviken laughed. "Now you know how it works, so I will no longer teach you the rules. Was Nastauria's child a daughter or a son?"

"A daughter."

"Good. Why did she travel to Enatherr?"

Restarian hesitated. He could not avoid these new questions. They were open ended and leading. He resisted and chose to remain silent. Suddenly the pain gripped him differently, squeezing every fiber of tissue and causing him to gasp for air.

"Oh, yes," Radviken said, "there *is* one more rule I failed to mention. Failure to answer brings a different pain. Shall I ask the question again? Why did she travel to Enatherr?"

"To steal the Blossom," Restarian sputtered, and the pain ceased immediately.

"Yes..." Radviken trailed off, savoring the moment. "That is my favorite rule of them all." He licked his wrinkled lips, wetting them with anticipation.

"Who was with you in the cave?"

"Torian," The prince replied.

"Is Torian a Fainne?"

"Your Searcher tested him!" Restarian cried defiantly, the pain once again burning every nerve ending.

"Answer the question."

But he didn't know the answer and so he guessed. "No, he is not." The pain soothed immediately, so he assumed he'd spoken true.

"Who, then," the king asked with excitement, "is Torian's mother?"

The answer to this was now evident to him. "Clíodhna, Queen of the Deamhan."

The king leaned back in his chair with a grimace filling his face. "So she gave me a child as well," he muttered. "Now that you're cooperating, young prince, let's begin the real inquisition!"

The pain gripped Restarian without even a question asked. He closed his eyes and wished he wasn't always the weakest as the Storm Rider had said. But somehow that was always the case. When he opened his eyes, he told Radviken everything he knew and answered every question in stark detail.

CHAPTER TWENTY-ONE

I've yearned to reveal my secret to Alistaria, she deserves to know the truth about her mother.
– Lamentations of Nastauria

Alistaria awakened to shouting. It wasn't angry voices she heard, merely the vocal sounds of disapproval. It reminded her of the times she had watched the guardsmen train, and someone stepped wrongly. The entire squad would get a dressing down for one man, and the sergeant ensured he spoke loud enough to train the troops looking on as well. Blinking her eyes against artificial light, she found a woman with a round cheery face smiling down.

"Hello, dear," the woman said gently. "You've been through an awful lot and it's best to lie still. You'll be awfully sore, you will. Your fever's broken, but you need rest to recover."

She looked around, taking in the room and its lack of craftsmanship. A simple table with two chairs stood in the corner, and the rest of the furniture was boxy and bland without the intricate carvings of her home. The bed she lay upon was stiff – with a straw packed mattress that poked her side when she tried to roll.

"Where am I?" She asked, surprised to find her voice had turned raspy in her sleep. *A barn,* she remembered. She had fallen asleep in a barn. Memories suddenly flooded in and she also remembered the farm and the funeral pyres. *The Ganshees!* With alarm she felt the wounds all over her body. Her heart suddenly raced with an anxious desire to get on with her journey.

"Please, relax," the woman said sweetly. "You're safe at Tamee's boarding house. You're lucky Piotr and Boyd found you when they did. You might've died out there in the Tempest!"

The Tempest, Alistaria thought. *How many days of it remain? I must find it now or wait another cycle!* She tried to stand but found dizziness instead. Collapsing onto the bed she let out a groan. The shouting in the other room stopped just as suddenly. As her eyes refocused, three more faces appeared in the doorway.

"Aw, she's awake, then!" The woman standing in front of two young men was quite a bit older than the young woman at Alistaria's side, with sternly carved features that spoke with authority.

She must be Tamee, the girl reasoned.

"We're glad to have you among the living," she said, and when she spoke this time, Alistaria's thoughts were confirmed. Hers was the voice from the other room.

"I've got to be on my way," Alistaria tried to explain, holding her head against a spinning sensation despite her head lying still.

"Not in your condition, you won't be. Although these bumbling buffoons normally foul up everything they do, they did right by bringing you here." The two men at her side shied under her chiding, and stared at the ground like scorned children. "Really, Piotr, I figured at least *you'd* have more sense to get you boys inside during Tempest!"

The taller man – slender and lean with a patchy beard that showed signs of never filling out properly replied, "I tried, Miss Tamee, I really did. We were bedded in a tavern the first night, we were."

"In a tavern, eh, Boyd?" She eyed the shorter man with seething eyes that seemed to bore into his soul. "What happened, did you toss with the keeper's daughter and get you both thrown out?"

He was a silly sight then, shifting his stocky frame from foot to foot and nodding along. He wasn't ugly, Alistaria noticed, but he wasn't at all attractive. She found it odd that the young woman sitting beside her seemed to stare at him with adoration. Perhaps he was the standard of male beauty in the Human Realm.

"I never touched his daughter, ma'am!" He shifted his weight again nervously, "Or at least I don't think she was his daughter. I think she was the scullery wench..."

"Enough!" Tamee cut him off. "I don't care for the details." She turned to Piotr. "How often has that been happening?"

The taller man shrugged and said honestly, "Too many times to count, really."

"I can't help it!" Boyd cut in. "The women love me!"

The younger woman patted Alistaria's arm and handed her a steaming bowl of porridge. The Fainne's stomach immediately rumbled with hunger. "This will help give you strength," the woman said, but never took her eyes off the shorter, stockier of the two men. Alistaria noticed that she stared at him as if he had the same effect as the bowl of food did on her.

Tamee looked toward the woman staring longingly at Boyd and quickly sent her off. "That's enough Margaret! You can go upstairs with the others."

"Right away, mum!" The girl leapt to her feet and rushed from the room.

Tamee turned her attention once more to Boyd. "That behavior won't be tolerated around here, either. I've got several new girls and I can't have them wasting their time on you."

"Yes, mum."

"Now, why were *you* out in the storm young lady?"

Alistaria realized the woman called Tamee had refocused on her. "I have to get to..." She abruptly broke off, unsure what she should say. Caution echoed in her mind. *Never trust a human,* her mother's voice urged. *Their hearts are full of deceit.*

"Are you a criminal?" Tamee's voice was harsh but not unkind. "It's okay if you are, but I need to know now, if the Storm Riders will be knocking down my door to arrest you."

"Storm Riders?" Alistaria had never heard the term. "I've no quarrel with anyone. I'm not from around here."

Boyd's eyes lit up. "See! I told you she's a..."

"Enough of that!" Tamee said, cutting him off abruptly. "Dear, what is your name?"

"Alistaria."

"I am pleased to meet you, Alistaria. My name is Tamee, and these bumbling fools are Piotr and Boyd. That skinny young lady you met before is called Margaret, and she's the only one of my girls allowed around Boyd because I doubt he'd find her interesting." She leaned in as if confiding a secret, "I swear, they never get the real work done with him around."

Boyd tried to protest but Tamee cut him off with a harsh stare. Piotr, recognizing the look, hurried his friend from the room. After they had left, the woman continued.

"Those two are like sons to me. I raised them myself – foundlings both of them. They aim to be thieves, but are rather inept at the practice. They're loafers who always seek the easy path, but you'll find their hearts are pure and usually make the right decision when it comes to others. I know you're eager to be on your way, but you are truly weak. I ask only that you eat and build up your energy for the rest of your journey. Where is it, you're headed? We can point you in the right direction."

"Norgaard, ma'am."

"Well then, that *is* quite the journey. You won't make it alone during Tempest so you should stay the night. Those two will see you get to the capital city in one piece tomorrow. I'll trade them my wagon. It has proper walls and a roof to keep the storm off your head. I'll also find fresh horses to speed the trip."

"How long was I asleep? How many more days remain in Tempest?"

"They said you were out when they found you," she nodded. "They made the trip from Enat in a day and part of tonight. That makes three days and half a night of the storm have passed."

"Then I really must be going tonight." Alistaria tried to rise from the bed and once again found she hadn't the strength."

"It won't be tonight. Get some rest and let's talk again in the morning." With that the woman rose and left the room, shutting the door firmly behind her.

Alistaria rolled over and closed her eyes, accepting she would need her strength after all. She found that she could sleep some more, and soon found herself drifting off despite more loud voices from down the hall.

"You girls get back upstairs," Tamee said. "You'll be leaving Boyd alone!" After a few seconds of scurrying feet up the stairs, the boarding house fell silent and Alistaria drifted into slumber.

Chapter Twenty-Two

If she had given birth to a son, the curse would have broken and the Fainne would have fallen once more to the Deamhan. I confess I gave in to her incessant begging for one, and fell into her plan out of a simple desire for peace from her nagging. I never truly expected the seed to take hold.
— Confession of Radviken

Torian awoke, lying on the barn floor and shoulder stinging from the fall. He flexed his hand, trying it and pleased the damage wasn't serious. After flexing also his elbow, he knew his recovery would be swift. Looking around to find his bearings, he realized he had lost a full day. He had no way to know which of the cities he had seen was Norgaard, nor how to find the palace when he did find it.

A nearby grunt revealed that the troublesome beast had returned – quietly eating in his stall. Further inspection revealed his saddle sagged upside down, installed too loosely and the cause for the Fainne's pain. If he were to try again, he would have to cinch it tighter. Torian suddenly hated the animal. *I'd rather fly,* he mused.

By his calculation three days remained of the Tempest. It roared overhead. Through the open door flapping in the wind, he watched shingles ripped from rooftops and trees shaken between the buildings. These had been stripped of their leaves by the winds, naked and exposed to the ice pellets falling from the sky. Since sundown the temperatures had dropped significantly. The Tempest wind had turned icy, and it had formed a thin coating around most of their branches – weighing them heavily and threatening to tear them away from their life-giving trunks.

Just then, a human form appeared in the doorway, looming large in the opening and holding a chopping tool in his hand. Torian noticed the man walked with a limp and had been recently wounded. Rage filled his eyes and roared with his voice. "Who's breaking into my barn during Tempest?" Gripping the weapon he stood ready. "Show yourself!" He commanded.

Torian stood, slowly rising to his feet and drawing his sword. The newcomer blocked his escape, forcing him to face the man in combat. Setting into his stance the Fainne lied, "My animal was ill, and had to leave it outside of town. I needed another. I chose your barn as a place to rest, and meant your property no harm."

As the man's eyes adjusted to the lack of light, they focused on his black armor and swam with confusion. His eyes twitched to the cut leather along Torian's ribcage but only briefly. After a moment his face took on a look of shock and his trembling hand lowered and then dropped the tool to the ground. "I'm sorry, my lord! I had no idea you were a Storm Rider!"

Confusion clouded Torian's mind as he reasoned the man's behavior. He started to speak while the man nervously eyed the beast in the stall.

"He's terrified, my lord!" The man said of the animal. "Your mere presence has worked my horse into a lather, it has!" The man rushed to attend to the dangling saddle. We must let him rest. Please come be a guest in my home for the night! We can attend to him in the morning and see if he is well. Then I will gift him to you as you leave about your duties."

"I cannot impose," Torian said.

"I must insist," the man continued. "I cannot leave a Storm Rider to bed in my barn without offering him hospitality within! Please sir, my family would be honored."

The armor, Torian finally understood. *He believes me one of the men from the cave. I cannot accept this offer, not without risk of exposing the truth.* "I must be about my duties tonight," he insisted.

"Please, lord," the man begged. "We have a spare bed and stew on the stove."

Torian paused. Bedding and food in his belly were enticements he could not refuse. "Just for the night," he agreed. *But not an hour longer, or my hopes of catching up to Alistaria will be in vain.*

The stew was so delicious Torian devoured a second bowl. The owner of the home laughed and motioned for his wife to fill it a third time.

"Look, Jaana," he said with a smile, "someone likes your cooking!"

She shot her husband a wary glance and replied, "Careful, Markey, or you'll be cookin' for yourself."

Markey replied with a wink and raised his own bowl to his lips – slurping so eagerly it ran down his beard. "Actually," he said to Torian, "everything she touches is perfect. I love that woman!" Though the hour was late, his young son had joined them at the table.

The boy stared wide-eyed at their visitor, mouth agape and saying nothing throughout the meal. He finally found his voice and asked, "Are you one of them?"

"Hush, boy," Markey commanded. "Show some respect. Of course he's a Storm Rider!"

"That's not what I mean," the boy argued. Turning to Torian he asked, "Are you a Searcher?"

"So what if I was?" He replied.

The boy's eyes grew even wider – something Torian didn't believe possible. The child suddenly begged for answers to a flurry of questions. "What did you do to earn elevation? What does it feel like? How does the magic work?"

Suddenly regretting his response, Torian simply stared back in silence. He was saved by Markey. "That's enough of ya, child. Get off to bed!" The boy tried to argue, but Jaana quickly returned to usher him upstairs. Once they had left, Markey leaned forward and quietly asked, "How'd you get the armor, son? Did you find him dead along the side of the road, or what?"

"I... I don't know what you mean."

"You ain't no Storm Rider and we both know it."

Torian's eyes darted to his sword, hanging useless from a rack near the front door. "I never claimed to be. You said that I was, not I."

"That may be so," the man said, "but you never denied it as false."

"When did you know?"

"As soon as I laid eyes on my horse..."

Torian felt his gut twist upon itself.

"'Twasn't a Rider's rig," the man continued. "'Twas one of my own! Any true Rider would have salvaged his saddle and carried it off to find another mount if his own had gone lame." Markey explained. "Besides, 'twas obvious you've never even saddled a horse."

"You're wrong," Torian protested.

"By Shadow, boy! You didn't even fasten the bit or the reigns!"

"That's why you invited me indoors," Torian realized. "What will you do with me? Will you turn me in?"

"Turn you in?" Markey laughed. "Turn you in to whom? King Radviken? No, son, not yet. I want to know how you came across that armor." He leaned in closer, suddenly sinister. "How'd you come about it?"

"I killed the previous owner."

Markey abruptly slammed his fist on the table. "Truth, boy! Was he dead from the storm? Did you find it lying about?" Torian stood, causing the homeowner to also jump to his feet. In a flash the man's knife was drawn and the big man growled, "Whatever you're thinking, do it slow-like."

Torian lifted the chest piece just enough to reveal punctured leather across his armpit. "I stabbed him here. The other Rider I kicked off a cliff."

The man stared at the wound, but something in his eyes betrayed acceptance. He nodded his head toward the blade by the door. "Git your blade, boy. Don't unsheathe it, just place it on the table and sit down."

Torian complied, lifting it from its perch and setting it down carefully.

"Now, back up," Markey ordered.

Once he was clear, the man sheathed his knife and drew the sword, leaving the sheath on the table and marveling at the craftsmanship of the etchings on the hilt. "This blade is fae silver," he commented.

"Aye, but how do you know of it?"

"Because I was once a Rider, myself." His eyes narrowed as he asked, "Are you a fae, boy?"

Torian paused. *What would he do if I am?* Thinking also of his encounter with Clíodhna, he added, *But what if I'm not?"*

"Defend yourself!" The man shouted as the blade swung through the air. Torian ducked instinctively, responding by grabbing the sheath from the table. He parried a return stroke and jabbed with the metal tip, striking the man in the solar plexus and knocking him backward. The tiny kitchen was no place for a duel – and the sword should have been a great disadvantage in the tiny space – but Markey wielded it like a master.

Torian shoved hard against the table, shoving it into the man's legs and toppling him over. As Markey grabbed the nearest chair for balance, Torian brought the sheath across his hand to loosen hold on the sword. But the man pushed into the blow, shoving the table into the shorter man's stomach and winding him slightly. Torian staggered toward the cutting block and a knife Jaana had left behind. He grabbed it and spun, bracing for a blow.

Markey instead placed the sword on the table and sat. "Well, you have the instincts and training, so perhaps it's true you killed him."

Slightly out of breath, Torian asked, "You were testing me? Why?"

"No one has ever killed a Storm Rider except for me. I had to know if you could do it."

Torian raised an eyebrow. "And now? What do you think?"

"Well, since you're wearing the armor, I'll have to simply believe it for now," the older man replied. "But as for the fae sword... That means you must be sounded – checked for any fae blood." He drew out a small crystal from a chain around his neck and pointed to the knife in Torian's hand. "Prick some blood for me... just a wee bit will be fine."

The boy's hand shook as he held the kitchen knife above his palm. *What will he do when he discovers?* He wondered. But he complied, and in a flash the blade moved and revealed a small line of crimson.

Markey held the crystal above the wound and waited. Torian held his breath. After a while, nothing happened, and the large man returned the necklace over his head. "Your room is at the top of the stairs." He said. "Feel free to stay for breakfast. I'll ask any questions I have for you at that time."

"Why not now?" Torian asked.

"I have to think of the questions before I can ask them," Markey answered honestly.

Chapter Twenty-Three

*Her sorrowful wails should have heralded another queen,
but instead it was a son unblemished and harking a lift of the
curse. My confession is that I wish he had been stillborn like
the others. I find it interesting that Nastauria stole him away.*
— Confession of Radviken

After Tamee was certain the girl had fallen asleep, she gathered
Piotr and Boyd into the kitchen. Growing up in the boarding house,
they both understood this was the room in which she conducted her
most serious business. Piotr looked around, noticing how little had
changed in the few years they'd been traveling. He let the nostalgia
wash over him — it was good to be home, even if for a while.

The boarding house really *had* been home to them — despite the
goings on there weren't found in normal homes — and Tamee had
indeed been a mother to them both. Her stern manner was a front,
one that her many children and her working girls easily saw through.
She conducted her business fiercely, but her heart was purely gold.
She had held her children when they needed comforting throughout
the years, taught them how to be street smart so they would have
a chance at life, and raised them with a conscience — albeit a bit
skewed since she encouraged their thieving profession. If Piotr could
say one thing about Tamee and her boarding house, it was that she
loved her *little foundlings*, as she called them.

Standing with her in the kitchen brought back a certain memory
that stood out the most. That had been the day she sent them off
into the world to make their way — two young men with so much

potential that it overshadowed their lack of ambition. They didn't understand then – and Boyd might never – but it was finally clear to Piotr. They had grown too comfortable and dependent upon Tamee and her boarding house, and that threatened to prevent them from growing into responsible men. Four years in the world had done wonders for them both, and Piotr was ready to settle down and plant roots. He only worried how to tell Boyd.

"You were right," Tamee said to Boyd. "She's definitely a fae."

"I knew it!" The stout man explained.

"Wait," Piotr said, "I thought fae had golden eyes and gold-flaked skin. Also, where are her wings?"

"As far as the skin and wings, those only appear in their own realm. Here, she would appear human. As for the eyes, I've seen several fae with blue, green, even brown eyes like hers."

"So how do you know?"

"First off," Tamee said, "the cut of her clothing. Fae cloth has a different feel and look to it. They don't grow cotton or sheer wool like us, nor do they cultivate silk. She was certainly wearing flax, something we don't grow enough of to make cloth. Also, did you see that embroidery?" Both men nodded. "That was spider silk, something only the fae know how to spin. Of course," she added doubtfully, "I'd have to perform a dowsing to be sure."

"How do you know so much, Tamee? And why did you say you've seen several fae? How many have you met?" Boyd asked.

"Because I run a brothel," she said. "I'm the unofficial midwife in these here parts and I've delivered every baby in Crosston and several of the surrounding farms. I've seen every child in this region, and I've learned to recognize when one's a changeling."

 Piotr's ears perked. "What's a changeling?"

"A changeling is a fae child who's been swapped out with a human's. It doesn't have to be a fae, either. Sometimes the Luchorpán leave one of theirs, as well."

"Why would they abandon their children?" Boyd asked.

"Why do the magical folk abandon their children?" She asked. "Why does anyone?"

That was a question Piotr had often wondered, but about his human parents. Why had he been abandoned and left to be raised by a brothel madame? Why had Boyd? He knew that sometimes one of the girls in the boarding house fell into the family way, and Tamee cured their affliction with potions – something she despised doing at any cost, and always gave the girls the option of keeping the bairn. Most of the time she gave them drinks to prevent conception. To those who chose to keep their child, she gave them a dowry and sent them out to start their own lives. That was the last they had seen of Jaana and Markey – she was with child and he left his job as a bouncer to escort her up north after the incident.

But the neighbors and nearby farms often found themselves with unwanted children as well, and those were usually the foundlings left on Madame Tamee's doorstep. When he was younger, Piotr would imagine he was the son of a lord and a young lady, instead of a farmer, and that hopefully they would someday realize their mistake and seek him out. Of course, he grew out of that fancy as he grew older, and no one came bearing his landed titles and knighthood. As such, he settled into a life of bumbling thievery beside Boyd.

"Tamee," Piotr asked, "where is it she's headed?"

"She said to Norgaard, but that implies she's aiming to break into the lord's palace."

"Why in Radviken's name would she do that?" Boyd asked.

"The story we told at the tavern," Piotr realized. "Is it true that Radviken stole the fairy Blossom for his own?"

The woman nodded. "As I understand the legend, his magic once belonged to the fae."

"She wants to return it to her people, then." Boyd said, "Is that such a bad thing?"

Tamee lowered her tired body into a chair and pointed to a kettle. "Brew me some tea, and I'll tell you a different story. None of us lived at the time of the king's ascension, but the stories of when the

Shadow Realm walked Enatherr have survived three generations. My grandmother once told me a tale I believe will explain how he brought balance."

Radviken's story began a thousand years after King Octavian had broken neutrality to fight alongside the Luchorpán. After King Calug's betrayal of the humans, occupants of the Shadow Realm had crept into the land, ravaging all villages from Norgaard to Rivania. Only the Port of Enat offered safety from Draugar and Skinwalkers that roamed each night, and the bustling seaside town swelled with poverty as the northern towns evacuated. But even that respite failed, as creatures of the realm found their way into the surrounding forests.

King Rashmere reigned during this time, but was nothing more than a terrified child with regents and a strong witan vying for control over his kingdom. The future of the dynasty appeared tenuous to all, even the commoners who worked the land. Rumors of the end times flourished, filling the coffers of the priests who profited by warding off demons in every shadow. The boy monarch had no one he could trust and no friends except the few children of his servants.

Radviken was one of these. Before he ascended, the young man lived a simpler life as a squire to a pikeman. He had grown alongside Rashmere, and spent his childhood roaming the halls of the palace with the young king. When the royal family had been driven from Norgaard, Radviken's had followed, leaving behind their home and carrying memories of the green valleys and whitecapped mountains surrounding the capital. Caught up in the refugee flood southward, the boy king and the young squire conspired on ways they could drive the shadow from Enatherr and regain control over his kingdom.

Octavian's stories of the Fairy Realm had lived on through his writings – keepsakes that passed forgotten until the boys had rescued them from a dusty library in the palace of Norgaard. They brought these south and learned the secrets of traveling between the realms, uncovering also the secrets of monsters and creatures they would encounter. In the end, they decided to risk it all and try to steal the Bláth de Deamhan.

They journeyed northward into the forest until they found a fairy ring. Though circles of mushrooms are common, Octavian had written there would be a certain shimmer to the air when they approached an actual ring. *Look for the growth of blossoms nearby,* he had recorded, *especially daisies and irises that thrive even without direct sunlight.* They rested that night in the center with their backs to each other as they endured hours of circling foes.

The Draugars snapped their rotting teeth – growling and threatening, but could not enter the ring itself. The young men knew they must sleep to complete the passing, but sleep proved impossible with the threat of death all around. After several days their supply of water and rations ran out. Exhausted they remained in the ring, praying sleep would come and deliver them into the Fairy Realm. Eventually fatigue won over, and the boys awoke in the foreign land.

Each had suffered from the ill effects of traveling the portals, but Rashmere had fared far worse than the squire. The journey had proven too difficult for his delicate frame, and death clearly awaited the king. He selflessly bid his friend to continue without him, and removed his signet ring – thrusting it into his friend's hand.

"Take this," he urged. "Continue our quest and recover the Blossom. Only you can save our realm. My kingdom is to be yours."

But Radviken refused, and fashioned a litter for his friend. He dragged him for two days through the forest as he searched out the fairy city – finally realizing on the morning of the third that his friend and sovereign would surely succumb to death. Reluctantly, he placed the signet into his pocket and made preparations for burial. A voice in the forest gave him pause.

"You could have returned your friend through the portal," a dark man with velvety skin had said. He was a Síth, and master over the beasts. Alongside the specter hovered dozens of pixies who craved the flesh of the dying man. "But you chose to keep him here and so his soul is mine. Everything that dies in this forest belongs to me."

Radviken stood with his sword drawn and prepared to fight off the Síth. "He is a king, and you have no claim to his body," he argued.

"Since you were unfamiliar with our laws, I will allow you a boon in exchange for his soul. What is it you seek here, human?"

"I promised my lord I would find and take the Blossom de Deamhan. I demand you take me to the Deamhan so that I may recover the source of their power."

The Síth merely laughed. "You are ignorant in many things, but that request I can honor." He led the young man away, diverting his eyes as the pixies devoured his friend's flesh. "Come," he said to Radviken, "and meet the Queen of the Banshees, but you will not find any source of power residing with her."

Piotr interrupted the storytelling. "Tamee," he said. I thought King Calug had left the Blossom with the Deamhan. Why would the Síth tell Radviken he wouldn't find it there?"

The old woman smiled and patted his hand across the table. "You listened well, then. Lord Radviken shared your confusion all those years before. The Fainne were greedy and coveted power in every form. They had eventually found a way to trick their cousins and steal their relic – replacing the Blossom stolen by the Luchorpán. As punishment for conspiring with outsiders the Fainnen king marked them – turning them into the grotesque apparitions of the Banshees we see during Tempest."

Both Piotr and Boyd both nodded silently. They remembered well the apparitions flying around their cart during the journey to Crosston. The shorter man visibly shuddered against the memory.

"So he did not find the Blossom with the Banshees? The Síth had tricked him?"

"Yes, but Radviken was wise even when he was young. He quickly won over the queen with his wit and charm, learning from her the history of her people and how they became so marked."

"That must have been awful," Boyd remarked, "to live among such hideous creatures." He shuddered at the memory of their sharp teeth.

"Actually, the queen was quite fair. The Fainnen King had granted that she and her direct female line would always retain the beauty their people once possessed – as a reminder to them all of his dominance."

"So she was beautiful?" Piotr asked.

"Very much so."

"What did he do after learning the Fainne had claimed the Blossom?"

"He summoned the Síth and tricked him into helping him steal back the relic."

Boyd snickered, "How do you fool a Síth?" He asked.

"You offer a trade," Tamee explained. "The Síth require souls to retain their magic and longevity, and Lord Radviken offered his own upon one stipulation. He could claim it after the natural completion of his life. Only," she added, "as soon as he possessed the relic, Radviken knew he would hold power over his mortality. He retains his soul because the Síth is powerless to claim it."

Piotr nodded. "So he took him to the Fainne as promised?"

"Yes," she agreed. "And our king found the source of their power, and brought it to Enatherr. He sealed our realm from that of the shadow."

Piotr turned his eyes to the doorway, thinking of the sleeping fae in the guestroom. "Why haven't they tried to steal it back before now?"

"I don't know," Tamee said. "But we cannot let her succeed in her quest. You boys must pretend to aid her, but watch her closely instead. Learn her plans and interfere if you believe her successful. We cannot allow her to open Enatherr to the Shadow Realm. Despite my fondness for the fae, I'd rather not deal with Skinwalkers and demons far worse."

Boyd yawned and stood to stretch, indicating he was ready for bed. As if on to his cunning and intending to head off his defilement of her girls, Tamee stood as well. Steering him toward his room she warned, "I'll be sleeping with my door open across the hall from you, so I'll hear anything moving about. Also keep that mangy mutt with you, so it don't crap on my floors."

Piotr stifled a laugh as the two departed, leaving him behind with an empty mug. He stared at it wantonly, but decided it would be better to be up earlier than the fae girl. Instead of topping it off, he drew her journal from his satchel. The beautiful script called to him, drawing him toward the secrets revealed within. He yearned for more than he had already read.

The fae were real. He knew that now, despite a lifetime of believing, and knowledge had a way of changing perspective. To listen to Tamee's endless tales was one thing, but to find a girl wearing their clothing and bearing their silver was another. To find this book upon her person was convincing even without the other clues. He had to know more, so he opened the book and read a story about regret.

He had once assumed the journal contained the story of the girl, but quickly learned it was of another – a woman once beguiled and taken advantage of for her love. He slammed the book shut when he came across a single name… *Radviken*. His lord… his king… but his story from the viewpoint of the other realm?

Tamee had just warned them against helping her, but, if these pages were to be believed, it was crucial they recovered their Blossom. With trembling fingers he found the page upon which the name was written – and proceeded to read.

Part Three
The Blossom of the Fainne

(hapter (Twenty-four

*I learned of the boy's survival from the Síth. Such vile crea-
tures, they. What trade did Nastauria pay for his interference.*
– Sorrow of Clíodhna

Rough hands shook Restarian awake. Adjusting to his surround-
ings, the prince looked around wearily. The grueling day and night
had sapped his strength and the boy longed for rest. How long had
he been asleep? It felt like minutes though it must have been an
hour or more.

The guards pulled him to trembling feet and half dragged him
toward a tub. It steamed with scalding water and all Restarian could
do was laugh. *More burns?* He wondered. *What more can heat
do to torture my skin?* His nerves were numbed by the hours of
endured flame under Radviken's interrogation. He could handle a
bath – unless they planned to drown him, in which case he welcomed
the water.

No, he had decided he would rather die than go back to
Fainnotheria. How could he return to his people after telling their
secrets? How could he face Alistaria? He had freely given his captor
everything asked of him – the population of the Fainne, the troop
strength of the Kern, and how the healers tended the roots of the
great trees. What powers of theirs still lingered. Worse, he had also
revealed the location of every Fainnen Ring, helping Radviken determine where Alistaria might have emerged.

The gruff attendants stripped him of his clothing and lifted
him helplessly into the air. They dunked him harshly into the tub,

splashing water everywhere as they righted his mouth above the waterline – he was too weak to have attempted to do so himself. As he sat, he realized he had been wrong. He could still feel the heat of the bath, and his nerves had been heightened not numbed. Strangely, he found himself too apathetic to scream.

The water had been scented – he found that oddly pleasing – and lye soap sat on a stool nearby with which they expected him to scrub. *Why bother,* he wondered, *when I should simply submerge my head one final time, and wash away my sin against my kind.* But the guards did not allow even that mercy, as one of them grabbed the bar and rubbed it vigorously against his skin. It would welt in places – he knew but did not care.

Finally the second dunk came as a pair of hands thrust him beneath the surface wet his head. He did not try to breathe before, but he did this time. They pulled him choking and gasping above the surface, too soon before he could fill his lungs while under – a missed opportunity. They scrubbed his mane with such force he saw strands floating in the water. Another dunk and they pulled him free of the bath still dripping with lather. The drying was worse than the washing, as one had to hold him up while the other attacked his skin with rags – he had no more strength to stand much less help, so he yielded.

Torian would surely die because of him. Radviken had been displeased at the prospect of siring a child upon Clíodhna, although he found it amusing to learn Alistaria had been born to Nastauria. Despite his rough handling, he found a smile while thinking of Torian's demise – the spilling of Deamhan's blood would prove to dissuade future pretenders amongst the prince's people. How his father had tolerated his presence among them, he would never understand.

Once he had dried, the dressing proved less invasive. The undergarments were simple layers atop which his guards dropped a robe of regal worth. Deep purple in any realm depicted royalty, and Restarian wondered why he would be honored as such here. Their duty completed, the guards left him to rest upon a comfortable chair as they exited.

What would become of Alistaria? Surely this king would track her down with jealousy. No royal bastard should be allowed to live when the ruler himself had no heir. *I would do the same,* he considered, *if I had sired a child I did not wish to rule.* He would also discharge the life of Torian. *Why let the child of your enemy walk freely, when you can disrupt their legal accession?* Clíodhna had done the same to *his* family – by seeking out and killing his father to prevent him from inheriting the throne.

A thought struck the prince, and his eyes grew wide. *Why didn't she kill* me *when she had the chance?* She could have ended the line right there at the Fainnen Ring, but she chose to send him through. *Why does she wish him to follow Torian unless...?* He marveled at the possibility. Of course, she could be waiting for Restarian to return to their realm. He *would* cross over in nearly the exact location as her palace when Tempest waned. Why would she charge him with simply observing and following her son unless... *Unless she has doubts he is truly her son?*

Restarian sat up in his chair, suddenly pondering several thoughts at once. *My father's a schemer,* he knew, *and so is Aunt Nastauria.* Either one could have tricked Clíodhna – *would* have tricked her – given a thread of opportunity. Suddenly rejuvenated, he charted each possibility in his mind. *Two women,* he considered, *giving birth in the woods near the same time, yet both children raised by the Fainne.* What trick was pulled over the Banshee Queen? What would drive a woman to perpetual warfare against a stronger foe? Sure, she had numbers, but the fighting strength of the Kern was clearly more effective in battle.

The locked door to his quarters suddenly opened, and two young women entered. The taller of the two wore a flowing gown of scarlet that accentuated her long raven hair. The shorter had curly locks of wavy red that complimented her emerald dress. Both smiled as they entered and Restarian found energy to rise to his feet.

"Thank you, your highness, but there is no need to stand," the taller woman urged. "We are here to attend to you, and not the other way round." Placing a hand atop her heart she said, "My name is Clarise." Gesturing with an open palm to the shorter woman she added, "This is Niamh."

"Please to meet you, royal highness," the redhead said with a blushing curtsy.

Restarian stared at both women, unable to find the words to greet them. He had not expected such a warm reception after the ordeal of the night before. Though he stood, his legs grew weak once more and he fell into his chair. "I'm sorry," he muttered. "I'm not myself today."

Niamh placed a gentle hand on his shoulder while Clarise placed one on his arm. The redhead began to gently massage his neck muscles while the taller woman whispered, "We understand, your highness. Lord Radviken can be very..." she paused then added with a smile, "demanding on his subjects. But he has invited you to have breakfast on the patio, a rare invitation for which we have come to escort you."

The girl rubbing his neck had moved her hands downward from his neck and now pressed against the knots between his shoulder blades. She leaned in close as she did, and he breathed in her light scent. The closeness and her touch quickened his heart as she rubbed, relaxing and soothing away pain from the night before. After a while her tender fingers moved upward to his head, massaging his scalp and finishing by rubbing his ears. He leaned back into her hands and sighed, finally relaxing.

Niamh whispered flirtatiously, "This regal color suits you. Are you truly the king of the Fainne?"

Her question caused him to pause and consider his own future. If Radviken had dressed him so, and the young women sent to attend him believed him such, then the human king may have a plan that included the prince. With eyes closed against the euphoric touch of her fingertips he whispered truly, "Not yet."

King Betarian stirred. He had landed hard, but softer than he would have without the carnage left by the Deamhan. He would not have survived the fall down the stairs, save for the piled Kern bodies below. The calculated ambush caught his army unaware – cut down too easily. Several bodies had stacked atop his, and he pushed these aside to roll onto his knees. Pain surged through his body as he moved.

Part of his chest plate had bent from impact, and it bit into his ribcage and restricted his lungs. He fumbled with the woven flax ties and freed a gasping breath. The air soothed his lungs, filling them and restoring his vision as the room came into focus. The battle had truly ended, and the Deamhan had journeyed elsewhere. The entire palace echoed with the silence of their abandon.

Fainnotheria, he realized with regret. *Left alone and undefended, the vile creatures would have attacked with impunity.* But he knew as long as the shield held, his kingdom would survive their assault. If it failed, he would sooner die than return to face the destruction of his people. He knew he must return regardless. A stumble and a gasp for air told him he would not.

He pushed to his feet, but abruptly collapsed. His right ankle had apparently broken during the fall. Flashing pain in his wrist and shoulder announced he had other injuries as well. He fanned his wings to test those, and paled with realization when they failed. The radius bone to each had cracked cleanly, leaving them to dangle useless. He would not return home without healing, and each of his tenders were left behind during the attack.

He tried to regain his footing once more, willing himself to stand upon unsteady legs. Limping along, he made his way through the Banshees' nest. They had been a great people, once – not rats piled upon each other for warmth. He knew their unraveling had been the work of his ancestor, but felt nothing for them in the way of pity. All he could muster was contempt for their repulsive existence. If only he could have eradicated the vermin as planned – if only his ancestor had done so years before, instead of simply marking them as the savages they were.

An empty crystalline structure loomed before Clíodhna's throne. This was also the handiwork of Girtrán the Great. Exhausted he sat upon the throne to await the queen's arrival. He thought now of the story of Girtrán – not the false history told by the elders, but the true and actual history passed down by his father and eventually to his own children.

Girtrán zipped above the canopy, unseen by the Deamhan tending the forest below. Most would go about their duties without looking up, as the Fainne were no threat after the Great War. The rest would be in the palace, deep in their cups and awaiting the royal birth. He aimed to slip into the palace during the revelry and steal their precious relic for his own kind.

The boy had been present when King Calug turned on Octavian, stealing the Bláth de Fainne for his own people. The coalition between the human and Luchorpán kings had humiliated his father, and reduced their once mighty nation into groveling subjects – working at the will of their masters. The human king had not expected the move, and he found himself suddenly fighting two fronts in a war he had already won. As he fled into undignified retreat, Girtrán had watched as his father did nothing except hand over his sword to the Deamhann King – the boy had also hoped to find him drunken and vulnerable within the palace on this visit.

He landed atop the nearest spire, briefly admiring the view of lush forest below. The trees here were even larger than in Fainnotheria, a sure product of the longevity of the Bláth de Deamhan – it was as old as the realm itself. The palace itself was wondrous. The towering bastion of beauty had never aged despite standing for generations, and the gilded steeples reflected sunlight above the canopy of tree-tops – he aimed to topple these as well.

Girtrán would destroy their entire civilization once he had their Blossom – teaching them a lesson that would last generations. The hatred in his heart bled contempt for his enemies, yet he would not trample them completely underfoot. He knew exactly what he would do once he held their magic, and stealing their relic was only the beginning of his revenge. Once he brought it safely to Fainnotheria he would have enough power to challenge King Calug, and the Fainne would enjoy the power of both Blossoms as the Great Spirit had intended.

He crept down the twisting staircase into the great hall below. The magnificent splendor reflected golden stenciling and glowing statues that stood high over a central throne room. Thousands of Deamhan danced in the shimmering light reflected by the spires, completely unaware of the child entering their midst. As he descended the staircase, he passed by many guards – each set of eyes focused on the revelry and drunken on the excitement below. Those who did notice his arrival mistook him for one of their tenders returning from his chores.

The throne sat upon a dais before the Blossom. Upon it rested the king, drunken by fermented grapes – a gift from King Calug and a sign of his spreading corruption. The Bláth grew within a silver planter's pot, polished to a shine. The crystalline bush billowed out the top and spread leafy branches in all directions. From the center branched seven stalks, each adorned with a gem.

As Girtrán neared the Bláth, he recognized each one. In his people's possession they had been blooms. Some represented the spirit: a red rose for healing, the white lily of resurrection, and the green hydrangea of sight. Others reflected the elements. But he saw a garnet instead of the begonia of fire, an aquamarine in the place of the hyacinth for water, and a lapis replaced the starry aster of air. The sight that drew him in and brought excitement to his heart, however, was the onyx in place of the black iris. Reaching out a trembling hand he plucked it from its stem.

It flashed briefly to an iris but changed back into a gem as soon as it left the bush. Gripping it with excitement he quickly plucked the remaining stones. Each transformed briefly just as the first, but returned to their final form. In all he stood holding eight stones: a ruby, a pearl, the onyx, an emerald, a vivid garnet, aquamarine, a diamond, and a lapis. The bush now resembled an intricate ice sculpture left barren without its blooms. It's glow slowly faded.

One of the guards finally noticed his trespass and cried out with alert. "The Blossom is taken!" He shouted. The entire room turned its attention upon the thief.

Girtrán waved the pearl in the air and asked the Spirit to bestow sleep upon the turning heads. He had correctly chosen the white lily and deep slumber overtook the room.

"What is the meaning of this?" A groggy voice asked from the throne and the boy turned to face the king. "Wait," the king said with squinted eyes. "I know you. You do not belong here. You are a cursed Fainne!"

"And you are a vile Deamhan," the Fainnen prince accused. "For how many years have our people warred over these relics? For what purpose have we been forced to deal with the greed of the Deamhan?"

"Our greed?" The king asked. "Have you not been taught your own history, boy?"

"I know of your people's treachery, and how you've invaded our realm and cursed our prosperity."

"You have it wrong, child," the king explained. "Our people are the same. We trace the same ancestors to a division long before recent memories. Our forest had grown over populated, and two brothers agreed to peacefully split the empire. The first prince remained in Fainnotheria."

"My people," Girtrán argued.

"No. The Deamhan remained to tend the forest. Yours followed the prince through the Fainnen Ring into the realm of humans. There you tended roots grown from seeds of the Tree of Life. A great forest sprouted, until strife with the humans threatened your existence. Your people split once more."

"I don't believe you," the prince growled.

"Whether you do or not," the king said, "history cannot be changed – only rewritten by those who ignore the warnings of truth."

"Then explain how my people came to rule over Fainnotheria before the Great War!" The boy growled.

"By pushing mine out of the city with treachery!" The king spat as he rose to his feet. Completely sotted, he fell immediately upon his face – wine goblet tumbling toward Girtrán.

The boy gently nudged the vessel with his toe and approached the drunkard. Kneeling he whispered, "This day should be a great celebration for your kind, but I am here to spoil the hopes of your child's birth. The curse over your people begins when they awaken from this great slumber. I shall not kill you or your brood, rather, I shall corrupt your very being. He raised the onyx stone and waved it over the room, then searched the palace to find the queen.

He found her in the midst of childbirth. Her attendants knelt beside her, but with a wave of his pearl they slumbered like those in the hall. The woman on the bed stared up with fright as he entered, and pled for his mercy.

"My mercy is indeed yours, your highness, and that is why I am here – to bestow that mercy upon your child." With a broad grin he sat across her in the room and waited. "Please go about your birth," he commanded.

"I cannot birth alone. The child or I will surely die."

Girtrán waved his hand dismissively. "I assure you the child will not die if it is a princess," he promised. "If it is a daughter, I will provide healing when the time comes."

His words terrified the queen, but she found bearing to face him. "If you are here," she asked, staring down at her sleeping aides, "what of my husband and our people?"

"They slumber just like your attendants. They also have been marked by me, as the holder of the Blossom."

"So you took it, then?"

He nodded. "I did."

"How have they been marked?"

"You will know soon enough, but fear not," he vowed, "I will spare many of your offspring, but each generation originating from your womb will receive a different curse." The young prince smiled and said, "Your screams of childbirth shall be the language of your people, and your wails will also be theirs. I condemn all but your female descendants to this misery – to them I grant infinite beauty. You shall only have queens until such a time your people have suffered their penance. As such, all males in your line will die in the womb until the time to lift the curse has ended. When a king is finally born, he will herald hope, but only briefly."

The queen, not fully understanding his words, screamed as she pushed – eventually bringing a daughter into the realm. Girtrán rubbed the diamond over the forehead of the infant, bestowing the mercy he had promised.

He waved the onyx stone and pointed down at her maids – now transformed with greyish skin and a bulging bone structure. Their teeth grew needle sharp and orange with corruption.

The queen screamed agony into the room, suddenly aware of the plight of her people. But her screams subsided as Prince Girtrán handed over the child – beautiful and unmarred, since it was a girl. She looked down to find her attendants still asleep on the floor and wearing the corruption her people were now forced to wear. Her wails of pain and sorrow were the first sounds her child would hear.

King Betarian touched the crystalline structure that once held the eight blooms. His ancestor had returned with them and planted them beneath the Tree of Life – bleeding over them to provide life.

The Bláth de Deamhan had resprouted as the Blossom of the Fainne, and he had sealed the city within the shield. By the seventh day the Deamhan had awakened, and many destroyed their fellow creatures out of fear before they realized their curse. Thirty days later they had fallen into another slumber – all except the queen – and the Tempest emerged to destroy their half of the realm. Thus it has been ever since.

Betarian lifted his head. A clatter of claws upon the spire announced the arrival of the Deamhan on the high rooftop above, and he leaned back to await their arrival. He was dying, so there was no point fighting with any weapon except the truth.

Chapter Twenty-Five

*I hope to be forgiven once the truth has been discovered, but
no greater sin exists than to separate a mother from her child.
Who will remain to grant mercy once mine are revealed?*
– Lamentations of Nastauria

Alistaria stretched her muscles against the darkness, assuming
it was morning but unable to tell through the shuttered window.
Everything about her body hurt. Her neck and ribs were the worst,
but the ghostly pain of her missing wings rivaled that ache. How
long had she slept? Suddenly aware of fleeting time, she jumped from
the bed and searched for her clothing.

They were gone, replaced by a set of traveling breeches and a soft
tunic. Pulling them hurriedly on, she also found a pair of leather
footwear. Rubbing the sore pads of her tender feet, she marveled
how such a creation could be so comfortable despite restricting the
toes. Deciding they were far better than strips of cloth and tree bark,
she pulled these on as well.

The quiet of the house echoed with every step as she crept downstairs – intent on fleeing before the others awoke. That hope was
dashed the moment she reached the eating area. The woman called
Tamee was already there, dishing out helpings of eggs and sausage
to the two men from the night before. The shorter, stockier man was
shoving his face when she walked in, and grinned up at her with bits
of food in his beard and teeth.

"Well, look who's up, Piotr!" He announced with excitement,
food splattering as he talked.

The taller of the two picked at his eggs, something worrying his sad eyes as they stared at the plate. He looked up as well, and feigned a warm smile. Something indeed troubled him. With a polite wave he gestured to an empty chair as Tamee place a breakfast bowl on the table. "Please join us," he offered.

"I can't," she politely refused. "I must reach Norgaard before Tempest wanes."

Boyd nodded with a messy smile. "We'll get you there! Piotr and I, well we know that route like the back of our hands! We'll get you all the way to Radviken's palace if you want!"

She felt a slight rush at the mention of their ruler – her father – but quickly settled and hoped the others hadn't noticed. Keeping her voice calm, she asked, "If it's no bother, I'd appreciate if you'd point me in the right direction. I don't know where anything is."

Tamee walked by and placed a tender hand against the girl's back. "The boys will help you. Trust them," she said, "they're good boys and will serve you well."

Trust. The word caused Alistaria to cringe. She prayed silently the reaction wouldn't be mistaken for recoil against the woman's touch. *Trust no human,* her mother had warned on so many occasions. She turned toward the men and wondered, *Surely, these are good people. They brought me here when I was near death. They found help to nurse me to health.* Changing her mind, she nodded her agreement, "I'll gladly let them guide me," she said.

Boyd grinned ear to ear while Piotr laid his fork on the plate. "I'll ready the wagon," he said, and rose to his feet. Without looking back he pushed open the door and stepped out into the storm.

"Boyd?" Tamee asked gently. "What's eating Piotr?"

"I asked him the same thing." He replied taking another bite.

"Well, what did he say?" She pressed, impatiently waiting for him to chew.

Without bothering to chew *nor* swallow, he said, "That he read something he found didn't set well."

"Hmm," was all she replied.

Piotr drove the wagon while Boyd rode sword-side. Tamee had even found them both weapons to wear. One of her knacks had always been resourcefulness. No doubt some customers had forgotten purses from time to time, and she made them pay by leaving their steel as collateral. Boyd relished his cutlass – waving it about like a swashbuckler – while Piotr cursed his dagger. He never much cared for blades.

"I think it makes me look like a pirate," Boyd bragged, brandishing it about.

"Put it away before you stab yourself in the foot," Piotr snapped. He was in a dark mood and Boyd's behavior irritated him more than usual.

The book had indeed been a journal, one with secrets about two women – one of whom did several awful things to the other. She had done something else that troubled him deeply, something he found hard to sympathize with, despite her situation. He couldn't understand how any mother could give up her child. He did pity the girl in the back of the wagon, though. Looking over his shoulder he watched the girl staring out the back, eyes fixed on the disappearing sights of Crosston.

"Sorry," he told his friend. "I'm just cranky." In a whisper he added, "I don't like this."

Boyd nodded, sheathing the blade. "I know, but Tamee's right," he replied in a low voice. "Besides, we'd be rewarded handsomely."

Piotr nodded. It made sense turning the girl over to the palace. They *would* be rewarded, possibly given land and titles. *Sir Piotr* had a nice ring to it. Besides, it was Tamee's idea and not one of Boyd's hairbrained schemes. This *actually* had a chance to work. But after what he'd read during the night, he didn't see how they *couldn't* help the girl, no matter *what* she was up to.

"Something's different on the wind today," Piotr suddenly realized.

"Aye," Boyd agreed, looking around. "It's quieter."

The girl strained her ears to listen, obviously soaking up the howling and cracking trees. "It sounds awful to me," she admitted. "How can you say it's quieter? Is it waning?"

"No," Piotr replied. "It ain't that. It's just that they're not... there's no... wails this time."

"That's right!" Boyd exclaimed. "You think those Banshees really left?"

The girl sat upright, drawing her silver dagger from its sheath and turning to face the rear entrance. "Banshees?" She asked with slight panic, shivering as if her skin crawled.

"Yeah, they flew out of the trees and up into the sky yesterday." Boyd explained, "Liked to have scared our britches brown, they did!"

"I hate Banshees," she admitted. "They're horrible beasts and foul vermin!"

Piotr chuckled, "You act like you've met them."

Realizing she'd said too much, the girl clamped her mouth shut.

"It's okay," he said tenderly. "We know what you are, and it doesn't bother us."

She spun around with knife drawn and pointed at him. "What do you mean?" She asked with a mixture of fear and anger behind her eyes. "What exactly am I?"

"You're fae," Boyd said. "Tamee reasoned it out. That knife was a giveaway since everyone knows about your Deamhan silver."

Alistaria hissed and jabbed the blade in his direction. "I'm not a Deamhan, I'm Fainne!"

She doesn't know, he realized. Playing along he said, "Oh right, I'm sorry about that. I'm always switchin' you guys up in the legends."

"The Deamhan are despicable beasts," she spat. "They're uncivilized and disgusting! They'd sooner tear out your heart to feast than speak civil. All they do is shriek and wail."

"So the Deamhan really *are* the Banshees?" Piotr asked. "Tamee told us that your kind were the same, once. Until your king cursed them, that is."

"Same?" Her lip curled into a snarl. "We're nowhere near the same. And he didn't curse them; he revealed their true forms. Forced them to reveal the demons they are." After a pause she asked, "How do you even know about them or us?"

"We see the Banshees on every Tempest, so everyone believes in your realm. In fact, not a person in Enatherr lives that doesn't know the stories of your kind – or of your war with them. King Radviken spread many of the stories himself, to help spread his legend." Piotr tried to remain calm as he talked. If he spooked her, she would run off and they'd never have a chance to turn her over. "King Radviken even told us of your history, and what happened after King Octavius' war."

"So he's boastful, is he?" Her dark eyes grew sinister at mention of the king's name.

Piotr decided to press. "Are you here to steal the Blossom?"

"You can't steal what's already yours," she retorted. "He stole it from us, and it doesn't belong here."

"Well, I guess that's fair." He watched her face closely as he talked. "What will you do with it, if you take it back?"

"I'd defeat the Deamhan forever," she said through gritted teeth, sliding the knife into its sheath.

Too bad she doesn't know, Piotr decided. *I'll have to return the book to her.* That bit worried him, especially since she was just beginning to trust them. "I understand," he said, "but what about our world?"

"What do you mean?"

"You may not like King Radviken, but we do. He's our savior and lord. He claims he took your relic to save our realm from certain death. He claims the Blossom keeps the Shadow Realm locked away."

She appeared to consider Piotr's words. Finally she answered. "He's a liar," the girl said with hatred burning in her face. "He lusted for our power and took advantage of those who trusted him. He betrayed that trust, and I won't believe he wished to save his own world. Yours did fine for thousands of years before stealing our relic."

"Look, we'll help you get into the palace, if that's what you want. I'm just saying not to judge him based on his action without considering his reasons. Maybe when you meet him, he'll accept a compromise."

"Well," she said quietly, relaxing in the wagon. "He did show us mercy,"

"How so?" Boyd asked.

"He tore out the bush by the root, but left a single vine and the rose of healing," she admitted. "I never understood why he did that for us. If he was as evil as the elders claim, why did he take care to leave us with any power at all?"

"If he left you that boon," Piotr asked, "why didn't you heal yourself?"

"That power won't reach me in this realm. I can sense it from afar, but can't feel it in the roots or the ground."

"Maybe you have different powers in Enatherr," Boyd offered hopefully. "Lord Radviken can bestow his powers to anyone he wishes. It's common knowledge he gifts magic to the Searchers to do their work alongside the Storm Riders. Maybe *that* can reach you?"

Mention of the Riders caused Piotr to sit up straighter. The men were notorious bladesmen, and he and Boyd would be no match for them. As for the Searchers, they would take the girl without offering a reward.

"I doubt it," she replied.

"How *does* he use the power of it then?" Boyd asked. "If he stole it from you, how does he use it here and you can't?"

"He planted the blossoms, I guess," Alistaria replied. "Once he planted the bush in your realm and fed its growth with his own blood, he had dominance over it. He can either share it out, or keep control for himself. But I won't be able to feel it just because of my presence." She rubbed her finger. "The bush remembers his blood, that's why he has the power."

But the journal mentioned something about the Deamhan having ability to sense the power in the Human Realm, and there was even a story about Radviken's children sharing that power through his blood. Leaving that out, Piotr asked, "What if he dies?"

"He won't because he has the Lily of Resurrection. But even if he did, I'm hoping his offspring would inherit the power." She seemed to ponder on that, and Piotr watched as silent thoughts spun as wheels within her head.

She's hiding so much, he knew. *But so did her mother. This poor girl's so alone.*

Alistaria watched the men closely as they rode. She had already said too much, and her mother's words of caution echoed in her mind. *Never trust a human.* Or was that warning due only to her own experience with Radviken? What if humans were mostly good? These men seemed helpful – they *did* save her from certain death, and didn't seem to care that she was a Fainne. What if Nastauria had been wrong? What if her mother was simply a scorned lover who failed to see how truly benevolent he was? If these men were correct, he saved his entire world from the Shadow Realm.

The storm abruptly intensified, and several dead branches ripped from trees along the road. Piotr pulled back on the reigns and they stopped. She hurried to the front of the wagon to look out, terrified of what she may find in their path ahead. A large trunk lay across the road, blocking their way. She relaxed and drew a deep breath.

"It'll take some time to move it," Boyd suggested.

Piotr nodded his agreement. "Unhitch one of the horses while I dig under the trunk. We'll tie it off and drag it from the road."

As they rose from their bench, Alistaria felt a wet nose touch her arm. "Hello, Lucky," she said, reaching up to scratch behind his ears.

He whimpered a reply and closed his single eye as he pressed closer, nuzzling for either warmth or comfort.

"I have no choice but to trust them, do I?" She asked. "They seem like capable men able to aid in my quest. What do *you* think?"

He whined and then let out a snort that could have been a chuckle, but settled into her lap.

A sudden explosion of light in the distance caused them both to jump. Several seconds later, the sound of roaring thunder shook the valley as she stared at the clouds above. Tiny fingers of light branched out in all directions. It was only lightning, but she felt something odd in the storm. Just as she felt the roots she had tended in Fainnotheria, the air around her seemed to pulse with living essence. She shuddered against the eerie realization the Tempest was alive.

But what is it? She thought.

Chapter Twenty-Six

It was a simple act, the trading of a soul. To ease the conscience of your action you need only focus on the value of the trade.
– Journal of King Betarian

Torian was up early but Markey was already packed for a trip and waiting for him to come downstairs. He paused when he saw the older man was dressed in the same ebony armor as he. But, while his own was haphazardly worn, the true Rider bore his sharply and with dignified fitting. The Fainne suddenly felt awkward and unbefitting.

"So you really were?" He asked. "You were a rider of the storm?"

"A Storm Rider, and yes."

"Then why are you offering to help me?"

"I still haven't decided if I will, young Torian. I've only decided I'm not letting you out of my sight. You're not a fae, yet you carry a sword made entirely of Fainnen silver. I'll take you to Norgaard, and decide your fate along the way."

"I could run away," Torian declared.

"You could," the man agreed, "but I'd find you easily enough. My dowsing crystal already has a taste of your blood. It will track you for me and then I *would* clamp you in irons before the warden."

Torian fell silent. He did not trust Markey, but he needed the man's help. Three days of Tempest remained, and he was no closer to aiding Alistaria. *I don't even know how to find Norgaard, much less the palace without his help.* He nodded his agreement. "How does that work," he asked. "The crystal, I mean."

"I'm told it's a part of a relic once held by the Fainne. King Radviken blessed them with the power to identify Fainne whenever they cross into our realm."

"But it told you nothing of me?"

The Rider narrowed his eyes. "Should it have?"

Torian flinched. "Of course not," he lied. "But I was with one, why are you helping me instead of patrolling?"

"I've been asking myself the same question since I went off to bed. Originally, I had figured on enjoying a simple dinner with my wife since I was in town. But you're right, I *should* have arrested you immediately and brought you before the Storm Wardens for the crime of murder and interfering with public officials. They, in turn, would have turned you over to the Searchers and eventually King Radviken for trial."

"Why didn't you?"

"For the same reason my life was spared, long ago. It's rare to best a Rider in combat. The fact that you did makes you a very special case. No, I reckon I'll escort you to Norgaard but for a very different reason. But as to why I was home and not out patrolling during Tempest, well, that's a more difficult answer – one you've not earned." He pointed to a bowl on the table. "There's your breakfast. I recommend you eat up whether you're hungry or not. Fill your belly full. It's a hard ride north, especially for someone with no experience on horseback. We'll not stop to eat again until midday."

Torian nodded. He wasn't hungry, not with the overwhelming amount of nerves swimming in his gut, but he ate every bite. "How did you become a Rider?" He asked. "Were you always one?"

The big man started to answer but turned his attention to Jaana entering the kitchen. She shot her husband a look of caution as she pulled two sacks from a cupboard. He watched her for a moment, fondly taking in the beauty that a husband holds for his wife. "No," he said finally. "I had a different line of work once. I was employed by a boarding house and provided protection for the... residents. I grew up there, really, so I felt a kindred bond with each of them."

He shared a look with his wife and gave her a wink. "That is, until one captured my heart."

"Wasn't much of a fight, as I remember it," she replied.

"No, that was the only fight I ever lost, and mind you I entered many a scuffle. I was no more than a brute at times, beating men over non-payment and the like."

"But you also protected the residents and intervened on our behalf more than once," she reminded.

"Aye," he agreed. "That I did."

"One Tempest evening we were visited by a Storm Rider – a mean and nasty bloke. He roughed up some of Miss Tamee's girls pretty badly. He left without even paying for damages, claiming it was within his right as a Rider and to take it up with King Radviken."

"What did you do?" Torian asked.

"I followed him outside with an old blade Miss Tamee had laying around and challenged him there in the street. I thought we were alone, but they always ride in pairs and sometimes have a Searcher among them. On this night both his partner and the wizard emerged from the shadows to watch the fight – laughing at the young man challenging the trained swordsman."

"But you won?" Torian asked.

"Won?" Markey chuckled. "You can say that, but I call the outcome lucky. He whipped me solid with the sword, knocking mine from my hand early. He bid me to leave them be, chiding me as a welp not ready to take on a master."

"But you showed him," Jaana replied with a shy smile, remembering the night with pride for her husband.

"Aye," he said.

"What did you do?"

"I challenged him to put away the blade and take me on like a man – fist to fist. At first, he merely laughed, but he was an evil man with a dark heart and relished the opportunity."

"So what happened?"

"And so we fought in the street under a fierce Tempest. Our ruckus drew Banshees even, swooping down from the clouds to cackle at our brutality and Ganshees hungry for a meal. The man was a seasoned fighter for sure, but wasn't ready to take on a man who had made fighting a career from early on. I finally cracked his skull on the cobblestones, but it wasn't my intent – I was aiming to subdue him, but I was stronger and had the advantage when we grappled. I wasn't sorry I'd killed him, but I figured I'd be arrested by the others standing around."

"What did they do?"

"The other Rider did nothing except gather up his friend's armor and horse, leaving the corpse for the Ganshees. But the Searcher... He stepped right up and twisted my limbs within his magic, bound me so that I couldn't even talk."

"Did he arrest you?"

"Not at first. He tested me on the spot." Markey absent-mindedly touched the divining crystal hanging around his own neck when he recalled the memory. "He first thought I might be a fae, so he examined my blood to determine how I bested one of Radviken's warriors. After he was certain I had used no magic, he forced me to come with them. I stood before the Storm Warden and even the King himself."

"What did they do?"

"They were appalled by the Rider's actions. Apparently, he violated several of the King's laws and I was granted clemency – but with a price. They tested me further, thinking maybe I was a Deamhan instead. Satisfied I wasn't, they sent me home to get my affairs in order and to return before the next Tempest. That's when Jaana and I wed before moving north to Middleton from Crosston. She set up the household with a dowry from Tamee while I trained in Norgaard and joined the Storm Guard. Eventually I became a full Rider."

Pointing to the storm beyond the kitchen door Torian asked, "If you're one of them, why aren't you out in it then? Why aren't you..."

He paused, unsure how much the man knew and how much would be forgiven.

Markey cleared his throat and changed the subject, "I promised I'd have some questions for you by morning, so let's begin with the sword. Where did you obtain Fainnen silver?"

"It belonged to my traveling companion. A young... a young *man* I met in the mountains and escorted over the pass."

"Why were you out in the mountains?"

"I was hunting and lost track of time. Tempest caught me and I decided to hide in a cave until it passed," he lied. "I heard the boy's cries for help and guided him over the falls. It became so treacherous that we camped in another cave intending to stay until the storm passed. That was when the Riders attacked."

"And you – a man of Enatherr – fought back in self-defense against an agent of the king?"

"They gave me no choice. They did not identify themselves, but did not allow me to surrender. They attacked immediately without warning and I defended."

"Hmm," the man replied, nodding.

Torian squirmed in his chair. His lie would seem plausible, but was filled with too many holes. Also, he had recited it like it was practiced. Surely the man would see through the story – especially being a Storm Rider.

"Where did you get the sword?"

"The boy had given it to me as payment for assisting him over the pass. I didn't know it was fae, only that it was valuable, I swear."

"You're a terrible liar," the human said. "But, nonetheless, you bested more than one Rider two nights ago, and thus have few options."

Torian froze. *Two? How does he know about the second?* His eyes reached out for his sword still on the middle of the table where Markey had left it the night before. *How does he know?* And then he understood. The image of the second Rider's face came into recollection as he flailed his arms and toppled over the side. It was surely Markey.

"You knew it was me." Torian asked. "You're the man I kicked over the edge, aren't you?"

"Aye, 'tis me. But that changes nothing so let's be off."

"Why? So you can turn me in?"

Markey turned swiftly and barked, "No! So I can do for *you* what someone else did for *me* years ago. Killing a Rider is a capital crime worth hanging in Norgaard."

"Then why would I go with you?"

"It's a hanging crime, unless you take the place of the Rider you killed!" Markey said. "I'm taking you north to hand you to the Storm Warden, yes. But not as a captive, as an apprentice. It's the only choice you have."

"Why would you do that for me?"

"I'm not doing it for you," Markey snapped. "I'm doing it for Blayse. I owe it to his memory to elevate the man who bested him."

"But what if you're wrong?" Torian asked. "You dowsed me, and it determined I wasn't fae, but what if I was? How would you be honoring his memory then? The Storm Warden would surely know, and you'd be taking me to my death."

Markey waved his hand dismissively. "Dowsing's never wrong. Whatever you are, you certainly aren't Fainne."

Torian felt the blood leave his face. *The dream of Clíodhna,* he remembered. *What if I'm really not a Fainne?* He bit his lip and said nothing.

"Look, I don't know anything about you, but you not only bested me, you bested the greatest swordsman in the Realm. Blayse was next in line for Searcher, and he was captain of our regiment. Your showing up in *my* barn last night wasn't by chance – it was certainly fate, and I have to make a choice. I can either turn you in as the fae Radviken is looking for, or as the human who bested two Riders. Since you aren't a fae, then there's only this."

Torian thought again about Clíodhna's words in his dream – if it really *was* a dream. *She suggested I was her son,* he wondered. *But who, then, would be my father?* He paused with a question on his lips but unable to get the words out.

"Well?" Markey demanded. "Spit it out!"

But Torian couldn't, not this one. Instead, he asked himself. *I wonder if dowsing works on Deamhan?*

Markey grew tired of waiting and rose to his feet and kissed his wife goodbye. He nodded to the door and led Torian to the barn. Two horses were already saddled, and the man finished tying their rations to each. He pointed to the smaller of the two.

"You'll be ridin' Sally," he said. "She's a gentle mare, perfect for a beginner like you. Hold her reins to the right to turn that way, and left to go the other. Don't let go of them no matter what or she'll bolt like Racer did last night. Pull back when you want to slow or stop, and give her sides a gentle kick when you want to go."

"I figured out the kick," Torian muttered quietly.

"Yeah, I guessed that you had." Markey laughed but showed him how to climb onto Sally's back.

Once he was firmly seated, Torian found that horseback riding wasn't too difficult – although Sally was a much more docile beast than Racer. Markey led both horses into the storm and closed the barn doors securely behind them. Mounting his own, he turned the steed north. He led Torian at a trot as they rode out of town.

"How soon will we reach Norgaard?" Torian asked. "Is it far?"

"A days ride is all, but it will take all day to get out of Midlandis and we'll need to stop once to eat along the way. We'll briefly camp in the forest at mealtime."

"Why the forest?"

"There will be other Riders on the roads, and maybe a Searcher or two along the way. I aim to avoid them if I can."

"But you're a Rider. Won't they let us pass?"

Markey ignored the question and spurred his horse forward. Torian felt a sudden rush of anxiety as he did the same, focused completely on staying on its back. Soon they were riding north a steady gallop. They travelled for some time before veering west into a row of woods along the foothills. Once the nervousness atop the horse subsided, the young Fainne relaxed. At full gallop, the sensation was as close to flying as he had felt in several days.

Chapter Twenty-Seven

This trade I made was worthy, exchanging weakness for a stronger blow upon our enemies. For what use is passing on a dull blade? Strike when the edge is sharp and protect the newly forged.
– Journal of King Betarian

Restarian followed the two women into a banquet hall. A grand table was set with servants attending and spread with rich and luxurious foods, many of which the prince had never imagined. The aromas filled his nostrils and his stomach rumbled with anticipation as he realized it had been some time since he'd eaten. His suddenly weak muscles also reminded him as he nearly fell into the chair Niamh had pulled out. She chose the seat to his left for herself, and Clarise walked around the table to the far side, standing beside a comfortable chair placed at the head.

The woman with red hair softly touched his hand and smiled. She slid a small bowl of appetizers toward him and encouraged him to eat. "Our lord will be here soon, but you needn't stand when he arrives. You've been through much since your arrival, and he wishes to shower you with comforts befitting a future ruler."

He winced at mention of Radviken, and his skin suddenly surged with remembered heat. He shivered as the pain endured at the hands of her sadist king suddenly shot through his body – as if he really *could* have forgotten. With a trembling hand he reached for his fork. After dropping it to the table once or twice, he finally grasped it firmly and selected his first taste of human fare.

On the plate Niamh had offered he found a small gamebird wrapped in a fatty meat and drizzled with a mixture of honey sauce. His mouth salivated while awaiting its arrival. Once consumed, he was not disappointed. His tastebuds reacted with splendid acceptance, and he forced his body to remain composed as he ate – savoring each bite with pleasure.

Inside, he yearned to attack the feast with the exuberance of a Ganshee, but managed to maintain dignity as he ate. *I'm to become a king, and this is my first diplomatic dinner,* he reasoned. *But my true test of bearing will come when I face my captor in person after enduring his tortuous ministrations.* He did not have to wait long for that test. Radviken arrived with fanfare.

The man who strolled through the door had noticeably changed. He appeared healthier – younger even – than the night Restarian had first encountered him. He bounced with an energy of confidence and the servants bowed deeply as he approached the table. Clarise pulled out his chair and he sat. She joined him by choosing the seat on his right.

"Ah!" He said to the prince, "I see you've already discovered the bacon wrapped quail! Such a delicacy does not exist anywhere in the world except within this palace. Sadly, it will only be us who dine tonight, as my other guest seems to have already departed."

Radviken took his place at the head of the banquet and snapped two fingers to set the servants in motion. They scurried about their individual tasks – whether it was lifting a platter to their shoulder or bearing a flagon for the pour, they anticipated every desire of their master and his dinner guest. One paused beside Restarian and filled a crystal goblet with a golden liquid. The king lifted his own and offered a toast.

"To Fainnotherr!" He announced. "May splendors shine forever in your realm!"

The prince raised his glass and replied, "To Enatherr, may you survive after we've stolen back the Bláth de Fainne and returned it to Fainnotherr. He braced for the king's anger and downed the liquid, finding it sweet with a slight burn. It was an odd drink, but quite good. A waiting servant immediately refilled his goblet.

But Radviken did not lose his temper, rather he seemed quite amused. He roared with laughter and raised his glass against the air before downing the contents. His was promptly refilled as well.

"No doubt you are angry over your treatment last night," the king said. "I assure you the methods were not savory for me either. Rather they were a means to efficiently obtain the information I desired."

"And which I aptly provided," the prince retorted.

"Which you aptly provided." Radviken agreed. "So, tell me about my children. What are they like? Do they know of me?"

"Alistaria does, but Torian does not. He... I don't think he even knows he is the son of Clíodhna."

"But she knows and told you, I assume? I wouldn't have imagined Betarian would have allowed her male child to remain in his kingdom. Not with the corruption written all over his face. That awful man's a bigot, one who hates any race who isn't Fainne." He sipped his glass slowly, pondering a memory from long ago. "He hated me the moment I entered his city. He knew I was human by the way I walked... I never did learn how to use those silly wings properly. They were blasted awful, really. I always had a sideways cantor to my flight." He laughed again.

Restarian sat up, keenly aware that his mind had somehow been muddled by the drink. He stared down at the glass and remembered what Alistaria had said about the human habit of fermenting grapes. "What do you mean, wings?" He asked. "Surely you had no wings in Fainnotheria."

"I did indeed," the king replied with amusement. Everyone passing into your realm takes on your form entirely. I had the gold-flaked skin and your ears as well." He soured at the thought. "I hated those. Always in the way when I tried to sleep on my side. Needless to say, I took what I had come to find and returned with haste. Then I sealed the realm so your father couldn't follow with his Kern."

Thunder cracked so loudly outside that Restarian jumped. Stealing a glance at the window he said, "Except during Tempest."

"Except during Tempest," Radviken agreed. "The only time I must protect my realm is during Tempest. Any of your kind who visit must return upon its termination, and Deamhan can only appear in a ghostly form without the help of your people." He snickered. "And we all know there's no chance of that happening." Looking at the prince over his glass he narrowed his eyes and said seriously, "Until now."

"Until now," the prince muttered.

"How *did* my son and daughter even manage to meet up, much less travel together? Surely Betarian and Clíodhna haven't formed an alliance?"

"Surely not. Nastauria sent Torian along to aid Alistaria."

"But not you."

"No."

"Because you're too valuable?"

Restarian felt the truth drench his insecurities. It certainly wasn't due to his value, and he admitted such to Radviken. "Because I'm useless. I cannot fight because I was born a root tender."

The laugh came from deep inside Radviken, galling a nerve within the prince that had already been pricked by Nastauria's choice of Torian.

"The grandson of Betarian..." The king roared with glee. "Is a root tender? Come now, isn't this the richest?"

"Surely the root tenders have great purpose," Niamh said, coming to Restarian's aid. She touched his arm and smiled warmly. He only shook his head with shame.

"Heavens, no," Radviken said with laughter still edging his words. "Root tenders are weak in form and worthless as an army, especially against the stronger form of the Deamhan. Now, I'll grant this – their healing powers are unmatched in power. I'm sure Restarian can heal any bruise or cut you endure, but he will most certainly never aspire to Kern." He paused to chew on a thought before taking a melodramatic sip and smacking his lips. "Did your father ever achieve that rank? Last I saw him he was a mere sentry guarding the Skygate. You probably inherited your weakness from him."

It was too much to bear. Restarian dropped his diplomatic air and allowed emotion to rush in. He grabbed the knife from beside his plate and leapt onto the table – sprinting toward the king and sending the dishes flying in his wake. Niamh and Clarise screamed out their alarm and nearly fell from their seats in their scramble to safety.

But Radviken never flinched. He remained calmly composed in his chair while the prince approached him with speed. With the slightest wave of his hand, a gust of wind sent Restarian flying off to the floor. Abruptly the king curled a finger and the boy twisted and contorted on the ground.

"Do you feel that?" Radviken asked. "That is what I truly stole from your people – their power. You have none against me for I possess it all." He rose from his chair and calmly downed the remainder of his goblet while the prince stared up helplessly with eyes pleading mercy. "Go ahead and try to reconnect with the healing rose, root tender! Find even a fraction of power from your connection and try to wield it against me in whatever fashion you may choose. You will fail no matter what you try because I've severed any connection you had through the portal. It matters not that the blood of your father possesses the rose, because you cannot use it in my realm." He leaned in and whispered, "You're useless here, and so is your precious Alistaria. Nastauria was wise to send the brat named Torian, because at least he has a chance to wield his father's power through his blood. But I will find them both soon. And when I do there will no longer be any stain of my previous indiscretions in either world."

Restarian's vision swam as the light flickered out around him – eclipsed by the aura emitted by the wizard king. Blinded with Radviken's power, he heaved a heavy sob and passed out from the pain.

Restarian awakened with a gasp, struggling to catch his breath and blinking his eyes against darkness. *Surely, I've gone blind,* he thought, trying to calm his nerves enough to find reason. Eventually he found air to breathe and settled where he lie, staring at the ceiling and trying to process every thought that raced through his head. Slowly his sight adjusted and so did his rational mind.

If he had ever doubted the king's power, there was no longer any reason. The threat posed by Clíodhna paled when compared to this human, and he no longer considered her more than a nuisance – neither her nor her son. Time was running out and he must achieve what he came here for. He must aid Alistaria in her mission and steal the Blossom for their kind.

Surely, she's nearing the palace by now, he thought. How much time remained before Tempest waned and his father's Kern would have to wait another cycle for opportunity? *Not much,* he reasoned, *two days at most.* But nearing the palace was not the same as residing within its walls. It would be up to him to steal the bush and complete the mission. All he had to do was pluck the blossoms – no, they were gems in this world – and wait out the end of Tempest.

Before standing he flexed his muscles slowly, feeling for any damage to his body and found none. As intense as the pain had been, it was completely gone except for the ghostly burns that lingered. He may forever feel the scorching heat from Radviken's interrogation, and he trembled at the brief memory. *That power belongs to my kind,* he thought angrily. After he had returned the Bláth de Fainne to its rightful place, he would himself raise to Kern and return to destroy this pretender.

Placing both feet firmly on the ground, he tested his legs and found only the slightest wobble. Good, he was sturdy enough to try. Pushing up from the bed he stood upright, swaying but holding steady. The ill effects were of the fermented grapes, he realized, and hoped they'd wear off soon. He had consumed only a little, but the damage had clearly settled. He would have to work hard to keep his wits about him.

Carefully he crept toward the door to his room. Trying the handle he was shocked to find it wasn't locked. *He has no reason to fear me,* he realized. *I'm nothing to this man but a flea on a dog's neck.* Then another thought struck him. *Or am I the dog? Does he keep me as a pet or for some more sinister purpose?*

He pulled the handle and peered into the hallway, expecting to see guards but finding none. He remembered a little of the layout to the palace, enough to know his way to the throne room and the banquet hall. The Blossom, he knew, was in the private chamber just off the throne room. He shivered as his skin seared with ghostly heat as he imagined the inside of the chamber. He would never forget that room.

The entire palace, it turned out, was asleep. Here and there a few candles illuminated just enough of the hallway that he wouldn't stumble or bump into walls. *No doubt so the residents can find the privy at night, he thought.* Thinking of the privy made him realize he had not used even a chamber pot since the banquet. The fermented grapes protested inside his belly and he quickly searched one out. He found it near the end of the row of guest quarters.

It was a small room on the exterior wall of the castle – an afterthought by the builders, he realized. The structure rose the height of the brick with a similar construct on each level. Each would deposit their droppings down a vertical shaft to a pit below that workers would occasionally clear. He opened the door and found a smoothly carved wooden seat with a hole in the center. This rested above the shaft – only the best for the guests of Radviken.

He peered down as he did his business, staring at the darkness in the void. *Only a fool would think to attempt an escape that way,* he thought. It was too wide for one man to reach the other side to shinny, and he would certainly plummet to his death if he tried. Perhaps if he tied together the bedding? Wrinkling his nose he realized there were other reasons not to try. Frustrated and feeling just as trapped as before, he went about his task of finding the throne room and thus the private chamber.

He remembered it was several floors up and he ascended each step of the stairway cautiously. At every turn he expected to find guards, but thankfully had not encountered any – even outside the doors to the throne room. He never ran into servants either, since any that were up would be in the kitchens several floors below. Finding the room, the prince placed a shaking hand on the door handle and pressed.

During his first visit through the throne room, he hadn't taken time to notice the tapestries. They adorned every wall, each depicting a different scene of Enatherr's history. On one he viewed the Luchorpán King Calug carrying away a bush from the Fainne. *That's not right,* he thought. *Our history teaches this differently.* He paused to examine it carefully, but concluded that was indeed what it showed. Instead of stealing the Blossom from the Deamhan, he could clearly be seen taking the bush from beneath the roots of the Tree of Life – in Fainnotheria.

The other tapestries were interesting as well, clashing with what he knew of his own history. The Great Spirit was in one, bestowing three trees just as the legend was told. One went to the Luchorpán, another to mankind, and a third to the Deamhan. That was wrong as well, but the next panel was pure fantasy. It depicted a civil war between the Fainne, with the losing side crossing through a portal into the Human Realm.

His people, he realized, had pushed the humans – no more than hunters and gatherers – from around the Tree of Knowledge, and settled there to live. Around them the forest prospered, while the humans cut down their trees to build villages along the rivers.

The next series showed the rise of those villages into cities, with human armies joining with King Calug to drive what was clearly the Fainne from their realm and following them to Fainnotherr – pinning them between him and his human allies and their ancient enemies the Deamhan. He gasped when he realized his people bore a Blossom gifted to mankind from beneath the tree and through the portal. *That's why the king pursued them!* He realized. *We stole what was first given to the humans!*

With a gasp he finally understood what Calug had actually stolen from the Fainne. *The Luchorpán stole the gift given to the humans, not to us! Ours remained in the hands of the Deamhan. They must have taken us in after the war, treated us as refugees and reformed the alliance!*

The next panel confirmed his suspicion, as warfare resumed in the fae realm and the Deamhan were driven from Fainnotheria by the very refugees they had allowed within their walls. At one point they had stolen back the bush, but it was retrieved by a single man – *King Girtán the Great! My ancestor!* He left behind the stain of corruption that marked the Deamhan as Banshees. Restarian paused. Before the king had arrived the Deamhan had done something bold with the Blossom.

A mighty storm grew over their palace that crossed through the realms and into that of the humans. *The Tempest,* he realized. *They created the Tempest – but why? And why did my ancestor leave it to form over their palace every cycle?* His eyes furiously followed the pattern into the next panel. The reason was clear. The Tempest was what protected the fae realm from the encroaching Shadow. With the imbalance caused by the missing human Blossom, they had created a way to keep the evil from their world – thus protecting both them and the Fainne.

A sinking feeling entered his gut, and he thought about how his own people had erased this telling from the lessons given to their children. *We covered up our transgressions against the Deamhan,* he lamented. *They were never the aggressors, not one single time! According to this, we were!*

He kept following the chronicle around the room, viewing the Shadow Realm cross over unabated to attack the humans. That was when he clearly recognized Radviken cross into the fae realm with a king who would die upon exiting the portal. After the Ganshees claimed the regal body, Radviken had left to retrieve the bush. He searched both the Deamhan palace and finally Fainnotheria. *He is a hero to his people*, Restarian realized.

Anger abruptly swarmed the prince's heart. *No. None of this is true and all of it the vile lies of a tyrant!* Hatred for Clíodhna and her brood finally cleansed him from her lingering spell, and any compassion he felt for her was gone. *No wonder my father hates them all! Human and Deamhan are truly evil, and I will survive to restore our true history as I was taught.* He carefully pushed open the door to the private chamber.

Chapter Twenty-Eight

*For is motherhood not merely a title at all – worth
more as the actions instead of the act? I raised, taught,
and nurtured her without fail, so she is truly mine.*
– Lamentations of Nastauria

Alistaria felt the wagon veer off the road, suddenly bouncing as it left the cobblestones. The horses heaved them forward, trudging along as they made their way into the trees. Fear coursed her veins and she sat upright, straining to see what had caused them to leave the road. Turning back to the men riding up front she searched their faces for a reason for the detour. They stared straight ahead as if nothing alarming had forced the change.

"Why are we leaving the path?" She asked.

Piotr betrayed no concern as he replied, "'Tis a smugglers path up ahead and in the trees. I expect Riders along the road, and this is the best way to avoid them."

"Riders?"

Boyd nodded. "Storm Riders. Awful fellas, those are. Some are decent fellas, but we've seen some that aren't."

"Are they soldiers?"

"You might say that, but even the city guards and constables fear them. They work directly for Lord Radviken – do his bidding, so to speak," Piotr explained.

"Have you ever seen any?" She asked him.

"Once or twice. We saw some back in Port Enat before we happened along you."

"What would happen if they caught us?"

"Nothing to Boyd and me, but it's suspicious to be out during Tempest, so they usually stop those who are and rough 'em up a bit. They're searching for fae, though, so I want to avoid them on your account."

She felt her heart skip a beat. "They can detect my kind?"

He nodded. "They test your blood with a crystal."

Boyd nodded and held up his hand, making a slicing motion across the palm. "They make you bleed and then hold this necklace thing over it. Did it to me, twice."

"But not Piotr?"

"Nope, He's always the lucky one." The dog whined at its new name.

She shivered at the sudden chill on the air, and pulled Lucky closer in her lap. He snorted a brief protest but resettled quickly. "Can we fight back?" She asked with a shaky voice.

"I've only seen it done once," Piotr admitted. "Back in the day at Tamee's. Our friend, Markey, stood up to one who had his way with one of the women and refused to pay. He followed the Rider outside, and they fought in the street. He killed him, but not on purpose. Anger took him and he couldn't stop. That's when a Searcher tested his blood, and they took him away up north."

"That's awful," she said, shifting her weight and peering out the back of the wagon once more. "Did you ever see him again?"

"We did right before the next Tempest. He came home to fetch Jaana, then left for Midlandis. They decided to make him part of the Storm Guard within the palace. But Tamee said not to worry, that he would be fine." Piotr explained. "She almost found it amusing that they'd given him the option."

Boyd nodded. "She actually seemed worried before when they took him, but apparently all they did was test him over and over to ensure he wasn't fae. Satisfied, they offered him the job."

Not wanting to think about testing blood for Fainne, she changed the subject. "So tell me about this smuggler's path. Is it safe?"

"Sometimes you'll come across a constable or two, but those are usually the ones looking for a bribe," Piotr explained. "I've not tried it during Tempest, but it makes sense the constables would all be snuggled in their cozy homes for the storm."

"That's right," Boyd smiled. "'Twas my idea to leave the main road and try the path." Piotr seemed to flinch at his words. He suddenly appeared worried.

By the time they reached the trees, Alistaria had settled again. Even her nerves had calmed, but the lingering doubt in her mind echoed discomfort. *Why would two men take a young woman into the forest,* she worried. *Away from the main path and knowing she's a Fainne?* She was at their mercy, she knew – the mercy of two thieves. Two *bumbling* thieves, as Tamee had put it. What was it she had said about Piotr and Boyd? What was it that Piotr had said? *That none of Boyd's hairbrained schemes worked,* she remembered. A shiver ran down her spine as she understood Piotr's sudden worry over the path.

An explosion abruptly sent the horses rearing, as a tree fell across the road behind the cart. They took off on a dead sprint down the path, wagon wheels no longer hindered by the deep mud and finding solid bedrock in the grooves of the smuggler's road. The entire vehicle careened on two wheels then crashed hard on all four as they came out of a turn, nearly losing Boyd over the side. He clung to his seat for dear life.

Piotr fought to control the horses with the reins, pulling them back to slow and urging them to halt. "Whoa!" He commanded, but they would not listen. They were blinded by a fear fueled by the storm.

Alistaria looked upward at the clouds. The lightning trailed across the bottom of them now, as if it were following their progress. When it reached the spot directly overhead, it formed a perfect circle as if revealing their location. She marveled as it lingered, then recoiled with hands over her eyes as it exploded as a ball of light. Fully spooked, the horses reared once more – overturning the wagon and sending Boyd and Piotr sprawling into the woods. The girl clutched Lucky as she flew end over end within the wooden confinement, crashing into walls and roof until it finally settled where it landed.

She was certain she had died – the second time in this awful realm when she had nearly done so. Luckily, she had survived and without any serious injuries. She flexed her limbs to be sure, then ventured from the vehicle to find her companions. Lucky, also unharmed, trotted faithfully beside her. She scrambled to where she had last seen her companions.

She found Piotr kneeling over Boyd. He had fallen hard and broken bones in both his arm and his leg. The look on his face screamed agony.

"Tend to him," Piotr commanded. "I have to fetch the horses and re-hitch them to the wagon. The break in the leg is bad, and if we don't get him to Midlandis soon, he may never walk!"

She nodded her understanding and watched as the taller man scurried off to retrieve the animals. He wasn't wrong, the break in the upper leg was clean and the bone protruded through his trousers. What he didn't realize was that it had severed the artery supplying blood to his leg. If she couldn't heal him, Boyd would certainly die on the forest floor. She looked around for a source from which to draw power.

Nearby she spied a large mulberry with trailing roots branching outward beneath a thick trunk. Grabbing the man by the collar, she dragged him until they were close enough to touch the branching taps. Kneeling, she placed one hand on the tree and another on the man – hoping the Great Spirit would allow her to feel lifeforce in both. But the thrum in the root was gone, and all she felt was the weakening beat of the man's. She looked upward and prayed.

Another thunderclap rolled across the clouds, reaching like branches and raising the hair on her neck as it passed overhead. When it was directly overhead, she felt her skin crawl and chest palpitate. Her heart momentarily missed a beat as she gasped against the sensation. Frightened, she watched as it surged once more, bright fingers searching for something – perhaps even her. This time the channels were focused, the gap between narrowed and directly above. The energy above crackled and Alistaria recognized a pattern in the electricity. It was alive with a noticeable thrum and beating with its own lifeforce.

No, she thought, suddenly understanding. *It cannot be this easy!* The power that had once belonged to her kind had changed when it committed to the Human Realm, and this terrifying new form was as alive as the healing rose of home. When it flashed once more, she felt the blood within her heart respond – stirring and yearning to accept the power wielded by unseen forces. Radviken maybe? *No, he would send others to search them out.*

"Go," Boyd whispered, voice barely audible over the thunderclap. "Searchers are here."

"I can't leave you," she protested. But she could. She had no loyalty to this man nor his friend. She could save herself by fleeing into the woods.

"I'll be okay," the stout little man said with a feigned smile. But he would not. His wounds were grievous, and would kill him if she couldn't set the bones. Even without the magic of the Bloom she could do that much for the man.

With nervous fingers she felt his arm, feeling for the break. Finding it clean and not splintered, she picked up a thick branch laying nearby. "Bite down on this," she ordered. "There will be pain, and you cannot draw the Riders down on us with your scream."

Boyd nodded and did as she commanded. Smiling up with teeth tightly clenched he winked his approval and braced for the pain.

Relying upon healing knowledge learned and guided by the Fainnen Rose, she trusted her instincts. Just as the lifeforce would have once channeled through the roots to snap his bones into place, she both pushed and pulled the broken pieces to do the same – feeling the audible pop of success. Beneath her, the man on the ground screamed silently. Overhead, lightning left the clouds and struck the mulberry.

The explosion was deafening as the tree overhead split in two. Luckily it fell away from the pair laying amongst its roots, and the full energy of the blast channeled away. But it proved enough for Alistaria, confirming what she had realized before. The energy was alive and wielded somehow by hands that once bled on the Blossom of her kind. Her own blood responded to the energy with yearning.

The trunk beside her sizzled as the sap within turned to vapor. Charred and blackened, the bark smoked as it rendered heat toward the sky. The tree would perish quickly from its wounds, but she detected a distinct thrum within its core – not of its lifeforce, but of the energy of the bolt that split it in two. This thrummed and called toward her own. Placing one hand against the steaming bark she placed the other against the bone she had just set. She felt it respond immediately.

Boyd's eyes grew wide with shock as he felt his arm mend, and Alistaria shook her head slowly. "Lie back," she said. "I've much more work to do."

"I feel it," He replied with amazed wonder, speaking around the branch still between his teeth.

"Brace yourself," she commanded, feeling the shattered femur in his leg. It had snapped in two different places, crushed beneath the wagon when he fell. "This wound is much more serious," she explained. "I will have to draw upon more power and cannot set it first."

The man nodded his understanding, but she knew he did not fully. He would surely pass out from this pain, and death remained a possibility. She felt the trunk for the energy within, finding it dissipating rapidly. She would have to work quickly. With a deep breath she concentrated on drawing it all, sending it toward the wounds deep inside the skin beneath her fingers. It came with a rush.

The healing exploded from within Alistaria, but the power fueling the magic was not the tree itself. Her body surged as a conduit between the energy in the storm clouds drawing it down into the trunk and through her hands. She felt the femur snap into place.

Jagged edges of bone no longer scraped against the severed artery or the surrounding muscle, allowing the tissue to meld quickly on its own. Boyd roared with pain; his body wracked by convulsions that seized his body into rigor mortis – his muscles rigid throughout.

Overhead, the lightning formed a perfect circle directly over Alistaria and her ward. From the center, a steady stream of energy poured. The young girl had never felt so much power in her life, and the rush she felt was unmatched. She instantly yearned for more.

If I find the Blossom, she mused as she healed, *my kind could wield this magic against the Deamhan and finally drive them from existence.* Hatred for the Banshees crept into her thoughts and Boyd's skin turned bright red where she touched him. The branch fell from his mouth and he screamed in agony, begging her to stop. Realizing her task was completed and she was now doing harm, she released her grip and the power ceased pouring from the heavens. The lighted circle in the clouds remained – no longer glowing white but with a crimson hue the color of blood. Somehow, she immediately understood the Searchers had found her.

Piotr found the horses a half league from where they had bolted and left the wagon. Spooked, they were pressed together under a tree and shivering from the lightning overhead. He gathered their reins and stroked their long noses, speaking words of comfort in the most soothing voice he could muster under the circumstances. Inside he shared their terror and worried about his friend. He had left Boyd lying on the ground with the fae kneeling over him. Of course, she had no powers in this realm, so he wondered what little aid she could offer.

After a while the electricity overhead had focused on one spot in particular, no longer fanning out beneath the clouds. This calmed the animals, and he turned their heads and coaxed them forward. They resisted, but finally cooperated and followed him to the wagon.

Their eyes though – like his own – were fixed securely on the circle of energy above where the wagon had tipped.

The Searchers, he worried, *have found her!* He knew little of their ability to seek out the fae, only that their power was cloaked in the storm. *If they take her,* he thought, *then my problem is solved. We can return to Tamee's and enjoy the dry warmth of her boarding house while waiting out the remainder of Tempest.* He held back on the edge of the clearing, watching as three dark riders approached Boyd and the fae. *Take her,* he urged silently. *Take her and leave Boyd.*

To his horror three Riders leaned over and tested the blood of both Alistaria and Boyd. After a brief discussion, they bound only the girl and set her atop a spare mount – leading her away into the storm. His friend, he noticed, appeared to have suffered no injuries after all – or he had been healed. He jumped to his feet and brandished his cutlass, waving it about and challenging the Riders.

One of the newcomers stepped forward. With his own sword drawn, he quickly rendered Boyd's hands empty. With a heavy boot he kicked the thief's chest and sent him sprawling hard onto the ground. While he caught his breath, one of the trio stood over him.

"I'm not here for your kind," the Searcher growled. "Run now back to your king and tell him Radviken is coming for what is rightfully his." Turning with a flourish and explosion of light that caused both Piotr and Boyd to shield their eyes, the Riders were quickly mounted and suddenly off at full gallop.

Piotr waited until they had left before approaching his friend.

"Come on," he said, reaching out a hand.

"Come where?" Boyd asked, eyes fixated on the Riders growing small in the distance.

"Back to Crosston and Tamee. Let's leave this wild scheme to the Tempest, and start planning how to weather out the next one," he replied.

But Boyd shook his head. "No. That girl..."

"That *fae,*" Piotr corrected.

"That fae girl just saved my life," he agreed "and I'm fixin' to repay the favor."

"How will you do that?" Piotr asked his friend.

"We're thieves. I'll break into Radviken's palace and set her free. That is," he added, "after I help her steal back her flowers."

Piotr opened his mouth to protest, but instead touched his hand to the journal in his breast pocket. *Radviken* won't *be kind when he finds out she's his daughter, especially when he learns she's a Deamhan.* His friend was right. They would have to find a way to help her succeed.

Chapter Twenty-Nine

*In the end the frayed edges will be remembered, not the ends
I had bound. Hidden in plain sight and under my very nose, they
were my undoing. I confess I could have done more to stop them.*
— Confession of Radviken

Torian had finally found a comfortable rhythm with his horse
by midday. He was nowhere close to a master rider like Markey, but
Sally obeyed his rein commands and he had finally figured out the
perfect heel pressure to nudge her into a gallop. He also hadn't fallen
off, and that was a wonderful sign. Nonetheless, he was happy to
dismount for lunch.

Markey showed him how to loop the reins around a tree limb so
that the horse wouldn't bolt, but allowed him to easily remove them
if they had to leave in a hurry. Torian liked this man, but couldn't
explain why. Though also true that if he hadn't needed his help so
badly, he would have run off, hidden, and tried to find Norgaard
by himself. But the Storm Rider had been kind and compassionate
despite knowledge he had killed at least one of his comrades.

"Go ahead and light the fire, boy," the Rider commanded.

"With what?" Torian asked. Without fairy sparks he was unsure
how to create one, much less in the pouring rain.

Markey grunted and stepped under cover of a large branch.
Crouching down he pulled dry tinder from a satchel and placed it
on the ground. Digging under some leaves he came away with dry
sticks for kindling. These he piled atop the tinder and pulled out a

stone and piece of steel. After several strikes against the rock, sparks soon ignited the bundle.

"There, now hurry back with more dry kindling and some fallen branches that aren't too wet. Don't grab anything living or it won't burn well... Just recover whatever the pixies haven't cleaned up yet."

Torian nodded and hurried about his task. It felt good to be doing *something* of importance – he was beginning to feel that he would never find Alistaria in time. At least this gave him a sense of worth.

"You don't know much about horses nor outdoor survival, do you?" Markey asked.

"I really don't," Torian agreed.

"Didn't your father teach you?"

"I never had one," he replied. "I was raised in a nursery... an orphanage and only ever learned how to fight."

The Rider nodded what he thought was understanding, assuming he had meant with the other children and not as a sentry of the Skygate. "Children can be cruel, that I understand. Well you fight with some skill; I'll give you that. Not bad for growing up without sword lessons."

Torian noticed that look had returned to Markey's eyes, the same he had seen when he saw the badly saddled horse and when they had fought in the kitchen. What it meant he didn't know, but hoped it wasn't lingering mistrust. He tried to divert the subject.

"Well, you don't know what it's like to grow up an orphan, but thank you."

Markey laughed – not a chuckle but honest letting loose of sound. "Remember I said I grew up in a boarding house. I was a foundling, as Miss Tamee used to call me and the others. No idea who my mother and father were and with no other parent than she. But she took care of me all right. She taught me most of what I learned over the years."

"Oh," Torian said softly. "I didn't realize."

"No bother. I grew up and so did you." He slapped the boy on the back and stood to retrieve a pot. He filled it with water from a skin and set it to heat on the fire. To that he added some dried soup and handed Torian a hard piece of bread.

It was strangely inedible, he found. He placed it to his mouth and bit down, nearly breaking a tooth. This set Markey to more laughter.

"You really *don't* know much, do you? It's called hard tack. Wait for the soup to warm, then dip it in to let it soften before eating it."

Torian lowered his eyes with embarrassment. "Oh," he said. "I really didn't know."

"Well, I ain't judgin'. Just tryin' to figure out how much you actually *do* know, in case I need to depend on you for real out here." After a few minutes of sitting in silence, the soup had warmed, and Markey had divided it into two bowls. The tack rations melted just as he had said, and soon Torian's belly was full. "You go ahead and snuff the fire and load the horses. I'll walk down to the creek to wash the bowls."

"I can do that for you," The boy offered.

"Folly, that. Your greenhorn self would get lost trying to walk twenty steps back to camp. I'll go, you tend to the easy tasks."

Once he was alone, Torian turned his thoughts to fleeing on Sally. *I could do it,* he reasoned, *if I take both horses and leave him now.* Of course, he still didn't know his way, and time was running out. Instead he did as he was told and stood waiting with both reins in his hand for the Rider to return. It was like this – with his hands full – that rendered him unable to defend when the men emerged. There were two.

A blade rose immediately to Torian's neck, pressing him against the tree with his nose pointed upward so as not to have his throat sliced. Overhead the lightning flashed and revealed both men wore hooded cloaks exactly like his and Markey's.

"Where'd you get that armor and that horse?" One of the Riders pointed to the larger with the Rider's saddle. "Who's your escort and why did he leave you alone?"

When he didn't answer, the second Rider said to the first. "You reckon this is the one we're looking for? The one who killed a Rider last night and sent one missing?"

"If he is, then he's a Fainne. Get out your crystal and dowse him, I'll draw some blood."

The tip of the sword pressed into his throat, not enough to kill him, but enough that Torian feared it might. Without Alistaria to heal him, any serious wound here could wind up fatal. He felt the coolness of his warm blood trickled down the chilled skin of his neck as it ran toward his chest. The second man held the crystal aloft and frowned at the result.

"He's clean," he said. "Ain't no Fainne, that's for sure."

"Well, is he a Deamhan, then?" The first Rider drew Torian's silver sword from its sheath and held it aloft. "Only a fae would carry such a blade, or am I wrong?"

"Can't rightly tell. If he's not a full blooded fae, then the sounding may not be accurate." He shrugged. "Or could be he's a halfling."

"Or a changeling," the first Rider replied with a sneer. "Either way he's fair game to haul before Radviken. If he turns out to be the one who the king seeks, then it may just be us who're elevated to Searcher."

"Unhand the boy," Markey's voice boomed from the edge of camp.

"Well, look who we've got here," the second Rider said. "You've been reported missing, Markey O'Malley." His green teeth seemed to glow under the flashing lightning strikes. "Did you run off or join up with him after killing Blayse?"

"This is just a boy I'm escorting north on my way to Norgaard, Smythey. He's no concern of yours."

"Well too bad for you, because he's our prisoner now. We're turning him over to the Storm Warden to curry favor." Smythey said.

"On what grounds?" Markey asked.

Rider number one held the silver sword aloft, training it level to Markey's throat with his right hand, while his left held tip to Torian's throat. "Here's our grounds, mate. This sword alone is worth elevation to Searcher. But I think he turned you against Blayse. You stabbed him in the back, most likely, and this one promised his sword as payment for aiding his fae business. Or at least that's what I'm telling the Warden."

Markey said nothing, just stared intently at his fellow rider as if planning his move.

"Wait a minute," the first Rider suddenly said with a grin. "You already knew that didn't you? You're taking the boy in by yourself, no matter what you did to Blayse. You killed your partner, now you're turning on him and taking him in yourself."

"Easy now, Gother. I know what you're thinking, and there's no reason for us to fight over who gets the bounty or rewards. Just hand him over and no one else need be hurt tonight."

Gother grinned back at Markey, as if evaluating what he knew from the sparring grounds and sizing him up. Torian felt the pressure on his throat ease as the Rider's sword arm anticipated throwing up a parry. "You'll have to take him, Markey," he said with a snarl, "and there's two of us against you and a kid."

"Yes," Markey agreed, "a kid who killed Blayse."

Both Riders turned to Torian and gave him a quick sizing. Markey took advantage of their diverted attention and attacked with an upward cross that Gother was able to bat out of the way with the fae sword. Unfortunately, his body was turned awkwardly, and couldn't swing his strong arm in time to counter with his own. Torian shoved him off balance and darted out of the way of Smythey's attack from the side.

By then Markey had slipped behind both men and dragged his edge across Smythey's hamstring, dropping him to one knee as he bellowed out pain. Torian thought fast and dove at him from the side, knocking his sword free and grappling with the man on the forest floor. The Rider was stronger, but lacked the strength he would have had with two solid legs. In no time at all Torian was on top, with hands wrapped around his throat. A silver sword hit him with the flat against his temple, knocking him free and sending him sprawling to the dirt.

He looked up just as Markey managed to plunge the tip of his blade into Smythey's chest before placing his foot beside it and drawing it out. *He doesn't even flinch at killing,* Torian thought. The man had already rounded on the remaining Rider and stood ready for a two bladed attack. It came swiftly.

The smaller man swung both blades like a master, sending Markey into a furious retreat of blocks and jabbed parries. But he deflected each blow as he avoided the onslaught of arcing slices and chops. And then he suddenly wasn't where Gother had expected. At the last moment he ducked under a tree branch which the Rider hadn't seen. What should have been a killing blow stuck deep in the wet wood and stuck. While he tried to wrench it free, Markey swung from the side and struck the man solidly across the arm. Torian could hear the cracking of bones over the rumble of thunder.

Gother turned with fury in his eyes, lifting the silver blade and renewing his attack against Markey. With one arm dangling useless at his side he should have been slowed, but anger mixed with fear drove him forward.

"Grab it, boy!" Markey called to Torian, meaning the Rider's sword laying discarded in the leaves. He scrambled toward it, head swimming from his earlier blow. By the time he reached the blade, Gother had somehow gained the upper hand in the fight. He charged the man from the rear, forcing him to turn his attention and duck a swipe from over his shoulder. Thankfully, Markey had anticipated the move and jabbed his tip deep into the Rider's chest, opening his eyes wide with shock at the speed of the move. They left him lying in the leaves while the Ganshee descended to begin their feast.

"We have to go," Markey barked. "Gather those bowls while I fetch the horses. Hopefully they haven't run far."

Once they were mounted, Torian pulled alongside the Rider. "Thank you," he said, "for what you did back there – for what you're doing. But I can't let you continue to risk your life for me. You just killed two of your own Riders – people you knew! Please just point me in the right direction and I'll go on alone."

"That's not possible now," the man replied with only slight unsteadiness to his voice. "Now I *have* to hand you over to the Warden."

"Just get me to the palace and I'll find my own way in. There's something I must do."

Markey wheeled in the saddle, causing Racer to shift his weight and snort. "That's not an option for you. Like it or not, you've only got two choices now. You can follow me to the palace and apprentice to the Riders or hang from this tree! But the first option fulfills my vow and helps you with whatever it is you Deamhan are planning."

"Deamhan?" Torian felt his skin crawl as he froze in place. "Why did you say that?"

"Because that's what I think you are. That's the *only* reason Radviken would send out an entire legion of Riders to find three fae. At least one of you has to be Deamhan."

"Why would he be more afraid of Deamhan?"

"I overheard Blayse and the Searcher Cainnech talking before we jumped you in the cave. In our realm, Deamhan can use his magic because his relic once belonged to them."

Torian suddenly understood why Nastauria sent him along with Alistaria. She *knew* Clíodhna was his mother. *Of course she knew! Clíodhna said she had stolen her son!* But one detail continued to trouble him. *If I'm Deamhan, why don't I look like the rest of the Banshees?* Turning to Markey he asked, "What if I was sent here to kill Radviken?"

"You weren't. No, you're after the source of his magic, that Blossom thing."

"And that wouldn't trouble you?"

"I don't give two damns about his magic! My only worry is to keep my head on its shoulders and food in Jaana's and my boy's bellies. Now gather the bowls while I fetch the horses!"

"When," Torian asked, "did you doubt my story and begin to think I'm a Deamhan?"

"The moment you said you were out hunting, but then didn't even know how to start a fire. But the silver sword was a dead giveaway that, if you aren't Fainne, then you're a Deamhan."

"Why do you keep saying I am? I'm not!"

"I assumed you and your friend travelled together. A Deamhan can't cross through the portal without a Fainne, and as useless as he was, I figured you dragged him along."

"And it doesn't bother you if I am?"

"I personally don't care if you are or aren't. Besides, you wouldn't be the first Deamhan to cross over and hide amongst us – or become a Rider."

"How do you know?"

"Because I know of another, but since he was half human, he slipped past both the Searchers *and* the Warden. I don't know what would happen if you're full blooded. But you don't look like the other Banshees, so I'm guessing you're half."

Torian let the man's words sink in. He had no intention of staying on and apprenticing as a Storm Rider in Blayse's stead, but the man's plan could get him inside the palace. Markey spurred Racer forward, and he nudged Sally to follow. *Even if I find Alistaria, will she want help from a Deamhan?* She hated them as much as he.

CHAPTER THIRTY

I waited until her son was born, mesmerized how such beauty was born despite her curse. I bade her to sleep, then, and she did. I approached in order to steal the child, my own grasped tightly in my arms. I never expected what came next, as her second child began to arrive. What I did next is my greatest lamentation.
— Lamentations of Nastauria

Alistaria eyed the aquamarine stone on the pommel of the Searcher's sword. The light blue reminded her of water as she stared, wishing for blue skies to return and the sun to reflect off the raging river to her right. It would have been a beautiful sight at any other time, but Tempest raged above – washing the world with a greyish hue that almost made her forget color existed. *How much time remains?* She wondered. *One? Two days?* She thought it was two.

At least her captors were taking her north to the palace, even if she had already grown tired of their company – actually missing that of Piotr, Boyd, and Lucky. Though she didn't trust any of the humans, at least they had provided conversation and, especially in the dog's case, a little bit of friendship. These others were hard men with set jaws and eyes that had seen violence. The only hint of humanity from any of them had been their excitement over turning her over to a man they called Storm Warden.

"One of us will be elevated," one of the Riders said to the other. "What do you think, Searcher Cainnech? Will you present us for elevation?"

"Cease your foolery!" The Searcher commanded. "It was I who found her, just as I found the boy Fainne. Neither of you are worthy for elevation, not like the swordsman killed during the first night of Tempest. Each of you were useless except to lift her atop the horse. It is I who shall receive a second power from our master." The Riders immediately stopped their musings, and remained quiet for much of their journey.

Boy Fainne? Suddenly worried, she considered her friends. *Could it be that Torian has already been captured?* She had seen Restarian push him into the ring just before the flash of light as she travelled.

"Do I hear correctly," she asked, "that a Fainne swordsman defeated one of your Riders? How is that possible with you there to empower them. It seems Radviken would have elevated you for capturing my friend – had you not lost one of his swordsmen."

"Friend..." The Searcher chuckled at the word, testing it out once more. "Friend? You call your sworn enemy your friend? Surely, he aided you to travel and nothing more. As for Lord Radviken's displeasure, that was over the quality of my find. The Fainne boy was weak and worthless as a fighter. He merely cowered in the corner while the true fighter defended him. No, Betarian's son surely does not take after his father."

Betarian's son? Understanding twisted her gut as she realized Restarian had been the one captured. Swallowing her fear she tried to cloak her worry in the bearing of her mother. "What of the warrior? Did he prove too powerful for you to capture? Is that why you were sent back into the Tempest? Radviken wants the true threat captured, and not the prince?"

"True threat..." The man's voice rang with amusement as he laughed off her chides. "The only true threat in our realm on this night is you Deamhan."

The air suddenly gasped from her lungs and she swayed in the saddle. "What do you mean, by calling me a Deamhan? Do I *look* like a Banshee?"

"No, but neither did the warrior who defended the prince. But the Storm Warden will figure out how you're disguised in our realm."

"I'm curious," she said, "how you come to believe I'm a Deamhan."

His laughter was joined by the two Riders, this time. He refused to answer.

"Furthermore, how did you find me? Since I'm in your custody, what harm is there in telling me these things?"

"Be silent," the Searcher insisted. "I do not reveal my ways."

"Or you don't know how it works," she said, "and are only following the power truly owned by Radviken."

The man wheeled in anger – proving she was right in assuming his arrogance was his weakness. "Finding the Fainne is easy, as their stench travels miles. Even the lowest Storm Rider recruit could have found the prince," he admitted. "But finding you... Oh you were so stupid to channel the lord's power from the storm. The heavens revealed your whereabouts, if you must know." He pointed upward and she lifted her eyes. Bolts of lightning flashed from his fingertip and joined the clouds, fanning out in every direction. "I had already detected your presence using my power over the water in the storm clouds. But I located your precise position when you were stupid enough to draw your Deamhan magic through the Tempest!"

"I am not a Deamhan!" She screamed! "I hate the Deamhan! They are what is wrong with our realm! Their corruption is vile, nearly as grotesque as your king! No one compares me to them, for I am their opposite! My existence represents harmony and balance in the forest. I *am* a Fainne!"

Searcher Cainnech smiled broadly. "No, stupid girl." He drew a chain necklace with a dangling crystal from his armor and held it for her to see. "You most certainly are *not* a Fainne, and only a Banshee can draw healing power from the Tempest your kind created!"

King Betarian sat atop the throne and waited. The heavy flapping of Deamhan wings caused his heart to beat faster, aware he would be trapped alone with the brood, but no longer caring if he died – as long as he took her with him. He sheathed the sword in his hand and drew instead a silver dagger that he hid within his sleeve. It was much more appropriate for the task ahead, as he would not last long in a fight against them – but he could assassinate their queen with ease.

He watched the vermin descend the staircases, the host assembling in the great hall and curling upon each other like animals in a den – huddled for warmth and protection. He was so close he could smell the corruption on their skin and winced against the putrid aroma. Luckily, none had yet noticed him where he sat. His hand absently felt the sharpness of his blade, savoring the edge and careful not to spill the wrong sort of blood.

Voices and more wings turned his eyes upward and he watched as two women landed. The first was clearly Clíodhna – a vixen cloaked in the same beauty once worn by her mother. In her hand she held a red ruby, turning it over in her hands and eyeing it carefully. When she finally held it to the light, Betarian felt his stomach sink and bile rise into his mouth. Swallowing hard he understood she held the last bloom of the Bláth de Fainne.

How? He questioned. *How would she have entered Fainnotheria?* Of course he knew the answer lay in the slain forms of his soldiers scattered throughout her palace. The Kern had not been there to protect against her onslaught. *But even then,* he wondered, *how did she breach the shield without help?*

He did not have to wait long to learn of his daughter's treachery. She emerged from behind the Banshee Queen and followed her down the descending stairs with an air of nonchalance.

"How will you use it, now that it is yours?" Nastauria asked.

"I will repair my realm, and journey to his to retrieve the rest of what belongs to my kind," Clíodhna replied. "I'm assuming you will aid me to cross the portal if your daughter fails?"

"I am certain Alistaria will succeed in retrieving what was once and now again is yours," the traitor said. "The survival of both our people hinges on her, as King Girtrán promised."

The queen wheeled on her guest, staring her down with eyes that warned caution. "The *redemption* of my people depends upon my son, the herald of a new age. Stealing him from my birthing bed did not prevent the collapse of yours, Nastauria. Tell me why I've allowed you to live?"

"Your son did indeed survive as Girtrán promised a king finally would. But his birth was not the herald of a new age, Clíodhna. His birth heralded the redemption of both our people. Fainne and Deamhan will once again unite under the birth of Alistaria."

Betarian froze, suddenly aware that his daughter's treachery was not new, but indeed began in her childhood. He recalled the first time he had caught them conspiring in the forest – meeting secretly as friends and neither caring about the vast differences between their kind. He had demanded immediate audience with Rhíodhna, the Banshee Queen at the time and this one's mother. Together they agreed on one accord and finally put a stop to their rendezvous. But it was apparently too late – the corruption had blinded Nastauria to nature of their enemy.

He waited until the two women walked into view of the throne before speaking. "Fools!" He growled. "You both play at fanciful games, just as you did as children."

"Father," Nastauria began, trying to say more but cut off by his rage.

"Enough!" He roared, causing the drowsy Deamhan to stir and begin to rise.

Clíodhna hissed and turned to her warriors. "Finish this old man," she commanded, "and ease my ears from his insolence." To him she added, "How dare you sit upon my throne and command me in my house?"

"You will stay your warriors," he said with a laugh. "For I know more about your son than Nastauria."

Both women paused and the Banshee Queen raised her hand. The soldiers held off, pacing anxiously, and grinding their teeth as they waited for her to change her mind.

To Nastauria he asked, "What have you told her about that day you birthed Alistaria?"

"Only what she says now," Clíodhna admitted with a hiss. "That my son was born first before her daughter. She believes him to have heralded her own spawn of Radviken. But I know he wasn't left stillborn on the forest floor as Síth Morkur claimed. That was a lie conspired by the lot of you."

"That's not what I claim…" Nastauria tried to speak once more, but was cut off again, this time by the queen.

"I know it's a lie because the Síth later told me the truth," she said. "You lurked in the forest as I birthed, watching and waiting to see if he was born alive or dead. He was a tiresome birth, but I held him in my hands and felt his heart beat and his tiny breath upon my face. The first living boy born to a Deamhann queen since Girtrán, and as beautiful as the line of royal women had been before him. My son was free of both curse and defect."

"That part is true," Nastauria agreed. "I watched from the forest as you languished with pain. After you fell into slumber…"

"A slumber *you* inflicted upon me!"

"Yes," Nastauria admitted, "a slumber I entranced you with. I picked up your son and held him as well, gazing into his blue eyes and watching him smile up at mine. Your son *was* born healthy, and I took him away and bade the Síth to lie in exchange for another life freely given that day. But Clíodhna," she pleaded, "you *must* hear the rest. So much more is at stake here, and these facts concern both our people."

"Yes," Clíodhna agreed. "The fact that you sent *my* son away with *your* daughter to retrieve the Blossom that rightfully belongs to my people."

"That is not what I did," Nastauria argued. "Please listen to the rest."

King Betarian broke in with laughter. "Daughter you are a fool! You dream of cooperation between sworn enemies, just as you did when you were a child." Turning to the Queen of Banshees he said, "And you dream only of stealing back what your people stole from our own."

"It belonged to us first!" Clíodhna argued. "It is ours!"

"Exactly my point," he said with a grimace. "You're blinded by the desire to hold the power, but that ambition is misguided. It is ours, and we must restore the Blossom of Life to its proper place beneath the tree of the same name! That is the reason it thrives as a vine with its true form of beauty, and why I took steps to ensure neither of your dreams bear fruit." Drawing and pointing a silver dagger at Nastauria, he explained, "I too made a deal with the Síth, when I gave him the life of my son. That weakling had already given birth to my grandson and I found him... dispensable."

"You gave my brother over to the Síth? Is that how he fell in battle?"

"Yes," he said without remorse. "By my own blade that pitiful Skygate guard fell upon the forest floor and my deal was complete."

"What deal?" Nastauria asked slowly, piecing together the events in her mind. "What did you ask in return for killing my only brother?"

Pleased with himself he turned toward Clíodhna to watch her face fall at his explanation. "I bade him to exchange her son in the realm of humans. Morkur left him as a changeling and swapped her child for a mortal."

"My son," Clíodhna worked out, "was taken to the Human Realm? "I don't believe you, Betarian." She moved, raising her hand to signal her warriors and they ceased pacing, bracing themselves to lunge. "Not when your daughter admits to sending him along with her own."

Betarian laughed at the shock on Nastauria's face. "No, you did not know that when you sent him to aid Alistaria, did you, traitor? That sentry you sent was not her son. Hers was left behind as a mortal and surely has died there by natural age. Your daughter's escort is a mere human raised in our nursery – enhanced by the gift of longevity and enchanted like all who arrive through the portal.

A voice caused them all to turn. Standing to the side was Síth Morkur. "What he tells you is true, Clíodhna, though not every word of it. I carried your son through the portal as part of our deal, but not to the same timeline. Your son is very much alive, and now aids the children in their mission to retrieve the Blossom."

"How," Nastauria asked, "did her son remain in their realm and not return following Tempest?"

"I enchanted him to remain, and he will do so until one of Radviken's heirs bleeds for the Blossom. He is destined to aid the effort to return all three Blossoms to their rightful places."

"Three?" King Betarian felt a wash of confusion pass through his mind. "Three Blossoms, like the three trees bestowed by the Great Spirit?"

"The same," he replied.

"So the trees themselves..." he trailed off.

"Were only great trees. The true power came from which Blossom was planted beneath its roots. Ask your daughter," the Síth commanded, "she had figured this out on her own."

Nastauria nodded. "And why I helped Alistaria by sending Torian with her." Turning to Clíodhna she swore, "I truly believed him your son, and hoped by sending them both there would be twice the chance of their success. One of them must bleed on the Blossom to open the portals for you, and any one of Radviken's heirs can steal back the gems for replanting your Bláth de Saol."

Clíodhna stared back with confusion. "You don't call it the Bláth de Fainne?"

"That is not its name. It is truly named the Blossom of Life, and was gifted to the Deamhan who once owned the land we wrongly call Fainnotheria. It was my people who stole it from yours and named it of the Fainne."

"To the victors go the spoils," Betarian interjected. "The land is ours as surely are the powers contained in the bush!"

Ignoring her father, Nastauria added, "I tried to make things right by finally reuniting our peoples. I believe Alistaria will see that through." To which the Banshee Queen scoffed.

"By stealing away my son, the harbinger, and allowing Betarian to hide him away? Of course the Blossom belongs to me, and I could have brought peace to my realm on my own. Even now I feel it calling me through the Tempest!"

The Síth turned to Clíodhna and said, "You are right to feel connected to that Blossom, though it truly belongs beneath the Tree of Life and not in this palace. Fainnotheria is the ancestral home of the Deamhan, and your people must work together to restore what belongs to each of you."

"What belongs to each of us?" Betarian demanded. "If the Tree of Life is hers, then which belonged to the Fainne? Was ours stolen by the Luchorpán, then?"

The Síth sighed. "Your people chose to leave this realm long ago when two princes peacefully came to accord. Yours gave up this realm, and then again fled as refugees from the Human Realm. You do not belong here."

Betarian seethed with anger at the spirit's trickery. "Lies!" He cried out. "Fainnotheria was ours!"

"Your kind had stolen what once belonged to the race of man, uprooting the Bláth de Eolas," Síth Morkur explained.

Nastauria translated. "Blossom of Knowledge?"

"Yes." The spirit nodded his approval of her wit.

Clíodhna blanched. "The Luchorpán took the second Blossom. Are you saying they now hold twice the power? Both their own as well as that of the humans?"

"Yes," the Síth agreed, "and that is how they opened the portal to the Shadow Realm and set it loose against the humans. That Shadow was the reason the Fainne were forced to flee to your realm, taking the Bláth de Eolas through the portal."

Betarian spat. "Then what *actually* belongs to the Luchorpán?"

Síth Morkur nodded to Nastauria who answered, "The Bláth de Cumhacht," she said, "the Blossom of Power."

"So says *you*," the king hissed at the Síth. "You've filled my daughter's head full of lies! All of this is untrue!"

"Just because certain knowledge goes against your values does not make it untrue, Betarian. Opinions may vary, but facts do not. Claiming something is fact is not the same as what really *is*... or what really occurred. Do not try to obscure the past with your embarrassment over the actions of your ancestors. Study their mistakes and learn from them. Do not hide them or remove them from your sight."

The king collapsed in the throne, suddenly weaker and more exhausted than before. Pain entered every muscle and broken bone – surging with each breath he took. "What is happening to me?" He asked.

"I am claiming the soul Nastauria once traded to keep her own child safe," the Síth replied.

Betarian suddenly understood the war was lost, and his enemy held both the relic and the high ground. "What will happen?" He asked. "When Alistaria returns with the Blossom and you claim it as your own, Clíodhna."

"I will reset the order of our realms."

Nastauria placed a hand on the king's arm and said, "Sins of the past will begin to be corrected, and not out of emotion, but because it is rightful and just, Father."

He found the energy to recoil one last time, pulling away from her touch. "Do not call me that now or ever."

"I have said too much and must depart," Síth Morkur professed. "I only arrived to claim the next soul owed to me by Nastauria. I believe this arrangement like many of your others was upon his natural passing. Well, I believe that time has arrived."

She nodded toward her father and said, "Take what I have given to you and go, then. We will no doubt meet again, I'm sure." "Undoubtedly," the Síth replied as he stepped toward Betarian. "And quite soon."

Realizing he had been given over, the king succumbed to his wounds and breathed his final breath when he said, "My only hope for the Fainne is that my grandson succeeds instead of your daughter, Nastauria."

She leaned in close to his ear and whispered. "Alistaria is not *my* daughter, Betarian. Know this in death – in the end it was your arrogant hatred that allowed your own daughter to defeat your bigotry. I actually bore you a grandson, and he was also spirited off so I could hide Alistaria within your kingdom. That is the price your soul has paid, that of your own deceit."

The king's eyes grew wide with understanding and his gasp became his final breath.

CHAPTER THIRTY-ONE

*The death of a king brings winds of hope as well as sorrow,
unless the branch has withered and the tree no longer
produces viable fruit. In that case, cut it down and burn the
root, there's no reason behind waiting for another harvest.*
– Journal of King Betarian

Restarian entered the private chamber of Radviken, careful not
to make any noise, and cautiously ensuring no one was alerted on
the other side of the door. He looked to both the left and right,
scanning the room for danger. Other than a warm fire burning in
the hearth, there was no movement and not a single light. Certain
he was alone, he continued inside.

The Bláth de Fainne was unguarded where it had been the night
before, shimmering with its power and seeming to glow from within
its crystalline stalks. All he had to do was pluck each gemstone and
carry them away. He paused. There were no guards on his room, no
one in the halls, not a single sentry on this chamber. It was *too* easy,
almost as if it were a trap or the king was testing him still.

He thought about the fiery torture and the contorting magic
he had endured just that very evening. Radviken *would* test him in
just such a way. *Is he lurking nearby?* He considered. *What is he
expecting me to do?*

When the king stole the Blossom from the Fainne, he had ripped
it out by the root and carried it off. An examination of the delicate
structure revealed that wouldn't work, not in the state it had taken
in Enatherr. Perhaps if he plucked one of the gems. He slowly reached

out a hand and chose the diamond. *Power,* he thought. *If I choose power, I could own it all and turn it against him!* He found it warm to the touch.

He pulled and nothing happened. It was firmly attached and part of the structure. He tugged harder, wiggling and pulling while willing it to break free. Again it held fast. Restarian ran his finger along the vine, searching for the secrets hidden so well. Suddenly a thought occurred. Every Fainne child must prick their finger before the elders when they are presented. They bleed for the bush to determine if it has chosen for them a gift. Before the other blooms had been stolen, a child may have known one of many opportunities to connect. Not all are healers.

If he had wrenched it from the ground as a bush, Radviken would have pricked his skin, he thought. *Perhaps that is how he can channel it now!* He reached down timidly, feeling along the vine and softly testing the tip of a crystal thorn. Closing his eyes tightly he braced himself. With bated breath he allowed the tip to pierce his skin, just as the vine beneath the Tree of Life had done when he was a child. Pulling his finger away he gazed down at a single drop of blood upon the tip. He placed this against the Diamond of Power.

The blast was both unexpected and forceful, sending him flying across the room and slamming him against the far wall. Abruptly the room burst into laughter, suddenly filled with twenty or so people dressed all in black. Among them was Radviken. No longer watching behind a veil of magic, each person was bent over and giggling at his plight. Some touched a hand over mouth while others slapped their knee or held their gut. The only person in the room who *didn't* laugh was Restarian. He stared at them blankly. No, that's not quite true. Niamh was also stoic, and she stared back at him with curious interest.

She had changed out of her emerald dress, wearing instead a long-sleeve tunic and a pair of matching trousers dyed a deep onyx. Her red hair was pulled back in a tight bun that made her face appear stern. Only her eyes were soft, staring down at him with tender mercy instead of pity. Her hand was clenched around the hilt of a long dagger at her side. On its pommel was an emerald as green as her eyes.

Restarian tried to climb to his feet but staggered instead, unsteady and nearly falling again to the floor. He turned to run away, but the exit was blocked by two guards clad in the same black leather as the pair the night before. *Had they been there the entire time, as well?*

"Oh, Prince Restarian," the king cackled. "I must thank you, for I haven't laughed like that in many years. To be honest," he added, "I didn't think I ever would again! Thank you for bringing our entertainment tonight!" He approached the prince and grabbed him by the shoulders, turning and shoving him down into a chair by the fire. "When I replanted the bush, I added a touch of my own design and now it only obeys my blood. I can bestow it upon others, at my choosing, as tonight's ceremony was planned. But it wasn't you who were to receive my blessing and the Bloom resisted you."

"Who..." Restarian stammered. But he found he really didn't care. The boy was exhausted, beaten and humiliated once more by the arrogant king.

But Radviken answered his unspoken question. "Tonight Niamh ascends to Searcher," he explained.

"Suh... Searcher?" He stammered again, so confused by the events around him. "What's a Searcher?"

"A Searcher is what every Storm Rider yearns to become. They spend years proving their worth as my soldiers and enforcers, keeping our realm safe from the other realms – realms like yours." He took the young woman by the hand and led her toward the Bláth de Fainne. "Her final test was to woo a young prince and prove she can work more covertly and not only under the shadow of Tempest. I believe I will put her to work wooing my noblemen for information."

He reached carefully toward the crystalline structure and pricked his finger atop one of the thorns. Drawing forth blood in the same manner as Restarian had, he let a drop fall upon the Emerald of Sight and the gem came to life with a brilliant glow. Radviken nodded and

Niamh stepped forward to do the same. She pricked the exact thorn, then sacrificed a drop to the glowing stone. The light extinguished immediately. Those gathered clapped wildly and the young woman bowed to her king. He drew a raven cloak from a table nearby and placed it over her shoulders and tied it in front. After she had resumed her posture, Niamh turned to face Restarian.

"Are you ready for your final test, Searcher?" Radviken asked of her and she nodded she was. "Good. Since you have chosen sight as your power, reveal to us the true form of this fae."

"Right away, my king," she said with a devilish smile and approached the prince. She leaned in softly and whispered, "You enjoyed the massage, didn't you fae?"

He froze, unsure of what she was about to do and worried it was more torture. He finally nodded that he had, staring back at the others with embarrassment. He watched for their reaction and they laughed as fiercely as before.

"I noticed something was missing when my hands caressed your head and back," she said. "Do you know what it was?"

Terrified by her seductive calmness, he worried what she would do next. He shook his head, "no," despite his suspicions.

"First, I noticed the color of your skin was wrong." She ran a finger along his arm and a trail of golden flecks appeared in a line that lasted several seconds after she pulled it away. "Then, I realized your ears were simply the wrong shape." She leaned forward and kissed him gently upon his right one, tugging slightly with her lips before stepping back, leaving him aware they had regained their fae form.

Despite the other people in the room, the boy felt his heart beat fast at her touch, the same feeling as when she had massaged his back. He felt both awkward and wrong, but was entirely in her mercy and control.

"But most of all," She said with puckering lips that he suddenly yearned to kiss, "I wondered about your wings." Her hands flashed like lightning as she reached out and spun him around. Just as fast, she had drawn her blade and cut the back of his tunic from his collar to his waist. When she had stepped backward, she also gave him a shove to his knees.

He was suddenly fully aware that his wings had returned – spreading and fanning like a butterfly emerging from chrysalis. They would not yet be ready for flight, he somehow knew, and his legs were too heavy to stand and run away.

Across the room Radviken applauded and the others joined in after. "Wonderful," he praised. "Simply wonderful... and excellent form! I would have adopted a less seductive method, myself, but that was marvelous! You have the child shaking in his boots and unsure if you'll kill him or kiss him! Oh, Niamh, you will make an excellent agent in my court!" The smile on his face abruptly disappeared and the sinister sneer from the night before returned.

Restarian, now reduced to the child he actually was, began to tremble and whimper and cry. "No," the boy pleaded. "No more, please! I just want to go home!"

"Oh," the king said cruelly, "you will, eventually, but not in this form." He snapped his fingers and the mob descended like birds flocking to scattered seed.

The sound of drawing blades caused the Prince of the Fainne to wet his trousers and curl into a ball. Any effort to fight them off would be futile, and he prayed to the Great Spirit the pain would be superficial like the night before. But that prayer fell unanswered as the first blade drew flesh from his wing. Soon another followed and then another. And so it went as they flayed.

After they had removed all of his skin from the spread bones of his wings, they mutilated his ears – laughing all the while over his screams. He only passed out once – and when he did, they revived him so they could go to work scrubbing the golden scales from his skin. During that he fainted twice. After he had awakened the second time, he felt his body grow distant and soul grew restless to depart his worthless flesh.

As he died, he heard the king proclaim, "Don't worry, I can resurrect him so that you can finish the job."

Part Four
Redemption of the Deamhan

Chapter Thirty-Two

*Three lives were granted and the first life was given. The second
was traded, and the third one stolen. I now weep for all five.*
– Lamentations of Nastauria

Alistaria had ridden in silence the rest of the trip, shivering
against the cold. The rain had fully changed over to snow this far
north, something she had heard about but never fully imagined. It
had quickly covered everything ahead, including the road. But the
horses seemed to know their way home, and kept easily to the path.

The view had taken her breath, but the harsh man ahead had
stolen her passion. His previous words had cut and rendered her
mute – how dare he call her a Deamhan – leaving her fearful of
what other lies he would conjure if she pushed. Instead, she had only
listened to the clapping of hooves and the howl of the wind as they
climbed the slope to the city. The only sound she herself had made
was when she recognized both the city and the palace ahead – and
that was a gasp.

She had never seen anything like Norgaard, and had never imagined such a sight existed. The city itself was a sea of tall houses with
steeped rooves A single waterfall cascaded over the mountains far
in the northeast, with that single river splitting in two as it flowed
around both sides. Beyond the winding roads and alleyways – and
standing high upon a hill overlooking the rooftops – the palace was
indeed the tallest structure in Enatherr.

The man's words crept once more into her mind. *You most
certainly are* not *a Fainne, and only a Banshee can draw healing*

power from the Tempest your *kind created!* It couldn't be. She'd rather end herself than face life knowing she was a Deamhan. *He was lying, for sure!* There was no way it was possible, for Nastauria was her mother and Nastauria was also Fainne. She wished she hadn't lost her mother's journal. *The answers lie in there, or she wouldn't have given it to me!*

Thinking about the journal brought another memory, one she had nearly forgotten. Even with hands bound she was able to feel a pocket sewn into her waistband, and touched a tiny bulge. *I still have the spores,* she realized, and it was a comforting thought. No matter what happened in the palace, she could still lay the circle and draw in Betarian and the Kern. The mission hadn't been worthless, and she was about to make it inside.

Movement caught her eye. She lifted her head and strained to make out a creature resting casually by a fence post. Its long black fur contrasted the brilliantly white snow, causing it to stand out. At first, she thought it a hare, but it was unlike any she had ever seen. It's long hair more resembled a bearded old man than a rabbit. Even its limbs seemed oddly long for a hare. Its eyes were oddly human as well.

She eyed it curiously. "What sort of animal is that?" She asked the Riders, gesturing with her bound hands.

"Where?" came the gruff reply of indifference from her left.

"What does it matter?" Replied the other man riding on her right. "Are we sightseeing now?" Both men laughed at his joke, but she ignored their sarcasm.

The animal locked eyes with her then, and winked as if it shared her view of the two men. Then it shrugged as if wishing it could offer help in her predicament.

"I swear it just winked at me!" She suddenly blurted out, causing both men to scan the area.

Seeing nothing, the man on her right warned, "Don't be trying no tricks, now. There ain't nothing out during Tempest. Even the animals have sense to take to their dens."

"I swear it's right there," she said. "It's there against the fence and staring right at me."

"What?" The man on her left asked. "That fence?" He laughed. "There ain't nothing there at all. Now you be quiet or we'll knock some quiet alongside your head."

"It may be a Puca, you see." Searcher Cainnech muttered. "If one has revealed itself, then someone close to you has died – or *is* dying. They're the harbingers, for sure, but have other uses if one's chosen you."

She stared at the animal questioningly. Slowly, it nodded its agreement with the man's words and winked again. "What's a Puca?" She asked.

"You know them as Skinwalkers – shapeshifters and spirits from the other realm."

The Rider on her right said, "Oh, a Puca..." He pointed. "Against that fence over there?" He abruptly drew his sword and screamed, spurring his horse at a gallop toward the spot.

Alistaria watched as the odd beast barred teeth into a hiss and exclaimed, "Sharp things!" Then it was gone – disappearing completely without a trace.

Both Riders shared revelry in the joke and laughed at the horror on her face. "What?" The man said as he sheathed his sword. "'Twas only a joke. There wasn't nothing there."

Ignoring him she turned to Searcher Cainnech. "I thought Radviken sealed Enatherr from the Shadow Realm. How can a Skinwalker be here?"

"Some were already here, and found themselves trapped on this side. We purge those who cause trouble, but ignore those who comply with our laws. Their mere existence seems to keep the villagers and town folk in remembrance of the King's benevolence."

"Why could only I see that one? Who died?"

But the Searcher didn't answer. He turned his head to focus his beady eyes on Alistaria, and with a sly smile he winked – oddly resembling the gesture of the animal. She shivered at the eeriness of the oddity.

Only a few miles away, high in the upper levels of the palace, Restarian had died again. The first time there had only been blackness when he passed, quickly replaced by the sudden brightness of life returning and Radviken standing over him laughing. Once he was restored, the others had taken to carving again – slowly removing every ounce of muscle and tendon from his wings. They were careful about that business, taking great care to nick every nerve upon which they could inflict pain.

The second time he died he had crossed over longer in the blackness – enough time that his mind adjusted to the dream around him. Only, it wasn't a dream. By the time he had awakened to Radviken's vile laughter, he had realized he'd glimpsed the Shadow Realm. The gathered Searchers continued carving at the King's order, and he fought hard to ignore the pain. But soon he succumbed once more and immediately found himself in the realm.

He stood in a dark forest – not unlike the great trees around Fainnotheria – except the ancient trunks were gnarled and twisted by corruption. The air shimmered with the same, a ghostly vapor parting aside as he walked deeper into the dreamlike world. Overhead the sky was a deep scarlet and he saw movement above in its vastness. At first, he assumed he had seen strange clouds swirling and descending. His skin crawled – not from the ministrations of Radviken's cruelty, but with a dread feeling something or some *things* watched him closely from the mass. The storm was moving toward him.

It was truly a storm, but different than the Tempest. But as he strained his eyes to focus on the swirling forms within, he felt his body rendered rigid with terror. Like the Tempest in Enatherr swirled with the ghostly forms of Banshees, this shadowy maelstrom churned with trapped souls. As unseeing eyes came into focus, he trembled at the sight of hands reaching out of the clouds toward him. He turned and fled as fast as he could into the waiting forest.

All at once the trees came to life, reaching leafless branches that clawed at his skin. These he dodged – ducking and weaving as he searched for a clearing. It was just ahead. Would he make it?

He felt the heat from the storm as it grew closer. It thrummed with a cadence of lifeforce as it fed off the souls within. Their wailing and gnashing of teeth reached his ears and his skin burned from the closeness of brimstone burning within the clouds. He tried to flap his wings and fly, but only their skeletal uselessness remained. They were in this realm as they were in his own, and would remain so upon waking under Radviken's laughter – if he bothered to revive him once more.

A shape stood in the clearing, a Fainnen soldier – no, a Kern! The soldier stared off at the distant horizon, oblivious to the raging hell storm in the sky.

"Fly!" Restarian yelled, but the man either hadn't heard or simply hadn't heeded. "Fly away from here!" He pleaded. This time his grandfather turned – dazed and with a look of confusion painted across his hopeless features.

"Grandson?" He asked. "What has happened to your wings? We must set the healers upon you at once," he insisted.

"Do you not see the storm, Betarian? Fly and save yourself," he begged.

Slowly the older Fainne turned glossy eyes toward the hells above. "I see my son," he said drowsily. Calling out he cried, "Justarian! I am here!" And to Restarian he smiled. "Your father is there," he pointed. "He beckons to me, Restarian." He took a step toward the advancing souls but the boy caught his arm and turned him away.

"Why are you here?" He pleaded. "You are king and must be saved!" He felt himself fading as his skin turned translucent and the wisps of corruption swept all around. Radviken's laughter could be heard in the distance. With tears in his eyes he pled, "Come with me!"

"No, my time in Fainnotheria ended today. But if you are return-ing you must avenge my death."

"Who?" Restarian asked with urgency, staring up at the storm. "Who killed you? Was it Clíodhna?"

He shook his head solemnly, "No. My death is on my hands, and I have only myself to blame. But treachery surely runs rampant in your kingdom – and it is yours now, for sure. Avenge the traitor who betrayed our people. Kill Nastauria when you return, for she has colluded with our sworn enemy. Trust not the Deamhan, not now or ever. Allow not a single heart to beat in their corrupted chests, starting with their wicked queen and finishing with her daughter." As soon as he finished speaking, King Betarian was caught up by the hands of reaching souls.

"Whose daughter?" Restarian asked, falling backward. "Clíodhna does not have a daughter, Grandfather! Surely you don't mean Alistaria!"

But Betarian did not answer, and the prince stared up with frightened eyes as they bore the king upward, devouring his flesh for eternity within the brimstone prison of the storm. For a moment, their wails turned to glee as they feasted. Restarian closed his eyes as the searing heat grew closer. When they finally opened, a different king stood over him, cackling with glee at the terror frozen forever on his face.

"My word," Radviken said, "it seems his hair has turned completely white! Perhaps we've pushed him past his limits, my friends. What's this? You have more skin to flay? Just one more time, then. Have another go with your blades, but be quick about it for I am growing bored."

Restarian closed his eyes, determined to remain alive this time no matter what. He *must* live. He *shall* avenge Betarian. Every Deamhan shall die – all of them no matter who.

Chapter Thirty-Three

That my people knew my affection allowed me to enjoy their approval throughout my reign. They never betrayed me, no – that act came from outside my realm. My single mistake was leaving behind a child in the act of love and without consideration of my legacy. But most certainly I should not have given a child to a Fainne.
– Confession of Radviken

Torian despised Norgaard immediately. He hated the city almost as much as giving up his wings when arriving in Enatherr – and for the same reason. He felt trapped. He preferred the forest of Fainnotherr, and the feeling of being dwarfed by the tall buildings filled him with doom and a strong desire to flee. The lack of wings denied him the sky, rendering him grounded, weak, and vulnerable. The structures closed in around him, adding to that weakness and making him feel like an insect on the forest floor – vulnerable to trample. The only landmark which brought any sort of joy wasn't even in the city. The towering waterfall in the distance thrilled his heart and lured him to travel northward.

"Magnificent, isn't it?" Markey said of the falls.

He shrugged and tried to act like it wasn't impressive. "So where's the palace?" He asked, changing the subject. Now that they'd arrived in the city he hoped to separate from Markey, and find Alistaria on his own. The man may be telling the truth about not turning him in, but even so he didn't relish the idea of apprenticing to the Riders.

"It's there on that hill on the far northern tip of the city, right where the river divides," Markey replied. "But we're not going there straightaway. I've someone for you to meet, first."

This unsettled Torian. "I'd rather not," he said. "I'm in a hurry and want this ordeal to end."

"Not dressed like that, you're not. Rider's armor was fine for turning heads the opposite direction during Tempest, but I can't present you to the Warden wearing Blayse's armor. You also need a change of clothes that doesn't scream fae. Clurich can help with that as well as... other things."

"What other things?" Torian suddenly felt more uneasiness pass through his gut. He was a trained soldier – nearly a Kern – and a fighter learns to master his instincts and trust them as well as a honed blade. They currently screamed caution.

"You'll see. Just follow me. Just don't be put off by how he looks or acts – Clurich is a strange one, but I trust him. He's helped me many times during investigations in the capital city."

"He informs for you?"

"Aye, he does a bit of that as well." Markey led him off the main road and down a twisting alley with bridges overhead.

Despite people hiding out Tempest in their homes, Torian could tell right away this lower district was of the seedy type – had this been a normal day he would be surrounded by the worst sort of humans. *What am I thinking?* He asked himself. *All humans are bad...* He briefly glanced at his riding companion. *No matter how helpful or friendly, they're all as evil as Radviken.*

"Here we are!" Markey finally exclaimed.

Their destination turned out to be a gathering place for travelers with rooms to rent and a large common room for drinking and gaming away the wages of the locals. Torian raised his eyes to the swinging sign hanging above the door. It read, *The Lucky Luchorpán.* He wrinkled his nose at the debauchery coming from within, a joyous revelry which even drowned out the howling winds of Tempest – now a full on blizzard raging around them.

Despite the storm, a man of small stature – short but stocky with stout arms and legs that had surely seen physical labor – lay past out drunk on the steps. He was smaller even than the children of the Fainne, reaching a full height that only came to Torian's naval had he bothered to stand up and greet them. He slept comfortably, oblivious to the raging snowstorm and covered with a woolen blanket. His thick beard was coated in frost and icicles of snot hung from his nose.

"Is he dead?" Torian asked.

"Not likely as dead in body as he'd wish." Markey chuckled. "No, he likes the cold and often pokes his head outside and forgets to go back in."

"Does he live here?" Torian asked.

"Live here? He owns the place."

Reading again the name on the sign, Torian wondered. "He's not really a Luchorpán, is he?"

Markey laughed. "I actually don't know because I've never asked – would be considered rude to do so – but I've never dowsed him because I never had call to do so. Doesn't rightly matter to me if he is, as long as he abides by the law. Besides," he added, "he's proven a right helpful fellow at times when he's sober."

Furrowing his eyes to the empty jug beside the little man, Torian asked, "How often *is* that?"

"Not very," Markey admitted. Getting down from his horse he gently nudged Clurich with the toe of his boot. "Get up, friend," he commanded.

The words that replied came out slow and slurred into one mess of a sentence. "Whoooo gooooooes therrrrrre?" Clurich demanded.

"An old friend," Markey replied.

"Dooyee have ale?"

"No, but you do. Serve us up."

They found a quiet room in the back of the tavern, warm and cramped but distinctly private. Once they were all seated, Markey opened a fresh bottle and poured them each a glass. Torian was instantly repulsed by the foul smelling liquid within, but sipped it to be polite in company of the proprietor – not that he seemed to care. The little man downed his mug as soon as it hit his lips, then smacked them and slammed it down for more with a smile. As it turned out, a touch of the drab was what the little man needed to clear up his speech.

He smacked his lips again and said, "A hair of the dog be all I need to think clearly, Markey! Thanks for the pour."

"Hair of the dog?" Torian inspected his own mug for any canine fur within.

"'Tis an expression, is all." The little man said with laughter. "The day after a drinking spell, all a man needs is the hair of the dog who bit him the night before. Then everything's right in the world once more! What brings ye to mah tavern, Markey Boy?"

The Rider pointed at Torian, and the tavern owner squinted his eyes in examination. "What about him? Seems normal to me."

"Remember when we first met?"

"Gaw, I kin barely remember breakfast."

"That's not for another hour," Markey assured.

"Well, then I kinna remember my last drink. Do a lad a favor and top thissun off?" His friend complied and he drank it just as fast as the first before wiping his whiskers and saying, "I be pullin' yer leg, Markey Boy. Of course I remember. It ain't often I meet..." He turned a quick glance at Torian, suddenly unsure of what he could say, then finished, "... someone like you. Are yah here for the same reason Tamee sent yah the first time?"

"I found this young man in a cave with this sword," Markey explained, pointing at the table for Torian to draw it out and lay it down. He did, and placed it before Clurich.

The little man eyed it greedily, with green eyes drinking in the iridescent silver as if it provided a larger addiction than ale. "Fainne silver," he said with a whisper.

"Aye. He fought both me and Blayse off like an expert, killing him and wounding me. But when I dowsed him, he wasn't a Fainne."

Clurich's eyebrows lifted with sincere sympathy. "Blayse is dead, then? That's too bad, Markey. I know he's yer only friend besides Jaana and me." His eyes returned to the silver blade on the table. "So you'll be presenting this young man to the Warden as a proxy for him, but first want me to tell you if he's Deamhan?"

Markey nodded solemnly.

The little man thought for a moment then added, "Of course, why would 'ee be travelin' with a Fainne if not to gain access to the realm." His eyes shot back to Torian, examining him with unfettered amusement. "It ain't often I get to study one of 'em, freshly come," he admitted, "'tis been a *long* while."

Just then the door opened and a beautiful tavern maid entered. She was tall and graceful with long red hair and perfect skin free from any blemish except a few perfectly placed freckles along the bridge of her nose. Her green eyes danced merrily around the room as she handed them another jug of ale. "I figured he'd already downed the other, so I brought reinforcements for you and your friend, Markey."

"Thank you, Deirdre."

The girl settled in next to Clurich, wrapping her arm lovingly around his shoulder and kissing him gently on the cheek. "He sobers up quickly when you come, don't 'ee, Markey?"

"Aye, that he does."

Torian leaned in close to the Rider and whispered, "Should we be having this conversation with... a visitor?"

Markey only laughed. "We can speak freely around Deirdre. She's Clurich's wife and knows all his business. Even if we hid it from her, she'd know soon enough after we left, isn't that right, dear?"

She nodded with a smile. "Don't be worryin' none 'bout me. My husband's secrets are safe enough in my heart that I kin hold a few more." She looked down at the sword. "So where'd you dig up Fainne silver, Markey?" She pointed at Torian with her thumb and added, "Do it belong to him?"

Torian couldn't believe his ears – how easily these humans accepted he was Fainne... *If I actually am a Fainne,* he thought. "Is it possible," he asked of Clurich – unsure how much the man could know about the dowsing, "for a Fainne to escape detection? Like if he's halfblooded?"

"Oh now, the process is quite thorough when detecting Fainne. They originated in this realm and are only cousins to the Deamhan. But the dowsing is *highly* accurate."

"So how are Deamhan detected?"

"The same way fer sure, but that *would* be affected if the blood sample wasn't pure."

Torian whispered, "like if he were half-human?"

Both Markey and Clurich nodded and exchanged a knowing look. "Especially if he was half-human."

The Storm Rider agreed.

Clurich continued, "But even a full-blooded sample is hard to detect, since they're not of this realm. And a Searcher would have to confirm with a second reading. But even their magic is less accurate when human blood is mixed in."

"How do you know? You speak like you've tried this before."

The two men exchanged a second look that seemed to punctuate the first. "Before we get into that... if we even do... I need the truth of your origin. Tell me *what* you are – or what you *think* you are – and how you came to that cave. If I'm to take you before Radviken I'd better be sure you're undetectable. Otherwise his Searchers will see right through your blood."

Torian swallowed hard. *This could still be a trap,* he thought.

"I'm sorry," he finally said. "You've been nice enough, but I don't know if I can trust you fully. I still don't know if you intend to turn me over instead of presenting me as a recruit. What if I *am* a Deamhan? Especially then? How could I place my life in your hands when we just met?"

Markey sighed and looked to Clurich and nodded. The little man nodded back and explained, "Because you wouldn't be the first

Deamhan I've dowsed for Markey O'Malley. Ye might say he's got a fondness for them, one almost as fierce as his duty to his partner Blayse." Pointing to the rider, he added, "I trust this man, fer he's got a heart o' pure gold. He's a fighter, sure, but his loyalty be to his family, and not to the king he serves." To Markey he asked, "'Tis that a fair assessment?"

"'Tis," the Rider replied. "I do my job, but I don't relish in the politics of it. But I know the law – *am* the law in this realm, and Blayse was my friend. You either replace him or hang for him, that's all I truly care about."

Torian thought long and hard, unsure how to proceed. Eventually his mouth worked through the details on its own. "My name is Torian, a sentry of the Skygate in Fainnotheria," he admitted. "I was raised an orphan in the court nursery, ignorant of both lineage and without a clue of my parent's identity. My entire life has been focused on one goal – acceptance into the Kern. I was sent by Nastauria – the divested daughter of King Betarian – to watch over her daughter who travelled to Enatherr to steal back the Bláth de Fainne from her father, Radviken the Vile."

Clurich smiled at the knowledge with eyes that begged for more. Dierdre also listened with keen interest, as if she were hearing a bedside story. Only Markey drank the words stoically – unflinching and impossible to read. "Go on," he gently commanded.

"Alistaria stepped into the Fainnen Ring alone, but the portal didn't work. Restarian, the grandson of the king, had followed us into the forest and assumed it failed because of her human blood. When he saw Banshees approaching, he shoved me into the ring to aid her travel. I blacked out, and awoke next to him, but with Alistaria nowhere in sight. Together he and I crossed the mountain pass in hopes we'll catch up to her before Tempest ends."

"You only have until the next dawn. Today and tonight are the waning winds, and it will be over by next morning," Dierdre informed him sadly.

He nodded. "As I feared." Turning to Markey, he asked, "Will you still help me? I just admitted to planning to steal the Blossom."

The Rider stared at the table, picking at a splinter with his fingernail. "Radviken is an awful man," he agreed. "But he brought stability to Enatherr. The old folk speak tales of before he brought back the relic, and the images painted by their words are miserable. Crops sometimes failed, horses and cows would go lame, and rain often forgot to fall or flooded unexpectedly."

"And women were sometimes barren," Diedre added, "or the children stillborn."

"Aye," he agreed, "or those things. No, young Torian, I can only agree to help you find your friends, but I cannot allow you to take the Bláth de Saol, for it does not belong to your people.

Clurich cleared his throat and said with profound seriousness, "Nor does it belong to yours, Markey. Remember what Tamee warned you of years ago."

"It serves us well as it currently stands, my friend," The Rider said with a nod. "But I'll turn the gift down, if offered."

"What if he doesn't offer you a choice?" Diedre asked.

"Well," Markey replied, "what if Tamee was wrong? What's the worst could happen?"

Clurich shrugged but Dierdre whispered, "Your wife and son would pay the price."

This visibly stung the Rider, his love for them obviously greater than his duty. Turning back to Torian he said, "Let's see that satchel of yours. Empty the contents here so we might remove what gives you away. We can't have any trace of the fae world once we step foot in the palace."

"You still intend to take me?"

"Aye, 'tis my duty to the law. I'll remain quiet as to your plans, and let you figure out your own path once you're presented."

Torian nodded and complied. He did not carry many belongings, only Restarian's waterskin and some rations. These toppled out without much sound. But a loud clunk resounded with crystal resonance as an object struck the wooden table. All eyes stared at the strange object.

"What is that?" Markey asked.

"I truly don't know!" Torian exclaimed. He was as confused and curious as the others. He reached to pick it up but Clurich stopped his hand – grabbing it off the table and holding it to the light.

"That be part of a Bláth!" He said. "If ye didn't place it there, who did?"

"I don't... I don't know," he stammered. But then he thought of his dream. "Restarian was the only one near my satchel at any time since I packed it. It wasn't there before you and the others arrived at the cave – I know because I had pulled out rations to eat – and he was beside it when we fought."

"So he put it in," Markey agreed. "What does it do?" He asked of Clurich.

The little man appeared deeply worried as he stared down at the crystal. "Have you had any strange dreams lately?" He asked.

"As a matter of fact, I have," He admitted. In a soft voice he told them of the meeting with Clíodhna, and how she had led him to believe he was her son.

"That would be why the dowsing didn't work," Clurich said with a nod. "If he's half Deamhan and half human, then he would be difficult for a Searcher to detect as well, as we rightly know already." His eyes grew wide with excitement. "Markey, if this is true and Clíodhna's blood touches the Blossom..."

"Aye," Markey agreed. "We'd have bigger problems for sure." His hand flashed like lightning, just as a thunderclap sounded outside.

Torian jumped from the table, but it was too late – what blood wasn't on the Rider's knife dripped from his sliced hand. "What was that for? Do you injure me then? Do we fight now?" He demanded angrily.

But Clurich had already leaned over to inspect the blood on the blade the Rider held and both men ignored Torian. While he peered down, he drew another crystal from a necklace around his neck.

Explaining without lifting his eyes, he said, "This shard is from the Bláth de Eolas, the Blossom of Knowledge that once belonged first to man and then to the Fainne. If you are even partly Deamhan it will reveal your true nature."

Everyone in the tiny room watched with bated breath as he dangled the pendulum over the knife. They waited for several minutes but nothing happened. All eyes returned to Torian.

"What?" He demanded. "What does that mean?"

"You, young Torian, are a human," Markey explained. "A *full* blooded human, and you now only have one option."

Torian felt sick.

"Leave his belongings with me," Clurich said with sober clarity. "I'll keep them safe until his fate is decided by Radviken."

(HAPTER (THIRTY-FOUR

*Facts are easily erased and history rewritten, but truth never
disappears entirely. We may hide our actions, but evidence is
woven into the tapestry with every cut upon the weaver's fingers.
Search for the blood and let it guide the framing of forgiveness
and understanding, but what truly matters is to never forget
the bigger picture. View it often and bring everything to light.*
— Lamentations of Nastauria

The palace stood high above the city, dwarfing every building and
forcing them to kneel in rows to its splendor. The city literally paid
homage to King Radviken, and the palace represented his supreme
rule over both the landscape and the lives of all dwelling in Norgaard.
Alistaria could not help but feel overwhelmed.

There was only one entrance to the palace grounds, and those
were protected by high unscalable walls. Once beyond that gate,
snow covered gardens awaited the replenishment that followed
Tempest. Now on its final day, the Ganshees had made their way
north and currently devoured rows of roses and other flowering
plants and hedges among the gardens. Her skin crawled and old bite
wounds throbbed with the recent memory of their teeth.

The walls of the palace were just as slick and high as those encir-
cling the gardens. The single portcullis loomed over armed Storm
Guards, each holding a pike or carrying a sword. Even if the king
had opposition, a frontal assault would prove impossible. Torian
and Restarian would certainly not be joining her, as there were no
other entrances to the castle and they'd never make it past the guards
unless also as Radviken's prisoners.

She pointed to several protruding structures on the higher level. They looked like stone balconies that had been completely enclosed – each with a stone chimney protruding from the center and continuing to ground level. "What are those?" She asked.

"King Radviken is all knowing and splendorous," Searcher Cainnech explained. "In his wisdom he constructed his fortress with indoor privies. Bed pans and chamber pots are not even a worry for our lord. Indeed this palace holds all kinds of luxuries which you will sadly miss out on in the dungeons."

Her heart raced at mention of dungeons, and a wail from the uppermost level sent shockwaves of fear through her body. Then a shout and a cry for mercy rang out, that echoed into the gardens and caused her skin to shiver with raised bumps. The voice almost sounded like Restarian. She prayed to the Spirit that it wasn't, but her gut told her it was. At least he was alive.

Time was running out, and she would hopefully find a suitable place to scatter the spores and grant her grandfather entrance. A glance at the sun and she realized dawn had already passed by two hours. Soon it would be midday and then evening. The portal would be useless by the next dawn, so she had to find a suitable spot quickly – but even then, she did not know how quickly the ring would grow.

The Searcher interrupted her thoughts. "Dismount here," he commanded. They had reached the portcullis and he presented her to the guards. They replaced her bindings with iron shackles that burned her skin.

Anything but iron, she cried out in her mind. Agony wrenched her insides the moment it touched her skin, for iron alone was torture enough for a Fainne. She gathered her bearing and raised her head with dignity the way her mother had taught, entering the palace with head held high. "Take me directly to my father," she demanded.

At her words the guards looked around nervously and turned to the Searcher for guidance. "Ignore her," he said. "Take her to the dungeons and grant *me* immediate audience with the king."

A disembodied voice echoed through the palace, shaking mortar from grout lines and sending the Storm Guards into action. "Bring my daughter before me at once," Radviken ordered.

Alistaria, upon hearing her father's voice for the first time, merely smiled and nodded to the guards. They treated her with awed reverence as they led her up several staircases to their king's quarters above.

Radviken the Great stood in the throne room, wringing his hands anxiously and waiting for the girl to present herself. He paced for what felt like an eternity, eager to look upon her face and hear her speak. Though he had seen her arrival through the emerald, seeing her in person would bring more joy than he had expected. It was odd feeling so nervous to meet his own daughter, much like the first time he met Nastauria.

Would she be amiable? Could he sway her from Betarian's loyalty and ensure an heir for Enatherr? He hadn't expected the need of an heir, not when his body could restore itself with each Tempest. At this moment, for instance, he already felt as young and vibrant as he had when he met Nastauria, and planning for his kingdom now seemed a distant thought. But each thirty day cycle grew more taxing on his body, and he knew he would someday perish before the Tempest could revive his lifeforce – for that he must plan.

The ability to draw upon the life taken from Tempest had been the only reason he had lain with the Banshee Queen. The Síth had promised him a prolonged life, but that required his and her union before replanting the Blossom. He had explained, in order to draw life as a Síth does, one must be able to create a life in the fashion you wish to consume. Just as the Síth consumes souls, Radviken had developed a connection to the storm and the lifeforce absorbed within. The Tempest was, after all, a creation of the Deamhan, and use of it required a consummation with Clíodhna and their ultimate conception.

Though she had been beautiful, he did not love her like he did Nastauria and that was how he had broken free of her charm. She was a means and a way to achieve his goal – nothing more. Prince Restarian's news regarding a child born alive to her intrigued him, but not with the same enthusiasm as meeting his child with Nastauria. *The other from the Deamhan must surely die,* he knew.

His connection to the Tempest, despite its benefit to his longevity, had prevented him from blocking the Deamhan access to the Blossom like he did to the Fainne. Indeed, as long as they could bleed upon and draw from its power, they were all dangerous to Enatherr. *If one were to also contain my blood,* he thought, *that would be even worse.* Because then she and her army could enter the portal without aid of her enemies.

The door to the throne room opened and he turned to greet his daughter.

Radviken was an attractive man – distinguished and certainly athletic for his human age. He was stronger than any Fainne, muscular and healthy. His features were broad like Torian's, and his eyes the same icy blue. Alistaria could see right away the attraction her mother had felt for the monster who had destroyed her realm.

"Greetings, Alistaria! I hope you were well treated by my Riders."

She had not expected such a warm and inviting welcome. It actually caught her a bit off guard, but she set her jaw in the way she had seen her mother do so many times before. It was finally time to act the princess her mother had trained. With confidence and bearing she said, "My reception has been warm, but these irons are not necessary. What trouble could I cause that you alone could not handle? Why would they believe I would challenge you directly?"

"I agree there is no need for those, and I apologize for the use of iron against your bare skin. I recall now your mother had explained the pain it causes your people." He motioned with his hand for the guards to remove the shackles and they jumped to comply. In less than a minute they had been removed.

She rubbed her wrists - now red and showing raised welts – but tried not to appear as pained as she felt inside. Iron had a way of working into a Fainne's body and causing long-term problems that lingered. She doubted the brevity of this wearing would do the same, but she already felt a bit lightheaded from the time they touched her skin. She swallowed against nausea as well.

"Thank you," she said, looking around the room and feigning interest in the many tapestries. "Is this a historical account of some sorts?"

"It is, actually, the true account of both your people and mine."

She leaned in closely to examine one. "This can't be," she said aloud. "Many details are wrong."

"I assure you otherwise. Your King Girtrán did not stop at corrupting the Deamhan. He immediately rewrote your history to fit the narrative he hoped would turn into his legacy." He paused to consider something then shrugged. "I might add it was a venture he was wildly successful at bringing about."

"But this suggests the Fainne were not originally from Fainnotherr. It depicts a different view of events suggesting we stole our Blossom from the Human Realm and eventually fled through the portals."

"Yes, heartbreaking, isn't it?"

Alistaria watched the king's face for amusement at her own response. *I'll give him no such satisfaction.* "Heartbreaking?" She asked him. "The only part of your story I consider heartbreaking is that you seem to believe these lies. King Girtrán did not corrupt the Deamhan, he merely revealed to our eyes the corruption already existing in their hearts."

"So your kings have led you to believe."

She turned with graceful bearing, holding her back straight and chin set. *He's testing me,* she thought. *Testing to see how I react, but why?* She eyed him defiantly but betrayed not a single emotion with her words. Gesturing to one of the tapestries she asked, "Do you expect a child of the forest to believe the Deamhan controlled Fainnotheria before us? That we came through the portal and pushed them out? How can you expect such primitive minds – unable even of proper speech – to develop and build such a fine city as the home of the Fainne? Have you not seen their weapons compared to our own?"

Radviken smiled with satisfaction. "Yes," he agreed. "Theirs are simple iron while yours are a fine silver made unbelievably strong."

"Exactly."

"Because what better way to inflict injury on your enemy than to cut with the metal most painful."

She paused.

"Have you not thought to wonder *why* their weapons are made of iron? After all these years fighting against a stronger, more advanced foe, they've chosen simplicity because it truly causes lasting damage when it cuts. Yes, you may heal your wounded after each battle, but the effects of the iron weaken your warriors with each attack." He walked casually to his throne and leaned against the high back of the chair, crossing both arms with a relaxed regality that projected confidence. "The metal is poison to your bodies, added to what your own rulers have already fed to your minds. I assure you the tapestries depict the truth."

Alistaria was losing the sparring match – finding herself up against a master manipulator and king of deceit. She felt the need to fully confront his motives and move the conversation along. "Is that why you commissioned these tapestries? You created monuments to make gods of your ancestors and to perpetuate the lies they constructed." She gestured around the room. "These monuments to your false history should be destroyed."

"My dear, Alistaria, I applaud the conviction with which you speak, but you are very much mistaken. I may have done evil things – all of which will damn my soul, but for which I offer no apology over my actions. I believe the things I've done for my own people far outweigh my crimes against yours – both past and present. Could

I but find a way to retrieve ours from the Luchorpán, I would return the Blossom of Life to Clíodhna's."

"It never belonged to her people," Alistaria hissed.

"But again you are wrong. Both about ownership of the Blossom and of the origination of these tapestries. These were found in the old palace when I expanded the structure to become as you see today. I did not create them to sell lies to my own people, I displayed them in case you or others like you ever wished to know the truth. Ask Nastauria – she knows the truth of your people, for her father had told her the exact story I heard from Clíodhna. Now I will tell you the same of Girtrán's treachery – your elders could do the same, but choose instead to avert their eyes from the truth of actual history."

"What is history except the narrative pushed by the victors?" Alistaria demanded. "Every time a war is won history is rewritten."

Radviken smiled. "I am pleased that you understand and accept my point, daughter. That is why I've brought you to face your history as told by your own kind." He pointed at the tapestries. "These were spoils of the Great War, brought back by King Octavian during his hasty retreat from Fainnotherr."

"Spoils of war?" As confusion began to clear, fear of understanding threatened all she believed.

"King Octavian took these from the halls of Fainnotheria, Alistaria. Look closely at the threads with which they're woven."

She turned slowly and approached the nearest – taking it in her hand and feeling the fine woven flax therein. "Flax thread is common," she said, "and could have been woven here."

"And the embroidery?" He asked.

Realization lifted the veil of her denial. "Spider silk," she whispered.

He nodded. "Woven by Fainne hands."

Alistaria felt her knees weaken and her head swim. She felt faint. So many ideas clashed within her mind. Even if the tapestries truly told the story of her people, how could she trust this man who – by his own admission – was damned for the evil he has committed without remorse. As if those evils had manifested into sound, a wail could suddenly be heard from the next room. This time she clearly recognized the voice as Restarian's.

"What have you done with the prince?" She demanded.

"I assure you what has been done to him was not against *him*, but his father."

"Bring Restarian to me at once," she demanded. "I wish to inspect his wounds and speak to him alone."

The king bowed. "I will send him to you at once." He turned with a regal flourish and strode through a door to a room beyond.

As soon as she was alone, Alistaria dug into her pocket for the small pouch of spores. Stepping behind the throne she quickly drew her waterskin and poured it in a perfect circle on the floor around her. Stepping from the center in case the magic worked instantly, she carefully lined the circle with the spores and waited. Nothing happened.

The door to the private chamber opened abruptly and she spun around, shoving the empty pouch into her pocket and gathering her composure. The creature who entered was barely able to stand on his own feet and wobbled precariously as if he would collapse. She ran to him, eyes filling with tears at the wretched state of Restarian. He fell into her arms and they toppled together onto the floor.

Clamoring out from under him, she climbed to her knees and looked him over to access his needs. The first thing she noticed were his wings – once splendid and full, they had been carved of every piece of useful flesh. What remained was a skeletal display of jointed bones that would never again taste the winds of flight. She ran her hands across his back, mournfully sensing the infection beneath the skin. Her heart broke when metallic odor reached her nose – finding its way to her mouth and under her tongue. Whoever had done the flaying had used knives of iron.

She had to work fast – the wounds would fester not only with infection but also with the corruption of the metal. Despite the urgency she paused. Her cousin would never be the same, even if she could heal his body. His mind was no doubt broken by the torture, and he would surely have left much of himself in the room this had happened. With a deep breath and focused concentration, she set her own mind to healing what she could.

This deep in the castle she struggled to feel the storm as easily as she had in the forest. The thunder outside was muffled – a distant rumble she could barely perceive. She closed her eyes and listened instead for the thrum of the energy, finding it lingering in the static around the room. The power was there, she only had to channel its form through her own.

She marveled how the air around her had become like the roots of the forest, drawing it into her body and gathering the healing properties from the Fainne world. *Only it isn't, is it?* Truth of her people's history was in doubt until she could confirm these new details with Nastauria – if she was ever given the chance to do so. Pushing thoughts of hopelessness aside, she went to work healing her friend.

Chapter Thirty-Five

Do not be shocked when the truth is revealed, for my intentions were never to hide it from you forever. I merely desired you view the world with a different lens once the curtain was lifted.
– Lamentations of Nastauria

Alistaria did not look up when Radviken returned, but she knew he was no longer alone. A hooded man in black armor and cloak had also entered and now stood next to the king. The two were engaged in a low discussion that she could have overheard if she had bothered to listen, but by this point she was focused only on healing her friend and only snippets reached her ears.

"Strange how she seems to actually care for the prince," she heard Radviken say.

"Odd behavior toward one's sworn rival for sure," the other man replied. She had gathered by now he was some sort of general or high marshal by the adornment on his uniform. "You'd think she'd let him die instead of healing his body. She'd have so much more to gain if she displayed malice instead of mercy."

"Yes," the king agreed. "She is so unlike her *mother* in many regards. I'm now as equally shocked the prince tried to protect her as fiercely."

Of course you tried to protect me, Restarian, she thought. *You've always been more of a brother than a cousin, and I will do the same for you.*

"I am disappointed," Radviken whispered, "but it seems Searcher Cainnech spoke truly about her origins."

By this time she had managed to mend Restarian's broken ribs – of which there were many – and also a punctured lung and several bruised organs that bled internally. She also tended to his brain which had shockingly hemorrhaged despite no obvious head trauma. But any effort to regrow tissue around his wings had proved wasted. He would never fly again, and his bare bones would be exposed for the rest of his life.

She gently rolled him over and studied his face. A deep burn had been left upon his skin, most likely a product of her father's interrogation. This she healed cleanly, but the scar would remain – marring the gentle arc of his cheek. Both of those had grown gaunter and dark lines had formed under his cheekbones – carving them so profoundly he appeared far older than his young years. But what troubled her most was the hair atop his head – turned stark white by whatever brutality these humans had forced him to endure. It had affected Restarian so terribly it would become a forever reminder of his trauma.

She smiled down lovingly as he blinked his eyes open, trying not to alarm him with her worry. But she gasped with shock as they opened, for she did not expect the change in their color. These had transformed from their usual emerald to a dark crimson. Restarian would never be the same.

"Alistaria?" The boy asked, blinking up at his friend.

"Easy," she cautioned. "You'll be weak for some time, so don't try to get up."

"I'm sorry," he said.

"Don't be. This makes twice you've protected me, once at the Fainnen Ring and now by enduring the brunt of his wrath."

"It was for naught," he explained. "I've told him everything – about you, about Torian."

A tear formed in her eye as she nodded gently and forced a smile. "I know, but it's okay." Leaning close she touched his arm and whispered so Radviken would not overhear, "I did it, and soon your father will arrive with the Kern."

Restarian shook his head. "No, they won't come because grandfather is dead. He has died and Nastauria is a traitor. She's joined with Clíodhna and allowed her to steal the Blossom of Healing." Something changed in his expression and he suddenly recoiled from her touch as if struck by a viper. "And you are Deamhan," he hissed.

"Don't be silly," she begged. "He will come. How could you possibly know what has happened in our realm while we've been here? Don't believe the lies told by this human."

The prince's eyes flashed between the king and his general and then returned to Alistaria. "I did not hear this news from *his* lies, Alistaria. I met my father in the Shadow Realm and he told me himself. He told me of Nastauria's treachery, and warned me of Clíodhna's daughter."

She didn't understand his words, pushing them aside as rantings from a previous fever. She refused to accept them. *Delirium*, she thought dismissively. After collecting herself, she said, "I had to repair many injuries and even mended several in your brain. Do not believe the dreams you may have experienced under his hand."

"It is true, Alistaria," Radviken said from across the room, a sneer replacing the once broad smile across his face.

She shook her head violently. "No!" She protested. "I will not believe such insolence! You're only trying to turn him against his dearest friend!"

Another man – a palace guard – entered the throne room via the main hallway. "My lord, Storm Warden," he said to Radviken's general. "A Rider has returned with the other you seek."

"A single Rider you say?" The general lifted an eyebrow toward the king. "This could be the missing Rider from the other night, the soldier left behind and presumed missing by our careless Searcher."

Radviken nodded. "Bring them *all* before me in my private chamber," he commanded and the man departed to follow the guard. Turning to Alistaria he gestured to two others by the door. "Clamp her again with irons and bring her before me as well. It is time we get some real answers since the prince's knowledge proved false."

She stood with alarm, but the men grabbed her forcibly and shackled her wrists with the vile metal. "What can you gain by my torture, Father?" She asked. "Just a few moments ago you spoke of enlightening my mind to our history. Do you no longer wish to reach accord with your daughter?"

He paused, turning slowly and with a sincere look of sadness on his face. "The Searcher who found you also recovered Prince Restarian, but his incompetence allowed the death of one Rider and the disappearance of another. This *incident* allowed for the escape of the prince's travelling companion."

Torian bested his Riders! She realized. Her heart fluttered at the possibility he was still alive.

"When he returned with you, he reported witnessing a channeling of healing power through the Tempest, I was skeptical then, for I did not believe his words after his integrity was already compromised. But now I've seen you perform the same healing with my own eyes."

"That means nothing. In Fainnotheria I was a powerful healer!" She decried.

"That may have been so, but would prove an impossible task here unless you are Deamhan. But I must wait and fully test you later because now it seems that missing Rider was a hero to the crown. He has returned with the third member of your party."

"I am no threat, so why do I find myself suddenly in chains?" She demanded.

"Because one of your fellowship was a Deamhan and, until you healed the prince, I had not realized that abomination was you. You are my offspring through Clíodhna."

Restarian stared up at his friend and cousin standing beside him in irons. It was true, what Betarian had said, and Radviken now confirmed it as well. He remembered his grandfather's words while in the Shadow Realm. *He bid me to kill every Deamhan, even her.*

The guards hauled him to his feet as well, leading them into the private chamber – still filled by the gathered Searchers. They looked on with eager smiles, pleased he had been fully healed and was ready for more of their brutality. Rough hands shoved both him and Alistaria onto the floor, forcing them to kneel before Radviken as he sat casually by the fire. Behind him stood the Blossom – the relic their party had sought was so near light reflected off of it and flickered in Alistaria's eyes.

She had come so far only to fail. Even if she planted the ring, his grandfather was unable to come through. This spot in their realm was surely the location of Clíodhna's palace, and she had bested Betarian. No Fainne would ever reach that portal. A thought suddenly wrenched his stomach and choked his breath with an audible gasp.

"What is it?" Alistaria asked with concern.

"If you laid the ring then she may come through." He said. "He fears her most because she can work his magic in this realm. They all can… *You* can…" he broke off suddenly understanding why his cousin was securely locked in iron chains. She had worked Deamhan magic to heal his wounds. *Allow not a single heart to beat in their corrupted chests,* his father had commanded, *starting with their wicked queen and finishing with her daughter.*

"Why," she asked with tears forming in her eyes, "do you keep saying I'm Deamhan!"

She doesn't believe or understand, he realized. He suddenly pitied her, raised among her enemy to hate her own kind. *She may never understand.*

The doors opened and several more people entered. A new Searcher had arrived, but he appeared less confident than the others. Restarian looked back and forth between this man's face and that of Niamh standing behind her king with a knowing smirk. Beside him were two other men dressed in Storm Rider armor. One had his hood down and was clearly a middle aged fighter who had seen many years of battles. His face was hard and eyes confident. Behind him was Torian. Restarian did not recognize him at first with the hood over his eyes, but as his face turned to look directly at the prince, he could see it was surely him. The guards shoved all three to the floor beside Alistaria. She too had recognized Torian, and Restarian could tell her heart was breaking.

"Searcher Cainnech," Radviken said to the trembling man who had entered first. "You recovered my daughter and the prince, and surely wish to attain a second gem."

The man eagerly smiled, his nerves settling a bit as he clearly yearned for additional power. "Yes, my lord! I do desire your blessing."

"But how is it," the king asked, "that you allowed this boy to kill Blayse, the most skilled swordsmen among my Riders?"

"He too was an expert swordsman, my lord! He bested them both."

"But were you not also a Rider before you elevated? Have you not skill with the blade that matches or exceeds that of a mere Storm Rider?"

Searcher Cainnech tried to speak, but the words caught in his mouth.

"You were afraid, weren't you? It is my new belief that you snatched the Prince and cowardly ran after he bested Blayse."

"No, my lord!" the man protested.

"You possess the power of water *during Tempest*, yet you fled when the boy demonstrated skill. Why did you not strike him down with lightning?"

His eyes turned to the floor and said nothing.

Radviken's blue eyes turned icy with anger as he turned to the Rider kneeling beside Torian. "You, Markey O'Malley, Rider of the Storm. You were there, what do you remember of this man's actions?"

"After the boy had sent me over a small cliff, I saw a flash of light within and this Searcher flee with the boy."

"What happened to the swordsmen to allow this Searcher escape with his life?"

"The boy was blinded by the energy and could no longer fight."

"So you are telling me Searcher Cainnech fled for no reason? That he could have easily dispatched the blinded swordsmen?"

"Easily, my lord."

"And what of you? Why did you not dispatch him?"

"I tried, but had sustained injuries in the fall. By the time I found my way up the cliffside, he had fled as well. I trailed him, and finally caught up in Midlandis. I dowsed him, found him to be human, and brought him here to be judged for the death of Rider Blayse."

"I assume you wish elevation as a boon for your service?"

"No, my lord. I am older than most Riders – close enough to retire. I only ask you grant this boy an appointment in the Guard. He killed Blayse, the greatest swordsman of us all, and deserves clemency and appointment to the vacancy he created as written in your law."

Radviken laughed but the Storm Warden spoke for O'Malley. "This Rider is idealistic. He himself entered the ranks after killing a Rider, but he's been loyal many years and no doubt believes what he's asking is fair. He does not know the history of this boy nor his identity, and clearly sees elevation as redemption for his fallen comrade's memory."

"Is this so?" Radviken asked. He frowned, studying the man kneeling at his feet. "Yes, I *do* remember you. But surely you understand this is not a man but a fae. You dowsed him, but did you not realize he may be a Deamhan? Did you take him into your custody without questioning why he travelled with a Fainne?"

"Not at all my lord. I travelled several days with the boy, and learned much about him. He is certainly *not* a Fainne, nor is he Deamhan."

Radviken motioned for the guards and they forced Torian to his feet then hauled him forward. One forced him to hold out his hand where a bandage covered a fresh wound on the palm. "Cut that away and let's have a look."

They complied and fresh blood soon oozed from his palm. The king removed a necklace and held it aloft. At the end of a long chain three crystals dangled in a single fixture the shape of a triangle. As he suspended the setting over the blood a single stone glowed brightly. All eyes turned toward Torian.

"Well, Prince Restarian," the king said aloud. "It seems your lies were many told, even under the most persuasive of measures. But he is neither Fainne nor Deamhan, but a simple man." He turned toward the Storm Warden. "A changeling perhaps?"

It took several heartbeats for Restarian to understand what they were saying. *A changeling? Torian? Of course!*

"I think I see now what has happened," The king said. "The prince tried to protect the real Deamhan's identity. Why he did, I cannot presume. What I don't understand is how you came to travel with the prince," he demanded of Torian.

"I was hunting in the wood when I lost track of days. Tempest hit, and I sought shelter. This boy happened along, and I aided him over the pass and we camped in the cave. I did not know he was a Fainne," Torian lied, looking at Restarian as he spoke as if willing him to back his story.

What is he doing? The prince wondered, considering his lie. *He is protecting Alistaria, but why is he protecting me also? Does he think he can earn trust with this madman? Of course! He does not yet understand Alistaria is truly a Deamhan, and also believes Nastauria's lies!* He turned mournful eyes toward his cousin, recalling their many happy memories and wondering how Nastauria could have hidden her heritage. He pitied her ignorance as well, but could not forgive her true heritage.

"Is this true?" Radviken asked of Restarian. "Not that your words hold sway, son of Betarian."

He nodded, suddenly sorry for doubting Torian before, and now compelled to see him spared. "Yes. I met him just below the pass. I had jumped stupidly into a raging river and he pulled me out."

Radviken turned to Niamh who nodded. There was enough truth in his words to fool both her gift of sight and his lingering compulsion spell. "Searcher Cainnech," the king called out. "Rise and present yourself to your king for judgement."

The Searcher did – although it was clear to everyone in the room, he was unsure if he were to receive punishment or reward. Radviken also stood, walking toward the Blossom. He stood before it as he had the night Niamh was elevated, and Restarian wondered if this man would be as well.

"Your cowardice is unforgivable," Radviken declared. He felt along the crystal vine until he found a particular thorn – needlelike and stained forever pink with the Searcher's blood. It was below the green emerald of sight. His fingers moved in a flash and the thorn was plucked, held between the king's fingers above the floor. Everyone in the room watched with bated breath as a single drop of blood fell slowly to the marble beside his feet.

Searcher Cainnech fell to his knees with hands to his temples, obviously in agony as his power left him.

"Take him away to the dungeons," Radviken commanded the guards. "He's not fit, even, to wear the armor of a Rider." He waited until they had dragged him from the room then added, "Stand, Torian, and present yourself to the Storm Warden."

Chapter Thirty-Six

I confess my destruction came by my own doing, without thinking in youth of future consequences for my careless actions. Again, I do not lament a thing, nor do I seek absolution. My confession is for my own cleansing – to remove the stain I acquired in another realm.
– Confession of Radviken

Piotr drove right up to the palace gates. They had found some shovels along the way, and these and an empty wagon were all they had – even their food had been lost in the accident. He swallowed hard and looked the nearest guard in the eye. Neither spoke, they only stared. When the guard blinked, Piotr blinked. When the sentry cleared his throat anxiously, Piotr demanded, "Well get on with it! Why'd you call us down during Tempest, man?"

This completely confused the guard, stopping him midsentence and sending him into a tirade of thoughts and uncertainty. He quickly motioned his buddy over, and this man seemed less easily convinced.

"Get on with you!" He screamed over the howling winds – angry at being summoned from the guardhouse during the storm.

"Get on with *you*!" Boyd screamed back.

"Did you really call us out here, only to forget you did?" Piotr chastised. "That's not a way to treat us, not during Tempest and not *ever!*"

Both guards blinked with confusion. After a moment one of them asked, "Well who in the blazes *are* you?"

Boyd pointed a thumb at the shovels in the back, as if that explained everything. Piotr nodded his agreement and waited. Finally, the first sentry said he had to call his Sergeant.

"That's finally the best idea I've heard all day!" Boyd said with oozing sarcasm. "While you're at it, why don't you call Lord Radviken himself down, and you can explain to him why his privy's backed up!"

"The... privy?" Both guards asked at once.

"The privy!" Boyd and Piotr answered also in unison.

Piotr pointed at the various outcroppings from the upper levels and their long chutes to the ground. "They don't shovel themselves, you know!"

The guards exchanged another confounded look and then the second spoke. "I don't know nothin' about shovelin' a privy!"

Boyd rolled his eyes. "That's why they called us! We're the shit shovelers, or didn't you know?"

Both sentries shrugged and shook their heads. "We didn't, actually."

"Well we don't appreciate bein' called out in a blinding Tempest, so our bill will be double this time! Just point out the Royal shit chute and we'll be done and on our way. But hurry up about it, so we can get home to our families!"

"We really need to call the Sergeant," the second man said with more uncertainty.

"Go ahead and do just that," Boyd said, "So we can explain to him how you held up the shovelin!"

"Look," the first guard said, "we don't mean to say you're not who you claim to be, it's just that we don't have any way to prove it."

Boyd leaned across and narrowed his eyes in a most serious expression. "Good sir. Who in their right minds would not only *claim* to be shit shovelers, but *also* be downright proud of their work?"

"Uh, I don't *know?*"

"Exactly. Now, the crux of it is, have you ever seen shit shovelers shovel shit during Tempest?"

"No, I actually haven't."

"Exactly. Because that would be a shitstorm of a mess, one that neither you nor I want to deal with, if you know what I mean. Now, the fact we were called out during Tempest should let you know just how much of a shitstorm this would become if you don't let us work as called! Do you get my meaning?"

Both guards looked into the back of the wagon, again seeing only shovels. A quick look underneath revealed no contraband there either.

"Well, they don't have weapons," the first man said.

"And I don't want a shitstorm," the second man said. They both shrugged and waved Piotr and Boyd through. Lucky gave the sentries a thankful bark as they were on their way.

"So which is it?" Piotr asked over his shoulder. The first man pointed to a privy on the top floor – six stories up. Only a fool would try to shimmy that high up, but this *was* Boyd's idea. Piotr tipped his hat in thanks and they made their way to the rear of the castle.

"That was easy," Boyd said.

"This was all a *horrible* idea," Piotr complained.

"But not my worst."

"No, not your worst."

It didn't take long to reach the base of the king's privy. Nor did it take long to learn that king behind-leavings smelled exactly like those from commoners. They pulled alongside the bin and Boyd hopped down. Lucky followed. Piotr maneuvered the wagon so it'd be easier to shovel into – they had to actually perform the job in order to sell their legitimacy as well as clear a way to get into position to shimmy up the flue.

The two guardsmen watched for several minutes as they worked. Surprisingly, the men had spent so many Tempest nights in smelly barns far worse than this and the smell hadn't bothered them as bad as they'd expected. Boyd even hummed along as they worked. After a while the guardsmen lost interest – convinced the shovelers were either legitimate or seriously committed to their lie – and stopped watching their every move. That was when Piotr stuck his head inside the flue and measured their chances.

"It looks doable, Boyd. They built it so no man can shimmy it alone, but if we put our backs against each other and lock elbows, I think we can literally walk up it."

Boyd popped his head in and frowned. "I dunno," he said. "How will I get Lucky up there?"

"You don't! Lucky isn't even our dog. He's been following us around, is all. Besides, we'll be back down eventually, and ride out with him if he hasn't wandered off."

"Nah, I want to bring him up." He walked to one of the wagon wheels wrapped with twine to give extra strength. This he quickly unraveled, then fashioned a harness to slide under the dog's legs and belly. "I'll just hang him from my belt, see? Then we'll climb up with him dangling below us all the way up."

"What if he barks?"

"He never barks."

"He barked at the guards when they let us in," Piotr reminded. The chute was just large enough that two men could comfortably stand two abreast. The men turned their backs and locked elbows.

"Funny thing, that. I thought he was sayin' his thanks for lettin' us pass."

"Dogs don't have manners, Boyd."

"Dogs have manners plenty, Piotr. It's people who forget pleasantries." The men slowly walked their feet outward until they touched the wall.

"Well, I'll give you that. There're times when I'd much rather deal with a dog. Their kind are certainly much appreciative," Piotr agreed.

They cautiously stepped in unison until they were off the ground. They found as long as they kept pressure against each other the going was rather easy. Pretty soon they found themselves several feet above the ground with Lucky standing beneath them. He whimpered once as if to protest the pending disappearance of gravity, but was soon dangling above the floor of the bin and spinning in a slow circle.

"You always know where you stand with a dog," Boyd went on. "If he doesn't like you, he doesn't mince words. He either growls or avoids you entirely. If he's extra offended, he skips right to a nip or in some cases a full on bite."

Piotr grunted as he took a step, then said, "Cats are certainly less amiable, for sure."

"Exactly. You never know how you stand with those critters. They rub your legs for food one moment, luring you into false friendship. Then they roll over on their backs for you to rub their bellies, only to bite and claw at you the moment you do."

"And then decide you *must* give them attention when it's absolutely not the best time for you."

"Sorta like people, Piotr." Boyd explained.

"How so?"

"Oftentimes they act like your friend only because they need something. Then, once they get it, they're off and you never hear from 'em until they're hungry again for more. No sir! Give me friends who put me in my place and tell me how they feel!"

"Boyd?" Piotr asked.

"Yes, Piotr?"

"You know I'm your only friend and you're mine, right?"

"There's a reason for that."

"Yes," the taller thief agreed. "I reckon there is." He looked down at their starting place. They had travelled at least halfway by then. "Never expected to be climbing a shit chute with anyone else, that's for sure."

"Don't forget Lucky, Piotr. He's part of the team now." The dog was too busy spinning slowly on its rope to reply, but he seemed to be content enough watching the bricks pass by his eyes.

"I just wish he didn't smell so bad."

"You mean like us after this job?"

"No, I mean when he gets comfortable and destroys my nose with the fragrance from within his arse, Boyd."

"See? That's what I mean about manners. You've gone and lost yours. He's just a dog. He don't pick his meals, he takes whatever comes. He also don't lie to you about how comfortable he really is around you."

"So when he farts, it's really just him saying he's satisfied with my company?"

"Not at all, Boyd. He farts because he's gassy. Here, it seems we've reached the top."

The top of the privy turned out to be a wooden platform with a carved hole. Atop that someone had carved a wooden seat for comfort. Boyd examined the opening.

"I didn't think about that," he said.

"What?" Piotr asked.

"There's only one hole and two of us... not to mention nothing to hold onto except the top. Only one of us will get through there, and the other will have to hold his legs."

"That's impossible! The weight would be too great for the other to climb up."

"There *is* another way," Boyd suddenly realized. "But it will make a *lot* more noise."

Piotr looked six stories down the chute below, past the spinning dog and at the sudden stop they'd meet below if they lost their footing. "This was your idea again, wasn't it Boyd?"

"Aye. But this one's gonna work."

Chapter Thirty-Seven

To know my son had lived brought me sorrow, knowing his heritage would be stolen away just as she had taken his body. It brought relief in the end to learn Betarian had sent him to the Human Realm, for at least there he'd be free of the hatred lurking in the eyes of Fainne.
— Sorrow of Clíodhna

Radviken called for Torian, and Markey met eyes with the boy as he stood. *He knows what to do… why am I so worried?* They had rehearsed for this moment many times with the aid of Clurich, who assured them their plan would work. It all depended, however, on a single decision going their way. Would Radviken seek to elevate him? He prayed he wouldn't.

Torian knelt before the Storm Warden who stripped him to his waist. Storm Guard garments were brought in, and these were slipped over his head. Garbed as an apprentice with no sword or armor, Markey thought of his presentation many years ago. *They'll allow him to stay for the ceremony, but then he'll be taken to the barracks for initiation.* His skin still stung from memory of his own.

"Rider O'Malley," the king's voice boomed.

The defining moment had arrived and Markey held his breath.

"It seems I have an opening for a Searcher, and you are chosen despite your earlier protest. Cainnech possessed sight, but you are not bound by his former gift. You may also choose from fire, water, or air as a first level Searcher. Tell me now your choice and why."

Markey hesitated. All he was told by Tamee was to never accept the gift, but she never explained why. Elevation *would* increase his station, and with it would give Jaana greater comforts in which to raise their boy. He considered the gifts being offered.

The elements would assist him in his job for sure, even without power, but sight would aid his swordplay and ability to detect traps. Thinking of swordplay made him think of Blayse, and yearned for one final sparring round with the man to hone his skills further. When he finally spoke he meant to protest a second time, but instead his words surprised him.

"Sight, my lord. So I may see farther and better those things that are hidden. I choose sight so I may better identify the threats and sword thrusts of your foes."

Radviken nodded his pleasure. He would see the choice was humble, and worthy of the man's wisdom to spare the lad and take advantage of his usefulness. He turned toward the bush and pricked his finger on a thorn before squeezing a single drop atop the emerald. "Come forward and claim your gift."

Markey rose and began to walk toward the Blossom. He was surprised to find he could almost feel its power, even from this distance. It had a certain thrum to its shimmer, one that nearly beat in rhythm with his own heart. After he had taken two steps, however, he paused – eyeing a young woman just beyond the king.

Her face wore a stern expression, one accentuated by the tight bun in which her red hair was pulled. Her green eyes twitched toward the Blossom and exclaimed, "Your majesty! Do not elevate this man!" Markey stepped forward to prick his finger, anyway, but she stepped between him and her king.

"Why, Niamh?" Radviken asked, obviously taken aback by her interruption. "What do you see that I do not? I possess *all* power and do not see a threat."

"Test his blood again," she demanded.

"You suspect a Deamhan?"

"He *is* Deamhan," she seemed to growl.

She stepped forward and waved her hand over his face, stepping back again when nothing was revealed. She tried once more – face twisted with worry she had made a mistake. Markey held his breath each time. Finally, Radviken shoved the Searcher aside.

"Cease your insolence," he commanded, "if there was a veil you would have found it by now." But he must have decided to test him, and turned to Markey and commanded, "Present your hand, Rider."

Markey calmly complied, confident in Clurich's tests on him years ago. He felt the firm tip of the dagger against his palm, and the warm trickle of blood as it came forth. Above it the king dangled his three stoned amulet as everyone in the room watched. A single crystal glowed prominently and Radviken abruptly wheeled on the Searcher.

"He *is* human!" He said. "Niamh, you are new in your role, and your powers are fresh so I'll forgive this interruption, but you have a long way to grow before you'll be ready for this role. What did you think you saw that warranted such reaction?"

With a trembling hand she pointed to the door and explained, "I saw the Banshees enter our realm, my lord. His blood allowed them entry!"

"Hold him," the king commanded, and two Searchers complied. A streak of Markey's blood still stained his blade, and he touched this gently to a single thorn. The entire crystalline structure suddenly glowed brightly and the king stepped back with eyes wide. Turning to the Searchers he cried, "Bind him tightly!"

"I don't understand!" Markey said. "What does that mean?"

But Radviken ignored his question, returning his attention to Niamh. "I'm sorry to have doubted you, for you were right. Had he touched the stone we would have lost it all. Thankfully he has not taken my power, but I fear it was enough!" He abruptly turned full attention to the door, his own power over sight sensing his immediate future. "Searchers!" Radviken cried again, "Protect your king!"

Just then, a shriek in the throne room announced the arrival Radviken had most dreaded – the sound of Banshees spilling forth into the palace. While the Searchers formed a defensive perimeter by the door, Radviken's voice boomed throughout the palace – calling his guard and sounding alarm. In his anger, his stare settled on the girl kneeling beside the Fainnen prince.

Alistaria had not expected Banshees. Truly, she still expected her grandfather and a regiment of Kern to flood the room instead of the vile creatures. She looked to Restarian with confusion. "I don't understand," she said. "How did you know Betarian would not come? How did you know about the Banshees?"

"I told you, I met my father in the Shadow Realm," he said.

They both flinched as the Banshees flew forward, crashing into the line of fighters protecting Radviken. An explosion of light sent them crashing against the walls, but another line entered just as quickly. Alistaria watched with horror as everything slowly made sense. Feeling useless, she huddled next to Restarian.

He grinded his teeth and seethed with anger as he watched the battle. "That Rider with Torian," he said, "must be the son of Clíodhna. Only the blood of her child could have opened the portal for the Banshees!" Turning to her, he demanded. "Did you truly not know? Tell me now!"

She shook her head, terrified and still not fully understanding. "I didn't know," she said.

"It doesn't matter," he said. "You're one of them."

"Does it *not* matter if I am, though? If I'm truly her daughter, it *doesn't* matter! You know my heart. We've been friends for so long, would it affect how you see me?"

"I hate them all," he hissed.

"So do I," she said.

"I'll hate you as well."

"Surely you don't mean that?" She begged.

He gestured at the battle raging around them. "Soon they'll have the Blossom and we'll be dead either by theirs or *his* hand," he said of Radviken. He then eyed their silver weapons lying side by side on the table by the Blossom.

What will he do? Alistaria wondered. Her eyes fell to the Rider who had arrived with Torian. She watched as he fought the red-headed Searcher. Her gift of sight aided her sword as she parried or dodged his every swing. He was tiring, and would soon lose the battle.

"Alistaria!" Torian called.

She looked up to see her friend standing over a dead guard and holding an iron key. He held it up and pointed to her shackles. She nodded and he tossed it, sending it sliding across the floor toward her. Then he turned and drew the fallen man's sword, rushing to the aid of the Storm Rider named Markey. As she scooted backward to pick it up, a foot suddenly landed atop the key. She looked up, surprised to find Restarian glaring down.

"What will you do?" He asked. "Who's side will you choose now that you know?"

"Our side!" She said with anxiety flooding in. Time was running out. Radviken was across the room, fighting alongside his mages – each holding back the onslaught with a mixture of shimmering shields or lobbed fire and ice over their defenses. Guardsmen dueled off to the side with Banshees who had made it past the shield.

Restarian shook his head. "No," he said. "You'll choose hers, so I must stop her before you do!" With a kick the key slid to the far side of the room, toward the door to the throne room. It wasn't far, only about twenty paces – but it might as well have been leagues away. He rushed toward the table with the Blossom, retrieving his father's sword of Fainnen silver and turning to face the advancing Banshees. Though he held the weapon with confidence, they could tell he wasn't a swordsman. They circled and snarled, waiting for him to make the first move.

A body slammed into Alistaria from behind, knocking her to the ground. Stunned from the blow she looked around as the room slowly spun into focus. She tried to make reason out of the battle but it was now utter chaos – a free for all with iron clanging against the ringing of steel and bursts of magic exploding all around. Torian and the Rider had joined together and now stood back to back while fighting off several Searchers. Among those was the red headed woman.

Abruptly Radviken screamed. He stepped from behind the line of mages and roared, "Enough!" The power of his control over the Blossom was magnificent to witness and soon everyone was caught up in a shimmering cloud of corruption. They could no longer move, wrapped in the swirling embrace and muscles contorting under the spell.

Alistaria watched as the cloud grew, swirling on the current of battle and reaching out like an ethereal hand. She sucked in her breath as the shapeless form found Torian and his Rider friend. Their faces twisted with agony as the fighters fell to their knees along with the Searchers around them. Even Restarian fell, but he did not convulse – his face told Alistaria he already knew this particular pain quite intimately. Radviken spared no one, casting a wide net of power that ensnared all – not distinguishing between sides of war. It even found her.

She fought against the corruption that gripped her, feeling the oil slick cloud upon her skin and trying to understand its composition. It was so foreign to anything she had ever experienced – without a thrumming beat like her preferred art of healing. Her muscles twitched and knotted under his spell, and she whimpered at the hopeless feeling that had crept in behind the pain. *No one should wield such power,* she thought – and her eyes fell upon the Blossom standing alone. Her mind raced with options, trying to remember which gems would stand for each Blossom in this realm. Even if she could only get free, she would not have time to gather each and every one before challenged.

A ghastly scream entered the room, as a beautiful woman flew in upon an aura of her own corruption. This shimmering cloud was hers – repelling that which flowed from Radviken. She flew straight for the Blossom as Alistaria's ears rang with the ghostly wails of Clíodhna – inaudible at first, but soon becoming clear enough to understand. Her cries were an incantation, calling upon the energy of the crystalline bush as it thrummed.

It's true, Alistaria realized. *The history upon the tapestries was real, and the Blossom belonged to her people and not to us!* She marveled as it glowed under her command, pulsing as it had when the Rider's blood had lifted the curse barring the Deamhan. It strobed as she neared, yearning to answer the call of the Banshee Queen, but still held strongly under Radviken's grasp. He understood at once what she was trying to do, and turned his full attention to the queen. A powerful blast of power suddenly pushed her off course and into a wall.

Radviken stood over the woman he had scorned so long ago. "So it came to this after all? My plan to keep you both at odds has failed and you combined your strength against me?" He inclined his head to the Fainne woman now standing in the doorway "You, Nastauria, with your guile, and you Clíodhna, with your never ending need for vengeance. I should have known you would eventually work together no matter the effort I made to keep you at odds." He pointed at the Storm Rider laying twisted in corruption beside Torian and demanded of the Fainnen princess. "You hid him beneath my nose this entire time? How then, did you manage to send him to Enatherr?"

A voice boomed from behind Nastauria. "I brought him, Radviken." Síth Morkur strode into the room. "King Betarian traded his own son in exchange for me hiding the boy child here, all I had to do was pick the *when,* so he would meet these others at the right time."

"Of course," Radviken nodded. "He pointed first to Restarian and then at Alistaria. "But the others you sent were children and they ultimately failed." Alistaria felt the squeeze tighten around her body as Radviken continued to address the Síth. "But you claimed to be in search of balance when you coaxed me through the portal and promised me power."

"I coaxed King Rashmere through the portal, Radviken. You were nothing until you cowardly betrayed him, killing your own king and trading his soul to me. All of this," he said with both arms raised and meaning Enatherr, "was bought with his murder."

"And the Blossom?" Radviken demanded.

"Was purchased with your own soul, after the normal passage of time as we agreed. I am here to claim that today," the Síth explained.

"Not while I hold power over the Blossom," the king proclaimed, kneeling beside the Banshee Queen. He wrapped his hands around her throat and whispered loud enough for Alistaria to hear, "Do you see that girl over there? Our daughter? As soon as I've killed you, I will do the same to her." This made the Banshees wail louder, unable to save their queen beneath his weight.

Nastauria stepped forward, picking up the silver dagger lying next to the Blossom and holding it high above her head. Radviken did not see her as she approached, the only person in the room who wasn't twisted up by his corruption. She crept quietly but swiftly, ready to kill the only man she had ever loved. Alistaria cried as the woman she had called mother moved to save the mother she had called enemy. Restarian, well accustomed to the pain of corruption, let it wash over him as he rolled onto his knees. As he stood, he thrust his father's sword deep into his aunt's side, sending her toppling in death - the dagger chimed as it fell to the ground beside her.

Restarian immediately went rigid, then all his muscles slackened. He was suddenly freed of Radviken's corruptive spell.

"Thank you, prince Restarian." The king said as he released Clíodhna's lifeless form. "The price of your freedom has been paid, Tempest has ended, and you may return to your realm."

At that moment, Tempest indeed ended and the boy was gone – the only living Fainne in the room, he was instantly transported back to his realm.

Alistaria hid her eyes and wept, unable to move and not wanting to watch as both her mother's died. But a wet lick at her face and the smell of dog broke her mourning. She felt a soft click and the instant rush of relief as the iron shackles came off her hands. She turned onto her side and looked up as Boyd placed a finger across his lips and then pointed. Across the room, Piotr was beneath the Blossom, having crept past the king as he strangled the life from Clíodhna.

It won't work, she knew. *Only a Deamhan can touch the blossom without his permission – only a Deamhan or a child of Radviken.* She watched on with hopelessness as he reached a hand toward the Bloom. One by one he plucked the gems, each touch sending the crystalline structure into a pulsing fury. Radviken sensed the theft and looked up. Panicked, the thief missed the final bloom – the onyx of corruption, Alistaria recognized – and nicked his hand upon a crystal thorn. It turned pink with his blood, and the entire structure lit up with a brilliant glow.

As Piotr wrenched away the final gem, the cloud of corruption lifted and Radviken screamed. His life withered from his body as he aged there on the floor, the stolen years of youthful immortality gone in a single breath.

Suddenly free, Alistaria leapt to her feet and sprinted forward, scooping her dagger from the floor and meaning to jab it through her father's heart – but the redheaded Searcher jumped to her feet as well and whirled with a counter strike of her own, forcing Alistaria to duck. By then, Torian had regained his feet and drew away the attention of the Searcher. While they fought, she found herself in front of her father with blade in hand.

"Go ahead, then," he said, defeated, "Kill me."

She looked around. Torian and the Storm Rider – her brother, she now realized – had quickly won the quick skirmish. The Searchers were unaccustomed to fighting without their powers, and were out matched by the superior swordsmen. Led by the Storm Warden they fled from the room, leaving Radviken to face his own fate.

"Swift death is too good for you," Alistaria told him, "and I believe the Síth will claim you tonight whether by my hand or your own body giving out."

She turned to find Piotr holding out a handful of gems.

"These don't belong here," he said. "We know the stories and I read the tapestries in the next room before we entered. Take these to your realm and keep them safe."

"You claimed them, you won't try and keep their power for yourself?"

"No," he said, looking up at the Síth. Instead of fear at recognizing the mythical Master of Beasts, Piotr's eyes filled with awe. "I've seen you in my dreams," he said. "You told me to forget, but to always remember."

"I did," the Master of Beasts replied, "and apparently so did you."

"Who am I?" The tall thief asked, his blue eyes misting from the emotion of the day. "What am I?"

The Síth pointed to the body of Nastauria on the ground. "You are her son, and also his," he said as he gestured toward a very frail and wasted Radviken. "A prince of two realms but hidden away in a brothel and raised with a conscience, apparently, despite your occupation as a thief."

"We are quite bad at it," Boyd admitted.

The Storm Rider approached, placing strong hands on Boyd's shoulders and turning him to face him. "Piotr?" He asked. Turning to the shorter thief, he asked, "Boyd? Is it really you, boys?"

"Hello, Markey," Piotr said. "Tamee told us we might run into you again someday, and it seems she was right."

Alistaria realized the Banshees had not moved to attack, and stood instead watching her as if waiting. "What?" She demanded of them. "What do you want from me?"

One of them stepped forward. Alistaria recognized the woman, despite they all appeared similar with their appearance. She was the one who spoke to her at the farm. "Are you truly Clíodhna's daughter?"

"It seems I am," She said, turning away. "But I'm also *hers*." She knelt beside the two women joined in death upon the floor. With her back turned, she did not see the Banshee horde kneel to pay their new queen homage.

She gazed upon both women – scorned by the same man and cursed to the same fate. Neither had known their children, even if she didn't know how. It was Piotr who stepped forward, holding Nastauria's journal who offered explanation.

"Nastauria gave birth to a son on the forest floor," he said quietly, "but soon heard Clíodhna's wails of labor in the distance. She, too, had delivered a son. He pointed to Markey. You, I'm guessing."

The Síth standing over Radviken nodded.

"Seeing the Banshee Prince was born without corruption, she placed Clíodhna into a deep sleep, and held both boys, deciding their fates and meaning to take them both to freedom. But the Síth had also been watching, and emerged from the forest."

"I had come expecting her son to be stillborn like the other males in her line, but found him alive," Síth Morkur revealed. "As I turned to leave, she offered me a trade."

Nastauria held both infant boys in her arms above Clíodhna. *I can save them,* she thought, *and Clíodhna will assume hers died on the forest floor during her slumber – claimed by Síth Morkur and devoured by Ganshees.* But she found she could not leave. Her powers of healing revealed a life still inside the Banshee Queen's womb.

"You will deliver the third child, Nastauria, Princess of Fainnotheria?" The voice of the Síth had startled her, but she did not flinch from saving the child within.

"I feel I must," she replied.

Pointing to the healthy boy beside hers, he said, "The harbinger foretold by your ancestor King Girtrán has heralded her birth. If you return with three children, your father will have them all killed."

"Yes," she agreed. "But I cannot let this one die. Clíodhna was my friend, long ago, and I do not wish her or her people to suffer further. They do not deserve their current plight, and I wish there were something I could do to help her more than this."

"I am sworn not to interfere with your realms," Síth Morkur explained, "but there are actions we both can take to ensure my assistance."

"By offering you a soul?" She chuckled at the thought. Nastauria wouldn't dream of offering a life up to a Síth, no matter the boon. She certainly wouldn't offer him any of the children. Soon the girl emerged from Clíodhna's womb – perfectly formed and beautiful in Nastauria's arms. She laid her beside the boys and considered what to do.

"If I offered you a soul," she said, "to take one of these infants to Enatherr for safekeeping, what would happen to the child?"

"As a changeling?" he asked.

"No, as a foundling."

"I know of a places where foundlings are kept safe, they are rare and often the most unorthodox of homes, but the child would grow into a healthy adult."

Tears filled the young mother's eyes as she made her decision. "Then I offer you the soul of my father – the blood of my blood – to claim as yours at the natural completion of his life. Is that mine to offer in exchange for a favor?"

The Síth nodded. It was.

"Take my child, my son, and keep him safe. I shall raise her daughter as my own – so that my father's sworn enemy will be born under his roof and as one of his heirs. She will learn the false history he has pressed upon us all, but if she is truly the future of both the Deamhan as well as the Fainne, then she will someday learn of the true history of her people, as I will write down and pass on to her when the timing is right. Then she will understand, and hopefully have the power to bring about change as a unified kingdom."

"And the other? The harbinger? What of him?"

"I will return with him to Fainnotheria, but will not hide him from my father. I will let him know who and what he is, and turn him over to him. He will not have him killed, but he will not want him to remain under his roof. If he approaches you asking for a boon – to exchange him as a changeling – you shall not deliver him to this current time if it is in your power. Take him instead to a time he can aid his sister when the time is right."

The Síth nodded his agreement and carefully picked up the child from the softness of the forest floor.

"Please give him memories he *should* have experienced," she pleaded, "had he been raised here instead. Allow him to always experience what it would have been like to have been a fae, and let him also have family. I do not wish him to be alone. Let him have brothers, and many sisters, and a mother to love him."

He nodded that he would and turned with the child to leave. She did not watch him go, because her guilt was too great. Letting go of a child is the hardest thing a mother can do, and something no woman should ever have to face – much less a choice she chooses to make.

Chapter Thirty-Eight

*I never interfered with the realms, not in any way that would
have caused one to gain permanent power over the others.
As a Síth I cannot, in fact, interfere for my own gain – and
any benefit to myself must come as a gift. That's the way
with my role, to ensure balance by never allowing dominance by any realm.*

*Since creation I have merely done the bidding of the self-righ-
teous by helping sow their good-intended chaos along the
way. I never expected the sacrifice Nastauria eventually
made, for it was unexpected for any living being from any
of the three realms. Perhaps her compassion means there is
hope for balance after all.*

*Unfortunately for the world, her selfless actions are rare and
my work is never finished.*

– Síth Morkur

Alistaria stood in the throne room, not far from the two men
who, it turned out, were her brothers. Each had been just as surprised
as her at the revelation, and she truly wondered who had had the
better life – the two fae who had lived their lives as men, or poor
Torian who had lived his life as a fae. He waited nearby, eerily quiet
unlike Markey who was catching up lost time with Piotr and Boyd.

She had been studying the tapestries, comparing them to the
narrative left to her by Nastauria. The beginning had been her journal – the lamentations of a young mother who had given up her own
child and raised someone else's instead. She had not yet decided if the

decision was noble or selfish, for it robbed Alistaria of so much while giving also to her more. The second part of the journal had been a history of both the Fainne and the Deamhan. She found it matched perfectly with the tapestries, and felt entrusted with a knowledge she doubted either side would accept.

Much had happened following the battle in Radviken's palace. Radviken's body – and that of Nastauria – had already been carried through the portal by the Síth, since they were both souls who belonged to him. She was ready to travel through the portal and return to home, as well, but which home was Fainnotheria? *Is it the home of my ancestors or the home of the woman who raised me?* At least she was traveling with her own people now, as they had accepted her as their new queen without question – the Fainne, she knew, may not be so easily convinced.

"What will you do, then?" She asked of Markey. "You *were* born before me, so you are heir to his kingdom – unless you want to claim Fainnotherr as well."

"Truth be told," the older man said, "I don't want either. I was in good standing with most of the Riders, so I have support here if I want to claim the throne. But the Warden and his Searchers are at large, so I have quite a fight ahead of me." Pointing to the satchel at her side and the gems within, he added, "We'll be at a disadvantage now, but that one belongs to you."

"We can help you," she promised, "to take yours back from the Luchorpán."

"As much as I'd hate to fight two fronts right now, that may be an offer I'll take you up on." He pointed to the ring of mushrooms on the ground. "So that will work for me?" He asked. "Any time I choose to visit?"

"Yes, as both human and Deamhan, you should be able to cross through easily now, as will I. So will Piotr whenever he wants since he is fae and not restricted any longer by Tempest. Keep the portals safe from humans, though, as they will now be able to pass through without meaning to, as long as conditions are right. We will guard them also from our realm, and I've marked on your map the location of those in Enatherr."

"Thank you," he said, "and good luck."

"Just remember," she said, "you'll look and be quite different if you decide to pass through for a visit – and the invitation is open to do so. We have an alliance, don't we?"

"Aye," Markey said. "That we do." He smiled and gave Piotr and Boyd each a hug. "So you're going now?" He asked.

"You bet!" Boyd exclaimed. "I always wanted wings, and I'm eager to see what Piotr here looks like as a pixie."

"I'm not a pixie, Boyd." Piotr said with annoyance. "I'm a Fainne."

While they entered into a debate over the differences between Ganshee, Banshee, and Fainneshee, Alistaria turned her attention again to the tapestries. Speaking to Torian, she said, "I can't believe the entire history we were told was false. Why would the elders erase our past?"

"Perhaps they were ashamed," her friend said. He had been sullen since the end of the battle, and she knew it was due to his sudden knowledge of his true heritage. He loved living as a Fainne, and couldn't wait to return through the portal. "Or," he said, "they craved power, and the only way to convince an entire population to destroy their own thriving culture is to kill it from within and spread the lies that actually motivate hatred instead of ending it."

"Perhaps," she said, but she knew he was right. The Fainne had actually been the aggressors all along, preaching against the corruption of the Deamhan while spreading lies to ensure their own survival. Any who spoke against them were silenced, and only the lies decided upon by the elders could become the people's truth. "Many of the Fainne will fight against this," she said.

"Yes, but they have no choice. You hold the power now, and the only army left in Fainnotherr is at your back. Reunification is at hand, and as soon as the Blossom of Life blooms, you can remove the blinding corruption."

She took his hand and he squeezed reassurance. "So we're ready then." Everyone in the gathering nodded, and she stepped into the ring. One by one they were transported, reemerging in the Palace of the Deamhan on the other side.

Both Alistaria and Torian had expected to feel disoriented, and had warned the others before they left. But the journey was easier than before, as the unpleasant experience had been another trick by Radviken – a product of how he tracked them through the portal. She looked around as she arrived, hoping to find Restarian lurking nearby. But they wouldn't, though – his hatred and his family's inherited bigotry were a problem they would face at another time.

She stretched her wings as soon as she arrived and smiled to find Piotr doing the same. It felt good to be whole once more, their bodies returned to their natural form – only not all of them were. Her Banshee brethren stood off by themselves, unintentionally avoiding standing beside the others the moment they looked like again like Fainne. *That self-segregation will take generations to erase*, she feared. She looked down upon her golden flecked skin with sadness, suddenly aware how simply being born as a Banshee Princess had given her privilege over the others – a gift she could use for good once the boundary of appearance was removed. That would be her first priority as queen.

Laughter broke her musings and she looked up to find Piotr and Boyd bouncing in the air. Piotr had splendid wings, broad and widely spread like his mother's. That didn't mean he knew how to use them right off, though, and he flew awkwardly and bounced off bobbing and inverted Boyd. His wings were the strangest she had ever seen – circular in shape and seemingly too small to carry his weight.

Boyd's appearance in Fainnotherr had truly been the real surprise of the journey, holding Lucky in his arms and having taken on a different look than anyone could have expected. He was round in the belly but broad at the shoulders, with a full beard as orange as a begonia. His bushy eyebrows hid his eyes, and his impish face laughed behind his facial hair. He was also shorter than she expected, even smaller than he had been in Enatherr.

Had she ever seen one, she would have known right off he was Luchorpán – for he looked exactly how she expected a gnome to appear. But seeing him now made her wonder. Remembering the words Searcher Cainnech said to him in the forest made it clear. She would eventually have to tell him, but for now she let him bob around upside down since he was focused so intently on learning to fly correctly.

Free to soar without fear of attack by the Deamhan, they eventually took off and sped their travels – arriving quickly in Fainnotheria. But the journey had revealed the true extent of the corruption on the Deamhan realm. Everywhere they looked they found dying or rotting trees – covered by Ganshees or sick and awaiting their fate. The stories Nastauria had told her were true, and even the soil fell away from corruption in places, marking their world for eventual absorption into the Shadow Realm – reversing this decline would be her second business after the Blossom of Life had bloomed once more beneath its Great Tree.

Their arrival in the city was met with eerie quiet, as the Fainne watched her lead the odd menagerie through the open ceiling. Everyone stared at the Banshees, unsettled and wondering why they had travelled with her. But word was soon spread by the elders, and they all gathered around to learn more of their fate. Alistaria wouldn't leave them waiting long, she would address them as soon as she'd planted the Blossom.

She soon found herself before the Tree of Life, holding in her hands all eight gems of Saol. They sparkled in the eerie reflection of glow stone light, dazzling and reflected against her brown eyes. They were finally home, and she was ready to set things right.

"Go ahead, then," Torian urged. He was hovering above the ground, refusing to put feet to the ground lest he once again lose the gift of flight. He was certainly more fae than human here, despite knowledge of his blood – Alistaria knew it was what was in his heart that truly mattered.

She gently knelt before the patch of bare earth. "How do I do it?" She asked of Erania. "Is it truly as simple as planting them in the ground?"

The elder nodded and placed a tender hand against the girl's shoulder. "The important things in life are always the simplest. Place each gem into the ground and cover them with soil. Once they are all placed, you must water them with your blood to have control."

"Does it matter the order?"

"That is a question for those who cannot answer. Trust your instincts is all I can advise."

She chose to lay them in a circle, with the ruby at the top and in the following order going clockwise: Healing, sight, water, air, resurrection, fire, corruption, and power. Satisfied, she covered them with soil.

The voice of Síth Morkur rumbled into the chamber, causing everyone to turn. "Radviken had a different order when he planted, as did each of your ancestors and also the Fainne. I find it interesting that you have ordered a balance never before attempted. Why did you choose this combination?"

Alistaria cleared her throat and explained, "Healing is for our combined people as we find our way. Sight is for the clarity that knowledge brings – shedding light on facts that can only be viewed and not changed or hidden from view because we feel uncomfortable. Water quenches life. Air for the purity of our realm, and fire reminds our people that hatred and anger consume the flesh when held onto them too long. Corruption is for the eventual decay of everything that lives or is believed – as disgusting as the Ganshees, but just as useful. We must view it not as a weapon but as the harbinger of change."

"And power?" Erania asked.

"Power comes last, since it is the true corruptor."

"I see," the Síth said, obviously pleased by her explanation. "Now feed the Blossom your lifeforce to make it grow."

She drew the silver dagger and looked it over. It still felt strange in her hands, a physical weapon of destruction when she desired only to heal. Drawing it firmly against her palm she squeezed a crimson pool into her fist and dribbled it gently atop the pile. Almost instantly eight seedlings emerged and intertwined, twisting and combining their singular strength to form a woven trunk. Branches emerged in every direction while the assembly watched, reaching out to offer support for fragrant leaves that reminded Alistaria of lavender – soothing and restful was the smell.

To everyone's awe and amazement, eight blossoms emerged immediately, not constrained by the Tempest – The Síth later explained that was because they were in their natural home. The rose was first to appear, followed by the hydrangea, the hyacinth, aster, a begonia, a single white lily, and a black iris perfectly bearded with tips of yellow. Finally, the morning glory budded and bloomed, heralding the magnificent arrival of a new day and age. Alistaria looked down at her palm and was shocked to see her hand had fully healed with the emergence of the first flower.

"What will you order, now that you are the queen of the combined Fainne?" Erania asked.

Alistaria turned and gazed upon the collected faces, knowing already what the first command should be. She looked upon Torian, with his bold eyes of blue smiling broadly while awaiting her answer. Then she looked at Piotr and Boyd, each in awe of what they were witnessing. Boyd still flew upside down, but seemed quite content to do so. Lucky was at their feet, sitting and watching just as intently. But the onlooker who drew her gaze and locked eyes with the pride only a mother could give, was Nastauria watching her daughter expectantly, and bearing herself with regality – she wasn't there, of course, but her spirit would guide Alistaria always through the wisdom she had already bestowed.

She should be queen, not me, Alistaria thought. *Her daughter jumped over her succession and stole the crown.* But then another thought took hold. *But she isn't really my mother, is she?* Clíodhna the Banshee was her true matron, the Queen of the Banshees. *Is that who I am now? Am I a Deamhan or a Fainne?* She looked beyond the roots of the chamber to glimpse the hordes shuffling their weight outside. They would wonder the same of her allegiances.

"Come," she said to those gathered, "and I will let everyone know at once." Piotr and Boyd parted as she passed between them, grinning wildly and giving her a thumbs up. She couldn't help but smile back, despite the weight she now carried.

As she emerged with her following, a strange hush fell over the crowd. Fainne and Deamhan alike were gathered, all except the friend she would miss the most. Nothing would be right again, without Restarian and their exchanges of playful sarcasm. She privately hoped, in time, he too would come around.

"I was once close minded," she said loudly, startling herself with the command in her voice. Every eye was on her as she spoke, devouring each word. They would remember this moment for the rest of their days – when a petulant girl took leadership over their lives. "I was close minded and narrow in belief and tolerance. But I was ignorant to our true history, naïve to the importance of remembering our past."

She caught eyes with a Deamhan woman watching through the corruption painted upon her face. "I used to believe the curse Girtrán placed on the Fainne was to mark their true nature, and until recently was blind to the corruption in my own heart. For I was born to a Deamhan, and my blood is the same as theirs. I am ashamed of how I viewed my own kind, ignorant to our relationship. But we are truly the same, even if we originally come from different pasts and places.

"The bigotry and hatred were born the day Girtrán placed this veil, corrupting his cousins with his own darkness and not theirs. Today I remove that curse." She closed her eyes and sensed the magic all around and growing stronger. She sifted with her mind through the elements now fully available and felt for the vibrating thrum of corruption. With the wave of her hand she peeled the veil from those gathered amongst the Fainne, revealing their true beauty. The crowd murmured with excitement then, amazed by the changes around them. Fainne and Deamhan were finally again indistinguishable.

"From now on, we are one of form if not of thought. Let us embrace our differences and see not the surface, but judge only by the corruption demonstrated outwardly by individual actions. As of this day we are all one people of Fainnotheria. Embrace the faults of our ancestors and do not hide from them. Do not cover them up by toppling statues or erasing pages from our anthems. Open conversations instead, and learn to communicate and love equally – for we have a new history to forge."

The applause that erupted was deafening as the united Fainne rose into the air to clap their hands and beat their wings. The thrum they sounded shook the hall with their excitement, but over the roar she could hear Nastauria's voice in her mind. *Your work has only just begun, my daughter, my queen. I will never be able to put in words how proud of you I am. Thank you for making the death of my own child a worthy sacrifice.*

All at once movement above caused everyone to look upward at a single man, clumsily beating wings he had only just acquired. Markey descended awkwardly toward the roots, and landed hard beside her. The crowd silenced abruptly as he caught his breath and tried to speak.

"What is it, brother?" She asked.

"Our new alliance faces its first test, and we need your aid. The Shadow Realm has spilled over and Enatherr is under siege."

It was so quiet when he finished speaking that you could hear a leaf fall. Alistaria searched her thoughts for something to say. *I can't commit so quickly to another war,* she thought. She cleared her throat and started to speak, but was interrupted by a subtle *pfft.*

"Sorry," Boyd said with a shrug. "Lucky gets a bit gassy," he explained.

HOWLING SHADOW

CORRUPTED REALMS – BOOK TWO

"They came to us aboard a gleaming ship, slipping through the fog as if settling from the sky itself. They were warriors, clad in shining armor and bearing weapons equipped with powers unbelieved if not recorded in these tomes. Each and every Tuatha de Dannan was a god to us, truly people descended from the spirit Danu."
– The Annals of History Book III, Passage 12

The sun dipped below the horizon, casting perpetual shadow over a darkening forest. Not a single star shone in the sky and chilling breezes cut through the branches overhead. In the distance, animals screeched into the blackness—a sign either of life or one ending. Shivers ran down the arms of every fae gathered around the ring. Nervous eyes darted amongst the soldiers, betraying distrust and lack of unity. The shriek meant something different to each.

Not long before, that sound would have warned some in these ranks of approaching Banshee, hell-bent on destroying peace. To the others it bellowed defiance of oppression and bias against their visage. But the corruption marring the Banshee had been lifted by their new queen, Alistaria—a girl raised within the very walls of Fainnotheria as the granddaughter of the Fainnen King. She had issued a single command during her coronation, that both races must work together under a common name. Gone were the kingdoms of Fainne and Deamhan, for they were finally united as fae.

No longer at war, they discovered a new threat lurking beyond the portals in the Shadow Realm. Alistaria ordered immediate integration of both the root tender ranks and the newly formed military. Despite quiet grumblings by those with the most closed of minds, the unification had proved effective as both sides brought talent of equal measure. Former Deamhan demonstrated powerful abilities not only to heal and wield fairy spark, but also with swinging swords and spears. Though odd to see former Banshees wearing golden armor, these gathered comprised the first of the unified Kern—warriors of legend and the best fighters Fainnotheria had to offer.

Torian's mind raced with his own anxiety, but battle waited on the other side of the portal, and it cared not about race. Even now, as their general leading the charge, Torian was far different than his soldiers. He was a changeling, a human raised among the fae, but none cared as long as he proved the bravest and most capable leader. Besides, soldiers had a way of overcoming bias simply by sharing the dangers of a lurking threat—with trust won by teamwork and respect earned by selfless deeds.

He stepped forward, a signal to the men their attention was needed elsewhere, and they adjusted ranks around him. Under the late King Betarian, the Kern had been an elite force of single units whose best tactic was swarming their enemy with speed and agility. But this general had a new tactic to try—one better suited to fighting in the other realms. In Enatherr, flight would be a wanton dream, so he lined shoulder to shoulder to fight on the ground.

In this formation, their golden armor and glistening shields formed a wall ten soldiers wide by three deep with spears outstretched. If one fell, another could step forward into the phalanx and replace him. Likewise, each shield position could move in unison providing protection to any threatened side. More importantly, simple facing movements could redirect their attack with a single command, allowing them to outflank their enemy as quickly as they could retreat.

Though eager to test his army's recent training, he hesitated before committing them forward, one rank at a time, into the Fainnen Ring. He drew in a soothing breath of calm. Letting it out slowly, the general nodded to companions who signaled they were also ready.

He commanded their advance, and the first line fae stepped through the portal.

The blinding flash of light muddled his senses on the other side, but it was surely better than before. The first time he had crossed over, Torian had passed out from pain, awakening with muscles contorted and trembling against wanton spasm. But now, with Radviken's curses gone, the experience only mildly affected the travelers as they emerged in a melee of violence. He had expected the battle had already begun, but failed to anticipate the enemy's numbers.

Here, the entire forest crawled with Draugars who moved with greater speed than one would expect from the dead—a sure sign little was actually known about the Shadow Realm. The reeking bodies passed around his position while avoiding the ring, heavy with decay or advanced enough in their rot to resemble loosely constructed skeletal beings.

They had pinned down a small group of human Storm Riders in a clearing up ahead. Knowing the dead couldn't step inside its boundary, his squad took a moment to acclimate before taking up stances. He wished again for flight, but focused instead on the new tactics. The other line would emerge soon, so he looked around quickly to determine his action and a way to step out of the ring.

The Storm Riders stood shoulder to shoulder, forced to dismount, and backed into a line along the forest edge. Each a master swordsman, they cut down the advancing spirits as they came, pushed back by their numbers but clearly overwhelmed. There were only six against the horde, and Torian frowned at the small number sent by Markey O'Malley. Either the king underestimated the enemy's strength, or he had fewer men to spare. He had no time to waste.

"Shields! Ready!" He commanded, locking his with the fae on his left and each soldier doing the same. "Spears! Ready!" Their silvery weapons reflected the moonlight as they were raised, ringing a metallic resonance as they fell into place upon their shields. "Forward! Charge!"

The squad ran in unison toward the skirmish, crashing into the Draugar focused entirely on the Riders and pressing them into the backs of their kind pressing ahead. This enraged the spirits, and many turned to face the newcomers head on. The move split the enemy force, catching them squarely between the allies. Torian frowned at the iron weapons in their hands, surely meant to harm the fae with the metal's poisonous properties. *But not me,* he thought, *because I'm not fae.*

The dead suddenly parted, inviting his squad deeper into their mass of gnashing teeth, but his men had prepared for the move and held position.

They expected us, he realized, suddenly suspecting a trap. "Spearhead! Adjust!" His own line folded slightly, resembling the point of an arrow and facing the two fronts with an angular defense.

He didn't have to wait long for the second wave. More Draugar leapt from the underbrush and moved to flank. His eyes flashed to the Fainnen Ring as he wondered what delayed the second squad. Moments later the ring flashed and he breathed a sigh of relief. "Rank! Close!" he shouted, adding with urgency, "Shields! Turtle!"

The fae in his line moved as a single unit, pivoting, and placed shields all around the squad. Each soldier took advantage of the brief respite and waited, breathing in each other's body heat. The odor of battle was a mixture of metallic and musk as they listened for the signal to lower their shields and resume fighting.

"Squad two! Flanking! Break!" came the shout from the second squad, signaling they had emerged and were in position.

"Broken squad! Ranks!" cried Torian, and his squad broke into two rows of five, each facing a different direction and enemy. His line faced their attackers, now turned against the reinforcements. "Thrust!" Five spears attacked in unison while the line of Kern reinforcements did the same. The Draugar screamed into the night as they died. "Phalanx! Fall in!" he commanded, and his line turned to rejoin their original foe. The reinforcements fell into a line behind his and the two squads became one. He felt the reassuring heat of comrades behind him as they marched slowly forward, thrusting and stabbing over his shoulder at the animated dead. Soon, the third and final rank had emerged, bolstering his unit. After a few short minutes, his front line stared at six very thankful Riders with the fallen remains of Draugar beneath the feet of the phalanx.

"You came just in time," one of the humans grumbled.

"It appears so." Torian stepped forward with an outstretched hand which the Rider eyed suspiciously. *At least the* humans *view me as fae,* he thought, putting it away unshaken. "I'm called Torian, General of the Kern."

"I'm O'Donnel, Rider of the Riders." He must have made a joke because the other five Storm Riders laughed. None of them seemed happy to be fighting alongside fae, even if they *had* just saved them in battle.

Torian turned his head and eyed the carnage all around. Something was off. He looked down at the closest Draugar, a mere skeleton with decaying flesh stretched over bones. One of its eyes was long rotted out, and the other was a ghostly white. The long beard was coated with blood, but had been bright blonde at some point. The armor it wore was unlike any he had ever seen on either human or fae. It was beaten bronze and ancient in make. Whoever these dead men were, they were not recently passed. He pulled a vial of yellow paint from his tunic and splashed it on the chestplate.

"What are you doing?" one of the humans asked.

"Marking him in case he rises again."

The man's eyes grew wide with fear and he asked, "You think he will?"

"I have a theory, that's all." Torian looked around. "I know the Tempest hasn't returned this month, but what of Ganshee? Have you seen any since Radviken fell?"

The Riders exchanged more looks of worry, and one of them spoke while pointing upward into the trees. "The pixies are around, but they won't touch these bodies."

He pointed upward, and Torian spied several Ganshee hovering in the trees overhead, chittering and gnashing teeth with displeasure over the offered meal. *Odd,* he thought, as they were usually quick to devour decaying flesh. "Where do they go, the Draugar after they're killed?"

"We don't know. About an hour after, they simply disappear."

Torian nodded. He'd had the same experience with the other's he'd dispatched before. "Tell me why there're only six of you. Their numbers have obviously grown, and would've wiped you all if we hadn't arrived when we did."

"We haven't men to spare, fairy boy. We're spread out covering each city as well as these damned portals."

Torian ignored the edge to the man's voice. "Have you figured out how they're getting inside your realm?"

"How can we? By the time dark falls, it's as if they're here already! Tonight they popped up all around our camp as early as dusk!"

"Here?" Torian asked, pointing to the spot on which he stood.

"Yes." The Rider replied. "Well, not exactly. We were over there." He pointed to a small escarpment in the woods. It was devoid of trees but not of fauna. Through the dense brush Torian could tell the ground was higher here, a rounded mound, but nothing appeared supernatural or out of sorts. There were no caves or entrances he could find. He fanned out his squad to finish searching while he talked to Rider O'Donnel.

An animal howled in the distance—too guttural to be a wolf and lacking the high pitched whine for which that animal was known. The hairs all over Torian's body stood atop chilled bumps on his skin. The human standing with him laughed.

"You've never heard a hellhound's howl, have you?" the human asked.

"No," Torian shook his head. He'd heard of the beasts, but only in legend.

"Neither had we, until our Riders reported hearing one or two near the Port of Enat. It's said they're moving farther north each night, but those sounded close."

"Too close," Torian agreed. When he turned from scanning the tree line, he found the man staring questioningly as if he'd something more to say. "What is it?" he demanded.

"You're the human changeling, aren't you? The one they're sayin' was swapped for a fairy."

Torian flinched. Markey had told him he'd become a celebrity—the fae-trained warrior who had bested the greatest swordsman to ever serve among the Storm Riders. He tried to push by, hoping to avoid the usual questions, but the man stepped to block his exit. They were always the same—wanting to know how it was living among the fae, but failing to realize he couldn't compare this life to one he'd been denied. He knew nothing about being human. "What do you want?" he asked in a low growl.

"I heard something about Markey," the man said. "Maybe you can tell me if it's true."

Torian paused, suddenly aware all six pairs of human eyes stared while awaiting his response.

"I barely know your king," he lied, pushing past. He wanted to search the bodies of the Draugar. For what, he did not know, but even rifling through the pockets of the dead beat having conversation with humans.

"But you did spend several days traveling with him," one of the others pointed out, "and you *were* there when he killed Radviken."

"He didn't kill Radviken," Torian corrected, "the Sìth claimed him as part of their deal."

"But you were there," O'Donnel insisted, "so you can answer to the truth."

"What truth?" Torian whirled around to face him. "Which truth do you want to know? Every time I save a group of you Riders from the Draugars, I get the same questions: 'Are the Banshees coming back?' or 'Is Radviken really dead?' Well, he's gone and the fae are your allies now." He pointed to a squad of his Kern gathered around a flat stone. "They're fae, and look no different than you in this realm."

"What I wanted to ask," the Rider said intently, "is Markey really one of them?"

Torian felt his breath leave him at once and paused. He'd worried this question would emerge. "He's human by all accounts," he said, "and the son of Radviken. He passed every test your Storm Warden gave him."

"Then who's his mother?" one of the Riders asked. "We're hearing tales Radviken bedded the Banshee Queen."

That was a question the Kern general hadn't been prepared to answer. His eyes flicked back and forth between the men, each awaiting his answer.

"Is it true then?" O'Donnel asked. "Is our new king the brother of your Queen? Is he really a Banshee?"

Torian suddenly realized he had no answer. It was true, but the knowledge would damn his friend and ruin relations between the realms—at a time they needed to work together to push back the Shadow Realm. He finally found words and hoped they'd be enough.

"You all served with Markey O'Malley, rode and trained beside him for more than a decade. What difference would it make if he *were*?" In the distance another howl caused the men to perk their ears. It sounded closer than the first. "He's the son of Radviken, and therefore, your king. And right now your realm is under constant attack from dark forces and you need help from fae to fight." Another guttural bray was followed by distant barking. Torian felt his skin welt up with goosebumps and added, "At this point, what difference would it make if your king were a *hellhound*?"

Before the men could answer, a shout of excitement came from the escarpment and several Kern beckoned furiously. Thankfully, Torian broke away and hurried over.

They stood around a flat stone, partially uncovered from an ancient burial. He could tell it was longer than it was wide and still mostly buried in the earth. It was taller than a man and as wide across as one's shoulders, and probably had stood erect at some point in its distant past.

"There's writing," one of the Kern pointed out.

Torian saw it too, deeply inscribed with strange runes he couldn't make out. "We need to study these," Torian realized. "It's too heavy to take with us, and we've nothing to take a rubbing." Then he remembered the vial of paint. Laying down his shield, he took out the vial and dipped the tip of a branch into it, transcribing the yellow letters onto the silvery metal.

"The Draugar have disappeared," O'Donnel said from beside him.

Torian only nodded, too focused on copying down the runes. "You'll need to make a rubbing of this and get it to Markey," he told the Rider.

"I will."

After he finished, he waved the shield around in the air, hastening the paint to dry, then led his Kern toward the Fainnen Ring. "We'll send another squad tomorrow evening, and every night thereafter," he told O'Donnel. "Just remember we're your allies in this, and your king is a better option than Radviken." He did not wait for an answer and stepped through with the first squad. With a flash of light, Torian was gone. Back to the only realm he ever truly considered home.

Chapter Two

"They allowed us to continue caring for the forest, existing peacefully beside them, but never walking among the Tuatha de Dannan. Their shadows were too grand for our kind, and we appeared mere insects hovering beneath their grandness."
– Annals of History Book III, Passage 25

The roots of the great trees thrummed with vibrant life. Overhead the flapping of wings broke the gentle rushing of wind through leaves, and Alistaria looked up from her work. Where her eyes would have once found wailing Banshees among the lush canopy, she smiled to find birds had returned to the forest and their sweet chorus settled the girl's heart. The period of warfare between the fae had ended, replaced instead by uncertain peace. She would enjoy it as long as it lasted.

It had been several weeks since her tenders had removed the beetles hiding in the bark, and new growth had sprouted near ancient stumps and fallen trunks where much of the forest had recently died off. It wouldn't be long, she hoped, for rejuvenation to reach the ancient ruin in the far Northeast (the once home of her birth mother's refuge) called simply the Deamhan Palace.

It turned out Alistaria had two mothers, one she loved and missed dearly and the other she knew not at all. That she did not love Clíodhna did not mean she was incapable of bonding with her late memory. She yearned to learn more about the woman from who's womb she had been stolen at birth. She would stop at nothing to understand and unite both her people—those who shared her blood and also those belonging to the culture in which she was raised.

She returned brown eyes to the forest floor, pausing to watch tenders going about their work. Three young women were nearby, demonstrating to a boy how he should feel along the roots for life-force. She recognized these four as once being Fainne, and noticed how they made a point to avoid two other women listening from a distance. She shook her head with disgust and rose into the air with the barest vibration of wings.

"Do you have any questions?" Alistaria asked of the women listening on. They no longer resembled Deamhan, the once sworn enemy of the tenders. She spoke loud enough to shame the others who had shunned them. All eyes dropped to the forest floor, some with embarrassment and the others in reverence. Alistaria was barely a young woman, but bore herself with grace and dignity of a queen—an attribute learned from the late Nastauria. She addressed the entire gathering with gentle rebuke.

"We'll never recover our livelihood unless everyone works together and forgives the past," she warned. To the two women she said, "And you must not tolerate even the quietest slight, whether intentional or not." She quickly added, "But do so lovingly, as we must treat others with example. You cannot live in ignorance simply because they avoid your company. They only do so because their ignorance of you is greater than yours for their ways. They fear the future and can't let go of the past. *All* of us should look past who we once were and accept who we are together."

"Yes, Queen Alistaria," all six woman replied with eyes down. Only the boy looked upon his queen directly, seeming to fully accept the changes she had brought. *Of course the children understand,* she thought. *It will be the elders of our people who are slow to accept the new way of life. Change is easier for the youngest.* She knew she should end their rebuke there, the lesson taught by what she had already said, but added more for measure. "We are all fae now as we've always been. You've seen the tapestries I brought back. Are they not displayed in the Chamber of Life for all to view?"

"Yes, your highness," they each agreed.

"The true history of our people dates back even further than those, when we were of one people before splitting off to find their equal way. Though we may never know much before recorded times, I hope our kind are never fractured again. That is our future, for which we must strive."

Upon that she left them, wings beating and bearing her away to tend another darkness in the form of a damaged trunk. As she stole a glance over her shoulder she smiled, observing the larger group had accepted the women with newfound welcome. Busying herself with a burl, she continued to listen to their distant conversation with hope. She smiled inwardly after detecting quiet laughter and a lifting of their previous discomfort. It would take time, she knew, but full unity *would* someday be reality.

She suddenly frowned.

The cancerous knot bulging the bark was not of the usual kind. Though it appeared similar to the eye, the thrumming lifeforce rang with a resonance that failed to match the rest of the tree. She leaned in close and listened, waiting for the distinct off-beat vibration. There it was. Faint but surely present. Drawing upon the strength of both the healing rose and the morning glory of power at the same time, she tried to realign the thrum. It refused to respond to her ministrations, and so she called another tender over. The man she beckoned was named Korl, one of the most adept of tenders. He hurried to her side, his magnificent wings gracefully pushing against the air with the slightest of effort.

"What is it, Alistaria?" he asked, using her given name. She understood when some of the elders had left off her title, and it didn't bother her when some of the others skipped the formality. She was, after all, the same girl she had been before the adventure that resulted in her crowning. But it came as a surprise when one of the teachers, one she had herself been lucky enough to train under, dropped the honorific in front of young tenders. The slight almost sounded intentional and worried the young queen.

She pushed her insecurities aside and drew his attention to the problem. "Take a look at this burl and tell me why I can't heal it," she commanded.

Korl leaned in, placing one hand on the tumor and the other against the healthy portion of the trunk. "It seems the usual malady," he assured her. "You must simply realign the passage of lifeforce to work out the kink that is blocking flow. Now that we have access to power," he said, "you can force it into place like a broken bone if need be."

"I tried that," she explained. "But something is off and I can't explain it."

Distant shouting drowned out what he said next, and she flew off immediately to investigate. Leaving him to work, she made haste toward the Skygate. There, she found a group of male tenders had surrounded one of the sentries. He stood alone as his companions idled off to avoid getting involved.

"You don't deserve the silver," one of the tenders said mere inches from his face, slapping at the sword at his side and daring him to push back. But the sentry resisted, staring stoically ahead while the tender continued. "Just a few weeks ago you were attacking this entrance, you don't deserve to guard it now!"

"How do we know you won't let the enemy inside when they come again?" another asked.

"Yeah!" Agreed the other. "How do we know you don't have more Banshee hanging around the old palace?"

"Is there a problem here?" a commanding voice interrupted. The idle soldiers saw the newcomer right away and snapped to attention, but the others did not. Torian landed beside the guard and used his silver spear to push the tenders away. "I asked if there's a problem here. Is there?"

"No, sir," one of the tenders admitted, stepping away and leaving his friend to stand alone against the general.

A general, Alistaria mused. *My general,* she thought proudly. He had worked hard to rebuild the Kern to their glory, but also commanded the Skygate—the place he had once protected without regard for his own life. She was curious to see how he handled this problem.

Torian addressed the remaining heckler. "Is this how it is, then?" he demanded. "I selected this fae myself for this detail, do you challenge *his* validity or *my* authority?"

"Fae?" the tender sneered. "We both know what he is, even if our eyes are enchanted to see otherwise. He's a Banshee and doesn't deserve to guard the Skygate." He spat his disdain, leaving the spittle to roll down the silver armor of the sentry's chestplate.

Alistaria had heard enough and stepped forward. "Your name is Brechan, is it not?"

"Yes," the tender replied without taking his eyes from Torian. When the commander bowed deeply before her, the tender turned with surprise, not expecting to find the queen standing beside him. "I mean yes, *your highness*," he corrected.

With a wave of her hand she sent a cloud to wash over the tender. He shuddered under the cold touch of the cloud, then cried out in fear—unsure what magic she had wielded or the damage she may have done. Everyone gathered took a step backward, including Torian. She had worked the gift of sight and altered his appearance.

Brechan looked down at his hands, once slender and smooth, now coarsely heavy with thick hues of dark grey. He reached up his hands and touched his cheeks, once graceful and rounded, now bulging with bony protrusions beneath the skin. He touched a fingertip to an orange tooth and recoiled from the sharp tip of the incisor. His once bright green eyes stared up at Alistaria like two voids—dark pools swimming with corruption and as seemingly endless where his soul had once resided.

"It seems," she said calmly to the root tender, "you now have something in common with this Skygate sentry. Like him, you have worn a false veil of corruption which has blinded others to your true form. I could grant this gift forever, by using corruption instead of sight, so you may feel how it is to have ignorance hurled back, when your only transgression was to walk among others."

Brechan opened his mouth to plead the queen's mercy, but his voice had left him. In its place was the mournful wail of sorrow and pain. He swallowed and tried once more to speak, but his voice was rendered a screeching cry as Banshee wails poured forth instead of audible words. He wheeled on his friend, the other tender who had jeered the sentry. That Fainne fell backward trying to scramble away, shrieking and whimpering and wanting nothing to do with his friend.

Alistaria snapped her fingers. Abruptly the root tender stood as before, the veil lifted and looking once more like himself. His friends laughed at the look on his face, mocking and jeering as he fell to his knees and begged his queen for mercy. But she noticed the stoic sentry responded differently. His eyes held pity for the Fainne sniveling before him, and Alistaria immediately realized her mistake. She should never have publicly shamed the tender. In her attempt to sow empathy, she had inadvertently sparked fear. Brechan would blame the sentry and take it out on him if he ever had him alone—or was forced to heal him in battle.

"Go about your business," she commanded suddenly, and all in attendance scurried off except Torian and the sentry. "I'm sorry," she said. "I followed my instinct and let emotion guide my actions. I may have worsened the situation."

To her chagrin the sentry nodded agreement. "It is getting worse, not better," he said. "Though you've brought us together, a simple desire for unity is never enough. Many of the Deamhan feel entitled now to receive more than promises, and the Fainne fear they will be put under the boot if we are granted too much control over key positions."

"There's no more Fainne or Deamhan," Alistaria corrected. "We are all the same as we once were and are only fae."

The sentry shook his head sadly. "No. I'm afraid that kind of thinking is the problem. We've been forced to sleep in a nest, piled upon one another and huddled for warmth for so long. We are unable to vocalize our true needs and desires to those with power. The worse crime King Girtrán committed upon us was theft."

"Of your dignity?" she asked.

"No, my queen. He stole our voice. Without a voice, no group of people is ever equal to those in charge. We were judged by appearance, but our lack of voice further reduced us to savages in the eyes of the Fainne—even to you, I recall."

"You... recall?" she asked. She was confused. *Have I met him before?* He was not familiar in this form. "You saw *us* as savages, as well!"

"Yes, we saw you as blind, deaf, and dumb to our hearts and souls," he said. "I know because I came across you in the human realm. You were frightened, running from the Ganshee when you became tangled in the burial pyres."

"You spoke to me."

"I spoke to you *and* you understood, replying back in our language and begging for help."

"I remember," she said. "You were cruel with your words, claiming all Fainne deserved the fate they'd receive."

"That was not me," he replied, "I was the other. I said your pleas were in vain and left you to face your sins."

"Had we not wrought so much suffering on you, would I have received your mercy? I doubt that very much. But I *did* turn out a Deamhan. Do you still believe I should've been denied your aid?"

"Your blood turned out Deamhan, but you truly know nothing about living as one. You've been pampered here in Fainnotheria. True, it was no fault of your own, but you know nothing of our plight. Your hopes of instant and lasting peace are those of a child, foolish and blind to what goes on when you are not around."

Alistaria stiffened at his honesty. "You challenge my authority, then?"

"Not at all," he replied. "You are my queen. I merely worry you will take too long to discover the best path to this peace and unity you preach."

"What's your name?" she asked.

"I am called Maerlin."

"Torian," she said to the general standing by, "I want Maerlin to continue to guard the Skygate, but also to serve on my personal guard. Ensure he rotates several times a week, so we may continue this candor with more depth. And more often." Maerlin seemed confused. "I've spoken openly. I don't understand why you'd seek to place me closer to your person."

"I need to surround myself with truth at *all* times, but especially now. It's your council and company I seek. Especially your wisdom."

He opened his mouth to speak, but shouts from the forest floor caused her to turn with sudden alarm. Several root tenders were racing upward with someone draped limply in their arms.

"Who is it?" Torian asked.

She strained her eyes to identify the fallen healer, but couldn't tell from this height. When they stumbled onto the platform, she recognized Korl. Kneeling beside him, she demanded, "What happened?"

"We don't know. We came upon him just as he is, lying next to a tree and unmoving."

Alistaria placed a hand on the teacher and felt for his lifeforce. It beat slowly, but there was an odd rhythm thrumming out of sync with the rest of him. Whatever had corrupted the great tree had worked its way into Korl.

"Should we have left him for the Sìth?" one of the tenders asked anxiously.

"No," Alistaria replied, "at least I don't believe so. He's alive, but something's terribly wrong with his spirit. Take him to Chamber of Life, but for observation. Until we understand exactly what happened, I won't risk any more healers."

She suddenly wished Nastauria could give her council and felt starkly alone beneath her crown.

Thank you for reading *Wailing Tempest*. If you enjoyed my story, please leave a kind review so that others may find it. For updates about my writing and where I'll appear in person, please sign up for my newsletter at *tbphillips.com*.

Books by T.B. Phillips are found most places books are sold or by visiting *andalonstudios.com*

Chilling Tales
Ferryman (October 2022)
Don't Pay the Ferryman (Expected June 2023)

Corrupted Realms
Wailing Tempest (May 2021)
Howling Shadow (September 2021)

Andalon Saga

Andalon Origins
Andalon Project (April 2022)
Andalon Paradox (Epected Winter 2022)

Dreamers of Andalon
Andalon Awakens (June 2019)
Andalon Arises (July 2020)
Andalon Attacks (December 2020)

Children of Andalon
Andalon Legacy (September 2022)